The Wrong Game

By

Marc Powell

 New Generation **Publishing**

In memory of my father,

Derek, my best friend,

who left my life far too early.

Acknowledgements

A huge thank you to;

my mother for a lifetime of love and support;

my wife Zoe who is always there for me

through all of my ups and downs;

and Malcolm Winters whose encouragement

and advice through the early days gave me the

inspiration to turn my dream into a reality.

Prologue

When does a boy become a man? Mike Slater wanted so much to be a boy again. Back with his mother eating those melt-in-your-mouth chocolate brownies that she would cook for him each weekend, safe in her world.

The door slammed shut and, as the footsteps faded away, his eyes began to fill with tears. He slumped to the floor and began to tremble uncontrollably, his bottom lip beginning to quiver. He was now in a man's world, taken violently from his safe and secure life and thrown into this place of despair. Tears started to come quickly.

'No!' he said to himself, forcing them back. He knew that Dan was there close by, suffering even more than he was.

'I'm not going to cry in front of my best friend. Stay strong! I've got to stay strong,' he repeated in his head but he struggled to believe his own words. Unsure of his future and feeling scared to death, he tried to concentrate on not crying in front of Dan, but he failed horribly.

'How could it have come to this?' he said to himself, folding his arms in an attempt to control his shaking body. Tears poured down his cheeks until each drop had nowhere else to go, clinging to his chin, waiting for the next shudder to send them falling onto his chest.

His dream of a once in a life time football tour of Europe, to learn and experience different cultures in a team that he loved, had fallen apart. Instead, he'd now become embroiled with drug dealing murderers who wanted him dead. He'd risked his life and that of his family. Interpol had used him as bait to catch a killer and now the same killer had drugged and kidnapped him. He couldn't believe how helping a friend had thrown his own life into such a world of horror and hurt. His life now belonged to a man who would take it from him in an instant, without regret or remorse. His future looked bleak but this time his mum and dad wouldn't be coming to bail him out.

'Dan, are you alright? Speak to me!' Mike whispered, as if there was an ear pressed to the other side of the door, listening. Dan didn't reply. Mike felt his heart miss a beat. A small beam of light which filtered through a filthy broken skylight gave Mike just enough light to see four grey, stained walls and a heavy metal door. The room made Mike claustrophobic, the semi-darkness bearing down on him giving the feeling that the walls were moving in on him. He closed his eyes tightly, waiting in terror for the life to be crushed out of him. It never came. Opening his eyes he realised that his mind had been playing tricks on him. Leaning back against the wall, he took a deep breath and tried to compose himself.

Outside, the summer sun was shining, but here in his private hell its warmth could not reach him. Vigorously rubbing his arms, he tried to generate some heat and chase away the goose bumps that had turned his skin into that of a chicken. Stopping suddenly, he ran his fingers along his arm examining the foreign material that he didn't recognise. It wasn't his favourite tracksuit top that he always wore, but a thin paper-like material, a kind of paper suit that you would buy from a DIY store. Feeling around the rest of his body he realised that his clothes were gone. Dropping his head in despair, any remaining hope in him began to expire. He knew that without his clothes, and what they contained, any chance of being rescued had disappeared. Cold, confused, shivering and with his courage waning all he could do was hope for a miracle.

It was then he saw Dan, huddled in the foetal position with his head tucked into his shoulder. His dark silhouette didn't move, but Mike could see his chest heaving rhythmically and he knew that he was alive. *Thank God*, he thought. Crawling closer, he gently placed his hand on Dan's back. Dan moved in a sudden jerk which startled Mike, making him reel back.

'Shit, my head hurts,' Dan blurted out loudly.

'Shut up! Be quiet or they might hear us.'

'I don't give a shit if they do,' Dan answered equally as loud. Mike hadn't got the energy to argue, so he didn't reply. Moving closer to his friend, Mike could now make him out a little clearer in the gloom of their prison. Dan rubbed the back of his head, wincing when he touched the tender part.

'I've got a lump the size of a boiled egg. They needn't have hit me, the bastards! They could have given me brain damage!' Dan screwed up his face with pain as he pressed his boiled egg-shaped lump.

'You? Brain damage? Don't make me laugh. You've got nothing to damage.' Both boys chuckled and smiled at each other in the gloom and, for an instant, they both forgot where they were. Mike put his hand on Dan's shoulder, giving him a reassuring squeeze.

'Don't worry, we'll get out of this,' he said, in a vain attempt to reassure himself as well as Dan, but Dan was more concerned about the cold.

'God, I'm freezing,' he said pulling at his paper suit. 'And what's this thing I've got on? Where are my clothes?' Mike, annoyed with Dan's concern about his clothes rather than their predicament, shouted into his ear through gritted teeth.

'Sod you're bloody clothes! Dead men don't need them, do they?' The instant Mike had said it he regretted it. Dan didn't need to hear such things and

Mike knew that it had hit the wrong chord. His friend needed support and to be given hope, not scaremongering, but it was too late. Dan sat, head bowed, in silence. Both their worlds had been turned upside down and in their tiny cold and dark room they could only start to guess at their destiny. Two friends, side by side, suffering together but in reality each one alone, fighting to come to terms with his fate.

Mike's head overflowed with recriminations and what ifs. Over and over the events of the last week washed around in his mind, like clothes in a washing machine. Constantly throwing his thoughts this way and that, but always starting at the same point and ending at where he was now. He tried so hard to change them and wanted so much to open his eyes and be back in the safety of his room at home. Closing them tight he waited, hoping in anticipation that he would be transported out of this hell but, when he opened them again, nothing had changed. He'd failed. He let out a sigh, emptying every last drop of air from his lungs. But when he breathed in again it wasn't air, it was more desperation.

Trying to come to terms with his predicament, Dan sat with his knees up to his chest, squeezing himself into a ball for protection. He sniffed hard, the kind of sniff you only did when you were crying. Where it came from you never knew, but it was a scientific fact that when you cry your nose would run as well. Mike knew that Dan was crying but he didn't say anything; he just put his arm around his friend and squeezed him a little more.

Desperate, cold, afraid and with hope diminishing, Mike could only curse his situation.

If only I could turn back the clock, he thought to himself as the tears began to fall once more.

Nine days earlier it had all been so different.

Chapter 1

The alarm clock broke the silence with a synthesized sound of a bugle call. It was a present from his Uncle Jim two Christmases ago. He had hated the clock at first, but when he found out that it annoyed his parents he decided to keep it. His uncle always sent a present at Christmas and birthdays, but Mike hadn't seen him since he was five years old when his dad had taken him with him on some family business. For Mike, his uncle was no more than just a distant memory.

The 4.00am alarm flashed intermittently, lighting up the room with a florescent green glow. Mike rolled over and pushed the button on the top of the clock, plunging the room back into darkness. He was already awake, anyway, when the alarm went off - he'd been too excited to sleep and lay awake most of the night. He felt like a child eager to get up on Christmas morning and open his presents. He knew it was really silly for a seventeen-year-old to feel like this, but he just couldn't help it. The day had finally arrived and he was going to enjoy every minute of it.

Quickly dressing, he put on his new Nike tracksuit which his mum and dad had bought him for this special occasion. Sitting on the edge of his bed, he pulled on his gleaming white trainers and stared at himself in the mirror opposite. A huge grin appeared on his face and he blew himself a kiss. Still grinning, he picked up his suitcase and made his way downstairs. The kitchen light was already on.

Valerie Slater stood at the kitchen table, pouring tea into three large Newcastle United mugs. She looked up and saw Mike still grinning. She smiled to herself and carried on pouring the tea.

'Hello love. Do you want some breakfast?'

'No thanks mum, it's too early to eat.'

'Well, make sure you have something later. I've made you a sandwich to take with you and put a few of your favourite brownies in.'

'Thanks mum.'

Brian Slater appeared at the kitchen door, still in his pyjamas. Brian was forty-five years old, but healthy living normally made him look a good ten years younger. Valerie put it down to his lazy life style. Brian, however, would put it down to his boyish good looks, but at this hour of the morning there would be no argument as he looked well into his fifties.

Brian had been a very good footballer in his youth. He'd played in goal on a semi-professional level at non-league football club Wellington Town and, in those days, the standard was just below that of the big boys in the professional leagues. Mike's mum would say ask anybody who knew him at that time and they would all give the same answer: 'He could have made the big time, that boy.' Unfortunately, though, for Brian his career was cut short due to a pub fight. Some disgruntled fan had been a little bit miffed with a goal that Brian had let in and he had ended up going through a window, tearing the tendons in his right hand. The injury had forced him out of football for two years, and he never played a full game again. The hand didn't heal properly and the football club couldn't afford to send him to see the best consultants. So that was it - career over before it had begun.

Mike knew that this bitter memory chewed his father up inside. It must be so difficult for him, Mike thought, knowing that it was some drunken bastard that had ended your career. Each day his father's resentment would worsen as he watched the footballers of today, with their bulging bank accounts, cars that you only ever see in magazines and peas for brains. The bitterness just kept getting worse and it seemed that the only thing that kept him sane was the thought that his son would one day follow in his footsteps, only this time Mike would go all the way to the top. Luckily for Mike, however, his dad's bitterness was confined to the Slater household and as far as anyone else was concerned Brian Slater was just an unlucky guy who was in the wrong place at the wrong time.

'I thought I'd better make the effort and say goodbye. You all ready, son?' said Brian trying to stifle a yawn at the same time. 'You take care of yourself and focus on the job in hand. Don't let any of those other jokers lead you astray, especially that Dan Sharpe. I know what you're like!'

'Don't worry dad,' replied Mike. 'I'm a big boy now.'

'That's what I am afraid of,' his father replied, shaking his head at the same time.

Mike swallowed the last dregs of his tea, put his cup in the sink and gave his mum a hug.

'Don't worry mum, I'll be fine,' he whispered into her ear. Giving him a kiss on his forehead, she whispered back.

'I know you will, love.' With that, she gave him a hug that a sumo wrestler would be proud of and pushed something into his hand. 'It's just a little extra that you're father and me thought might come in useful over there. Now, go on, get yourself away. You don't want to be late.' She turned away quickly so that Mike couldn't see her eyes filling up with tears.

'Thanks mum, thanks dad.' Mike hurriedly put his little extra in his pocket. He thought it wouldn't be right to count it in front of them. 'I'm not going forever,' he continued, trying to sound upbeat. 'I'll be back as soon as you know it, and I'll call and let you know how it's going. Don't worry, I'll be fine.'

Picking up his suitcase in one hand, Mike held out his other to his dad. He gripped it and shook it the way his dad had taught him, nice and firm.

'Good luck, son. See you soon and remember what I said.'

'Yes dad, I know, concentrate.'

Mike smiled at his dad and wanted to give him a hug, but he couldn't. He loved his dad like any son loves a father, but cuddles were never part of their relationship. He'd have to settle for that man to man handshake instead.

Walking to the end of the road without looking back, he knew his parents would be watching. There hadn't been many times in his life yet where he'd felt grown up, but on this occasion he knew that he couldn't turn around to wave. A child would and he wasn't a child anymore. Keeping his head facing forward, he thought about the coming tour and politely pushed his parents to the back of his mind. He had guessed right, though - his parents *were* watching from the kitchen window. Valerie sobbed, wiping her tired eyes on a tea towel. Seeing her only child leaving home was too much for her to bear. Brian squeezed her shoulder, gave her a kiss on the neck and then when back to bed. As he climbed the stairs he chuckled to himself, feeling deeply proud of his son.

It took only five minutes to walk the short distance to the Fox and Duck pub from where the team tour bus would be leaving. It was an awful-looking pub built in the 1970s; the planners had tried so hard for it to blend in with its surroundings but had failed miserably. It looked more like a Swiss chalet that had been dropped right in the middle of a typical British housing estate. However, this never mattered to whoever drank there as, once inside, it was in every way a typical British pub with its typical British regulars. Brian would make

Mike laugh whenever the pub was mentioned.

'Bloody breweries,' he would say, getting himself worked up with the thought of them. 'Beer's expensive, food's crap and whoever did the interior design - well! Why they tried to make it look like an English farmhouse when we live in a city is beyond me.' However, it had never stopped him from drinking there.

It was 4.40am on a Saturday morning. The streets were deserted, all but for a ginger cat sitting on a gate post staring at him. Mike stared back and the cat seemed to look at him with disdain for having disturbed its sleep. It was mid July and there wasn't a breath of wind, but still Mike found there was a chill in the air so he zipped up his tracksuit all the way to the top and quickened his pace to warm himself up. As he turned the last corner, he stood for a moment and watched from a distance. The pub car park was full of cars. Parents were busy unloading suitcases and bags and chatting with one another. It could have been a Saturday night rather than the silent early hours of the morning.

He leant against a lamp post and felt proud that he belonged to such a team. He watched as big Tony Fletcher, the team's six foot two centre half, waved goodbye to his parents. The twins, Graham and Steve Loach, were playing head tennis until the ball landed on the chairman's Jaguar. Grabbing the ball, they quickly jumped onto the bus without the chairman seeing. Martin Cuthbert, the left back, was trying to pull away from his mother who had hold of his coat. She was trying to get him to give her a goodbye kiss, but Martin was having none of it. Mark Baxter, one of the midfield players, was talking with the team Manager and trying ever so hard to keep a straight face as Stuart Forster, his midfield colleague, was making faces behind the manager's back. Floyd Barnaby, the only coloured lad in the team, stood quietly talking to the assistant manager, John Dodd, or Ken as everyone else called him. Mike couldn't see anyone else and assumed they were already on the bus.

A Range Rover pulled up alongside. Miles St John, the rich boy from Northumberland, climbed out of the passenger seat. Mike didn't get on with Miles, mainly because, according to Mike, he was full of crap. You could never have a normal conversation with him. If you had done something, you could bet that Miles had already done it a lot bigger, better and quicker, so Mike had very little to do with him. Little Terry Grainger, or the Midfield Dynamo as he was known, climbed out of the back seat followed by the best header of a ball Mike had ever played with, Richard Green. Mike scanned the area for any others and, of course Dan, but he couldn't see them.

'What a great team,' he said to himself as he approached, feeling really proud to be part of something special.

He hadn't really taken much notice of the team bus but, as he got closer, he wasn't too impressed with what he saw. Not being exactly modern, it was one of those three-quarter sized ones that always looked out of place wherever you saw them. Lacking style and comfort, and with the looks of a white ambulance bus from the local asylum, the team would definitely turn heads when they arrived. *Well, it'll have to do*, he thought to himself.

A large pile of bags and suitcases sat untidily at the rear of the bus. Mike made his way over and couldn't help but stare when he saw the fattest man he'd ever seen bending down and placing luggage into the boot of the bus. *He must be the coach driver*, Mike assumed, *and the only coach driver to resemble a conference pear!* His head and neck were of the same circumference, which made him appear to have no neck at all. He wore a white shirt which must have been a size XXXL, but even that looked too small for him. Each time he bent down to pick up a bag it would ride up his back and show the crack of his backside. As for his stomach, it hung precariously over a thick leather belt, like an avalanche hanging over a cliff face waiting to destroy anything in its path. Mike gave a wry smile and thought that he was probably a very nice man once you got to know him.

The rest of the players were saying their farewells to parents and friends, and boys were giving kisses to mothers and fathers bashfully, not wanting to look soft in front of mates. Mike was glad he'd said his goodbyes at home.

'Look who's been eating all the pies! You seen the size of that driver's gut?' said a voice Mike knew very well. He turned and saw Dan standing there in a full Newcastle United away strip. His legs looked even paler than normal in the early morning light.

'What you got shorts on for?' Mike said with a smirk across his face.

'Well, I've never been abroad before and my old man says it will be hot over there.' Mike slapped him on the back of his head, but not hard.

'It's not going to be hot this time of the morning, you dipstick. And anyway, we're going to France not Tenerife.' Dan looked back, not amused by his friend's unkindness towards him, but also unaware that Mike was also wearing his shorts under his tracksuit bottoms, but of course Mike would never let on. Dan grabbed Mike's case.

'I'll give this to fatty and we'll get on the bus. Oi, Fatty, take this bag will ya!' Dan yelled across at the driver. Looking up, the fat man scowled making the skin ripple on his chubby forehead.

'You call me fatty again, boy, and I'll plant one of these on your chin, you cheeky little runt!' The driver waved a fist the size of a sledge hammer in the air. Mike winced as he imagined the fat driver thumping Dan. He would probably kill him with one punch.

'You'd probably die of a heart attack if you tried, fat boy,' replied Dan under his breath as he walked towards the rear of the bus. With that, he put Mike's case with the others and ran to climb aboard.

To anyone that didn't know them, Dan and Mike appeared an odd match for best friends. How they got to know each other was totally by chance. Both their dads had been involved in a car accident. Nothing serious, just a common shunt caused by an irresponsible rubbernecker. The damage wasn't major, but when the police arrived and breathalysed each driver Dan's dad was found to be over the alcohol limit. This was no surprise to Dan, as his father had a history of getting into trouble with the police. The problem was that Dan, being a juvenile, then became the police's responsibility and, if a relative couldn't be found to take him, he would have to be handed over to social services. Brian took pity on the boy. He couldn't let social services take him, they were worse than useless in his opinion. So, with Mike's blessing, Brian thought it best to take him home with them. The police didn't care as it saved them paperwork, so that was sorted and Dan came home with Mike.

The two boys hit it off straight away and the common theme that sealed the bond between them happened to be Newcastle United football club. They were two fanatics in love with the black and white of United. Statistics, players, club and history were given the full works and only when dawn broke the next morning did they decide to get some sleep.

Dan wasn't anything like Mike. He'd been brought

up by his dad after his mother had walked out when he was only seven years old. This was generally believed to be due to his dad's excessive drinking and gambling. He lived on the opposite side of the City to Mike, on a large housing estate called The Meadows. It was one of those housing estates where every third house had the windows boarded up. Crime was the main pastime and you'd dare not leave your car unattended for long otherwise some delinquent would have scratched his or her name in the paintwork. There was a time when a particular police officer had attended a call for a burglary, and when he returned to the Panda car he'd found it propped up on bricks. 'Fuck off Pigs' had been spray painted on all four sides of the car and the blue light on the roof had been smashed. Now the police only ventured onto the estate in threes. Some people said it was for one officer to watch the Panda car and two officers to deal with the incident.

A year separated them by age and, even though they later found out that they went to the same school, they'd never met. Where Mike was responsible and polite, Dan was rude and arrogant. Mike didn't drink or smoke but Dan, for a sixteen-year-old, excelled in both. Given no choice in his early life, he'd had to grow up fast. His father had surrounded him with the worst living environment possible and credit was due to him that he'd not followed in his father's footsteps. Streetwise he had to be and streetwise he had become. So on the whole they were complete opposites, an angel and a devil, but a bond had developed between them and they'd become brothers rather than friends.

Mike climbed aboard the bus first with Dan pushing him in the small of his back. They instantly made their way towards the rear, but the back seat was taken. Dan leaned forward and whispered to Mike.

'I don't want to sit too near the front, listening to

19

Barry waffle on about bugger all.'

'Well, we'll sit here then,' Mike said, directing the way. He pushed Dan into two empty seats three quarters of the way down the bus. 'Barry will probably sit near the front and bore the driver.'

'Oh, I hope so,' Dan said with his eyes glued on Barry. 'I hope so.'

Chapter 2

By the time the tour bus had been loaded and the rest of the team had said their goodbyes to family and friends it was 5.15am. The sun, not yet visible, was just beginning to change the colour of the horizon. Mike watched with tired eyes as it climbed slowly, like a hot air balloon lifting off the ground. Every minute it would change colour, going from red to orange and then bright gold until it became so intense he couldn't gaze at its brightness anymore. Looking at Dan, who was fast asleep, he decided to do the same.

Waking up when his head hit the window, Mike didn't know which made him jump the most, the noise his head made when it hit the glass or the instant shooting pain in his forehead. His tracksuit top had not made a very efficient pillow and, with the movement of the bus, it had fallen on his lap, leaving his head exposed to danger. Dribble on his chin had found its way onto his t-shirt, making a wet patch that glistened like a slug. He quickly looked around the bus to see if anyone had noticed. A few boys were playing cards on the back seat, Barry was rabbiting away in the driver's ear and the rest of the team were sound asleep. Mike, relieved, settled himself back into a comfortable position and re-propped his head up with his top.

The long drive was intermittently broken by motorway bridges and embankments. Mike stared drowsily at the countryside whizzing by, day dreaming about the tour. Suddenly his dad's voice popped into his head and started to give him a lecture on life.

'There are millions of kids out there that would give their right arm to be going on a football tour of Europe. You should be prepared to work hard. You can play about as much as you want when you get home.'

'Yeah yeah,' Mike said, trying his best to think of something other than his dad, but the advice didn't go willingly so he looked around for a distraction. The bus began to slow and he stretched his neck so that he could look over the top of the seats in front. A service station was coming up, so he gave Dan a nudge.

'What! Are we at the ferry?' asked Dan, more asleep than awake.

'No, don't be stupid, it's just a service station. Are you coming?'

'Yeah, I could do with having a piss.' Always straight to the point was Dan.

As soon as the bus stopped, Dan left his seat and sprinted off in the direction of the services. Mike casually followed behind, not wanting to be standing next to him at the urinal. Dan's aim was lousy and Mike definitely didn't want a yellow tinge to his brilliant white trainers.

'Hey Mike, look at these babies,' Dan shouted from the back of a car transporter neatly packed out with top of the range Mercedes cars. Mike looked across in disbelief, only to see Dan sprawled over the bonnet of a sporty convertible.

'Get down before you damage something,' Mike shouted. Dan just laughed. Climbing down, he kissed the wheel arch of one of the cars and rubbed it as though he was stroking a cat.

'Get me one of these one day when I'm a superstar. I might even buy you one if you want,' he yelled, chuckling to himself. 'I think I'll have the Mercedes and you can have a Skoda.' Jumping off, he walked over to Mike with a huge smile across his face. 'Then again, maybe I'll get you a Lada instead. Suit you down to the ground.'

Mike grabbed him around the neck like a wrestler

would grab an opponent and ground his knuckles into his hair, making him beg to stop.

'Sometimes I think you're a bottle short of a six pack, you know that?' Mike said, pushing him away. Both boys chuckled and hurried off into the services.

'Ten minutes only,' shouted Barry and everyone quickened up the pace. By the time the two of them had visited the toilet and the shop the ten minutes was up. They rushed back to the bus, where Barry was standing by the door pointing at his watch.

'You two ought to learn to tell the time!'

'It wasn't my fault!' said Dan as he clambered up the front steps. 'Mike was trying to chat up the girl on the till.'

'Very funny,' said Mike as he pushed Dan in the back, making him fall on the coach driver.

'Oh, it's you,' said the driver, recognising Dan. 'I hope you're not going to make a habit of pissing me off.'

'Sorry pal,' he boldly shouted as he ran down the centre isle of the bus to his seat.

When the last boy was on board, Barry did a quick head count and then gave the nod to the driver. As the bus pulled away, Mike made himself comfortable once more. Dan was reading Match magazine and his face was buried in the pages as though he was scrutinising every word.

'What you reading?' Mike said leaning over Dan's shoulder, trying to take a peak. Dan replied without taking his eyes from the magazine.

'You didn't want to buy it in the shop. You didn't want to spend any money. So why should I let you look at it now?'

'Give us a look, otherwise I'll give you a dead leg.' Mike clenched his fist and was just about to bring it hard down on top of Dan's thigh when Dan pushed the magazine towards his face.

'Here have a look. The last time you gave me a dead leg it was knackered for three days.'

Mike took the magazine, but made sure that both of them could read it. The headline read 'Bonjour Newcastle'. It was an article on the latest signings for Newcastle United; three French players had been spotted when Newcastle were on tour there in the previous summer break. Transfer fees in the Premiership were already crazy so taking the young talented ones from abroad kept the clubs money in its pocket. Seemed to make sense Mike thought, but as long as they are good.

'That'll be me one day! You watch,' Dan said as he lifted his head and stared upwards like he was suddenly in a hypnotic trance. Mike replied, his tone of voice was harsh and unforgiving.

'Hey! Earth calling! Get a grip of yourself! See those words there. They say, talented, gifted and intelligent. Not you! More like bullshitter, useless and loser. Think again, dreamer.'

Mike once more settled back in his seat. He looked at Dan's face. There was no expression at all; he was just staring into the seat in front. Dan's feelings had been hurt, but Mike thought that it did him good once in a while to be put in his place. He knew that Dan had great ability on the football pitch, but he needed to start taking life more seriously; otherwise, in Mike's opinion, he would turn out like his old man. A real loser!

The next hour of the journey they didn't talk. Dan buried his head in his magazine and Mike listened to his mp3 player while staring out of the window at the countless number of road cones until it gave him a head ache. On his many previous journeys up and down Britain's motorways with his dad, it had always puzzled him why there were so many cones. To enable one lone maintenance vehicle to work on the carriageway it seemed necessary, by whoever was in charge of motorways, that ten miles each way would be coned off. The traffic would pile up and next thing you would be sitting for an hour in a traffic jam. The tour bus started to slow up.

'I knew it!' Mike exclaimed, thumping the back of the seat in front in frustration. 'Bloody traffic jam!'

With nothing else to do but stare at the hard shoulder, Mike pulled the tour itinerary out of his pocket. He examined the front page with the Club's regal coat of arms taking pride of place in the centre. It consisted of a three-turreted castle on a knight's shield with an artillery gun dead centre and, written beneath in Latin, *Miles Gloriosus* (Glorious Soldier). A broad grin appeared on his face when he read the club's name. Fenham Indispensables always made him smile.

The club had been founded at the end of the First World War by returning Northumberland Fusiliers who wanted to restore some pride in the local community. The name 'Indispensables' came about because of the large number of females to males in the region after the War. Rumour had it that the fusiliers became indispensible to the local ladies, fulfilling many of their nocturnal needs. The club had grown from just one team of senior players through the twenties, thirties and forties to having junior and youth teams from the fifties onwards. Mike had got used to the name, as he felt it gave them style rather than the usual last names like United, Athletic and Rovers. It got the area noticed and seemed to give the team more credibility, wherever they went. Every boy in Newcastle wanted to play for Newcastle United, but first they wanted to play for the Indispensables.

Mike carried on reading down the page. There was a

message from the Club Chairman:

'I wish to thank the family of the Late Arthur Hughes, whose kind donation has made this tour possible. May I say on behalf of the players and staff at Fenham Indispensables that Arthur is a great loss to this club. He will be remembered with fond memories. We will all miss his presence and the encouragement he gave us in the dressing room before and after every game.

Edward Hayes (Chairman)'

Mike, like all the players at the club, knew Arthur very well. Every club had one like him. He looked after the dressing rooms, the kit, the balls; he made sure that you had what you needed before a game and, if he didn't have it, he would do his very best to get it for you. He'd been a player himself in the fifties and at the end of his career had stayed on at the club he loved so much. He became one of the football coaches and when he became too old to coach he helped out in the dressing room. Arthur had recently died and, when his will was read, it was found that he'd left a large amount of money to the club. Needless to say, his family were not very happy with his choice of beneficiary.

The chairman had deemed it appropriate that some of the money would go towards giving the young players in the club a taste of what it was like to play in Europe. The rest would go to a memorial plaque that would hang on the dressing room wall. Mike looked up to the sky.

'Thanks Arthur, much appreciated.'

The team had now been travelling for most of the day. With three other rest stops, it was not until 6pm when the bus reached the ferry terminal at Dover. Mike watched through the window as the driver positioned the tour bus in a long line of other coaches facing toward an empty ferry berth. To Mike, it felt just like going to an away match with his dad to watch Newcastle play. All the away fans would arrive by coach and park up several miles away from the ground at a predetermined place set by the police. The police would then escort the whole cavalcade to the ground. The dockyard at Dover resembled, in many ways, turning up at the away ground - the lights and noise, the multitude of vehicles, hundreds of people milling about. Yet there were a few important exceptions. No home fans hurling abuse, spitting and throwing bottles at the coaches. No police with dogs segregating both sets of supporters. But most of all, no feeling of intimidation.

Mike changed his mind. Dover dock was nothing like going to an away game.

As the bus came to a stop, Barry stood up with the microphone in his hand. Before he could say a word Dan yelled out.

'Go on Barry, give use a song!' The bus erupted with laughter. Someone else shouted 'Yeah, know any Barry White?' The laughter continued until Barry spoke and then quickly died away.

'Bus is full of jokers and don't think I don't know who said it. I will be having words later with Mr Sharpe and friend.'

Dan looked at Mike. 'Don't worry, he's full of shit. He won't do nowt,' he said, covering his mouth with his hand as he spoke so Barry wouldn't see him talking. Mike replied, trying to talk without moving his lips. His voice had a sound of sarcasm to it.

'Oh, I'm not worried. He likes me. It's you he thinks is a twat.'

'Thanks mate!'

Barry announced that the ferry was going to be late

because of bad weather in the channel, and that everyone should stay on the coach until he found out what was going on.

'Oh, that's just great,' Dan said with a sigh.

'Don't worry, I'll play eye spy with you if you get bored, little boy,' Mike said, patting Dan on the head. Dan pulled away, not amused. But then, like a rabbit startled in the headlights of a car, he looked up at Mike as though he'd seen a ghost.

'I hope it ain't going to be rough. I've only been in a boat once before and that was a trip to the Farne Islands in Northumberland to see some bloody seagulls. I puked up going there, got dive bombed and shit on while I was there and puked on coming back.'

'You need to grow up!' replied Mike. 'You do realise that this boat is a little bit bigger than the dingy you went to the Farnes on, don't you? But if you want, when we get on board I'll ask if I can reserve a toilet for you to use as your own personal sick bag.'

'Thanks a million, mate. I look for a bit of support and what do I get? Bugger all!' Dan slumped in the seat. 'Mike.'

'What!'

'Wake me up if something happens.'

'God, what did your last slave die of?'

'Go on, will ya?'

'Yeah alright, but don't snore otherwise I'll be forced to kill you.'

Dan turned, making himself comfortable facing towards Mike. Mike looked at him, feeling a little bit jealous that he could fall asleep anywhere. Thirty seconds later the snoring started. Mike didn't have the heart to nudge him, as he would be less trouble asleep. Putting his top over Dan's head, he hoped that it would drown out some of the piggy noises, but it didn't work. Outside it was just starting to rain and the noise of the rain drops on the glass took Mike's mind off his annoying friend. Looking out to sea, the sky looked ominous. The clouds were thick and nasty-looking, more like bellowing smoke than clouds. Occasionally a flash of forked lightening would light up the horizon. Mike thought about what Dan had said. He swallowed hard and he too hoped the crossing would be a good one.

At first the rain tapped at the window gently, like a thousand ants wearing tap shoes. It was slow a first, but as the intensity grew the water on the glass distorted the view of the docks. Mike pushed his face against the glass to make out the blurry figures outside. He could just about make out five other members of the team sprinting away from the ferry terminal, back towards the bus. He squinted to see what was following them. His breath was making the window misty, so he quickly rubbed it to get a better view.

A shadowy haze was moving like a rolling mist across the dock. He couldn't comprehend at first, but then he realised what it was. The storm was advancing so quickly that the heavy rain had become like a wave rolling across the land. Anything you could see was instantly consumed by this gigantic wave of rain. Splat! It hit the coach, enveloping it in an instant. The ants had changed their tap shoes for hobnailed boots and the noise inside the bus had become quite deafening. Mike threw himself back from the window in shock.

Two of his team mates had made it to the coach before the rain had hit, but three were caught. They ran up the steps of the bus panting, trying to get their breath back; they looked as though they had just walked through the showers in the dressing room fully clothed. Water dripped off their clothes as they walked up the centre aisle. Some of the others sniggered, but instantly stopped when water was flicked in their faces as a result. Mike felt sorry for them, but was glad that he'd stayed on the bus. His thoughts jumped to the passengers on the incoming ferry, who had had to ride out the storm. It must be hell, with the boat bobbing around on the sea like a piece of driftwood. There would definitely be some very sick people on board.

Dan slept like a baby, oblivious to it all.

Mike closed his eyes and listened to the rain hitting the window. It's going to be a long night, he thought to himself. The hypnotic rhythm of rain on glass was making him feel sleepy. He recalled being caught in a rain shower the week before at a car boot sale in Seaham, near Sunderland. He'd had to take shelter quickly and ended squashed under the canopy of a burger bar. But that's when it happened. She was gorgeous. He found himself staring at her: a vision of beauty, an angel he thought. The rain had disappeared from his mind; the world could be falling apart around him, but he was frozen until, of course, she made eye contact with him and his legs went to jelly.

He'd looked up at the menu board and pretended to be deciding what he would have, but he wasn't reading; instead, he was just thinking what he should do next. She turned to another customer and he quickly reapplied his gaze. She looked older than him, but to Mike that made no difference. Her hair was blonde and was tied back in a pony tail which emphasised her face. Her eyes sparkled like diamonds and, in the heat of the burger bar, her cheeks were flushed pink. There was a tiny beauty spot just above and to the right of her top lip. Mike thought how sexy it made her look. Her lips were bright red, perfectly covered in the glossiest lipstick that Mike had ever seen. She wore a tight, figure-hugging t-shirt and Mike couldn't help but notice her cleavage pushing its way out of the top, like two puppies fighting to get out of a paper bag. There was a name badge which said 'DONNA' in bold capitals with 'Have a nice day' written underneath. Suddenly she turned to Mike. His eyes were glued to her breasts.

'What would you like?' she said as she stood right in front of him behind the counter.

'Sorry - what did you say?' he replied, struggling to get his words out.

'Do you want something or not?' Her voice had an edge to it now. There were other customers waiting to be served and she stood there, impatiently staring at Mike. The words just came out, he couldn't help himself.

'Donna, you're lovely.' He regretted his words as soon as he had said them. He heard someone sniggering. He felt so embarrassed. He just wanted the earth to swallow him up.

'Yeah, you're not too bad yourself,' she replied irritably, 'but do you want anything? I've got other customers you know.' She leaned forward, unwittingly showing off more of her cleavage to all the customers.

'Just a coke,' he whispered back to her. She served him his coke, winked at him provocatively and ran her tongue along her top lip. Mike had tingles everywhere. Smiling shyly, with cheeks as red as tomatoes, he turned away. The rain shower had passed and he edged back away from the stall with his can of coke. Feeling aroused, embarrassed and humiliated all at the same time, he stood watching her from a distance until he had to leave.

Mike opened his eyes and smiled. He knew that he had made a complete idiot of himself that day, but he was on his own and nobody would be rubbing his face in his embarrassment. 'But my God,' he said to himself, 'she was gorgeous.'

Staring at the rain through the glass, he decided then

and there that when he got back to England he would ask her out for a drink. Whether his dad would approve of him going out with a lass that sold burgers would pose a bigger problem. Brian could be so opinionated sometimes with regard to others, especially the opposite sex. Mike recalled his dad taking him to one side once when he was seeing a girl who lived in an area that he didn't approve off.

'With women, son, you have to aim high,' Brian had said, putting his hand on Mike's shoulder. 'Go for the best you can get. If your aim isn't very good then you should still get yourself a decent one.'

Mike hated his dad saying that. What was he trying to do? Comparing women to darts or shooting? How stupid could you get? Mike knew that whoever he chose to be with it was because he wanted to, not because he was sticking to some sort of pathetic rule laid down by his dad.

'Anyway,' Mike had replied, 'mum was only a school cleaner. That doesn't look like aiming high to me.' Brian nudged Mike on his shoulder with his fist.

'She lied to me, son. She told me she was the headmistress, and anyway I had a lousy aim.' Mike laughed at the time, going along with his dad.

He woke with a jolt. He hadn't meant to drop off, but the bus was warm and the sound of the rain had helped him on his way. The storm had passed and the gentle tapping of light rain had resumed. Mike turned to talk to Dan, but the seat was empty. Looking up and down the bus, Mike scrutinised each seat to see if Dan was there but he couldn't see him. Instead, he noticed Barry making his way to the microphone again. Yawning and rubbing his eyes, he livened himself up for the coming announcement. Barry flicked the button to talk and a shrill of feedback caught everyone's attention.

'Listen up. I've just been informed that the ferry will be docking within the hour.' A unanimous cheer went up and some of the lads clapped.

'Ok, ok that's not all. Customs are putting sniffer dogs into the luggage space and in here to check for anything that shouldn't be there. So I hope for your sakes that nobody's been an idiot.' His eyes quickly scanned the faces that peered back at him as though he was looking for one guilty face. 'Also, Passport Control will be getting on and checking your passports. So have them ready, ok?' He went to give the microphone back to the driver, then thought twice and turned back towards the team.

'Where is Mr Sharpe?' he snapped, pushing the microphone right into his lips. 'Have you seen him, Mike?' He looked over to where Mike sat, his bushy eyebrows joining together as he frowned. Mike sighed and thought how typical it was that it had to be Dan. Standing up, he shouted back using his hand as a loud hailer.

'No Barry! I haven't got a clue where he is, sorry!' Mike replied as convincingly as he could, but he knew that if Dan wasn't on the bus then he would be somewhere else smoking a cigarette. Unfortunately for Barry but lucky for Dan, Mike hadn't got it in him to grass Dan up.

As Mike sat down, a Springer Spaniel ran up the stairs onto the bus followed by its handler. Everybody stopped talking and sat still. All eyes watched as the dog methodically sniffed above and under the seats. The dog made no distinction between human and furniture and both received the same amount of attention along both lengths of the bus. When it had reached the rear, the handler whistled and the dog turned and ran wagging its tail all the way back towards the handler. It couldn't have taken more than three minutes to complete the whole bus. Mike thought how impressive it all looked and in a way was glad that Dan wasn't there because, if the dog was going to find anything, it would be Dan that carried it.

'I wonder where that little git is?' he muttered under his breath. Then he had an awful thought. Maybe they'd found something on him? It would be just like him to do something stupid.

Next onto the bus stepped two men checking passports. Each boy handed over their passport in turn. The details were checked. The officer would look at each individual's face, say 'thank you' and hand the passport back. Not another word was said.

Once the passport men had left, Barry rose from his seat.

'No one else leave the bus,' he shouted.

Mike watched as Barry walked towards the ferry terminal with determination in his stride. Half an hour passed and there was no sign of him returning. The incoming ferry had docked and the foot passengers were making their way down the gangway to the terminal. The driver started up the bus and the air conditioning sparked into life. Mike knew Barry would be looking for Dan. I wouldn't want to be in his shoes when Barry gets hold of him, he thought. The tour was more important to Barry than anyone else on the bus and he wasn't going to let anybody or anything jeopardise it, especially Daniel Sharpe.

By now the ferry was empty and the line of cars started to move forward ready for boarding. The bus moved as well but not in the same direction as the cars - just to one side, letting the vehicles behind pass.

The driver announced over the microphone that, due to one of the players not being on the bus, they could not board the ferry yet. The atmosphere suddenly changed. Mike could hear Dan's name being mentioned.

'It's always him. He'll fuck this tour up for everyone,' Tony Fletcher said, sitting a few rows in front.

'I think he should be sent home,' shouted Stuart Forster voicing his opinion. Mike put his head in his hands, his face grimacing. *Dan, you're such a donkey.*

Chapter 3

Half an hour later, Barry, who was very hot, tired and extremely pissed off, spotted Dan with a group of dock workers having a cigarette. They were all standing under a moveable walkway which provided them shelter from the rain. If it wasn't for loud laughter coming from the group Barry would have walked right past them. Dan stood in the middle of the huddle, easily recognisable, wearing his team tracksuit and the only one without a high visibility jacket and hard hat.

A fire burned in Barry's chest when it came to Daniel and it didn't take much to make him angry. He walked with purpose towards the group, his mind in overdrive already rehearsing what he was going to say. He was ready to give this delinquent a piece of his mind.

Barry was fifty years old and still single. He had lived with his mother up until she died and now just lived alone in the house she had left him. Barry had two loves in his life, football and his religion. People would find it hard to decide which one came first. He had been brought up a strict Methodist by his mother, who had frowned upon him fraternising with anyone who didn't belong to the same church. This played hell with his love of football and, by the time he found the courage to stand up against her, his footballing aspirations had faded and died. Anyway, Barry had two left feet so he would never have made the grade. His talent was in his motivational skills and he was a genius when it came to tactics. He had spent so many lonely nights alone in his bedroom as a teenager reading, studying and digesting everything you needed to know about the game that he decided to take his football coaching qualifications. His mother flipped her lid, told him he was a bad son and that football was for the weak minded. It didn't make any difference; he took his exams, and passed and, by doing so, it eventually led him to the Indispensables.

He knew that people mocked him for his single life and his beliefs, even the players from time to time, but everyone knew that he was good at what he did. He became admired as a coach and a manager and gained total respect because he didn't bullshit. He gave the Indispensables the inspiration to be good on and off the field. Of course, except for one - Daniel Sharpe, who he believed to be a demon sent from hell to test his strength and faith. So Daniel became a challenge in more ways than one.

Barry never swore or, if he did, nobody heard him. He believed that swearing was for people who could not find the proper words to use and didn't have the intellect to communicate in any other manner. This time, though, it was going to be different.

'Sharpe! What the hell do you think you're doing?' he yelled as loudly as he could. Then under his breath he apologised to his God. Everyone in the group jumped in surprise. They turned around to see a fifty-year-old, ginger-haired man striding towards them with a look of rage written all over his face.

Dan stood dumbstruck with his mouth open. His cigarette had already hit the floor by the time Barry reached him. The dock workers moved away quickly and soon only Barry and Dan remained. For an instant nothing was said. Dan looked into Barry's angry eyes and didn't see the usual soft look. He didn't care, though. So what? It's only Barry, he thought to himself. However, seeing Barry so worked up and about to explode required a second to think before he opened his mouth; he was just about to tread into new territory.

'Do you ever think of anybody but yourself?' shouted Barry, giving Dan a look that would burn through lead.

'What's up with you?' Dan replied with an arrogant tone in his voice. 'I'm just smoking a tab!' Barry glared at him. 'You're not my old man, so it's got nowt to do with you.'

'You amaze me sometimes, you know that? You've been given a gift and you don't even realise it.' Barry moved closer, making Dan step back against the wall of the walkway.

'What are you going on about?' Dan replied, shrugging his shoulder at the same time.

'You're an excellent footballer, Dan, and with the right direction you could go far, but you are the most selfish, obnoxious and stupid boy I know.'

Dan sighed. 'Yeah, whatever!'

Barry felt himself getting warmer. A bead of sweat ran down his armpit. The anger inside was fermenting like cider in a barrel, and unless the pressure was released he would explode. I'm not going to let this boy get the better of me, he said to himself.

'You realise football is a team sport, don't you? You boy! Better start being part of this team otherwise you will be out.'

'You can't do that,' Dan yelled, stepping forward and trying to exert some of his authority over this man standing over him. Barry stood his ground and Dan shrank back against the wall.

'I can do anything I want. Don't you forget that!' Barry said, sticking his finger into Dan's chest. Dan smirked his couldn't-care-less smirk and suddenly Barry saw red. He would say later that he didn't know what came over him. However, without warning, and like a man twenty years his junior, he lunged forward and with his right hand grabbed Dan around his neck.

Dan grimaced with pain as Barry squeezed the force of his grip, pushing Dan's head against the concrete walkway. Barry's barrel had just exploded. Dan struggled to get free, but Barry had all of his sixteen stone weight pressed against the lightweight sixteen-year-old. Barry's left leg started to twitch as the adrenaline rush that he'd released flowed through his body.

'Listen to me boy!' Barry whispered between his teeth. 'I might be old but I'm not taking this shit from you. That chip on your shoulder is going to ruin your life. You better start getting wise and grow up and realise that what you do affects others.'

Dan gave up struggling and relaxed. Barry sensed it but kept a hold, increasing his grip. He needed to get what he had to say off his chest and until then Dan wasn't going anywhere.

'You've got the best opportunity to make something of yourself with this team, but the way you're going, boy, I might as well send you back to your pathetic life of sniffing glue or mugging old ladies. Isn't that what boys like you do? You won't get another chance like this, so if you lose it, you might as well crawl back under that stone you came from.'

With that, Barry let go. Dan rubbed his neck, his eyes glaring into Barry's. In that single moment he hated him with every ounce of malice that he had in his body.

'I'll have you for assault,' he growled showing his teeth like an angry dog.

'Oh yeah!' Barry said smugly. 'You think that the police will believe you? No, think again, it'll be the other way round. It's you that assaulted me, I think.' On hearing that, Dan's eyes suddenly widened in surprise. 'Then we'll see who they believe.'

Dan knew he was right. He'd been in trouble with

the police many times before and assault already figured on his criminal records. The name Daniel Sharpe would definitely be on the police computer.

Barry raised his arm and pointed in the direction of the bus.

'The bus is over there. Get on it! And we'll say no more.' Dan, not saying another word but still looking furious, headed for the bus.

Barry leant forward, putting his head against the wall. He knew that he'd won the battle, but not the war. He was ashamed of himself. He'd resorted to violence for the first time in his life and it made him feel sick. As he walked back to the bus he vowed to himself that he wouldn't let it happen again. Dan walked a few yards in front with his hands stuck firmly in his pockets. Sulking like an infant would do after a scolding, he muttered unintelligibly to himself.

The tour bus stood alone on the dock. The ferry was waiting, but for how long remained unknown. Sixteen angry faces focused their attention on the two figures walking towards them. Dan didn't lift his head; he knew they were looking at him. He tensed himself up, ready for the barrage of abuse, but first he had to show his passport to the extremely fed up-looking official standing at the door. Dan held it up and stood expressionless while looking into space, afraid to make eye contact.

'Ok, that will do. Get this bus out of here,' groaned the official.

As Dan climbed the steps there was silence. Nothing had to be said that hadn't already been said. Dan walked to his seat and sat down next to Mike. He stared at the back of the seat in front of him as the verbal abuse began. There was no way he was going to make eye contact with any of them. Willing them to turn around, he sat listening to their vented anger. There was no doubt about it: Dan was definitely going to be made to feel bad by his team mates.

When Barry had cleared the door it closed behind him and the bus began to move towards the ferry. Faces turned away, instantly lifting the veil of hatred that had momentarily descended over Dan. Mike gave Dan a nudge on his leg. Dan didn't respond.

Mike was annoyed with him for causing them all to wait, but he was happy to have his friend back. He knew something had happened between him and Barry, but what, he had no idea. Noticing the red blotches around Dan's neck he realised the seriousness of their encounter.

'You ok?' he said softly.

'Yeah, I'm alright,' replied a dejected Dan.

'Don't worry, we'll be on the ferry soon.' Mike gave him another nudge with his hand and then turned to look out of the window.

The bus drove up onto a ramp and into the bowels of the ferry. A man wearing bright orange overalls and earphones directed it to a position to the rear of the other coaches. As soon as the bus stopped, the ramp behind them started to close. A loud whining noise could be heard as the winches took the strain of the slowly gathering cable.

On the bus, anger had turned to elation. Everything previous had been forgotten. For many on the bus the tour had now really begun and the excitement of being on a boat such as this, for the first time, was hard to contain. Everyone chattered and giggled, eager to get off the bus and explore the boat. Coats and bags were dragged from their places of rest and towed behind as the excited line of young boys hurriedly made their way through the vehicle deck and up the nearest staircase. Mike and Dan waited until only they remained. Mike turned to Dan, finding it hard to conceal his own excitement.

'Come on, let's go! Forget what happened, we're on our way again. Snap out of it.'

Dan rose from his seat, grabbed his bag and, without saying a word, walked down the centre aisle towards the door. Mike followed close behind but didn't say anything else to him. Let him stew, he thought. Stepping from the bus, he watched Dan run off. A strong smell of diesel fumes hung in the air and Mike didn't want to linger around too long.

'Excuse me, Mike, can I have a word?' a voice said from behind.

Mike turned to see Barry. He was standing next to the luggage compartment, waiting for the driver to get a bag out for him. Mike walked over, taking small breaths so as not to inhale too many fumes. Barry grabbed his bag as the driver shut the compartment and they both met half way.

'I need to talk to you about Dan,' said Barry, covering his mouth and coughing several times. 'But let's get out of here quick before we choke.'

They both hurriedly made their way to the staircase and climbed the first flight. The noise of the vehicle deck had died down to a steady hum and the ventilation system was doing its job where they stood. Barry put his bag on the floor ran his hands through his thinning ginger hair, took a deep breath and turned to Mike.

'Mike, you know I'm a fair man, don't you?' Barry sounded nervous.

'Of course you are, Barry,' replied Mike, wondering where Barry was taking the conversation.

'I think that I've been a bit too hard on Daniel. I lost my temper with him.'

'Well, that's easily done,' joked Mike. Barry didn't laugh.

'I've done something very wrong and I'm ashamed

of myself.' Barry bowed his head and let his chin rest on his chest, then took a deep breath.

'I laid my hands on him, I just snapped. I grabbed him around the neck. He made me so angry. He's threatened to go to the police and have me arrested. It will finish me off, Mike, you know that don't you?'

Barry poured his heart out to Mike as though Mike was his equal. Mike listened intently, nodding in agreement, trying to sympathise as much as he could. For a moment he relished the promotion to adulthood. He was surprised at Barry, though. This was the man who never got off the bench or ran from the dugout shouting abuse at opposition players or management. Barry was always the gentleman, calm, relaxed and even more so in adversity.

'I'm telling you this in confidence, Mike. This is between the three of us and stays between the three of us. Do you understand?'

'Of course I do, Barry, but what do you want me to do?' Mike had suddenly been demoted to seventeen years old again.

'Talk to him. You're his best friend. If anyone can get through to him it's you.' Mike thought easier said than done. He'd known Dan sulk for a week. Barry gripped Mike's shoulder and stared at him in the face. Mike felt nervous, his safety zone breached.

'If he wants to report me, then he has every right to. I will take my punishment. God is my witness,' Barry said in a most serious tone of voice.

Mike moved backwards and Barry let go. Mike's safety zone existed once more and he felt relieved.

'Look, Barry, I can't promise anything,' Mike replied confidently. He knew he could wrap Dan around his little finger but he wasn't going to let Barry know this. 'You know what he's like. I'll do my best.' With that, Mike brushed past him and continued up the stairs. He didn't want to give Barry any chance of prolonging the conversation.

Mike climbed two flights of stairs until he reached the Promenade deck. The drabness and smell of the car deck gave way to fluorescent lighting which made him squint annoyingly as he stood at the doorway, trying to get his bearings. He recognised no one. The ferry was huge and sixteen excited boys would easily be lost in its vastness. He looked across the lobby to the plan of the ship which was hanging just to the right of the purser's office. Walking over, he started to look for the 'You are here' sign. Suddenly, from out of nowhere, a small boy of about three ran in front of him and dropped at his feet. Mike stepped back, worried. The boy was crying having a tantrum banging the floor. Without warning he decided to grip Mike's legs, thinking Mike was his mother. Pulling at his Mike's trousers, he had to hold on to the notice board for balance. A young woman appeared from behind him, dragging another child, a girl of about five. She looked harassed.

'Julian, leave that man alone! Come to mummy, please.'

The boy didn't respond. Other passengers stopped to stare at the commotion. Mike felt embarrassed. He bent down and gently loosened the boy's grip from his trousers and stepped away slowly.

'Oh, I'm terribly sorry, he's not normally like this. It's his first time on a boat you know,' said the woman. Mike just politely smiled and nodded his head, backing away slowly.

'Bloody posh cow, you need to look after your children,' he said to himself as he turned and walked briskly off around the corner. With all the commotion he still didn't know where he was and he cursed the boy and his mother. Peering gingerly around the corner, back to where he had come from, he felt relieved that they were gone. Resuming his examination of the ship layout, he wondered where Dan might be sulking. Looking down a list of what the ship had to offer, he noticed the word 'Amusements'.

'No doubt he'll be there blowing his money on some video machine or one armed bandit,' he said to himself. He ran his finger over the deck diagram and found that the amusement arcade was situated on the same deck but towards the back of the ship.

Dan wasn't there. Three other members of the team were busy encouraging a fourth who was riding a motocross bike video machine. Mike smiled as he watched from behind. Unknown to the rider, his entourage were leaning on to the bike purposely causing him to crash and lose precious time. The rider was so engrossed in his game that he was none the wiser.

Mike knew Dan wouldn't be in any of the bars or restaurants, so his next port of call would be the duty free shop. Again, Dan wasn't there. Mike leant against the glass window of the shop wondering where his friend could be. After a few minutes of pointless guessing he decided that he would stay where he was. The ferry was large - he could look everywhere and still end up missing him. No doubt Dan would come parading past in his own time and Mike would catch him then.

There was a vacant seat directly opposite to where he stood. He decided to take it as it had a great view up and down the exterior of the Duty Free shop. Beginning to people watch, he delved into a pocket and pulled out his last piece of chocolate brownie that his mother had made for him. Taking the brownie from its cling film wrapping, he took a bite. The taste was heavenly and suddenly he missed his mum.

Having been so occupied with looking for Dan he hadn't realised that the ferry had left port. The calm waters were behind and the ferry was starting to pitch and roll in the rougher seas. Mike's stomach turned and he wished that he hadn't eaten the brownie. He needed some fresh air. Finding it hard to push open the heavy exterior door, he made his way out onto the deck. Once outside he instantly drew breath and the cold night air hit him in the face like an ex-girlfriend's slap. The air was heavy with salt and now and again sea spray carried by the wind would drench him with a fine coating of sea water. Forgetting his nausea, he retreated to the rear of the ship and shelter from the side-on wind. A piece of chocolate brownie made its way back to his mouth and made him gag. Leaning over a guard rail, he took deep breaths and stared as hard as he could at the horizon. His dad had once told him that if he ever felt sick the best thing to do was to look at the horizon. He said that sea sickness was caused when the ears and the eyes sending different messages to the brain caused by the motion of the ship. Staring at the horizon allowed your brain to fix on to something, enabling it to readjust and take away the feeling of sickness.

Focusing on the departing port of Dover, he watched as the mass of buildings and boat gantries on the quayside changed from bright definable objects to a blurred mass. Within no time at all, the English coastline had diminished into the gloomy blackness of the night.

While close to land his dad's advice worked and, in conjunction with deep breathing, he started to feel better, but with the ever fading coastline behind him his sickness returned. He felt the wind on his back eating through his tracksuit top as if it wasn't there. That didn't matter, because it was the rest of the brownie making its way like an express train from his stomach through his open mouth into the vast expanse of ocean that was primarily on his mind. He groaned as his body uncontrollably convulsed, throwing solid and liquid into the waves below. His mouth burned with the acid from his stomach and bits of brownie languished between his teeth and gums. Using his tongue, he cleared his mouth and spat brownie and acid-laden spit into the wind.

Thump! A hand gave a heavy whack on his back as the last dribbles fell into the sea. Mike felt drained, too tired to turn around. He stood motionless, his arms using the hand rail as support.

'Been looking for you everywhere,' Dan said chirpily into Mike's ear.

'Leave me alone. I feel like shit,' Mike groaned back at him, not taking his eyes of the sea.

'I feel ok. Thought I might puke earlier on, but I feel fine now.'

'Well, bully for you,' said Mike, finally turning to see Dan standing there as bright as a button. 'I need a drink of something. Got any water in your bag?' Mike gestured to the bag Dan had over his shoulder. Dan handed him a half drunk bottle of Buxton Spring.

'Don't drink it all - it cost me bloody one pound fifty, the robbing bastards.' Mike took two mouthfuls, swilled his mouth, spat it out then finished the bottle off.

'Oh, thanks a bunch mate,' said Dan staring at the empty bottle.

'Don't worry, I'll get you another, two if you want,' Mike said, handing the bottle back to Dan. 'Anyway, last time I saw you it was from behind when you stormed off in a huff, and before you say anything I know what happened. Barry told me.' Dan lifted his eyes to meet Mike's.

'Well, if it wasn't for the next stop being France that

old queer would be behind bars now. You've seen what he's done to my neck.'

Mike felt his body slowly returning to normal, but annoyance was not far behind.

'You are such a drama queen, you know that? We nearly missed the ferry because of you. What were you doing anyway?'

'Just got talking to some of the dock yard blokes, you know, football talk, Man United, Liverpool, Newcastle. I just lost track of time, but I didn't deserve what Barry did to me. He was a nutter!'

'Well, listen to me, mister. If it wasn't for Barry you wouldn't be on this tour.'

'I don't understand,' said Dan looking at Mike puzzled.

'No you wouldn't, you never engage that tiny brain of yours. My dad told me a few days ago but he swore me to secrecy, but I suppose you have a right to know.'

'Know what?'

'The chairman wanted to leave you behind, something to do with giving the team a bad image.'

'What does he mean by bad image?' Dan shouted back at Mike.

'Shut up and listen. Barry fought for you tooth and nail to get you on this tour. Not because of you, but for your talent and what you can do for the team. The chairman even refused to pay for you out of the club kitty, so Barry paid for you out of his own pocket.' Mike turned and faced out to sea. 'Thirty years Barry has been at this club in one capacity or another, and in that time thirty-five players have made it to the big time. That is one hell of a record and that is why he's here, because he's good at what he does.'

Dan's face had changed from defiance to disbelief. 'I didn't know,' he murmured.

'But that's the problem with you, Dan, isn't it?'

Mike pointed his finger at him, prodding him on the forehead.

'You've spent too much time thinking about yourself, living in your own little world.' Dan moved and stood next to Mike, both facing out to sea. A young couple slowly walked past, causing the conversation to be momentarily interrupted.

'It's easy for you to say that, having a dad like you've got,' Dan eventually replied. 'Getting loads of support and help with everything you do, always being there for you. Well, I've had no one watching my back. My old man is a waste of time - if he's not down the betting shop he's staring at the bottom of a vodka bottle. He doesn't care what happens to me.'

Dan stared into the empty blackness. Mike could sense the emotion rising in his friend, so he waited until Dan was finished. 'I do things for me because there is only me, and if you and Barry don't like it, then tough!' Dan turned towards Mike who hadn't moved, but his reply was prepared. He stared at Dan with a sarcastic smile on his face.

'So you think my life is so great, do you?' Mike drew a large breath and continued. 'Oh, it's great alright! You know what it's like to be constantly worried about failure, living in the shadow of a man that nearly made it all the way to the top? But because he didn't, he now makes it his life's purpose to make sure that I do.' It was now Mike's turn for the emotion, but he wasn't sure that he could handle it as well as Dan.

'I love football and I love my dad.' Tears began to well up in Mike's eyes. Dan had never seen him cry before and he certainly wasn't going to now. He quickly turned back towards the sea, composing himself at the same time. 'Day in day out I eat, sleep, shit and piss football. There is not a day that goes by where I am not coached or directed or told or pushed to do something that is not to do with football.' Tears now started to run down Mike's face as he poured out his heart to his friend, but Dan couldn't see his face. Mike's head was bowed, shaded in the inky blackness of the night.

'I am so scared to make mistakes, but the more that I'm afraid the more mistakes I make.' Mike rubbed his tears away and wiped his nose on his sleeve. 'This tour is my chance to be me, not my dad or what my dad wants me to be. Just me! And I'm going to do everything possible to make sure that I do what I want to do, and if it means that I have to make sure that you don't fuck it up, well so be it.'

Mike's tears had dried in the wind and when he turned back to face Dan they'd left no trace. Dan looked straight into Mike's eyes.

'I didn't know. I'm sorry.' His hand rested on Mike's shoulder.

'I don't want you to be sorry, I want you to make the effort and think before you act. We are going to the top but as a team, you understand?' Dan nodded. 'Now, first things first,' continued Mike firmly. 'You find Barry and say you're sorry, ok!' Dan shrugged his shoulders. 'Ok!' Mike repeated.

'Yeah yeah, ok.'

The two friends headed off to find Barry, knowing just a little more about each other than they did before.

'Oh, by the way,' said Mike. 'Barry isn't queer - he was married once but she left him because of his mother.'

'How do you know so much about Barry?' enquired Dan.

'My dad told me. He's known Barry for years. They coached together once.'

When the boys found Barry he was sitting alone,

sipping at a large whiskey and watching an enormous plasma TV which was mounted on the wall behind the bar. Madonna provocatively danced around wearing very little but a smile, but Barry wasn't looking. The bar was called the Ocean View Bar and, as the name suggested, you could get a panoramic view on a clear day. At night, however, it didn't matter. Mike approached first and sat down on a stool to Barry's left.

'Alright Mike, did you find him?' Barry said, swirling the ice in his glass with his finger. Without a word Mike gestured to Dan, who came and sat down on the stool to Barry's right.

'What you drinking boys? I'm buying.' Barry got a ten pound note out of his pocket and slammed it down on the bar, making the barman jump. He scowled at Barry in annoyance. The boys looked at each other, stuck for words. It was Mike who broke the silence.

'Just a coke for me please, Barry.'

'And I'll have a beer,' said Dan.

'No!' Mike said, interrupting Barry just as he began to place the order.

'Dan will have a coke as well. We are both supposed to be in training, you know.'

'Pity about the cigarettes though, eh Dan!' whispered Barry as he sipped his whiskey. Dan looked away, embarrassed.

'It's a good job Mike is sensible, he'll go places with his attitude.' Mike blushed and smiled back.

Dan bit his tongue. He'd said enough already that day.

'Dan's got something to say to you, don't you Dan?' Mike flicked his head to encourage Dan to speak. Dan swallowed hard and looked Barry in the face. Barry stopped playing with his glass and listened.

'I'm sorry about what happened today, and I want to thank you for everything you've done for me.' Dan whispered, so no one else could hear his apology. Barry came alive. He stood up and put both his hands on Dan's shoulders, pulling Dan towards him.

'Thank you, Daniel, I appreciate that. That took a lot of courage to do. I'm sorry too for grabbing you the way I did.'

'Let's just forget it, ok!' Dan said, shrugging his shoulders which made Barry let go. Dan, apology given, turned away, picked up his coke and began to drink. Barry looked at Mike and mouthed 'thank you' to him. Mike smiled back and nodded once.

Barry's demeanour had changed. Rubbing his hands together, he started to outline the tour. The boys already knew the itinerary but both kept quiet as Barry, like an excited schoolboy, waffled on.

Three days' training in France followed by a match in Amsterdam, Holland, then into Germany for another game against an army team from Gelsen Kirken. Finally finishing in Paris playing a match against a Paris St Germain youth side. Barry couldn't contain his excitement. He jumped and swung around on his bar stool, laughing out loud.

'It's going to be hard work you know, boys,' he said looking at Mike and then swinging around to Dan. 'But I know you two have got what it takes and you won't let the team down, will you!' This time he only looked at Dan.

'No, Barry. One hundred per cent, Barry,' Dan blurted out. Mike smiled. The equilibrium had returned and all three parties sipped their drinks, relieved.

Ten minutes later, the two boys stood watching the wake of the ferry turn from a frothy mess at the propeller to a thin line of churned-up water trailing into the distance. Both felt an enormous weight had been lifted from their shoulders and were busy celebrating by seeing who could spit the farthest into the sea. Dan won the first round easily, but Mike had let him win to keep the momentum of his happiness alive.

Mike's nausea had disappeared, but the ferry still rose and fell with each wave that it cut through. Each time the ferry climbed a wave, for a moment, stillness could be felt as though it had been lifted by some imaginary giant out of the sea. Then the giant would let go and, with a shudder that sent vibrations through one's body, the ferry would drop back to the sea again.

The boys weren't aware of this giant playing with the ferry - they were too occupied in round two of their spitting competition. Mike's mouth was drying up. He'd used his best ones in round one and the dry wind was not making it easy for him to produce more spit. Dan was like a conveyor belt, churning out a constant supply of sticky gob. Mike blamed it on the cigarettes helping Dan to bring up all that horrible phlegm that was in his lungs. Dan disagreed unconvincingly.

Mike was just scraping the back of his throat for a final attempt that would see Dan off when he felt something hit him on his back and neck. It was like someone had just thrown a snowball at him, but he knew there was no snow in July and this felt warm. All he knew was that the substance that had hit him on the neck was starting to move downward underneath his tracksuit top. He quickly moved his left hand to stop whatever was going south. His fingers took hold of a chunk of something that, when squeezed, flattened instantly between them. Still with it between his fingers, he brought it round into view and held it up in front of his face, sniffing it at the same time.

'What's up?' said Dan when he realised Mike wasn't about to launch the winning gob. Mike didn't reply. His face had glazed over.

Even though Dan couldn't see it, due to the artificial light coming from the ship, Mike had gone pale. He watched as his friend, once more, lent over the rail and puked into the wind. He stepped back and saw a steady stream of previously drank Cola descending from Mike's mouth into the sea. Mike, spitting out the dribbles, turned to Dan. Gritting his teeth, he glared at him.

'Some bastard has just fucking puked on me!' he shouted, looking up to the higher deck to see if the culprit was still there. However, just like Mike's coke, the guilty party had disappeared into the night. Dan examined Mike's back but he didn't get too close, for even he was starting to feel queasy. From top to bottom Mike was covered with something that resembled finely diced mixed vegetables. He recoiled in horror and covered his mouth. Slowly, Mike removed his top and, without looking at it, hung it over the side of the boat and shook it to remove the remaining lumps.

'I don't believe it! Surely they looked before they spewed. Jesus Christ, this was new on this morning.' Mike whined as he shook away the veg from his top.

Dan didn't say anything. He gave Mike a sympathetic look, but really he was trying hard not to laugh. He looked down to hide his amusement and watched as Mike folded his top inside out and used it to wipe the residue off the back of his neck.

Still cursing at his bad luck and, with his extremely amused best friend, he made his way inside to find a toilet to rinse off the evidence. Dan walked behind, keeping his distance to disassociate himself from his friend but also to keep the stench at arm's length. When Mike entered the toilet more puke smell hit him. He held his mouth. His body convulsed uncontrollably again but he had nothing else left in him to bring up.

As he made his way to the sink, he grabbed a paper towel quickly wet it and, with one hand, held it to his mouth and nose. He needed to wash his top and get out as soon as he could, but the rancid smell of human sick was so intense he didn't know how long he could take it. Dan followed him in but, with an about turn that a Grenadier Guard would be proud of, disappeared back into the ship's lobby. Filling a basin with water, Mike did the best he could for his top. Dan was waiting for him outside the toilet.

'Don't say a word,' Mike said, holding his finger up as he strode towards the external door. Dan, in a fit of giggles, followed him out.

As the lights of France drew nearer and the ferry finally made port, Mike had been relegated to holding his tracksuit top in the wind. Dan left him alone to simmer gently, but now and again would comment how he could smell puke. Mike ignored him. Waving his tracksuit top in the wind, he stared ahead of him.

'This tour can't possibly get any worse,' he said to himself.

Chapter 4

When the ferry neared Dunkirk and began preparing to dock, a woman's voice came over the loud speaker system directing vehicle passengers to the car deck. Mike and Dan were standing on the port side, watching the furious activity of the dock workers getting ready to secure the ferry to the quayside. The tracksuit top by now was bone dry Mike had it draped over the rail. The mixed vegetables were no more, but it still stank to high heaven.

Mike felt absolutely miserable; he knew it wasn't the end of the world, but he just couldn't come to terms with the fact that, with all the passengers on board, why it had to be him that got covered. Dan had consoled his friend as much as he could, but it fell flat as with each caring word he couldn't contain his amusement. Fits of giggles would take over his body and his mouth would smirk uncontrollably each time he offered support. So for Mike, the last hour of the trip had been totally depressing. When the lady made her announcement an instant relief had washed over him allowing this painful experience to be forgotten, or so he thought.

Mike boarded the bus last but, as he climbed the steps, he noticed an unearthly silence and all eyes were on him. Did they know what had happened? he thought. No they couldn't have, there had only been him and Dan there, so he dismissed the idea. He had hidden his tracksuit top in a duty free carrier bag that he had found sticking out of a litterbin outside the purser's office. Hoping that no one would notice, he quickly made his way to his seat. Terry Grainger, the team's five foot nothing right winger, was sitting in the seat in front of Mike. He turned around and knelt on his seat, peering over the top at Mike.

'What you looking at!' Mike growled.

'It's not what I'm looking at, it's what I can smell. You Ming!' he said, holding his nose. Dan came walking down the aisle.

'Sit down, you little gob shite!' he said pushing Terry back in his seat.

'Fuck off, Sharpe!' shouted the right winger as he fell backward against the bus window.

'Watch your mouth, otherwise I'll fill it,' Dan said, making a fist sign with his hand. Grainger sat back in his seat and made no further eye contact with him. He'd had experience of Daniel Sharpe's temper before and didn't want to feel his fists again. Once had been enough when he'd fought and lost over a disputed penalty decision on the training ground.

'Always mister popular, aren't you?' said Mike, as Dan sat down next to him. 'Don't worry Terry, I won't let him touch you,' Mike shouted over the seat in front. Terry didn't reply - he was too busy watching the fat driver edge his way sideways up the aisle towards where Mike and Dan sat. By this time, others on the bus were complaining about the smell.

'Excuse me, son,' said the fat man directing his comment at Mike. He leaned over Dan like an enormous grizzly bear. The pressure exerted on his shirt by his stomach caused it to become untucked from his trousers and Dan felt the flabby, warm, sweaty flesh of his stomach touch his hand.

Oh my god, he thought as he pulled his hand back slowly, rubbing it on the bus seat as if he was wiping it clean.

'I don't know what you've brought onto this bus,' continued the driver, 'but with that stink it's not staying.' Mike leaned forward and grabbed the bag containing the tracksuit and offered it to the driver.

'I'm not touching it, boy,' the driver said with the look of disgust on his face. 'Follow me and you can put it with the luggage.'

Mike, with bag in hand, followed the driver off the bus. His team mates giggled like naughty school girls and held their noses in mockery as he walked past. His humiliation was complete; he would remember this trip for a long time to come.

On his way to the luggage compartment he told the driver what had happened on deck. The driver sympathised with him, explaining that some young woman, after a night on a hen party drinking binge, had once puked up on him when getting on his bus so he knew exactly how Mike was feeling. No, thought Mike, you haven't got a clue how I am feeling.

The driver handed Mike a bin bag as an extra precaution against the smell penetrating the other luggage. Mike wrapped it up and handed it back to him. The bag and contents were placed with the other luggage but, as the door was being shut, Mike noticed a small compartment with a mattress, sleeping bag and pillow neatly stowed away.

'What's that for?' enquired Mike pointing at the compartment.

'Oh, that's where I would kip if I have to do any night stopovers, but I can't get in there anymore. As your mate said, I'm too fat. Boss says I've got to sleep in it because he doesn't like me kipping on the back seat, but I don't care. Bloody claustrophobic little hole if you ask me.'

Mike imagined the driver wedging himself into the tight little space and getting stuck. The fire and rescue boys would have to be called to pull him free. What a sight that would be!

The driver slammed the door shut just as the main ferry doors were beginning to open. Every engine in every vehicle on board sprang into life in anticipation of disembarking. Mike and the driver walked back towards the door of the bus. The driver tapped Mike on the shoulder.

'You can call me Dennis, if you like.'

'Thanks Dennis, sorry for stinking up the bus,' said Mike apologetically.

'Ah, don't worry about it. This bus has had a lot worse,' he replied as he squeezed himself between the ferry wall and the side of the bus.

They climbed back on board. Barry gave Mike an encouraging slap on the back as he walked past. Everyone else had turned their attention to what was happening outside the bus, so Mike sat back down free from further embarrassment.

The excitement of disembarking soon faded as everyone realised that they had been last on the ferry, which meant they would be last off. Mike had disappeared from the team's minds to be replaced by Dan once again. Mike was past caring after the crossing he had had, and Dan didn't care what people thought of him anyway. So the two just sat like zombies ignoring everyone.

Eventually the bus moved slowly off the boat and down the ramp, following the line of vehicles in front. Faces were pressed against the windows to glimpse the first view of a foreign land, but first impressions failed to impress and all that could be seen was a mass of grey drab warehouses and container lorries zipping around in all directions. The early excitement faded as fast as it had arrived until French customs officers and passport control got onto the bus. Everybody came alive, not because of the passport checks but because of the guns being carried. The eyes of sixteen teenagers from the northeast of England followed every move of each officer. Automatic weapons, seen up until now only on television, were in touching distance.

For Mike it all felt so unreal; he had never seen a gun up close before and he was surprised how impressive the weapons looked. One officer wearing full body armour had a machine gun across his chest. Mike watched him closely and not once did he move his hands away from the gun; his eyes were fixed on his colleague in front who was checking passports with just a pistol for protection. Attached to the butt was a long flexible cord that connected the pistol to the holster which, in turn, had a leather strap that secured the weapon tightly inside to prevent unknown hands from withdrawing it.

Barry turned and watched the ritual of passport control being carried out on his boys. He'd never seen such politeness and courtesy from his normally loudmouthed and idiotic team. How it would be nice to have one of these guns, he thought to himself. He might get a bit more respect. *Then again, I'd probably shoot myself or I'd end up shooting most of them.* He chuckled and Dennis the driver looked at him as though he'd gone mad.

Dan pretended not to be interested with it all.

'I've seen loads of guns before. I used one once, just like that one,' he said to Mike, pointing at the machine gun edging closer down the bus.

'Oh yeah, and where have you used one of these before?' said Mike sarcastically. 'In your back garden shooting sparrows?'

'It's true I tell you! The old man had a mate who brought one to the house once, but he told me to get lost as he was talking business. I crept back into the kitchen when they were having a smoke in the garden and picked it up,' Dan explained as convincingly as he could, but Mike wasn't falling for it.

'God, you are full of shit, you know that?'

'Hey, that's not all! I accidentally pressed the trigger and put four holes into the fridge door.'

'Did you bollocks!' Mike said laughing.

'My dad came in and gave me a good hiding. Smacked me around a bit. Broke my nose, the old bastard did. I didn't have time to suffer. I had to stick kitchen wipes up my nostrils to stop the bleeding. We had to do a runner pretty sharp - me, my dad, his mate and the fridge to Wallsend and chuck it into the dock before the police arrived.' Dan was getting excited as he told the story, banging the headrest of the seat in front when he described how his dad had beaten him. He wasn't paying any attention to the customs officer with the pistol.

'Monsieur, Passeport s'il vous plait,' said the officer, gesturing with his hand for the passport.

'What's he say!' Dan said, looking to Mike for help. Mike whispered in his ear.

'He wants your passport, stupid!' Dan fiddled with his pocket trying to get his passport out. It had been a long shift and the officer watched with a blank expression until Dan produced it and waved it in his face. There was a grunt of approval and he moved on to the seat behind.

'Didn't you do any French at school?' Mike said, elbowing Dan in the ribs.

'Of course I did, but it doesn't interest me. What do I need French for, living in bloody Newcastle?'

'You are so narrow minded. The world is a big place and you may not spend your life living in one place. Oh, why do I bother? I'm wasting my breath talking to you.' Mike sighed out of frustration, then stared at Dan full in the face.

'What are you doing?' Dan said nervously as Mike examined him with his eyes.

'I'm looking at your nose. You've never had that

broken.'

'Yes I have and I can prove it.'

Dan grabbed his nose between his thumb and forefinger of his right hand and, with a sharp twist of his hand, his nose made a clicking sound.

'Don't do that again, you make me feel sick.' Dan's eyes were watering and Mike grimaced as though he was feeling the pain as well.

'Don't worry, I'm not. Friggin hurts each time I do it. It's never healed properly, that's why.'

'Anyway, I can still smell something,' Mike said, leaning over to Dan and taking a good sniff of the air.

'What's that then?'

'Bullshit and you reek of it.'

'Look, it's true I tell ya. After we left the house to dump the fridge the whole street was lit up with police lights and sirens going off. The neighbours had heard the shots and called the police. Bloody armed response units had the street cordoned off until they realised the house was empty. By that time the fridge was at the bottom of the dock.'

Mike smiled at him and sniffed once more. Dan thumped him on the thigh and mouthed 'Bollocks' in his face.

'You wait until we get home,' continued Dan, 'I still have the newspaper article and that mate of my old man is currently doing fifteen years for armed robbery. So believe what you want to believe.' Dan sat back and folded his arms, purposely turning away so as not to make any more eye contact with Mike. Mike smiled to himself as he watched the armed customs officers leave the bus.

By the time the bus pulled away from the dock the buzz of excitement had given way to fatigue. The bus had been travelling, including rest stops, for fifteen hours. The teenage adrenalin had finally run out. Boys sat with heads against windows, staring at the bland countryside of Northern France. Flat, lifeless field after field stretched out to the horizon, only to be broken by the occasional farmhouse or barn. The bus joined the A25 main auto route and headed towards Lille. Apart from a faint murmur from the hardened card sharks Martin and Stuart on the back seat, the bus was quiet and devoid of conversation. Barry thought it was a good time to announce over the speaker system that everyone needed to put their watches forward an hour. The microphone whined due to too much feedback and the dosing teenagers voiced their disapproval by telling their manager to shut up. Barry took the hint and sat down.

The sun, now low in the sky and fading fast, threw its last light onto the rear of the bus as they headed east. The shadow made by the bus covered the side of the road in a grey shroud, which would shorten or lengthen whenever the bus changed direction. Mike sat listening to his music when, all of a sudden, Dan leant over and nudged him on his arm.

'I need to ask you a favour.' Mike looked at him in annoyance and switched off his music.

'I hope it's no more bullshit,' replied Mike, sniffing the air once more.

'No, this is serious! I need your help.'

'Go on then, spit it out.'

Mike listened with amusement as Dan explained. When he'd finished Mike sat back in his seat and laughed out loud.

'What's so funny about that?'

'Let me get this straight. Your old man wants you to pick up some cigarettes for him, but not in France. Over the border in Belgium?' Dan nodded in agreement. 'And because you've been so lazy and not learnt any French while at school, you want me to come with you to translate? Oh sorry! Hold your hand.'

Dan looked at him with puppy eyes, the only thing he could do before he had to beg. Mike knew Dan wouldn't go alone. He was full of confidence on his own patch, but here in France he was out of his depth. Mike looked at him down his nose, as though he were looking at a beggar in the street.

'I'll think about it and let you know,' he said with an arrogant tone to his voice.

'You know I wouldn't ask anyone else. Go on, be a pal.'

'You're not begging, are you?'

'No, not yet.'

'Look! I told you I will think about it. Ok!'

Mike switched his music back on and raised the volume. He noticed out of the corner of his eye that Dan was just about to say something else, but he stopped himself and went back to staring at the seat in front of him, deep in thought.

Mike sat and pondered Dan's request. It must be something more than just cigarettes because, normally, Dan wouldn't take the time of day to do anything for his old man unless there was money involved. Dan's father was not the typical loving dad. If he wasn't sending his son to the off licence to pick him up twenty Benson & Hedges, then he would send him to a so-called business friend's home at some unearthly time of the night to pick up packages and things. Dan never liked it but, when a ten pound note was waved in his face, reluctantly he accepted. Mike thought that he would need to extract a little more information out of him before he would agree to anything. Doing favours for Dan's father usually spelt trouble of the worst kind, therefore more investigating would be needed.

As the bus drove on towards their first hotel, Dan had a dilemma - either tell Mike the truth and be turned down flat, or try and entice him another way. Mike, on the other hand, knew that Dan was up to something. Why would Dan be sent to Belgium to pick up cigarettes? Why not just get them at Duty Free on the way home? Ten minutes passed without a word being shared between them when Mike eventually broke the silence.

'So what's so special about these cigarettes that your old man wants you to get for him?'

'Oh, I'm not sure. I think it's because you can't get them in France. They're special or something,' replied Dan nervously, which didn't do any good for convincing Mike. Mike began to get a little annoyed with his friend as he didn't want to listen to some other bullshit story. He wanted no more yarns spun.

'You have one chance and one chance only to tell me the truth, or you are going on your own.'

'Look, if I tell you the truth you won't come anyway.'

'Try me!' said Mike looking directly into Dan's eyes.

Dan then told Mike that, just before he was going to bed last night, his old man came to him as usual but this time not to pick up a parcel from mates. He gave Dan a piece of paper with the name and address of a man in Belgium who he was to meet tomorrow afternoon and who would give him a package to bring back to England. Dan had asked what was in the package and was told cigarettes. He too questioned the idea of picking up cigarettes in Belgium and thought it a stupid idea, but nevertheless he'd agreed to do it when a promise of two hundred and fifty pounds was made to him with fifty up front.

Mike looked at his friend and suddenly felt sorry for him. How he would hate to have a scum bag as a father like Dan's. He knew his own father wasn't perfect, but compared to Dan's he was a saint.

'You know there aren't cigarettes in the package,' said Mike lowering his voice in case the seats in front and behind had ears.

'Yeah, I know.'

'Then why are you doing it?' persisted Mike. Dan sighed heavily, his face flushed.

'Because if I don't I will have to leave the Indispensables.' Mike looked shocked, but let Dan carry on. 'My old man's in trouble big time with some bad guys from the city centre. He owes them a lot of money from his gambling and if he doesn't pay them back... well, you know what, he will join that fridge at the bottom of the dock at Wallsend.'

'I don't understand why you will have to leave the Indispensables over you dad's fuck-ups.'

'Look, I hate my dad for what he has become,' Dan said angrily, 'but he's still my dad and I don't want to see him killed. I don't want to be left alone. Life isn't perfect, but I've got it the way I like it, ok?' Mike nodded but didn't interrupt.

'The point is that if I don't do what he wants we will have to leave Newcastle, because these guys will come after him if he doesn't deliver that package. Football and the Indispensables are all that I have and you are the only friend that I have I'm not giving them or you up.' Dan's voice trembled. Mike didn't know what to say. He had never heard such an outburst of feeling from Dan before and he felt truly touched. He knew Dan was being used, but he too didn't want to lose his friend.

'I'll come with you, right, but I know whatever is in that package has nothing to do with me once we are back on this bus. If you get caught going back into England, you are no friend of mine, ok!' Mike knew helping him was going against every sensible thought that he had in his head, but for some reason he couldn't let him do it alone.

'Thanks Mike, I really appreciate it. No one will even know that we've gone.' Dan's demeanour had changed with Mike's agreement; he was back to his confident cocky self.

The bus sped on eastwards, but on board one of the team was seriously wondering what he was letting himself in for.

Chapter 5

It was 9.30pm when the bus pulled up outside The Belle Époque Hotel in the small town of Bergues, fifteen kilometres from the border with Belgium. Barry stood up and asked everyone to stay put on the bus while he checked in. John Dodd, the assistant manager and Dennis the driver got off to unload the luggage. Tired eyes examined the hotel façade with interest. Part of the building was about a hundred and fifty years old with a steep pitched roof and tall Baroque-style chimneys. The front façade was of red brick on three storeys with a centrally positioned front door of typical Flemish design. The hotel had been damaged many times throughout the last century, first during the First World War and then in the Second during the evacuation of Dunkirk. The Restaurant had been a relatively modern add-on in the last thirty years, with its Mansard roof that made it stand out from the other buildings.

Barry could be seen in the foyer leaning against the reception desk talking to a woman wearing a green silk scarf around her neck. He carried the tour paperwork with him in an A4 sized leather wallet and was busy flicking through it. Ten minutes had passed when he re-emerged. Climbing onto the bus he told everyone to pick up their kit and make their way into the Hotel and wait at reception. Dan and Mike waited until last and then made their way inside. It was like stepping back in time; not one piece of modern furniture stood out and the walls were decorated in a pink carpet-like material. Pictures with thick guilt frames hung on every wall. All depicted some type of hunting scene from a hundred years ago. Dan covered his mouth with his hand and nudged Mike.

'Is this where they filmed the Addams Family?' Mike laughed then stopped when the woman behind the reception looked his way.

'You could be right,' Mike whispered back. 'She could definitely pass for Morticia.'

Barry clapped his hands and the chatter died down. He introduced the lady as Madame Bray, who owned the Hotel. Her husband, Philippe, was the Chef and they would see him later at supper. Barry called out the boys' names in twos; both would step forward, sign the register, get given a room key and were then pointed in the direction of the stairs. Once in the room they were to deposit their kit and come straight back down to the dining room for their meal. As to be expected, Mike and Dan were sharing, but poor little Terry Grainger had drawn the short straw and been given the unpleasant news that he would be sharing with Dennis the driver. He wasn't very impressed, but Barry promised that someone different would share with Dennis at the next hotel. Dan gave Terry a pat on his back when he walked past. Terry turned around and told him to 'Fuck off!' Dan just laughed and Mike stifled a smile.

Dan and Mike made their way up to the third floor and found room sixteen at the end of the hallway. Mike unlocked the door and stepped inside. He stood in the doorway with his mouth wide open.

'Here, let me in. Let's have a look!' Dan pushed past him into the room, dropped his bag on the floor and stood in shock next to Mike.

'What the bloody hell is that?' exclaimed Dan pointing at the wall opposite. Mike was dumb struck; he had never seen anything like it before. On the wall in front of them was a woodland scene, but not in a frame or on canvass; the whole wall depicted a forest.

Trees, shrubs and even the sunlight could be seen streaming down between the branches. The room had been wallpapered to give the occupier the feeling of being close to nature. That was the only explanation that Mike could think of that would account for such taste in decor.

'I can't sleep in here, that will give me the creeps,' said Dan as he walked over to one of the single beds and put his bag down on it. 'It looks so bloody real that any minute a deer will come running through it. I'm going to ask Barry if he will get our room changed.' Dan started to walk to the door but Mike stopped him in his tracks.

'Get a grip of your knickers, man! What do you think everyone else will say when they know that you are afraid of some wallpaper? Look, if it makes you feel any better you can leave your bed side light on, ok?' Dan agreed that it was a good idea, but swore Mike to secrecy because if this got out Dan explained that his reputation would be shattered. Mike wasn't going to tell anyone; the wall gave him the creeps as well, but he wasn't going to let on to Dan, so leaving a light on would be better for both of them.

Downstairs in the restaurant, Barry was the centre of attention. The Loach boys buzzed around him like two angry wasps looking for the best place to sting him. The twins weren't happy with their room either, not because of a woodland scene but because they had a wall depicting a giant Eagle flying high in the mountains. Graham was adamant that everywhere he went in the room the bird's eyes would follow him. Dan felt relieved that Mike had stopped him making a fool of himself and Barry told the twins to grow up; it was only wallpaper and no, he was not changing their room. He did mention it to the chef when he appeared to announce what was for supper, who said that all of the rooms had a wall depicting some kind of rural scene with some being more vivid than others. The previous owner had done it and as soon as they could all of the rooms would be redecorated. Mike instantly knew why they had been booked into this hotel; the rooms must be cheap because no one else would stay here.

An old lady appeared in the corner of the room pushing a trolley with a large china pot containing steaming hot soup. Everyone settled down to eat. Dan leant over to Mike and pointed out that the woman must have had a hard paper round. Mike told him to shut up and offer his bowl for it to be filled. Hot brown watery liquid poured into Dan's bowl. He put it in front of him and stared at it. Once Mike had been served, he turned and pointed to what was in their bowls.

'What's that!' he said stirring it around with his spoon. 'It looks like dish water.'

'It's French onion soup. It's meant to be like this with little strands of onion in. Look!' Mike lifted up his spoon to show the onions. Dan did the same; he gave the soup one more stir, filled his spoon and raised it to his mouth. Mike gave him a gentle nudge of encouragement and he began to sip at it. Slowly his face lit up.

'This tastes better than it looks!' he exclaimed as the sip turned into a slurp.

'The trouble with you is that you only eat crap,' said Mike, breaking off some crusty baguette that was in the centre of the table.

'Oh, I am so sorry. We don't all I have our meals cooked by our mummy,' Dan said, putting on the poshest voice that he could.

'Very funny. Just remember that you have a main course next followed by cheese and then dessert, so don't go filling yourself up with soup.'

'I'll eat what I want! Mummy! Ok!' Dan threw a

piece of crust into Mike's soup, making it splash onto the table cloth. Mike thumped him under the table. Dan was just about to retaliate when he saw Barry looking at him. He put his head down and carried on slurping his soup.

The main course arrived and, to Dan's amazement, it was to his liking. A mountain of the crunchiest fries with an inch thick burger topped with a fried egg. Mike had never seen him so happy. With each mouthful he would smile to himself contentedly before pushing the next load in. He never said a word while he was eating and, when the old lady came around with seconds, Dan held his plate up and got it filled to the brim again. Mike watched without giving comment; he knew that his friend's diet consisted of takeaways and convenience food and, for Dan, a fortnight in Europe was going to test his taste buds to the limit.

When the cheese arrived, Dan wasn't interested; he couldn't understand why you had to have cheese anyway, whether it being before dessert or after. Mike pushed some smelly Camembert under his nose and told him to try some as it tasted better than it smelt, but Dan said he didn't want to eat anything that smelt like one of his sweaty football socks. Dessert came and was devoured the same way as the main course. The strawberry tart didn't stand a chance. *Where did he put it all?* thought Mike to himself. Dan weighed the same as a middleweight boxer and had the same physique; it seemed impossible for him to have eaten so much, but he had and there was no sign of it either.

With dinner over it was time for bed. Barry informed everyone that they were to meet at 9am tomorrow morning in the reception in full training kit. Anyone late would be sharing their room with big Dennis next time. Dennis smiled. He didn't take offence whatsoever; it felt good to be one of the lads.

After the long day of travelling, sleeping in the woodland bedroom wasn't a problem. For the twins, Barry had arranged for a sheet to be pinned up to hide the Eagle's wondering eyes. That night, sixteen teenagers and two adults slept soundly. Barry didn't sleep so well; a phone conversation with the club chairman had given him some worries. The hotel in Holland had been changed. They had originally planned to stay on the outskirts of Amsterdam, but had now been moved into the City centre. As Barry looked at his plan of Amsterdam his head fell into his hands.

'Why there of all places? Why! Why! Why!' Barry felt distraught but there was nothing he could do about it. He lay there in the dark and, as he drifted off to sleep, he wondered how on earth he was going to look after fifteen teenage boys staying in a Hotel on the edge of the red light district of Amsterdam.

***

A loud knock on the door woke Mike. He yawned, stretched and looked at his watch. It was 7.30am. Dan was still asleep. Without making a sound, he picked up one of his training shoes and launched it in the direction of Dan's head. It missed but hit the headboard, making Dan sit up with a jolt.

'Come on, sleeping beauty, breakfast then training,' Mike said as he pulled on his tracksuit bottoms and picked up his wash bag from the bedside table. Dan just sat scratching his head and staring at the Black Forest in front of him.

On the coach, Barry announced that Floyd would be sharing the room with Dennis next time as Barry had had to drag him out of bed. Dan drove Mike crazy with his whinging on about how poor breakfast was. Mike informed him that they were on the continent and on the continent they would eat a continental breakfast of bread, cheese, hams and fruit. Dan stated that he couldn't train to the best of his ability without some bacon inside him. But Mike told him that he'd better catch the next ferry back home because good old English bacon wouldn't be on many of the menus.

Barry informed everyone that the training session would last for three hours and then they would go back to the hotel for lunch; then, if everything went well, the afternoon would be theirs and they could explore the town. A cheer went up. Dan looked at Mike and winked. Mike hadn't got a clue what he was on about. Barry added that he wanted to see one hundred per cent or no free afternoon.

'That's it!' Dan exclaimed with a big grin across his face. 'That's our chance to get this package.' Mike had forgotten, but it all came flooding back to him. 'We'll catch a taxi from the centre of town. Twenty minutes there, ten minutes to get the package and twenty minutes to get back,' said Dan, bouncing on his seat in excitement. He makes it all sound so simple, thought Mike.

'We'll see,' Mike said, far from convinced. 'Nothing ever goes right when you're involved.'

'It's going to be plain sailing, just trust me!' Dan said rubbing his hands together. Mike didn't know what to think; he just hoped that these guys with the package would hand it over quick and let them leave.

The bus pulled up into a car park next to a small football stadium. The team got off and were introduced to Monsieur Dupuy, the owner of Bergues football club. Barry got everyone lined up and Monsieur Dupuy and Barry went along the line introducing each player, and shaking their hand.

'Just like Royalty meeting the players at Wembley,' Dan said to Mike, just before he had his own hand shook.

Monsieur Dupuy, speaking in perfect English, welcomed them all to his club and then pointed the way to the training area.

The grass looked beautiful; it was perfect in every way. Mike couldn't believe his eyes; he was used to rough Northeast turf, with dried mud as hard as concrete in the goal mouths. There was no chance here of diving on a dog turd or piece of broken glass. Dan couldn't wait to get his boots on; he threw his bag against the fence behind the goal, quickly stripped to his shorts and ran off as fast as he could to the big onion sack containing the balls. The temperature was warm but not too hot, but no one cared what the weather was like. The sixteen boys on the pitch were just soaking up the luxury of training on such a surface. Barry had not seen such happy faces for a long time.

The session went well. Everyone gave one hundred and ten per cent, but when it was time to leave the disappointment was hard to conceal. Barry pointed out that they would be back tomorrow and would be training with the local team; so they should enjoy the afternoon off and, above all else, be good. Once back at the hotel, Mike and Dan quickly changed. Mike made sure that he had his mobile in case of an emergency. They excused themselves from lunch and sprinted off towards the town centre of Bergues.

Bergues was originally a fortified wool town dating back to the Middle Ages, but now tourism was one of its main incomes. The town was nearly totally encircled by ancient fortifications which, in the height of summer, would be bustling with tourists. Mike and Dan paid no attention to any of the history as they searched the town for a taxi rank. They could have been running through the concrete jungle of Coventry for all they cared. Mike was just about to be brave and ask a local, when they noticed an empty taxi sitting at a red light at the main junction opposite the town hall. Mike tapped the driver's window and it lowered slowly.

'Parlez-vous anglais?' Mike said nervously. The driver looked at him, expressionlessly, wound his window up and drove off. Mike's confidence took a blow, while Dan just ran after the taxi sticking his fingers up and shouting 'Wanker' at the top of his voice.

'Come back. He won't know what wanker means,' said Mike. Dan turned and kicked the curb.

'What next?'

'I don't know.'

After ten minutes of walking the streets, Mike had a brain wave. There would be taxis at the train station, but where was the station? They stood opposite a small Boulangerie. Mike drew breath and went inside to ask. When he came out there was a spring in his step once again. He was pleased with himself because not only did he ask the right question, but he understood the answer. Straight up the main street under the bridge and turn left. He was right. Three taxis were parked out front; two were empty of a driver, but in the third the driver was dozing happily until Mike tapped the window. He sat up, said a polite 'bonjour', got out and opened the door so they could get in.

Mike plucked up his courage and tried again with his pigeon French.

'No problem,' said the driver in English, turning around with a large grin on his face. Mike felt relieved and got the sealed envelope off Dan for the name of the village that they wanted to get to. He said the name to the driver.

'Vleteren? I know it, over the border, not long way,' he said in his broken English.

As the taxi pulled away from the station, the boys

sat back looking out of the window. Dan spotted Richard Green and Scott Dale crossing in front of them. He nudged Mike and both of them slid down in the seat so as not to be seen. Once out of the town, the driver thought that he would practise more of his English on the boys. He's friendly, thought Dan, as he explained about his knowledge of England. He'd spent three weeks in London once when he was a student. His favourite memory had been witnessing the Queen on her balcony at Buckingham Palace. He told the boys that he wished France still had a monarchy because it gave a bit of style to a country. Politicians were all corrupt and only thought of themselves, he added.

Mike pointed out that the French had cut off the heads of all their Royals and our Prime Minister acted like a President anyway, so there wasn't much difference between the two countries whatsoever. The taxi driver laughed and expressed how much he liked them both. Mike asked him where he'd learnt his English, and he said it was during the same three weeks. Mike couldn't believe it. He'd been studying French for two years and hardly remembered anything. This man spent three weeks in London and was nearly fluent. Mike congratulated him on his English. The driver smiled in the rear view mirror and said 'merci'.

Dan, on the other hand, hadn't listened to anything that had been said. He'd just counted the tenth canal when the driver asked for the name of the house in Vleteren. Mike gave him the name of Jean-Marie Dubois and was just about to give the address when the taxi driver pulled over to the side of the road. He turned off the engine and spun around to face them.

'What's wrong? Why have you stopped?' said a concerned Mike.

'Bad man! Don't go there! I take you back. No pay,' the driver said, looking very concerned.

'We must go!' exclaimed Mike, telling him that it was very important.

Mike thought that the driver was just about to kick them out of his taxi, when he offered to take them to the end of the road where Dubois lived but no further. He would not drive to the property. Mike didn't have to ask his reasons; he knew from the first moment that Dan had asked him to go with him that this Dubois fellow wasn't going to be a decent upstanding pillar of the community. Dan entered the conversation, saying that they wouldn't be long and could he wait for them? The driver agreed to wait and asked if they would pay for the first trip, just in case they didn't come back. The rest of the journey was in silence; only once did the driver offer to turn around again, but Mike said 'no'.

Ten kilometres later they pulled up at one end of a street named Roggestaat. The driver pointed to the house and barn complex at the other end and told them he would wait here as long as he could. The boys thanked him and paid for the one way journey. As Mike climbed out, the driver tapped him on the shoulder and told him to be careful.

'There are bad men in there,' he said finally.

Mike reassured him that they would be back soon and, with that, he and Dan set off towards the house of Dubois.

Chapter 6

It was early afternoon and the street was deserted; not even a car could be seen or heard. On each side of the street there was a mix of old and new style Flemish houses. Each had their own private entrance with gate and large garden.

A black Labrador dog jumped up at a gate as the two nervous teenagers walked by. It barked and wagged its tail; then, from behind, another black Labrador mounted the first and started to hump away in full view of the boys. Dan laughed and then made a comment about the size of a Labrador's dick, comparing it to that of Mike's. Mike wasn't in the mood for jokes. He slapped Dan on the back of his head and told him to concentrate on what he had to do.

'Don't worry! Let me do all the talking and when they speak French, you come in,' Dan said in an authoritative voice.

'I'll just watch and listen, right?' replied Mike. 'You're the boss. Look! Here's the gate now.'

They both stood in front of a large wooden gate. A sign written in Flemish, French and English in the centre of the gate warned of dogs. For a whole minute they stood staring at the buildings beyond the gate. They could see an old Flemish farm cottage to the left and directly in front was a large barn with one central enormous barn door. Mike noticed it first; a sign no bigger than a slot of a letter box was attached to the top of the gate. It said in English 'Visitors', with a small arrow pointing to the left. They walked in the direction of the arrow, past the small cottage where a further arrow directed them around to the rear of the barn.

Mike could feel his pulse racing as a nervous dose

of adrenalin had been injected into his veins. He didn't want to go any further but it was too late. As they rounded the corner of the barn, two men dressed in a uniform that the boys didn't recognise were waiting to meet them. The men had guns neatly secured in leather holsters on their waists. Without a greeting or handshake, both boys were roughly manhandled up against the wall of the barn.

Mike looked across at Dan; he was expressionless. One of the men spread Dan's legs and, just like in an American cop show, patted him down for weapons. The other stood behind his colleague, watching. Dan's demeanour was calm. Mike, on the other hand, felt fear and his left leg started to twitch uncontrollably. He closed his eyes until the search was over. Only once did he cringe when his mobile phone was felt in his pocket.

'Follow me,' said the taller of the two. Without another word being said, Mike and Dan were led through a heavy steel door into the large barn. Mike caught Dan's eye as they were walking through. Dan calmly waved his hand as if to say 'Relax, everything is under control', but that didn't help Mike.

As soon as the four had cleared the door, it slammed shut of its own accord. Darkness hit them the same as if a blindfold had been applied and Mike stumbled with the feeling of disorientation. A hand took him by the arm and he regained his balance. The air was filled with the smell of tobacco and, as their eyes became more accustomed to the dim light, row upon row of cigarette boxes all stacked neatly on pallets could be seen everywhere. At the end of a row of pallets they came to a staircase which led up onto a walkway just wide enough for one man at a time. With one man in front of the boys and one behind they made their way to a white door. With three loud knocks the door opened and the boys were pushed inside. From darkness back into light they came, both squinting, as they entered the room.

A man in his late fifties sat at a large desk. The light from the single bulb reflected on the man's head, making it look like it had been polished. Dan thought it was amusing, but Mike hadn't noticed; he was too busy worrying. A large Cuban cigar lay smouldering in the ashtray. The air was thick with cigar smoke and, had it not been for a small extractor on the rear wall of the room, working at full power, it would have been unbearable. To the left of the desk was a small window, but the shutters on the outside were closed. Only a single shaft of light penetrated through a knot hole in the wood, lighting up the cigar in the ashtray. The smoke danced in the light before making its way towards the ventilation unit.

'Welcome,' the man said suddenly. 'I have been expecting you.' Mike gave a sigh of relief; he knew that he wouldn't have to speak French.

'Henri, get our guests a chair.' The bald man waved his hand and the tall chaperone slid two metal folding chairs towards the boys. 'Sit! Sit! Do not be frightened, I am just a humble business man trying to make a living.' This didn't make Mike feel any easier; he just smiled politely, nodded his head and sat down. Dan was used to dealing with out of the ordinary situations; he'd had lots of practice each night when he collected things for his old man.

'You have something for me?' Dan said, oozing with confidence.

'So you are the football boy?' The bald man stared directly at Dan. Standing his ground and staring straight back, Dan repeated what he had said before.

'You have something for me? I would like it now so we can leave.' The bald man carried on talking as though he had not heard. 'I don't like football myself I think it's a woman's sport. A little bit of contact and they roll around on the ground pretending to be hurt. Rugby, on the other hand, is a man's game.' He lifted his cigar, took a long slow draw on it and then laid it back in the ashtray. He blew the smoke out in the direction of Dan, but he was accustomed to smoke and he never flinched once.

Mike was amazed at how cool, calm and collected Dan could be. It was all he could do to stop his own leg twitching than have a conversation with someone like Dubois. Dan's eyes didn't blink; he had his gaze firmly fixed on Dubois. Then all of a sudden, without warning, he let out a little chuckle.

'Yes, Rugby is a man's game, but I never could get used to the scrums. Having to put my hand between another man's legs seemed very homosexual to me.'

The bald man shot up out of his seat, laughing out loud. 'My name is Dubois. You have lots of spirit, boy, but remember where you are and do not underestimate who you are dealing with. I have your package. Do you have the envelope?'

Dan walked forward and took the envelope from his pocket and gave it to Dubois. He opened it, took out a single piece of paper and studied the contents.

Standing behind Dubois in the shadows was the figure of another man. Dan hadn't noticed him before but, as he stepped forward, the silhouette became evident. Dan didn't let it show that he knew someone was there. With a total change in his demeanour, Dan spoke again.

'Mr Dubois, we have travelled a very long distance and would be much obliged if we could collect the package and be on our way.'

'Very well,' said Dubois, and clapped his hands.

'Didier! Get the package for Mr Sharpe.' Dan looked surprised.

'You know my name.'

'I know a lot of things about you, Daniel, and a lot more about your father.' For the first time Dan looked nervous, but the atmosphere was just about to change. A minute late Didier, the second of Dubois's men, came back into the room carrying a package about the size of a shoe box. He placed it onto the table in front of Dubois and whispered something in his ear. Without touching the package, Dubois walked over to the window, opened it up and swung the shutters back. The room instantly filled with light. Dan had to squint until his eyes adjusted.

The unknown man at the rear of the room could now be seen. He wore a grey pinstriped suit, a light blue shirt with a white collar such as what a City of London banker or a solicitor would wear. His hair was mousey brown tinged with grey, but immaculately combed back. Dan reckoned he was in his late forties, but what he was doing here he hadn't got a clue. The man looked totally out of place. Maybe another business associate? Dan thought. He told himself that it wasn't important, then turned and looked out of the window like Dubois.

Mike, feeling fed up, wanted to get the package and get out of there. He hoped that the taxi would be waiting for them, as finding another, out here, would be impossible. He looked across at Dan, but he couldn't get eye contact. Dan was looking out of the window.

The window overlooked a large courtyard. To the right, a blue articulated lorry was backed on to what looked like a loading bay. In the centre of the yard a white mini bus had pulled up. Mike noticed the number plate was British and written on the side it said 'Budget Rental'. Several men with suitcases were mingling around the rear of the bus. One of the men saw Dubois at the window; he smiled and nodded in recognition.

Dubois turned, picked up the package and walked over to Dan. Dan held his ground, standing firm, as

Dubois approached. Dubois lent forward within an inch of Dan's face. His skin was potted and dark stubble was beginning to push its way through his chin. Dan could smell the heavy odour of the Cuban cigar on his breath, and when he spoke he could feel the spit droplets on his cheeks.

'Be aware, young man,' Dubois whispered so that only Dan could hear. Mike strained to listen but failed. 'Your age means nothing to me. Your family means nothing to me.' Dan could feel his temperature rising. He clenched then loosened his fists to try and calm his nerves. 'If this package does not get delivered in the same state that you see it now, this will come looking for you and your father.'

Dubois held up a single bullet, produced a pistol from behind his back, then opened up the chamber. He pushed the bullet into the gun, then closed the mechanism. Dan jumped as the mechanism hit home. Dubois thrust the package into Dan's stomach then, waving his hand, he told his men to show them out the back way.

It was such a relief to be out in the fresh air again. Mike took several deep breaths and thought again how much he detested cigarettes. Dan was in quiet contemplation, recalling what Dubois had said, when Mike prodded him in the back. It brought him back to reality. Dubois's two henchmen took them into the rear courtyard. As the boys and their chaperones neared where the mini bus was parked, Henri, the tall one, told them to take the gate on the other side of the yard behind the lorry.

'Let's get the fuck out of here!' Dan said breaking into a jog.

'What did he say to you back there?'

'I'll tell you later, come on.'

The boys started to run towards the gate when,

totally out of the blue, an English voice with a strong London accent called over to them.

'Here, you two English!'

'Yeah and who wants to know?' Dan replied in a petulant manner, but the question had been enough to stop him in his stride and he began to walk over to the stranger. Mike was still running. Seeing Dan stop, he slowed and shouted back.

'Come on, man! The taxi is waiting.' But it was no good. Dan's natural curiosity, or stupidity as Mike would say later, got the better of him.

'What's a couple of Geordie boys doing out here? Dubois must be selling cigarettes to kids now!' the Londoner said, smiling at Dan.

'Very funny, and what's this? An Age Concern day out in Belgium?' Dan retorted, showing an even bigger toothy grin. The Londoner laughed, then spoke again.

'No, seriously. You were in Dubois's office. You must know his set up pretty well, so I feel safe asking you.'

'Ask me what?' Dan said sharply.

'I'm looking for a couple of extra lads to help me move some stuff back into Britain. Are you and your mate interested? I could make it worth your while.' Dan loved the thrill of the situation so he played along for a while.

'So, what kind of business are you in, then?' Dan said, as if he didn't know.

'Oh, Dubois and me have an understanding. I bring him tourists to buy his cigarettes and, of course, anything else, if you know what I mean? Let's just say I earn a living from it.'

'No thanks,' said Dan gripping tightly to the package. 'I'm my own boss and we're a little busy ourselves at the moment.' He looked back towards Mike who, by now, had walked back across the yard and was in the process of leaning over to whisper into Dan's ear.

'What do you think you are doing? Playing gangster or something? Let's get out of here, now!' Mike couldn't hide his anger and Dan could sense it.

'Look, here's my card have a think about it.' The Londoner held out a business card. Dan took it and, without looking, put it in his pocket. They were just about to leave when a small grey-haired man wearing Bermuda shorts and a disgustingly red Hawaiian shirt appeared from behind the Londoner. For an instant even Mike forgot his anger as he stared at the peculiar sight.

'Excuse me, son,' the man said, waving a small digital camera in Dan's face.

'Can you take a picture of me and my mates, please? I always take them so I never get in any of them.' Dan and Mike looked at each other. Mike rolled his eyes as if to say 'Fucking hell!' Dan agreed.

He gave Mike the package to hold and took the camera, waiting for the group to get lined up. He moved backwards to get the entire group in the shot. They all stood arm in arm in front of the barn, smiling and waiting for Dan to take the picture. There were smiles all round when the camera flashed. He was just about to take another when a loud shout was heard. Dan looked up at the small window that they had looked out of earlier. Dubois was standing waving his gun and pointing it at the group below. Everyone but Dan froze where they stood. Even Mike stood staring at Dubois. Dan in that split second remembered everything Dubois had said to him minutes earlier.

'Run!' he shouted, as he grabbed Mike's arm and spun him around towards the gate. Mike, not realising, instinctively ran with him. They sprinted around the back of the lorry out of sight, but when they got to the gate it wouldn't open. Dan was starting to panic. He pulled as hard as he could, rattling the gate in its hinges, but it still wouldn't open. Mike joined in with one hand, the other still gripping the package, but it wouldn't budge. The sound of footsteps grew louder from the other side of the truck. Mike turned and saw that the doors at the back of the lorry trailer were open.

'Quick! In here.' Mike pushed Dan in the direction of the back of the truck. They ran past a small sign fixed to the right hand post of the gate. It read 'Push here'. It was the electronic opening device for the gate. In their panic they'd missed it.

They climbed in and, after scampering over several pallets of boxes, hid in a small space deep inside the trailer. The muffled sound of voices could be heard getting closer. The boys held their breath as best they could, straining to listen to what was going on outside. Mike could feel his heart jumping around in his chest as he struggled to contain his breathing. He put his hands over his mouth and took slow deep breaths. Dan had his ear pressed up against the inside of the trailer. The voices died away and they relaxed a little.

By this time, Dubois had entered the courtyard and his two men stood in front of him, like obedient soldiers taking orders from their commander. The tall one, Henri, spoke first.

'They got away, boss. We looked up and down the road but there was no sign of them. Just an empty taxi parked at the end of the road.' They'd mistaken the taxi for being empty because the driver was reclined in his seat.

'You fucking idiots! Find that taxi and you will find those boys.'

'Yes boss.' Both men replied at the same time then, turning towards the gate, ran off to find the taxi.

'What are we going to do?' Dan silently mouthed to

Mike, who sat on the floor with his knees pulled up to his chin.

'Wait a few more minutes and when the coast is clear we'll leg it over the fence, ok?' Dan nodded in agreement.

They sat there staring at the back of the open trailer, waiting for the face of Dubois to appear with gun in hand, but it never came. Ten minutes had passed when Mike gestured to Dan to follow him. They both rose from their cramped position, but all of a sudden footsteps and voices were heard again. It was Dubois with the man in the suit. A forklift truck rumbled into view behind them and placed a large wooden crate into the trailer. Mike and Dan didn't look so as not to give their position away. There was a lot of talking going on, but with the noise of the forklift it was impossible to distinguish. As they huddled in their corner, wishing for freedom, the worst possible thing happened. The back doors of the trailer were closed.

With the natural daylight shut out, they had to rely on the dim yellowy haze that diffused through the fibreglass roof of the trailer. Mike suddenly felt sick, as though a thousand butterflies had taken off in his stomach. An instant feeling of panic came over him. He was just about to shout out when Dan put his hand over his mouth. Mike's eyes fixed on Dan's face. He had his finger over his lips as if to say 'Don't say a word'. Mike nodded and Dan took his hand away.

'They'll kill us if they find us,' Dan said, looking right into Mike's eyes. For a split second Mike didn't know what to say or do. He was in shock. Dan put his finger over his lips again and Mike said nothing.

Dubois's men had returned empty-handed. They told Dubois that the taxi had gone and the two boys had got away. He banged on the side of the trailer in a rage. Inside the lads froze.

'For your sake,' said Dubois, pushing his finger into Henri's chest and then Didier's, 'let's hope that there is nothing on that camera that will do us any harm. Now get this truck out of here! We've got a schedule to keep.'

'Yes boss! Sorry boss.'

Dubois and the unknown man walked to the rear of the trailer. The unknown man produced from his suit pocket a small silver chain; he wrapped it around the two door bolts and sealed the ends together with a pair of unusual pliers. It was an official French Government customs seal, which meant wherever this trailer was going it would not be opened until it was at its destination. When this was finished, Dubois handed a file of documents to Henri who was sitting in the cab of the truck. He gave two hits on the door with the flat of his hand and then, accompanied by the unknown man, walked towards the white mini bus.

Henri started the engine of the lorry; the noise and vibration brought the boys back to reality from their frozen state. As the lorry pulled out of the yard, Mike sat with his head in his hands. Dan was already at the back door checking for a way out. There was nothing. In the late afternoon sunshine the blue lorry, trailer and unknown captives headed out into the Belgian countryside.

Chapter 7

Dan came back from searching the trailer and crouched down next to Mike, placing his hand on Mike's shoulder. Slowly Mike lifted his head and fixed him with a stare that made Dan feel uncomfortable.

'You had to fucking stop and be the big man, didn't you!'

Dan fell back, causing him to sit down. He knew that he'd done wrong and saying something wasn't going to help. Mike was furious. He wanted to grab Dan and pin him up against the side of the trailer, but it was no use; they were locked in the back of a lorry trailer going god knows where, so fighting each other wasn't going to help.

'What were you thinking of? We were home free, got the package, shown the way out. I just don't understand why you fucking went to talk to someone who you'd never met before. Tell me! Why?'

Dan looked at Mike apologetically. There hadn't been many times in Dan's life when he was lost for words, but on this occasion he was. Mike looked him straight in the eyes. His voice softened a little.

'Please Dan. Tell me why, because my brain is in meltdown at the moment, and by the looks of it we are totally up shit creek without a paddle.' Dan lifted his head and bit his bottom lip before he spoke.

'I don't know. I'm sorry. I just did it without thinking.'

'Well, that's a surprise, you doing something without thinking.' Mike laughed sarcastically and shook his head. He got up and climbed onto a palette of boxes and sat back down, facing the locked back doors. 'You are a complete twat sometimes, you know that!'

Mike said without turning round. Dan didn't reply.

With each twist and turn in the road the boys would sway with the motion of the trailer. Neither spoke for ages, or so it seemed. It was not until the truck stopped that the boys got back together again, huddled in their corner in silence.

It was two kilometres to the French border when Henri pulled the lorry into a deserted side road. Didier jumped down from the cab, unlocked a small compartment under the trailer and took out two blue flashing police lights. He clambered onto the roof of the cab and, with the magnetic bottoms, fixed them to the roof, passing the power cables down to Henri. Next, he carefully un-wrapped a large white adhesive sticker with the word 'Douane' written on it and with the help of Henri stuck it to the front of the lorry, just above the air intake grill. Both men then jumped back into the cab and the truck headed off in the direction of the border once more.

Mike, as always, broke the silence first.

'I can't believe you've got me into this.'

By now, Dan had had enough of taking all of the blame.

'Wait a minute, mister brains almighty!' he shouted out as he tried to assert himself over his older friend. 'You said hide in the truck. You can't blame me for that!'

'Someone had to think of something. That gate wasn't about to open on its own, and with men with guns running after us it seemed the best idea. So don't try and twist it back to me.'

'I'm sorry, ok! How many times do you want me to say sorry? Sorry! Sorry! Sorry!'

'Stop it! Ok.' Mike raised his hand, causing Dan to stop.

'I'm just a little bit angry with you, Dan, at the

moment. You can understand why, can't you?'

Mike grabbed hold of the side of the trailer as it went over some rough ground. Dan wasn't quick enough and his head hit a nearby palette of boxes. Mike smiled. Serves him right, he thought. By now the tension between them was starting to ease and both ceased shouting at each other.

'I panicked. I saw Dubois waving his gun at me and I ran. I didn't want to wait around to get shot.'

Mike for the first time looked at Dan with compassion; he could see the fear returning to his friend's face as he spoke.

'Those guys would have killed us,' continued Dan. 'I know it for a fact. Dubois told me that if the package wasn't delivered he would kill me and my dad, and you know what? I believed him.' By now Mike's anger had died. He still wasn't too happy about the situation, but he listened to his friend.

'Mike, I've said I'm sorry. If I could turn back the clock I would. You can have a go at me all you want, but let's try and get out of here first, ok?' Mike agreed and for the time being their friendship was harmonious again.

As the lorry passed over the border between Belgium and France and headed towards the sea port of Calais, the boys were at a loss as to what to do. Each square inch of the trailer had been scoured for a possible exit but in the end both decided that they were well and truly locked in. Shouting for help hadn't been an option as they didn't want to run the risk of alerting Henri or Didier, who still carried their guns. Then, out of the blue, Dan thumped Mike in the chest. It wasn't hard but enough to send him off balance, falling backwards against the side of the trailer.

'What was that for?' Mike said, grimacing and rubbing his chest at the same time.

'Quick! Your mobile phone! Have you got it?' Mike fumbled in his trouser pocket.

'Shit, I forgot.'

The mobile was turned off so Mike switched it on. Dan came alive with excitement. He sat in front of Mike like an expectant child waiting for the sweets to be dished out. Mike paused and looked perplexed. The phone lay in his hand but he made no attempt to use it.

'What's a matter?' Dan said anxiously.

'Who should I ring and what should I say?'

'Ring the police you idiot! Go on!'

'Yeah and say what? Hello, my name is Mike. My friend and I have been kidnapped by some gangsters. We are in the back of a lorry maybe in Belgium or maybe in France. No, let's say in Europe. Please come and save us.' Mike could not help but sound sarcastic in his reply.

'Ok, I get the message. So what are we going to do?'

The boys decided that they needed to find out where they were before ringing for help. Mike found a rusty nail on the floor and tried to make a hole in the side of the trailer, but his attempt was in vain. Dan thought that the fibreglass roof might be easier to penetrate but, with the movement of the truck, there was no way, even with Mike's help, to stay balanced and use the nail at the same time. Feeling defeated, they settled back down into their hole. Dan raised the topic of food. Mike didn't appreciate him bringing up the subject. He hadn't thought about his stomach, but now that Dan had mentioned it he felt incredibly hungry.

The mobile suddenly bleeped and vibrated. Mike looked at it. It said there were five messages. After listening to each one he sighed. Without saying anything to Dan, he gave him the phone so that he could listen. Barry's voice could be heard ranting and raving about their whereabouts. Mike deleted them and pondered whether to call him. When he finally did he, too, got an answering machine. He left no message.

***

The afternoon had given way to evening. Barry sat in the hotel restaurant staring at the two empty spaces. He looked at his watch for the tenth time. He put it to his ear to make sure that it was still working; it was, so he looked at it again. He had already called Mike's mobile five times, but each time it would go onto answer machine. It was eight o'clock when he finally stood up and addressed the rest of the team and asked if anyone knew the whereabouts of Mike and Dan. He scanned every face and waited for a plausible reply, but none came. The closest to an answer was when Richard Green said that he thought he saw them in a taxi, when he was crossing the road, but he wasn't sure.

Barry sat down and contemplated his next move. John Dodd assured him that Mike was a sensible lad and that they had probably not noticed the time. Both would be back soon full of apologies. Barry agreed half heartedly and then started playing with his food, shoving it around his plate with his fork. His appetite was lost, but his imagination had begun to come alive with what might have happened to the boys. He set a deadline in his head of nine o'clock. If they were not back by then he would act. How he would act he didn't know, but he had an hour to decide.

***

When the trailer violently rocked from side to side the two captives weren't ready for it. They had been chatting about girls to cheer themselves up and Mike had told Dan about his burger van chick, emphasising the size and shape of her breasts. Dan said that breasts were important but he was a bottom man, and he fancied his geography teacher Mrs Taylor because she had a lovely bum. Each time she walked past his desk wearing that tight black skirt and high heels it gave him tingles in his pants. Mike said he was sick in the head, but he did have a point - she had got a nice bum. Nevertheless, she was double his age and was much too sophisticated and intelligent to go out with a sixteen-year-old with a penis the size of a caterpillar.

Both laughed together for the first time in ages, but not for long as each dropped to the floor when the trailer threw them about. Unknown to them, the truck had passed over railway lines on its way into the Channel Tunnel Rail Terminal. As they picked themselves up, the lorry stopped and the engine was turned off. They sat in silence once more, listening for life in the outside world.

Henri and Didier got out of the truck, slamming the doors of the cab as they left. When their voices had died away Dan, with Mike's support and the rusty nail in hand, began to pick away at the fibreglass roof. Dan was perched on Mike's shoulders like some third rate circus act, both permanently wobbling this way and that to get their balance. Each time Mike looked up to see the progress he would get bits of fibreglass in his eyes so, after the second piece, he decided not to look up at all. Dan would swear out loud each time he jabbed the nail into the roof. It was slow work - the nail was blunt and every few minutes Mike had to let Dan down because his shoulders would ache. The hole was about the diameter of a coke can when they heard Henri and Didier returning. Mike let Dan down gently, but this time they didn't rush to their hiding place; they both sat on top of the crate that had been loaded last.

The sound of the truck seemed louder as it slowly moved forward. Every twenty seconds or so there would be a clunk and the trailer would rise and fall like it was going over a sleeping policeman. Mike and Dan sat, baffled as to what was happening. It was only when the light shining through the fibreglass got more intense that Mike began to have an idea as to where they were. Even though the truck was still moving, Dan got back onto Mike's shoulders and relayed to him what he could see through the spy hole.

He told Mike that he could see a silver ceiling which contained strip lighting. Mike dropped him down quicker this time.

'We're on the bloody train for the channel tunnel. Fucking hell! We're going back to England!' Mike said with the look of a startled rabbit caught in the headlights of a car. Dan mouthed the word 'shit' about twenty times before letting his head come to rest on the metal side of the trailer.

***

Barry had had enough of waiting. It was 9pm and there was no sign of the boys and no answers to his calls. He asked John to make sure that the rest of the team got to bed and to take no shit from the Loach twins about their eagle-eyed wallpaper. John assured him he would be ruthless, but Barry new that John was as soft as warm butter when it came to dealing with teenagers.

Barry felt nervous. He wasn't sure how to handle the situation because of the language barrier. He needed some help and the only person he could ask was Monsieur Bray, the chef and hotel owner. Barry wasn't disappointed. Monsieur Bray agreed, readily pointing out that his son was a teenager once and he knew what Barry was going through. Barry wanted to go straight to the police but the idea was a bad one according to Monsieur Bray. First they must visit all the local teenager hangouts in case Mike and Dan were there; then, if no joy they would go to the police.

For an hour they trawled the town. Cafes, bars, local parks and even the railway station were searched but to no avail. Mike and Dan were missing. Monsieur Bray suggested that they may have caught the train to Lille as it was just a short train journey away. That suggestion did nothing for Barry's sanity - it just made him more fearful for their safety. His hopes were raised a little when Monsieur Bray took him to an Irish bar which regularly televised English premiership football. The bar was empty but for two old French men drinking Cognac and watching the television. The two searchers could not help but look up at the television as well. The French version of 'The Wheel of Fortune' was being shown, and the two men and barman were transfixed by the busty blonde that turned the letters when a contestant had spun the wheel and picked the right letter. For a few seconds, Barry and Monsieur Bray were glued to the spot as they watched the camera zoom into the bouncing cleavage. Barry's attention broke first and he nudged Monsieur Bray who looked at him, blushing, failing to hide his embarrassment. Thanking the barman, they both left. Outside on the pavement Barry couldn't hide his frustration; he knew the boys were in trouble and he cursed out loud, blaming himself for not taking tighter control over them. Monsieur Bray put his hand on Barry's shoulder; he understood the meaning of Barry's outburst but he could offer no more help than what he'd already done. Barry smiled at him and together they made their way to the police station.

To get there meant passing the Town Hall and Barry could not help, even with the worry of the missing boys, but admire its splendour. He loved fine old buildings and this one was a beautiful example of seventeenth-century Baroque architecture with ornate windows, tall chimneys and exquisitely carved stonework. Lights shone from the pavement illuminating the front façade, giving it an even greater feeling of grandeur.

'Amazing! It must have been designed by extremely expert architects and built by craftsmen,' he said to Monsieur Bray, who just nodded a polite 'yes'. He'd seen it a thousand times and, to be honest, he found it ugly.

Rounding the corner, the police station came into view. *What a contrast*, Barry thought. This building must have been designed on the back of a cigarette packet and built to the same design of the prefabricated post-war houses. He wasn't very impressed by it at all, and even less so when the sliding doors parted and he went from architectural splendour to the clinical and plastic.

The middle-aged English man and the local Hotelier made their way into the reception and stood in front of a large counter. A young female Gendarme greeted them both with a welcoming smile. Pleasantries were exchanged and Monsieur Bray went to work translating for Barry. Everything, even down to birthmarks, were asked for. Barry felt uncomfortable giving the information because he wasn't a parent, but he gave what he could and the young lady logged it all on her computer. When she had finished she explained that the boys weren't exactly children and they hadn't been missing for very long, but as they were foreign nationals she would circulate a missing persons report for them both.

Barry felt a slight relief but now he was at a loose end. He had done everything expected of him and now he must return and take care of his remaining fourteen boys. In his extremely poor French he thanked the officer and left the police station pondering a further dilemma. Should he ring their parents?

***

As the train began to move, Mike and Dan could sense the rocking motion of the carriage. The temperature had risen inside the trailer and both boys had stripped to their t-shirts.

'Say cheese.' Dan held up the small digital camera that was given to him to take the picture of the cigarette tourists.

'Oh great,' Mike replied shaking his head from side to side. 'One minute gangster the next minute thief. You are full of surprises today.'

'I couldn't help it when we panicked.'

'Wait a minute, when *you* panicked. Get it right.'

'Ok, when *I* panicked. I had it in my hand and when the gate wouldn't open I stuck it in my pocket. I'd forgotten about it until now.'

'Well, stick it back in your pocket. We're in enough trouble being in here let alone getting done for theft when we get out.'

Dan did as Mike said and put the camera back in his pocket. He looked over at Mike's watch and asked how long before they would get to the other side. Mike wasn't sure - maybe three quarters of an hour, but they would know for sure when the signal came back on his mobile.

Mike sat deep in thought, working out in his head what he would say to the police about what had happened. He thought that they would probably tell him to piss off and stop wasting their time, but he had no choice but to do it. Dan sat thinking of more simple things like pizza, fish and chips or Burger King and then, out of the silence, he suddenly said 'bacon'. Mike accused him of thinking of his stomach when he should be helping him organise their rescue. Dan said sorry but still contributed nothing to Mike. As the train made its way through the tunnel, Mike dreamed of rescue while Dan dreamed of a Donner Kebab with loads of chilli sauce.

Thirty minutes had gone and Dan was growing impatient. They had no idea where Henri and Didier were so it was an ongoing chore to keep the noise down. Both were glued to the tiny screen on Mike's mobile, waiting for the little transmitter symbol to appear in the top left hand corner. When the signal reappeared, Dan was on him like lightning.

'It's back in signal! Go on, do it then!'

Mike entered 999 into the phone and after two rings it was answered by a woman asking which service did he require. With an unconvincing tone of voice, Mike asked to speak to the police. She instructed him to stay on the line and then, almost immediately, the ringing tone was heard again. As he waited for someone to come on the line everything that he had planned to say disappeared from his head. He felt a sudden panic grow inside him; his chest grew warm as the adrenalin flowed. He loosened his collar with his finger and took a deep breath. As soon as the voice came on the line he let fly at a hundred miles an hour, but in a quiet voice, relating their predicament. All the time that he spoke he looked at Dan for support, but he only received a nod of the head for reassurance. When he finally stopped the voice on the other end said something that he didn't expect.

'I hope this isn't a hoax call. We have the capability to trace and prosecute if necessary.' Mike took the phone away from his ear, looked at it, shook his head and then replied in an angry whisper.

'Look! Everything that I said is true. You have our names, you have this phone number. You have everything apart from my shoe size. We were kidnapped in Belgium and are now back in England, locked inside a blue lorry inside the Channel Tunnel Terminal at Folkestone. Please hurry! This lorry could be going anywhere.'

The voice on the other end told him to keep his mobile at hand and not to worry, someone would find them soon. The line went dead and Mike slumped to the floor feeling exhausted. In that three minute conversation he had used up every ounce of energy that he had and now he felt totally drained.

'Well, are they coming to get us?' asked Dan, as though he expected the back doors to open immediately and be greeted by a full rescue party.

'Wait! They'll find us, ok? I've done all that I can. Let's just hope they get to us before we leave the Terminal, otherwise how many blue lorries do you think will be driving up the M2 at any one time? It will be like finding a needle in a haystack.'

Dan didn't say anything. He, too, sat down feeling deflated and together they sat in silence, wishing for a swift rescue. With all the excitement of the phone call they hadn't noticed that the train had come to a halt. When the engine of the lorry started up, Mike closed his eyes and swore, while Dan was biting his nails nervously.

The lorry slowly drove off the train and, as it picked up speed, despair started to take over from hope. The two boys hadn't thought much about the consequences of being found in the lorry by Dubois's men. They'd taken it for granted that they would be rescued as soon as they entered England. Silence reigned once more as they sat listening to the sound of the engine, swaying in rhythm to the movement of the trailer.

When Dan's fingernails had all but been chewed and Mike felt at his lowest, the lorry suddenly stopped and the engine was turned off. The cab doors opened. Mike and Dan lifted their heads simultaneously. Henri and Didier, while laughing and talking, climbed out of the cab, shut the doors and walked away. Mike's mobile vibrated in his pocket. He took it out and answered it. A man introduced himself as Detective Inspector Sanderson of the British Transport Police and asked about the welfare of them both. Mike felt the hope that had disappeared returning. He told the Inspector that they were well and that the lorry had stopped after only driving for about five minutes from leaving the train. The Inspector asked if he knew anything more about the description of the truck they were in, but Mike could only say that it was dark blue and the tractor unit didn't have a sleeping compartment. He told the Inspector about Henri and Didier and, together with Dan, gave the best possible description that they could, not forgetting to mention the guns that they carried. The Inspector thanked them and said to stay calm, that someone would be with them soon. He told Mike that he would text his number to him and to try and conserve the life of the battery on his phone. Mike agreed and, once more, the line went dead.

Chapter 8

It had been two hours since Mike had spoken to the Inspector and in that time the lorry hadn't moved. Both boys sat in darkness, listening to the sounds of vehicles moving in the distance. Since Henri and Didier had left no one had come anywhere near the lorry. Both boys were getting tired and frustrated. *Surely the lorry should have been located by now?* Mike thought. Dan had drifted off to sleep, leaving Mike with the awful task of trying not to let nasty thoughts enter his head. For the last hour he had failed. Everything from a horrible painful death to how he would explain himself to his mum and dad had bounced around in his imagination. He was still daydreaming when he heard footsteps outside the trailer. Was it Henri and Didier? He held his ear to the side wall and listened. Instantly he was overcome with emotion as he heard two southern accents coming from the direction of the rear doors.

'Help!' Mike shouted at the top of his voice, waking Dan in the process and who quickly joined in with the chorus.

'In here! We're in here!' they yelled whilst banging on the back doors of the trailer. Excitement took over and laughter rang out between their yells, while their faces were lit up with huge smiles. Rescue was imminent but the gruelling part of explaining was about to begin.

The heavy bolt cutters made breaking the seal on the back door look easy. As the two heavy trailer doors swung open, two intense torch beams hit them in the face and both boys had to shield their eyes with their arms. It didn't matter, though; their captivity was over

103

and, with helping hands, they climbed down from the lorry.

'Well, you're the most ridiculous couple of asylum seekers that I have ever seen,' said a small, stocky customs officer as he walked them to a nearby car.

'Don't you want to ask our names?' Dan said looking confused.

'Oh, we know who you are alright. You fit the descriptions perfectly of the two drug smugglers that we're looking for.' Mike looked up startled.

'No, there's got to be some mistake. We're not drug smugglers.'

The officer looked at his colleague and together they laughed.

'Only joking, son. Don't get you're knickers in a twist. I couldn't resist it,' he replied, still chuckling to himself. Dan didn't find the officer's humour at all amusing.

'Fuck's sake! You nearly gave me a friggin' heart attack,' he said, angrily. 'It's no laughing matter, right.' All four walked to the waiting car in silence, but Dan could not help but notice the two customs officers smirking at each other.

After a short five minute car ride they were escorted into a drab, grey building at the edge of the Terminal. Mike asked where they were being taken to as they entered the lobby area. The customs officer, without saying a word, pointed to a sign to the right of a large blue door. Mike looked across and saw 'British Transport Police' in small white letters. Dan laughed when he saw the sign. Mike was accustomed to Dan's unusual behaviour so he paid no attention to him. The customs officer that had played the joke on them asked why he was laughing. Dan just commented that the British Transport Police weren't real police, it was just staffed by officers that couldn't make the grade in the real police. For the first time the smile left the officer's face.

'Don't think you are dealing with amateurs, sunshine. These boys have exactly the same powers as any other force. Be polite and answer their questions and you might not end up in as big a pile of shit than you already are.'

The reply made Dan's face straighten and, as he walked through the blue door, he swallowed hard remembering all the times he had been questioned by the police before. Mike didn't care about what was going to happen; he was prepared to tell the truth so he could get out as soon as possible.

The boys were led to a small interview room, which had been decorated white and consisted of a rectangular table with four chairs, two on one side and two on the other. One wall had a large mirror of about two metres long and one metre high positioned a metre off the floor. The customs officers told them to make themselves comfortable and that someone would be along to see them shortly. Leaving the room, they locked the door behind them. Dan stood by the mirror, pushing his face up against it as if he was trying to look through it.

'What the hell are you doing?' said Mike feeling annoyed. 'Come and sit down over here for god sake! Someone will be here in a minute.'

'You know this is a one way mirror, don't you?' said Dan. Mike looked across at the mirror; he hadn't really taken much notice of it. 'There'll be some nosey copper standing on the other side now, watching and listening to everything we do and say.' With that, Dan began to tap the mirror with his hand and shouted 'Anybody there, anybody there!'.

'Fuck's sake Dan, sit down! You're getting on my nerves.'

***

What a bloody awful place to be, thought Detective Superintendent Slater as he sat in his office, staring out of the window at the rail terminal below. He had jumped at the chance to be seconded to Interpol (International Criminal Police Organisation) from his position at SOCA (Serious Organised Crime Agency), but Interpol's headquarters were in Lyon, France. Great wine, beautiful women, fantastic food and, of course, better weather, but he hadn't expected to be based at the Channel Tunnel Terminal watching cars and trucks drive past. *What a bad move*, he thought. He knew he should have stayed where he was in London, but the prospect of broadening his horizons and working abroad had lured him away to join Interpol.

Trying to suppress his depression, he picked up a cold mug of coffee that had been sitting on his desk for the past two hours and forced himself to drink it. He ground his teeth together when he'd finished, wishing he hadn't drank it, then put the mug back onto the British Transport Police coaster behind his desk lamp.

It had been an extremely slow Sunday, but he'd used it to catch up on his mountain of paperwork. He had several cases on the go with a never-ending number of enquiries to be made for each. Being the boss meant delegation was the name of the game and, even though he was a hands-on detective, he had a good team of officers below him who knew what was required of them. So this Sunday had been pen-pushing Sunday and he was glad it was over. He made his way to the door and turned off the light. The latch was just about to click as the door closed when his phone rang on his desk. He thought about ignoring it but he knew that, whoever it was, would try to ring him on his mobile, so

106

he turned the light back on, walked to his desk and took the call.

Inspector Tony Sanderson greeted him when he answered.

'Guv, you know these two missing boys that we've been looking for? Well, they've been found safe and sound, but I think you need to come down to the customs area and take a look at what we've got before you talk to them.'

Inspector Sanderson outlined what had been found and the circumstances. Without wasting any time, the Superintendent said he would be down in five minutes. He threw the phone down, grabbed his coat and, with a brisk walk, made his way downstairs to his car. *Things could be looking up*, he thought as he walked across the car park.

When Superintendent Slater arrived at the customs area, the blue lorry had been cordoned off as a crime scene. Yellow police tape had been tied to nearby lamp posts and a young police officer was checking identities of everyone who entered the cordon. The local Scene of Crime Officer (SOCO) had already arrived and was busy photographing and fingerprinting the exterior and interior of the lorry. The Superintendent walked over, hands in pockets, taking in the scene. The customs officers had set up some extra lighting which made the lorry look like it was playing the starring role in a stage play. He showed his identification to the officer who quickly wrote his name on his log, lifted the tape and ushered him in. Inspector Sanderson stood waiting for him.

'What have we got then, Tony?' said the Superintendent without taking his hands from his pockets.

'This is the truck that the boys were found in. Note the official Douane insignia and blue lights. We've checked it out with our French colleagues and it doesn't exist. Somebody has gone to a lot of trouble to make this truck look as authentic as possible.'

The Superintendent listened intently and not once did he interrupt his subordinate. While still listening, he climbed onto the back of the trailer.

'When it was opened the customs guys sent the sniffer dogs in and they went wild,' continued Inspector Sanderson. He lifted the top of one of the crates that had been recently opened and ran his hand through its interior. Superintendent Slater watched as the Inspector lifted off a thick layer of bubblewrap to uncover what lay beneath. The crate was full of plastic bags containing what looked like little white tablets.

'So what are we looking at, Tony!' said Superintendent, pulling out a clear plastic bag the size of a bag of sugar and examining it up close. The Inspector produced his note book and read out what he had written earlier.

'A preliminary count has come up with,' he began, flicking through his pages looking for the details, 'ten crates, each one a metre cube in size containing, what we believe to be, five hundred bags of Amphetamine type stimulants (ATS) Ecstasy. Lab will verify which type.' He paused and took a breath, which made the Superintendent lift his head up from examining the bag. 'If I have done my calculations correct, sir, we are looking at two and a half million Amphetamines with a street value of about thirty-eight million pounds.'

There was no visible reaction from the Superintendent. He squeezed the bag in his hand and turned it upside down, causing the contents inside to drop to the other end of the bag.

'Well, Tony,' he said, throwing the bag from one hand to another. 'We've just pissed somebody off, haven't we?' A look of contentment appeared on his face as he placed the bag back with the rest. Both officers smiled in the knowledge that what they had discovered was going to make some criminal somewhere extremely unhappy. The Superintendent turned to walk away, but the Inspector stopped him.

'But that's not all, guv. This truck came through with legitimate French Government paperwork and an official French customs seal, which means it doesn't get checked by our customs, a kind of diplomatic immunity to coin a phrase. It was never meant to leave the terminal; it was just for materials resupply of the French Passport control this side of the channel.' The Superintendent butted in before he could finish.

'So you are telling me, Tony, that many more trucks like this could have passed through here undetected?'

'Yes, that's right guv, but it also means that either someone high up in the French Government is issuing the paperwork to allow them through, or there is an extremely competent forger with good connections. Not forgetting, of course, that there will also be someone this side of the channel ready for the pick up.' The Superintendent stood silent rubbing his chin, deep in thought, while the Inspector waited for his superior's reply.

'Tony, I don't like this one little bit,' the Superintendent replied at last. 'It's drugs this time, but what else has been brought through? Weapons, explosives, even asylum seekers? It worries me.' Inspector Sanderson raised his eyebrows in agreement. 'What about the driver, Tony? Any leads?'

'Believed two males in the cab, both dressed as officers of the Douane. They'll be back in France by now, unfortunately.'

'Seize the surveillance tapes for the last three hours through the tunnel and get me the full list of employees with access to this area. We might just get lucky.'

'Consider it done, guv.'

'I can see us having our hands full with this one. Good work Tony! Now, let's go and talk to the two boys and get this case rolling.' Superintendent Slater climbed down from the trailer and started to walk towards his car. The officer on the cordon lifted the tape once more. He stopped and turned to face his colleague, who walked a few paces behind.

'For the time being, Tony, I want a total press blackout and no leaks. You understand me!'

'Yes guv, leave it to me.'

The day was certainly ending well, thought the Superintendent as he fumbled in his pocket for his car keys. He drove back to his office building slowly, thinking how this find would raise a few brows in the senior ranks. He wasn't one for blowing his own trumpet, but he told himself that he was due some recognition for all the work and past sacrifices that he had made for the force. Customs would probably take the credit, but they won't gloat too much because they let the truck through without checking it in the first place. Nevertheless, the size of this find worried him tremendously and it wouldn't be long before he had to release the information to the press. *Better to do it officially*, he thought rather than let some underpaid Pc leak it to a national newspaper for a pile of cash. He pushed the accelerator a little more; time was definitely not on his side.

***

The phone rang on Dubois's desk. He took the cigar from his mouth and held it between his thumb and index finger. He picked up the receiver and held it to his ear. A low, hoarse voice on the other end of the line spoke. Slowly Dubois's facial expression changed from being calm and relaxed to livid and boggled-eyed. Crushing the cigar between his fingers, it crumbled into bits of dry, broken leaves and ash. He slammed the phone down onto the table then, standing up, picked the phone up with two hands and threw it at the closed window. The glass shattered with a loud crack sending shards of glass, followed by the phone itself, out of the window onto the barn floor below. His eyes were glazed in anger and a large blue vein bulged and pulsed on the side of his forehead as he leaned on his desk.

'They will pay for this. I will have their young hearts on a plate!' he shouted as he glared at the wall opposite. For Dubois, his day had certainly been ruined.

***

The door opened and Superintendent Slater and Inspector Sanderson entered the room behind the one-way mirror. Mike had his head in his arms resting on the table, while Dan sat next to him, examining the camera that he had accidentally stolen. The Superintendent turned to make his way into the interview room, when he suddenly turned around with a complete look of shock on his face. The Inspector looked at him, not comprehending what was going on. Mike had lifted his head from the table and looked towards the mirror.

'I don't believe it,' the Superintendent said, whilst banging his forehead with his fist. 'Tony, what I'm going to say stays between us two, ok?' The Inspector agreed without any reservation. He had worked with the Superintendent many times before and respected his judgment implicitly.

'That one there, the tall one,' Slater continued, nodding slightly towards his colleague, 'he's my nephew.' The Inspector's eyebrows rose to full height.

He took a deep breath and rubbed his chin with his hand, feeling the stubble against his fingers. He didn't know what to say and for a moment he was silent.

'You know what the chief will do, guv?'

'Yes, Tony, I know. If he finds out my feet won't touch the ground and I'll be pulled off this case immediately. No, I can't let that happen. Right, this is what we'll do.' The Inspector paused for a few moments, deciding on the best way forward. Tony, you interview with a wire so I can communicate with you. As far as I know those two in there could be totally unconnected to the case. If they are, fine, I stay involved. If not, I will have to withdraw from the inquiry.'

The Inspector agreed. Family and work didn't mix, especially in a court of law. He left Superintendent Slater staring through the mirror as he went to get his wire.

Ten minutes had passed when Inspector Sanderson entered the interview room with three large plastic cups of tea. He placed them on the table, said they all had sugar in and then introduced himself. Mike sat up and smiled. Dan wasn't so warm towards the Inspector.

'Am I under arrest? Because if I'm not I would like to leave. I know my rights!' He sat on the edge of the table swinging his legs in an attempt to show some defiance against authority. Mike looked across at his friend, scowling.

'Dan! For fuck's sake! Wind your neck in and sit down!' Jim Slater smiled at his nephew's comment from behind the mirror.

'Listen to your friend, Mr Sharpe,' spoke the Inspector, 'he's talking sense. But if you want to be arrested that will not be a problem. What shall we arrest you for? Possession of drugs? Conspiracy to supply? Drug smuggling? I could go on but all this will take a lot more time. So let us say for now you are helping us with our enquiries, ok?' The Inspector pulled up a chair and sat down opposite Mike, smiling kindly. Dan came and sat down but kept his arms folded to show his resentment.

The Inspector was polite and calm towards the boys. Mike took an instant liking to him but Dan hated him, mainly because he hated all police officers and what they stood for. Sensing this, the Inspector directed everything towards Mike, who was willing to answer every question once the threat of prison, homosexuals in the shower and a ruined life had been explained.

For the next sixty minutes Mike gave the Inspector the answers to his questions, describing every event that had happened and why. Occasionally Dan would look across at Mike and nudge him if he said something that he didn't like, but Mike said it anyway. He didn't care what he thought; it was Dan's fault why they were there in the first place. Happy with Mike's answer but still needing more, the Inspector needed to get Dan involved in the interview as, up until now, he had sat silent. The Inspector, with Superintendent Slater in his ear, decided to question them regarding Dubois, who happened to be very well-known to the British police as a veteran in organised crime and in drugs especially. Mike described everything from the unknown man down to the colour of the wallpaper in his office. Dan, still silent, was getting tired and irritable and the Inspector sensed it but he needed to press on.

'Let's talk about the package for your father, shall we Dan?'

Dan immediately livened up and paid attention. The time was right for the Inspector to tell the boys what the package contained. Their jaws drop when he said the word Ecstasy. Mike stood up and walked towards the mirror; he turned around and looked at Dan. His face was full of contempt for his friend for putting him in this situation.

'Your father can go to hell for getting you to do this,' he said, pointing his finger at Dan who, by now, had succumbed to his shame and hung his head.

'I came with you because you asked me as a friend. I knew that the package was dodgy and now I'm told this. You and your old man are a class act, you know that?' Mike shook, overcome with anger. His words dried up as he simply couldn't describe how he felt. He head butted the mirror to see if the pain would help him find the words, but it didn't.

Jim Slater watched helpless from the other side. He told the Inspector to finish off for now and organise some food for them. Concerned with what he'd seen and heard, he made his way back to his office. A plan began to formulate in his head and he needed time to think.

Back in the interview room the atmosphere was intense; you could cut it with a knife. Neither boy spoke, Mike through choice and Dan because he didn't know what to say.

As the boys tucked into some ham and cheese sandwiches from the canteen's vending machine, Jim Slater and the Inspector discussed their plan of action.

'Well, I believe them, guv. It seems to me those two were just in the wrong place at the wrong time.'

'Yeah, you're right, but it's Dubois that worries me. You know he's a man who bears grudges, don't you Tony? He's one hell of a nasty bastard.' Jim Slater looked with concern out of the window towards the two boys. 'I fear for their safety, Tony, but we need to catch Dubois. This bastard has been running rings around us for years.' The Inspector sat and listened, nodding in agreement.

'Guv, you know Dubois will be long gone by now?

He's surely to have been tipped off.'

'I know,' Jim replied, sitting back down in his large leather recliner. 'We need to bring him out into the open.' The Inspector agreed, but he felt uncomfortable with the knowledge.

'I'm sorry, guv, but you can't be thinking of using them as bait? He's your nephew!'

'Look Tony, I know how it seems, but just realise this - with us they will be safe. If they're on their own or locked up Dubois will get to them. I've no other choice but to throw them back to the wolves.'

The Inspector didn't like what he was hearing but he knew the Superintendent was right. Coming around to the front of his desk, Jim Slater leaned in close to explain his plan.

The Inspector listened intently and was quite struck as to how simple the plan was. Slater would play Uncle Jim and not the Superintendent. The boys were never to be told who he really was. Uncle Jim would turn up after being called by the police and escort them back to France. If the boys questioned why Uncle Jim was there it would be easy to say that he lived just down the road. Uncle Jim would then decide that he would use up some holiday and continue on the tour with them. It was simple; Uncle Jim could watch the boys at close quarters and, at the same time, look out for Dubois and his men.

'Do you think it will work, guv?'

'I hope so, Tony, because if it doesn't those boys are in a world of shit. This is what I need.' The Inspector immediately produced his note book and started to write. 'I want a fully-armed surveillance team to follow twenty-four seven. Don't worry, I'll get clearance from the top. I've got a few favours to call upon. You just sort out the team and equipment.'

The Inspector instantly knew who he would use and

began systematically flicking through his notebook for telephone numbers.

'We will need full cooperation from each European country,' continued Slater. 'Contact Europol to assist. Don't give them too much information because they might get in the way. This needs to happen quickly. You understand?' The Inspector nodded but stayed silent. 'I'm going to be with the boys most of the time so you call the shots on this one, Tony, ok? But keep me informed and I'll contact you when necessary.'

The Inspector stood up, put his book into his pocket and was just about to leave when Jim walked over to him.

'He's my brother's boy; we can't let anything happen to him.' There was a kind of softness in his boss's voice that he'd never heard before. Emotion was something that Jim Slater never showed to anyone.

'Don't worry, guv, I'll look after him.'

'Thanks Tony, I know you will. Oh, and one last thing. Get Northumbria Police to lift Sharpe's dad - we don't want him causing us problems.' The Inspector left the room leaving his boss, for the first time in a very long while, unsure of himself.

Jim hadn't seen much of Mike as he grew up and at this moment in time he felt as far away from him as he could possibly feel. The next bit was going to be hard - how to play the loving uncle. He was used to dealing with police officers and villains, but teenagers were something different altogether; but at least he liked football, so maybe that would bring them together.

When the Inspector re-entered the interview room he was greeted by a wall of silence. Neither of the boys had uttered a word since he'd left. He knew that a rift had been created between them and he needed to patch it up before they could leave. He asked them to sit down because he had something important to say. Mike sat back down cautiously; Dan moved his chair away, making it squeak on the vinyl floor.

'We believe your story.' Mike's face lit up instantly. 'But you are not out of the woods yet.' The smile disappeared.

'You realise the trouble that you are in, don't you. You are that close,' he squeezed his thumb and forefinger together to illustrate how close, 'to being put away. Dubois and ecstasy both mean prison.' Both nodded in agreement and looked solemn. 'This is a serious thing that you two have gotten yourselves into. With the country on tender hooks from imminent terrorist attacks from people that would love to bring in all sorts of weapons, here you two are found cheerfully smuggling drugs into the country. You would be crucified if you were put in the dock, but there is still hope.' Forgetting their differences, both Mike and Dan sat forward to hear what the Inspector had to offer.

'The deal is you go back on your tour and carry on as normal while we do some digging. You're not out of the woods because when it's over you'll have to come back and talk to us. Let me just say you are more important out of jail than you are in it, wouldn't you agree?' Nodding in agreement but not realising the implications, the boys' faces lit up. 'Now, patch up your differences because there is someone waiting outside to take you back.'

Mike and Dan couldn't believe it. What a rollercoaster ride they had been on. One minute off to prison, the next back on tour. Things said in anger were for the time being put to one side and they left the room full of smiles. The tiredness that they felt had disappeared and the former best friends were best friends once more.

Chapter 9

Jim Slater, the man who regularly stood in the Old Bailey putting hardened criminals away while standing face to face with them, was nervous. He stood tapping the side of his car with his hand as he waited for his nephew to appear. He didn't really know Mike and Mike didn't know him. He was family, he thought. How hard could it be? The problem for Jim Slater was that he didn't know how to be an uncle; he'd never had to. It had been so easy being a relative by post, but now he found being a relative face to face difficult to say the least. Criminals and coppers were his life; finding room for a teenager was going to be tough, especially without blowing his cover. He felt extremely apprehensive.

The metal side door swung open and drenched Jim Slater in florescent light. Inspector Sanderson led the boys down the steps. Both looked tired but smiles had returned on their release. Mike looked across to where his uncle stood but nothing registered. It took another ten seconds until they were nearly at the car when the penny dropped.

'Uncle Jim! What are you doing here?' Mike said with genuine surprise. He recognised him from the many times he'd spent with his dad looking through their photo album at home.

'Shouldn't I ask you the same question?' Jim replied, frowning at him. Mike blushed with embarrassment then got into the car. Dan wasn't paying attention to any of them; fatigue had a hold of him and within a minute of getting into the car he fell asleep. The Superintendent and Inspector gave each other a cursory nod; nothing more was said. As the car pulled away to catch the next train back to France Jim looked into his rear-view mirror, bracing himself for the onslaught of questions. He felt relieved when he saw both sets of eyes closed. Mike had fallen asleep just after Dan and both were now leaning against one another, heads bobbing gently with the motion of the car.

The two boys slept soundly and neither felt the change from road to rail when Jim drove onto the tunnel train, but as it approached Calais Mike woke up. Dan was still asleep so Mike eased Dan's head off his shoulder and leant him gently against the head rest.

'Do my mum and dad know?' Mike said to his uncle as he leant forward resting on the front passenger seat. While the boys slept Jim's mind had been working overtime, trying to anticipate the questions that they might ask. Luckily for Jim, he was ready for the first question.

'No, they don't know,' he replied in a whisper. Instantly relieved to get the first question under his belt, Jim let out a sigh but he stiffened up straight away when Mike asked question number two.

'How come it's you? I haven't seen you for eleven years and now you show up here.' Mike's voice had an edge to it and Jim had to consciously stop himself from talking to him as if he were one of the criminals that he normally dealt with.

'Look Mike, when the police called what could I say? No, he's got nothing to do with me, let him rot. Is that what you wanted?'

'No, of course not. It's just that you were the last person that I expected to see.'

'Hey! Count your lucky stars that I'm here, because from what I've been told you two should be behind bars by now.'

Mike didn't reply. He slumped back in the seat, feeling ashamed, but deep down he was glad his uncle had picked them up. To face his parents right now would be a nightmare.

As the car made its way towards Bergues and for the showdown with Barry, Uncle Jim explained why it was he who had come to their rescue. He told Mike that he lived just a few miles away from the terminal. The police had tried to get in touch with his mum and dad without success so he was the next family member on the list. Luck would have it that Uncle Jim had just taken a week's holiday from his accountancy firm so it was not a problem picking them up. Mike sat there listening while Jim spun his tale. Calling himself an accountant just popped into his head he hadn't got a clue why he had done it, but the rest of the lie came easy.

Mike sat looking blank. For an instant Jim thought that he was not buying his story.

'Look Mike, I know you don't want to go home and face your parents. I thought that it would be best if I accompanied you back to the tour and not some police officer. The Inspector explained everything that you've gone through and, hey, maybe it's time that I got to know you a little better. What do you think?'

Mike didn't react at all. Jim thought the worst. He stared at him a little too long in the mirror, waiting for an answer, which didn't come. When his eyes met the road again he had to swerve to miss an oncoming car. *Why is this kid being so difficult?* he thought, but he had to carry on with the charade and hope that Mike would go along with it. Jim needn't have worried, however, as Mike had taken the bait.

'Uncle Jim, I'm sorry.' The swerving of the car had shaken Mike out of his trance. 'I do appreciate what you are doing and thanks for not telling mum and dad. I've got no problem if you want to hang around for a few days. It's a great idea.'

Jim felt relieved that for the moment he was doing ok. He told Mike to close his eyes again and he would wake them both when they arrived at the hotel. Mike didn't take much persuading.

It was two-thirty in the morning when the car pulled up outside the Hotel in Bergues. Jim woke the boys. Dan lifted his head from Mike's shoulder and twisted his neck to loosen the muscles. Mike looked at his shoulder and then at Dan in disgust. A large wet patch was visible where Dan had dribbled on him. Dan smiled as he wiped the rest of the dribble from his mouth. Mike shook his head; he was too tired to argue.

The front door of the hotel was unlocked and the light in the reception was still on. The boys thought that they would sneak away to their room, but they failed when Barry and the hotel manager walked from the small office behind the reception desk. Unknown to the boys, Inspector Sanderson had phoned ahead to organise the Superintendent a meeting room so that he could explain the situation to Barry.

Dan closed his eyes and grimaced in anticipation of the onslaught of abuse that he was expecting from his manager. Mike, on the other hand, smiled as he was genuinely pleased to see Barry. Whatever the two boys had expected it didn't happen and Barry greeted them with smiles. He embraced Mike, giving him a hug as if he were a grandfather embracing a grandson. He put his hand on Dan's head, ruffling his hair. Surprise was written all over Dan's face as he pulled away.

'Look, I know what's happened, but we aren't going to talk about it now,' said Barry. 'There's a match tomorrow and you two need your rest. Go on, get yourselves off to bed.'

The three adults watched as the boys made their way to the lift. Dan looked at Mike and raised his eyebrows; he was just about to say something when Mike stopped him. He'd had enough of Dan for one day. He told him that he didn't want to hear anything more from him tonight. Dan didn't retaliate; bed was calling him and tonight the wild forest wallpaper wasn't going to bother him one bit.

***

At 8am sharp there was a knock on the door. Mike opened his eyes slowly. *Surely it wasn't time to get up already?* he thought to himself, as he turned to look at his watch on the bedside table. Dan had the pillow on his head, but Mike knew he was awake.

'Come on, shit for brains!' shouted Mike as he threw the sheets off himself and sat on the edge of the bed.

'Tell them to fuck off, will ya!' The muffled sound of Dan's voice could be heard from under the pillow. 'I'm staying in bed.'

Mike walked over to Dan's bed and pulled the sheets off in one go. Dan sat up in surprise.

'Hey, you dirty bastard!' cried Mike. 'You didn't get undressed, you minger!'

'I was knackered, ok? I just couldn't be arsed last night.

'Well minger, you better have a shower because I'm not sitting next to you at breakfast. You stink!' Dan responded by giving Mike a two-fingered salute and pulled the covers back over his head.

Breakfast came and went just like the day before. Lots of bread, ham and cheese consumed with the now predictable moans from Dan regarding the lack of bacon. Uncle Jim sat with Barry and John; occasionally he would make eye contact with Mike and smile. Mike would nod to acknowledge him but, in the cool light of day, he had begun to realise that maybe it wasn't such a good idea to have him on the tour. He was a threat to his independence. No other player had a relative with them so why must he? Nevertheless, there was nothing that he could do about it and it looked as though Uncle Jim was here to stay, so the least he could do was to be civil to him.

On the way to the football ground, Mike couldn't help but think about the day before. He knew it had happened, but now that he was back with the team it seemed so long ago. He watched Dan through the corner of his eye and couldn't believe what he saw. The little git was the same as usual. Yesterday threatened with murder, while today he was acting like nothing had happened and was back to his old self of talking bullshit and showing off. As long as Mike lived he would never understand him.

As Mike listened to what Dan was saying he shook his head in disbelief. Dan was explaining to Martin Cuthbert, the left back, that to be an attacker you needed more brains than a defender. He was explaining that up front you needed to be constantly thinking about your position and being aware of the players around you. Fast reactions were the name of the game with your mind permanently focused on the goal. Defenders just stood there waiting for things to happen and then, when they did, they were too slow in reacting. Martin took offence at Dan's remarks and challenged him to play in his position. Dan declined, saying that he liked to break into a sweat when he played football and playing at left back would hardly keep him warm. Martin took the comment as an insult and then added himself to the long line of people that have called Dan a twat, but he was so thick-skinned that it just washed over him.

When the tour bus pulled up at Bergues football ground all of the team, even Barry, were transfixed by the spectacle that they saw. The Bergues team were already warming up on the pitch, but that wasn't what drew everyone's attention.

'I don't fucking believe it!' said Dan to Mike as he pushed his face up against the window. The Bergues team wore a bright pink strip. The jersey, shorts and socks were all bright pink!

'They look like a bunch of fairies. How can we play against a team that plays in pink?' Graham Loach shouted down the bus.

'The same as if they were wearing the Sunderland home strip,' replied Barry seriously. Never before had the Indispensables played against opposition that wore pink. To them it was a bad omen, as pink was not a football colour in the North East of England. Black and white was their colour and to play against pink put a curse on the game before it had even started.

'Ignore the colour!' Barry shouted over the melee of abuse. 'It's just a training game, go out and enjoy yourselves. Oh and Stuart,' Barry looked across at Stuart Forster, one of the midfielders.

'Just because they are wearing pink doesn't mean that you have to be nice to them and not tackle them, ok!'

Stuart blushed and hid down behind the seat in front of him as the rest of his team mates blew him kisses. Stuart was a reasonable player when he got going, but a lot of the time he was timid and always needed some encouragement to enable him to rise to the occasion.

From the first whistle Barry cringed with every ball that was passed and every tackle that wasn't made. The first half just never got going. Both teams cancelled each other out. Few shots were taken by either team and Mike had to make even fewer saves. There was a total lack of commitment by the Indispensables and, for Barry, the word 'dreadful' wasn't even strong enough to describe the team's performance. When the half time whistle blew he sighed with relief that it was over.

On the outside, Barry's demeanour seemed calm and relaxed as normal as he followed his team into the dressing room. Inside, though, he was furious. However, he had a dilemma. Should he be hard on them? Or just accept that it was their first ever game against a foreign team on foreign soil? He needed to motivate, not annihilate their spirit, and he had an idea of how he could achieve this balancing act.

Heads were down when Barry surveyed his troops. He thought that he had better start on a high point; better to build them up before he knocked them down, but there weren't so many high points so it didn't last long. He began to describe the different styles of play between the British game and the European game but it failed to lift any heads, so he decided to go on to his next approach. Mike still felt tired from the day before and Dan, who normally could not be shut up, sat listless in the corner flicking mud from his boots. It was no use trying to give them excuses for their performance; Barry needed to change his tack.

'Right, listen up you lot!' Barry clapped his hands loudly, making them lift their heads. 'Look at me when I'm talking to you, and that means you too Daniel.' Dan looked across, but his face was blank. 'This is what I want second half.'

Barry shouted, rubbing his hands together as though they were cold. He needed to get what he wanted off his chest and time was running out. 'Second half we use the wings more. I want one and two touch football only, just like what we do on the training ground.'

Groans were heard emanating around the dressing room but Barry continued on, determined to get them motivated.

'Quicker movement of the ball out to the wings

from the midfield and I want you, Floyd, to dominate midfield.' Barry pointed at Floyd Barnaby, the tall West Indian lad. He looked at Barry, nodding in agreement, even before Barry had said anything. 'With your height it shouldn't be a problem. Miles and Scott, I want you two out wide on the wings and everything that you get will be through Floyd, ok!'

Miles didn't react but Scott smiled; he loved to play out wide. Barry continued, directing his comments at the two wingers.

'If Dan doesn't score with his head in the second half, all three of you will not play the next game.'

Miles and Scott looked at each other with horror, as if they had both been told to kiss each other. Dan started to speak but Barry shot him down, telling him to shut up until he had finished talking. Dan sat back with his arms folded giving Barry an evil stare. Barry knew that he wouldn't really deprive them of the next game, but they weren't to know that. A little blackmail now and again, used in the right place, was an excellent motivating tool, Barry thought as he surveyed the reactions of the other players. He knew that Miles and Scott wouldn't run the risk of missing the next game so, with the threat hanging over them, they would run their socks off to make sure that Dan got every available opportunity to score. In turn, Dan would be made to run around, with and off the ball to create the space for the wingers; the rest of the team would be lifted as none of them wanted to miss a future game.

Barry could see that his words had got to them but he wasn't finished yet. His final words were meant to shock.

'Bergues are better than you! Better on the ball, better tackling, better skills, quicker and you will lose!'

He could see that the last comment had hit home; the words 'bollocks' and 'fuck off' resonating around the dressing room. The tension was suddenly high and blood had begun to boil in the teenage veins. Barry had to shout as they left the dressing room.

'Well then boys, prove me wrong!'

His parting words had definitely set fire to a few stubborn North East hearts and, as they ran out for the second half, Barry could see real determination in their faces and he was pleased with what he saw.

From the whistle the touch paper had been lit. Dan had turned into an annoying little wasp in the opposition defence, buzzing in and out, twisting and turning, drawing players from their positions. The French players couldn't match his speed and determination. Within five minutes of the second half resuming, Dan had been brought down by the French centre half, right on the edge of the eighteen yard box directly in front of goal. Richard Green, the tall centre forward, stepped up to take the free kick. Dan wanted to take it so badly that he thought about running in before the whistle and taking the shot, but he knew that Richard was better than him when it came to kicking a dead ball.

Richard stood calm and collected, knowing where he was going to put the ball before he'd even placed it down on the grass. The French goalkeeper had positioned his wall perfectly and was now busy jumping up and down keeping on his toes, awaiting the shot. Richard was ready. His eyes were fixed onto the ball; he didn't need to look at the goal as he knew where everything was. Suddenly, nobody else on the pitch existed but him, the ball and the goal. The whistle blew; instinctively he reacted, moving forward towards the ball, building up speed.

There was silence all around; he could feel the wind on his face as he quickened his pace. When he was only a yard from the ball he slowed down, lifted his head for one last look then, with the grace of a ballet dancer, flicked the ball over the wall towards the top left-hand corner. The ball hung in the air. He watched, worried that the goalkeeper would make up the ground and intercept it before it hit the back of the net. His mouth hung open as his brain willed the ball into the net. Everyone else stood motionless and silent, hypnotised by the football gliding effortlessly toward its target; apart from Dan, that is, who tiptoed slowly forward, as though the ball had hooked him and was dragging him with it.

Richard closed his eyes when the ball hit the post. The disappointment of not scoring hit him like a steam train in the chest and he didn't even react to follow-up the rebound. It didn't matter, though; Dan was already there, easily a yard and a half in front of any other player. With the keeper committed, all it needed was a little flick of his head to connect with the ball and it would fly effortlessly into the back of the net.

Without stopping, he ran around the back of the goal celebrating, the rest of his team-mates in hot pursuit. With a little shimmy throwing his pursuers off balance, he ran towards the dugout where Barry sat. When he was ten yards away, still running at full speed, he dropped to his knees and slid effortlessly along the grass. Coming to a stop, he punched the air with his fist and put his finger up to show Barry that he was number one. Barry just smiled, nodded and then winced as the majority of his team-mates jumped on top of him to congratulate their goal scorer. Dan disappeared under a pile of bodies as Mike watched from his goal area

'What a nob head,' he said as he watched his friend celebrate. Mike wasn't one to get carried away on goal celebrations, but he was pleased for Dan.

Celebration over, it was back to business. The game had turned in favour of the Indispensables and they were now playing in fifth gear rather than the second gear of the first half. Two further goals were scored before the final whistle - another one for Dan and an own goal which Dan tried to claim to get his hat-trick.

Mike felt somewhat disappointed, not with the result but with his own performance. The Indispensables had dominated the second half and in that forty-five minutes he had only touched the ball four times - two goal kicks, one offside and a catch from the only corner that the opposition had. He hoped that the next game in Holland would be a little more of a challenge, because he was here to play football and not watch the game from his goal area.

For Barry, the game had been a success. He had worried before the tour that his team may not have the same quality that existed in Europe, but his philosophy on the two different styles of football between Britain and Europe had vindicated him. They could now all go forward to the next game with the knowledge that they were unbeatable.

Barry made the team line up, before they went into the dressing room, to congratulate the opposition. Pats on the backs and hearty handshakes were dished out by all of the Indispensables. He took the opportunity to thank the Bergues team for their hospitality, but he had to shout to be heard as there was so much noise coming from the away dressing room. The celebrations continued long after the game had finish but they had to come back down to earth pretty fast as the bus would be waiting to take them on the next leg of their journey.

Mike changed quickly and was ready to go before Dan had even had a shower. Dan had spent the last fifteen minutes reliving every move of every goal. Mike hadn't got a problem listening to him brag, he was used to it; the problem began when Dan started to sing his football hymns and dance around the dressing room like an annoying little gnome. For anyone looking in you would think that he'd won the World Cup single-handedly. Everyone else joined in until the noise was unbearable. Mike decided to get the hell out of there; no doubt he would hear every one of Dan's renditions again on the bus, but in the meantime he wanted to get his uncle Jim's reaction to the match.

Outside, his uncle was nowhere to be seen. He looked around the pitch and the next door car park but he couldn't find him. Mike knew that he was at the match because he had seen him with Barry just before the kick-off. He decided that he would catch up with him later on the way to Holland, but for now he would take a quiet five minutes on the bus listening to his music before the rabble caught up with him.

'Well, did you see my goals!' said Dan excitedly as he nudged Mike, causing him to open his eyes and turn off his mp3 player.

'Well, what do you think?' Mike replied, putting his music away. 'I *was* actually playing in the same game, so of course I bloody saw your goals. I've heard nothing else since.'

'Christ! What's up with you?' Dan replied, the smile disappearing from his face.

'Look, I'm sorry. I didn't really have a good game, ok? I had nothing to do but watch you perform, so forgive me if I can't get too excited for you.'

Dan thought it best to leave Mike for a while, so he leant over the seat in front and started to describe his performance to little Terry Grainger, who wasn't feeling his best either because he only came on for the last quarter of an hour. However, he would listen anyway; he had no choice, as Dan would make him listen.

Barry did his usual head count. The door closed and Dennis steered the bus out of the car park back to the

130

hotel. Mike leaned back in his seat, casually looking out of the window, when he saw his Uncle Jim talking with two men by the exit to the car park. He didn't recognise the men he was talking to and, as the bus pulled away, Mike wondered who in Bergues would know his uncle, but he soon put it to the back of his mind and went back to his music.

Jim Slater gave his instructions to the two surveillance officers that Inspector Sanderson had sent him. He hadn't worked with them before, but if Tony had sent them he knew they would be alright. The officers from SOCA were experts when it came to tailing somebody, and specialised in covert surveillance.

'I take it that Tony Sanderson has given you the brief on these two boys?' Jim said, now back in the role of Superintendent.

'Yes guv,' they both replied in unison.

'Stick to those boys like flies on shit, but I want to know who's watching them. You understand? Dubois will try and make a move for them sometime soon and when he does we are going to be there, ok?'

The two officers left to follow the bus and the Superintendent became Uncle Jim once more.

Chapter 10

On the bus the atmosphere was jubilant and even Dennis, the driver, had been roped into singing football songs, but how long it would last was unknown. They had a long drive ahead and the excitement would soon wear off. For Barry, though, he had mixed feelings. He was overjoyed with his team's performance, especially with young Daniel who played like a man possessed, but Amsterdam now became his main concern. There was to be one night spent in the city centre, a match the following day and then once more back onto the bus to head for Germany.

The next twenty-four hours were going to be tough and he knew very well what existed in Amsterdam. The thought of exposing fifteen young boys to its evil ways was beyond comprehension for him. To let them loose in Amsterdam would be a nightmare for him to control. He had the responsibility of being their guardian and he would not want any of their parents knowing that he had allowed them to run amok around the red light district of Amsterdam. He'd discussed the problem with John Dodd over breakfast and the general consensus was to confine the boys to the hotel, using the excuse of their busy schedule and that they needed rest for the match the following day. Both agreed that there would be some dissent from the boys, but there were enough sensible ones to control the not so sensible ones. As he sat back in his seat, listening to the chaos behind him, he couldn't help but fear the worst of what lay ahead. A divine helping hand was what he needed and under his breath he started to ask for one.

Dan hadn't taken his seat next to Mike; he was still pumped full of excitement from the game. The next five hours travelling and the coming night ahead, in Amsterdam, couldn't come fast enough. If he could have whisked himself forward through time to the next game he would have done so, and there was no doubt about it that the amount of adrenaline pumping through his veins would have carried him through another ninety minutes.

Mike, on the other hand, sat on his own oblivious to the mayhem that surrounded him. Uncle Jim had noticed this and made his way down the bus, squeezing his way past Dan who was trying his best to give a demonstration of how he headed the first goal into the net. As he sat down next to his nephew Mike turned, thinking it was Dan, and looked surprised when he saw his uncle sitting there.

'You don't mind if I sit here, do you?' Jim asked nervously, hoping that he would accept. Mike struggled to answer the simple question and, for a short moment, he sat with his mouth open not able to reply. Jim took it as a sign to leave and started to get up when Mike reached out, took his arm and pulled him back down.

'Of course you can, it's not a problem. Sorry, I was miles away,' he said, beginning to smile. Jim smiled back, feeling relieved, and took the seat next to his nephew.

'I'm sorry, Uncle Jim, I just find it all a bit difficult, you know. It's been so long since I've seen you and with all that has happened I feel a bit awkward.'

'Not as awkward as I feel,' Jim replied, showing a deep look of sincerity on his face. 'I haven't exactly been the best uncle, have I?' Mike could have answered that in a single, two-letter word, but he held his tongue and let his uncle continue.

'I'm not a man who finds family an easy subject, you know. I've spent too much time on my own, absorbed in my own work, to let anything else interfere.

133

So it's me that should be asking for your forgiveness and it's me that's sorry for letting you down all these years.'

'Don't be!' Mike replied shaking his head. Jim was taken aback by his answer.

'I've always known you were there, even if I didn't see you. Every Christmas and Birthday you remembered me. It should be me apologising to you. You knew that I existed but it was me that forgot about your existence.'

Mike leant across and put his hand on top of his uncle's hand. It was Jim's turn to struggle to find the words, but not only through emotion; there was a healthy portion of guilt mixed in as well.

'Shall we start from scratch?' said Jim.

'Why not,' replied Mike, 'but can I just call you Jim? At least while we're on tour, because it's a little difficult with all of my team mates around.'

'Not a problem at all. Uncle makes me feel old anyway and I understand how you feel. Having your Uncle Jim on board does nothing for your street credibility, does it?'

Mike laughed and the tension between them disappeared. Uncle Jim was now a friend and past history between them could be forgotten for the time being. Anyway, he would get a better conversation out of Jim than what he was used to with Dan. In that same moment Dan's head came into view above the seat in front; he'd heard them laughing and was feeling left out.

'You're in my seat,' Dan said glaring at Jim as if he was one of his peers. Jim just smiled a polite smile; he had ten different replies in his head but he couldn't use any of them. Mike quickly answered for him, in case he said something that he might regret.

'Do me a favour Dan, sit somewhere else for now,'

he leant forward to whisper. 'We've got a lot of catching up to do. You understand, don't you?'

'Oh, how wonderful, talking about old times!' replied Dan sarcastically. 'Well, you two have a nice chat and I'll sit here on my own then, shall I?'

'Thanks mate, I knew you'd understand.' Jim nodded his head in agreement with Mike. Dan swung around in frustration. Mike knew that he'd pissed Dan off, but so what? He needed a rest from him anyway. Mike leant forward and offered Dan his music system as consolation. Dan took it and a little 'thank you' was heard over the sound of the engine.

As the tour bus trundled steadily through Belgium towards Holland, Mike and Jim talked constantly. Mike talked about everything that had ever happened to him since he was five, starting from when he had last seen his uncle. It all came so easy talking to Jim, much easier than talking to his father; he was actually enjoying reliving his life for his uncle. Jim, on the other hand, found it hard to talk about his past because everything revolved around his police career and there was no way he could reveal any of it. He managed to make something up about being an accountant living in the South East and commuting up to London every day but, given the chance, if he could direct the conversation back towards Mike he would.

Mike's mind was alive with his past exploits, but as soon as his father came into the conversation Jim noticed that his demeanour would change. Words were more stuttered and prolonged; it was definitely hard for Mike to talk about his father. Jim pressed him a little regarding his relationship with his dad but Mike wasn't forthcoming, so Jim decided to take the lead.

'Your dad and I never really got on. Did you know that?' Jim said, changing the subject completely. Mike looked at his uncle innocently.

'No, I didn't know that. He never did talk about you a lot when I was growing up and when he did it was always with mum and not me.'

'I take it he never talked about your grandad either?'

'No, nothing. I haven't got a clue about who he was.'

'He was a good man with a heart the size of an ox. It's a pity you never met him.'

Jim saw in Mike's eyes that he wanted to know more. *What the hell?* he thought. *It's his grandad, he's got a right to know.* So Jim began to tell Mike the story of the grandad that he'd never met.

'Your grandad, Bernard Slater, was a tough old cookie that loved his football, especially Newcastle United. From the age of fifteen he started to work down the pit at Ashington Colliery, just up the coast from Newcastle. He hated working down the pit but in those days you had no choice. It was a father and son thing. If your father worked down the pit then so would you when you were old enough. Football became his only escape from a life of coal dust and sweat. He was an excellent centre half, hard as nails but an intelligent player, not like the idiots that we see in the Premiership today. If he wasn't down the pit he would be either playing football or watching his beloved Newcastle.'

Mike sat listening intently to his uncle. His father had never told him anything about his grandfather. He had overheard once when his parents were arguing that his grandad was a stupid old fool who took his foolishness to the grave. Mike had never questioned his dad because he had no reason to. So, for Mike, his grandad had remained unknown to him.

'Bernard married your grandmother Mary and not long after your dad came along,' continued Jim. 'For your grandad there was no question about it - your dad wasn't going to work down the pit, but the only way out would be to play professional football. That's where your dad's footballing career started, and as soon as he was old enough to kick a ball one was placed in front of him. Then it was my turn to be born, but while having me your grandmother died.' Mike looked shocked. 'It sounds terrible, I know,' answered Jim quickly. 'It was just one of those things in those days - the technology didn't exist to save people when complications arose.' Mike looked at his uncle with a serious frown upon his face. Jim could see rage building up inside him.

'Why, oh why has my dad not told me any of this?' he cried. 'It really pisses me off knowing that he's had every chance to tell me about his father and mother, but instead he's told me nothing. All he fucking talks about is that bloody fight which ended his career.' Jim butted in by putting his hand up. It broke Mike's angry tirade and he relaxed, sinking back down in his seat.

'Look, calm down,' Jim said patting Mike's leg. 'There's no point getting worked up over your father, is there? He must have his reasons and only you can ask him.' Mike took several deep breaths and nodded his head for his uncle to carry on.

'I've heard the story about the fight as well, but I'll get to that in a minute. Your dad became a fantastic goalkeeper and with your grandad's encouragement he had every chance to become a professional. For your dad, though, your grandad's encouragement became an obsession. Your dad was going to be a professional footballer no matter what it took. For me, there was no encouragement; I couldn't kick a ball so I spent all of my time at my aunt's house in Gateshead, ignored by my own father and building up my resentment of your dad. Of course, that doesn't exist anymore, it was just my juvenile jealousy at the time.

'Your father, though, began to hate criticism

137

because the more he got the more your granddad would push him. I got sick of it all and when I was old enough I left the Northeast completely. For me, football was just a sport and an entertainment to be enjoyed, but for your father his whole existence was dominated by it.'

Mike turned to look out of the window. Trees, cars and the countryside passed by as the bus travelled North on the Belgian Autoroute, but he didn't see anything. His heart suddenly felt heavy with the weight of his own father's expectations, a mirror image of the generation before him. Jim asked him if he was alright and started to apologise for what he had said, but Mike asked him to carry on. He had been set on a journey and he needed to know where it would end; for him it was filling gaps in his life that needed to be filled.

'Your dad told you that his career was finished by a drunken fan in a pub brawl, hasn't he? Well, it wasn't.'

'What do you mean, it wasn't?' Mike said, snapping back at him. 'You turn up in my life after eleven years and the first thing you tell me is that my dad's a liar.' Mike's anger had suddenly overflowed and it was aimed directly at his uncle. 'Bollocks to you! Bollocks to you!' he shouted, pushing his finger into Jim's chest. 'You just can't say things like that about my dad. Yes, he's a pain in the arse at times, but he's no liar, ok?'

Mike once more turned away, but he couldn't dismiss what he had been told. His own curiosity to know more began to get the better of him. Turning back around, he straightened his face and prepared himself for the rest of the story.

'I'm sorry Mike, your right,' said Jim gently. 'I was totally out of order. This is between you and your dad and it's not my place to tell you these things. I'll leave the tour when we get to Amsterdam. I'm sorry, ok?' Jim began to rise from his seat; he hadn't got a clue why he'd needed to tell this story to Mike, he just felt that Mike had to know.

'No, don't leave now,' Mike said grabbing his arm. 'You've started something that you need to finish. We have a long way to go yet and I want to know the truth.'

'I'm not trying to score points against your dad or trying to get one over on him, or trying to win over my long lost nephew. I'm just telling you my side of the story. I just think that there are things that you need to know and when I've finished then you can decide for yourself.' Mike took his hand away from his uncle's arm and waited.

'Your dad was asked to go for a trial at Newcastle United after he had been spotted by a scout. Newcastle at that time had a development team which tried out young talented players to see if they would make the grade before any were signed onto the books and given contracts. You father did well and was offered a contract to play for Newcastle.'

'Hold on a minute. You're telling me that my dad was signed up to play for Newcastle United? I don't believe you.'

'Let me finish and it will all become clearer.' Mike tensed up with the thought of his father playing for Newcastle. It was too overwhelming for him to comprehend.

'The night that your father found out, your granddad took it as a dream come true. He went up and down his street waking the neighbours and telling them of his son's success, while your dad went out on the town to celebrate. The problem was that your dad, liking a drink, got absolutely legless and on his way out of a nightclub fell down a flight of stairs. His hand went through a glass door at the bottom, severing his tendons. That's what ended his career, not a drunk.'

Mike didn't say a word. His world had been

suddenly turned upside down. Why had his father not told him? He wouldn't have felt any different towards him. It was just bad luck, surely?

'Why would he not tell me this? I'm his son for God sake!'

'Your father never told you because he was too ashamed. It was alcohol that ended his career, just one stupid mistake. The story of the disgruntled fan was for his conscience not yours.'

'But why?' said Mike, still shaking his head in disbelief.

'I don't know why a father keeps things from his son. Only he will know why and you will have to ask him one day. Maybe he thought that he was protecting you, I don't know.'

'What happened to my grandad?' said Mike, remaining calm and relaxed.

'This is the sad part of it all. Your grandfather took it the worst. He never forgave your dad for wrecking his dream and they never spoke again. Even when your grandfather died your dad never went to his funeral. Some things happen in life that tears families apart, although they are done with the best of intentions. I know about your life, your football and I know about your father and how much he pushes you. You can tell me to get lost if you want and I will stay out of your life forever, but if I can give you a small amount of advice please take it.'

Mike had been destroyed by what his uncle had said. Hearing it now hurt tremendously, but the thought that his father had seen fit to lie to him all his life made it even worse.

'How do you know all this about me? You haven't exactly been round for Sunday lunch very often,' Mike said sarcastically.

'I keep in touch with your mum. She lets me know

how you are getting on. She's always been a good friend of mine, even going back to my school days. We were in the same class, you know. But she fell for your dad and not me, but that's another story.'

Mike sat feeling bemused. All this information about his family had been thrust at him so quickly that he was in a daze. Why was he being put through all this pain? The events of the previous day, with gangsters, guns, police and drugs had been bad enough, but this made him feel even worse.

Mike was silent. He continued to look out of the window but he didn't really know what to do. He wanted the bus to stop so he could run away. What direction, it didn't matter. He just wanted to run until he couldn't run anymore and maybe then the pain would go away. He turned back towards his uncle, his face red. His temperature had risen but the anger that he felt was tinged with sadness. Sadness that such a big part of his life had been unknown to him up until now.

'You've just described my life, you know that?' Mike said in a whisper. 'And yes, I get annoyed with the constant criticism as well. It scares me to fail, you know. I try so hard in everything that I do, but it always feels that it's not good enough. I love football so much and playing in goal is my life. There is nothing that I would rather do. I know my dad pushes me but I don't hate him for it. He's my friend as well as my dad and we share everything. Without him I would probably be on the streets, hanging around and getting into trouble.'

'Look Mike,' continued his uncle in a softer voice, 'all I'm saying is don't be forced into places that you don't want to be. You have your own life to live and it's unfair for you to be living your dad's as well. He messed up his own career all on his own and his only consolation is the thought that you will complete what he couldn't. If you have a talent use it and don't let anyone get in your way, but use it on your terms and no one else's. You may only get one chance in this life, Mike, and when it comes you grab hold and hold on tight. But remember, take it for yourself not for your dad.'

With that, Jim got up off his seat he started to walk away. Then he turned and leaned forward until his face was just a few inches away from Mike's.

'I'm sorry for putting you through that. It was wrong of me, but I mean what I said. When we arrive in Amsterdam I'll leave the tour, ok?' Mike said nothing.

Jim walked down the centre aisle of the bus to an empty seat just behind Barry and dropped into it as if someone had pulled his legs from under him. He sat fuming because of his own ineptness at being family. Why had he gone so far? Mike was just a boy. What gave him the right to take the responsibility of telling Mike the truth? A voice began to shout at him in his head. *You are pathetic!* it said. *You've become like the scum that you deal with. Is it not bad enough that you're using him, but to break his heart as well? You are a sad, lonely man, Jim Slater.* He held his head in his hands. He didn't know how to make amends and, instead of getting closer to his nephew, he was as far away as ever.

As the Superintendent contemplated his future on the tour, he noticed a white car periodically drawing level with the bus; just as it appeared as though it were going to overtake, it dropped back behind. His police officer's brain sprung into life and the next time that the car drew level he took a good look at the white male who sat in the passenger seat. The man observing the bus wore dark wraparound sunglasses, but the rest of his face looked familiar.

Jim suddenly moved back out of sight of the

onlooker. The identity of the man had hit him like a bolt of lightning. Henri Lachaise, the number one henchman of Dubois, sat studying the occupants of the bus. Jim needed to get a message to his surveillance team. He hoped that they would have noticed the car for themselves by now, but he couldn't take the chance. Without being able to talk out loud and blowing his cover, texting was the only answer. He detested sending text messages, but he had no choice. *White Renault Laguna. Occupant Henri Lachaise + unknown other. Trace car. Inform Sanderson. Stay with car. I have the boys. Slater.*

It took him five minutes to compose the text, all the time swearing under his breath through his lack of dexterity with his phone. He kept looking to see if the white car was still there but it hadn't reappeared. He swore again in frustration that sight of the car might have been lost. His phone let out two loud bleeps and vibrated in his hand. He nearly dropped it on the floor as he picked it up to read the incoming message. *Eyeball on car. Info passed to Sanderson.*

Jim Slater relaxed. There was nothing else he could do. His officers were good; they wouldn't let him down. But, more importantly, he wanted Dubois. His henchmen weren't that important. The hope was that they would lead the police to their boss. Jim knew that Dubois wouldn't show himself easily. *But you never know*, he thought to himself.

Mike was feeling as lonely as he had ever felt; Dan had his music, so there was nothing that he could do to take his mind off his dad. He thought about trying to go to sleep, but he was too awake. His mind raced, working overtime on reason after reason why his dad would lie to him and keep the family history a secret from him. Then there was the second dilemma - whether to hate his uncle for blowing the whistle on his dad, or to thank him for telling him the truth. Mike's brain had been scrambled and he was totally confused about what to do. There was still a long way to go before they arrived in Amsterdam and, unfortunately for Mike, there were no easy answers to any of his questions.

Chapter 11

Barry winced in pain as he bit too much nail from his finger. He had made it bleed so he put it in his mouth to stem the flow of blood. The taste reminded him of the first time that he'd eaten oysters. It wasn't a fond memory as they'd made him ill. As he sucked his finger he got the same nauseous feeling, so he quickly took the finger out of his mouth and sat on his hand, hoping that the pressure would stop it bleeding. Thirty seconds later it had stopped, so he started to chew on another one. The divine help that he'd asked for hadn't materialised and, as the bus entered the suburbs of Amsterdam, all he could do was bite the remaining nails and anticipate a stressful night.

Dennis, the driver, was also stressed. His navigation device had directed the bus safely and without a hitch to the outskirts of the city, but now it became confusing. The roads into the centre became narrower and harder to manoeuvre through. The hotel was situated in the most densely populated part of the city and, with the endless number of bridges and canals to negotiate, Dennis was starting to sweat.

Mike had managed to catch an hour's sleep and when he woke Dan was sitting next to him. His eyes were closed but his head was swaying from side to side, humming a tune from Mike's music selection. Mike looked over the rows of seats to see if he could see his uncle. The top of his head was visible and he could see that he had his mobile phone up to his ear. He felt a lot more relaxed than he'd felt earlier and he knew that his uncle hadn't meant any harm by telling him the truth. What he couldn't come to terms with was his father lying to him, and it was that which caused his anguish.

Nevertheless, after an hour's sleep to recharge his batteries and the sight of Amsterdam approaching, the previous conversation had lost its strength and Mike thought that he'd better patch things up with his uncle before he lost him for good. How he was going to do it was the problem and he urgently needed to think of a way before the bus arrived at its destination.

Jim Slater, meanwhile, had spent much of the time since speaking with Mike sending texts to Inspector Sanderson regarding Dubois and his men. He'd now become quite proficient at sending text messages and was feeling pleased with himself. The latest reply was a voicemail from the Inspector informing him that the car that Henri was spotted in had been stolen earlier that morning in Blankenberge, a small seaside resort just south of Zeebrugge.

Even better news was that Dubois's stronghold in Belgium had been raided by the DSU, Directorate of Special Units of the Belgian Federal Police, the equivalent to the British armed response units. Of course Dubois hadn't been there, but he'd left in a hurry leaving behind a huge stock of alcohol, tobacco and Ecstasy which matched the drugs seized the day before. From now on, Dubois would be an extremely wanted man and not just by the police. He would be marked by the other criminal organisations that he associated with for losing so much merchandise and money.

Jim Slater smiled at the predicament that Dubois currently faced, but he knew that a wounded animal can be more dangerous. The prospect of Dubois harming the boys was now even more real and he needed to stick even closer to them. He suddenly remembered that he had told Mike he would leave the tour in Amsterdam and he began to regret it. Opening his big mouth could cost Mike more than just his relationship with his parents - it could cost him his life. He closed his eyes tight and cursed himself for being such a fool. He needed Mike to forgive him, but he was extremely doubtful that Mike would.

The traffic lights turned to red and Dennis thought that he would have a quick look at his GPS again to calm his nerves. He knew its system like the back of his hand and, as always, the hotel, name of road and surrounding neighbourhood appeared within seconds of him entering the details. As the crow flies it was under a kilometre away, but by road it was going to be more like four kilometres before they got to their hotel, and Amsterdam was never a city that was going to be user friendly to vehicles, especially coaches. If you lived on a barge or travelled everywhere on a bicycle it was perfect. Once you were off the main roads, however, it became a nightmare for anyone who didn't know their way around. The smaller roads were barely wide enough for one vehicle. Every road seemed to be part of a one-way system and, because of the design of the canals, most roads were split in half by a canal running through the centre of it. Cars seemed to park where they wanted and the cyclist ruled when it came to the right of way.

Dennis wasn't feeling too impressed with the idiot who had changed the hotel. He knew that he shouldn't be taking his bus through this part of the city, but now it was too late and he had no choice but to carry on. The traffic light suddenly turned to green but he wasn't ready - he'd been too busy concentrating on the GPS to notice. There were traffic lights for bikes, lights for cars and lights for trams, all became extremely confusing when you were unsure of your route. He decided to go, but he felt flustered and confused.

The gearbox of the bus let out a loud groan of metal chewing on metal as, in his panic, he tried to find the right gear. The impatient drivers behind him began to sound their horns at the bus blocking their way. Dennis was trying his best but his brain wasn't sending the right messages to his limbs and his coordination had gone haywire. The bus lurched forward then stopped with a jolt, making everyone on board jump with the shock. Sixteen juveniles cheered in unison at the misfortune of poor Dennis. The big man was beginning to sweat once more and he was instantly aware of large damp patches forming under his armpits, which did nothing to help his overwhelming feeling of embarrassment.

The correct gear was found and the bus moved forward, slowly picking up speed, as if it were one of the trams which were so popular in the City. Some of the boys in the rear began to clap, sarcastically congratulating Dennis's driving. His embarrassment had disappeared, but a small amount of anger had appeared in its place due to the disrespect being shown from behind him. He looked into his mirror to see if he could get a glance at the culprits. *That Daniel Sharpe has got to be one*, he thought.

He was right, but his thoughts suddenly changed when there was a loud cracking noise from the outside of the bus. Faces pressed against the window to see where the noise had emanated from, and even Barry and Jim had to look to ease their curiosity. Poor Dennis, while looking in his mirror, had driven too close to the line of parked cars. A wing mirror could be seen hanging from the door of a shiny black Audi TT Sports Coupé. Whistling, cheering and clapping could now be heard from the rabble behind him. In his thirty years of driving there weren't many occasions when he had felt so many differing emotions in such a short space of time. *Get to the hotel*, he thought to himself. He was sick and tired of trying to squeeze his bus through these ancient tiny backstreets and there was no way he was going to stop to report an accident. The hotel was only just around the corner and the owner of the damaged car wouldn't have far to go in looking for recompense.

All of the commotion had taken Mike's mind off his dad and he'd finally regained his music from Dan. Positive thoughts began to filter through his partial depression and the tour once again became the highlight of his life. Dan pulled the earphone cable from Mike's ears.

'What do you want?' Mike said, snapping at him.

'I'm just seeing if you are alright. I haven't spoken to you for ages and I was worried about you.'

Mike relaxed and gave his friend a smile for his concern.

'Don't worry about what you uncle said,' said Dan. 'He shouldn't be sticking his nose into your business anyway.'

'You heard what was said between us?' Mike said, sounding surprised.

'Only when you shouted,' replied Dan, all innocently. 'It was hard not to hear.'

Mike bit his lip and slumped down into his seat. 'Shit,' he said to himself. He hated the thought of airing his dirty linen in public and if Dan had heard surely there would be others. Dan leant across to try and put Mike's mind at rest.

'Don't worry!' he whispered. 'I don't think that anyone else heard. Besides, your private life is pretty boring anyway.'

'Charming,' Mike said punching Dan on the soft flesh around his bicep, giving him a dead left arm. Dan threw himself back onto the opposite seat grimacing in pain and clenching his arm. Mike grinned with pleasure at his friend's contorted face.

'What was that for? You git!'

'That's for eavesdropping on my private conversations.' Dan smiled back whilst rubbing his arm. Luckily for him the pain wasn't that bad, but he just pretended that it hurt.

Meanwhile, Dennis breathed a sigh of relief when he pulled up in front of the hotel. He felt that his luck had changed as the road didn't have a canal running through the middle of it. There was just enough space to park the bus and still let cars pass. He turned the engine off and got up from the driver's seat; his light blue shirt had become dark blue with sweat, so he quickly ran down the steps to hide his humiliation and to get a fresh one from out of his bag.

As the team exited the bus, Mike walked past his uncle without saying a word. He needed to find the right moment to talk to him and now wasn't the time. The white car, parked a few hundred yards to the rear of the bus, had gone unnoticed. Henri and Didier sat in silence, observing the excited teenagers. Didier had his fingers crossed, hoping that they'd made the right decision to follow the bus. If the two English boys weren't on board Dubois would not be best pleased with them, and they knew him well for his vicious temper and skill with a gun.

Henri smiled and tapped Didier on the shoulder when he saw Mike and Dan get off the bus. Their luck had changed and at least Dubois would be getting some good news. He'd been like a bear with a sore head since his shipment had been discovered and his house raided. His little empire had taken a huge loss along with his credibility and respect amongst his criminal fraternity. He'd not spent his life building up his drug, tobacco and alcohol empire just for two boys, from the north east of England, to tear it down and get away with it. He was determined no matter how long it took and, whatever it took, he would make them pay. While Henri reported in to Dubois, a high-tech camera with an extremely powerful telephoto lens was snapping pictures of them. The two surveillance officers were across the street recording their every move. Henri and Didier were blissfully unaware that, as they watched the boys, they themselves were being watched.

Jim Slater hung back on the bus. He knew from his phone that Dubois's men were close but he didn't want to show his face, not yet. Dubois was well aware of Superintendent Jim Slater of Interpol, and to be spotted with the boys this early on would not bode well. He couldn't take any chances with Henri and Didier knowing who he was. While the boys collected their bags he rang Sanderson, asking him to contact their Dutch counterparts to have them drive by in the hope that, if Dubois's men spotted the police, they would run. A police car arrived within minutes and, as expected, Henri and Didier made their exit but the damage was already done; Dubois knew exactly where the boys were.

Dan stood staring at the front of the hotel with the rest of the team. Barry had gone ahead to book the team in and the fifteen teenagers were left standing on the pavement to admire their next stopover. The Prins Hubert Hotel was formerly a merchant's house built in the seventeen century. It was typical of the old part of Amsterdam, with each roof of each adjoining house designed like the shape of a stairway. Dan thought that the hotel looked like something that he had seen on a biscuit tin lid that his granny used to have. Mike told him that he never had a granny because he was a test tube baby made from all the leftovers at the hospital. Dan didn't get the joke; he didn't know what a test tube baby was. Mike ignored him; he wasn't about to explain.

Barry appeared at the front door of the hotel and everybody moved simultaneously to pick up their bags. Barry approached the group, waving his arms as if he was flagging down a moving car. Sixteen bags hit the pavement and Barry must have felt the breeze in his face as all sixteen boys sighed in frustration at the same time. He didn't look happy. *Come to think of it*, thought Mike, *Barry seldom looked happy, so what was the problem?*

He broke the news gently to the team, but the response he received was more severe than he'd anticipated. Inside he was fuming. That cheapskate of a chairman had changed the hotel to save money. The boys had been booked into five man rooms which worked out cheaper than doubles. The five man rooms weren't the problem, though. The biggest hurdle to get over was the fact that the beds were doubles and they were going to have to sleep together. North Eastern boys sharing a bed would be worse than sending a Geordie to watch Sunderland play. The first hotel had given a cheap rate due to the need of renovation. This hotel consisted of double beds. So what was the next hotel in Germany going to be? Barry didn't want to think about it; his hands were full already. Dan, as always, was the loudest to complain.

'Just like being on a bleeding girl guide camp,' he shouted over the noise of the grumbling. 'We'll be sitting around the camp fire next, singing pathetic songs, toasting marshmallows and holding hands.' Everyone laughed and Dan was the centre of attention again. Barry didn't appreciate the comedy; he raised his finger and pointed it in the direction of Dan, staring right at him down his finger. Dan melted back into the crowd and the rest of the moaners got the message and calmed down.

'Does this face look like it cares, Sharpe? Right!

Inside, be quiet and show some respect. Remember you are representing your team, town and country.' Mike grabbed Dan around his head and ruffled his hair with his fist, then pushed him through the hotel entrance door.

Barry led the team into the lobby of the hotel, gave one person in each group of five a key to their room and told them to drop their kit off and come straight back down. He had something to tell them and they weren't going to like it.

Upstairs in their room, Mike got to the single bed first. There was no way that he was going to share with anybody, even Dan. Dan instantly began to sulk; he threw his kit onto the floor because he wasn't quick enough to get to the remaining double bed. He was left to sleep with little Terry on a fold-down sofa bed and it was obvious to the others that he wasn't too happy about the prospect.

'Don't you touch me when we're in bed, Terry,' Dan shouted at the little winger. 'Otherwise I'll smash your face in. You hear me!' Terry ignored him; he was used to Dan's threats. Mike laughed out loud but Dan wasn't in the mood to be laughed at any more. He stuck a single finger up to his friend and stormed out of the room.

Downstairs in the dining room a large table had been set for the team, but this time there were other guests present. Barry clucked around the boys like an old mother hen, making sure that they all behaved themselves. Dan sat there in silence, still in a mood about the sleeping arrangements, so at least for Barry there was one mouth less to keep quiet. The hotel had organised a set meal for them all but, when the foreign substance was placed in front of Dan, his silence suddenly broke.

'What the hell is that?' he said to the waitress, at the

153

same time lifting the food with his fork and letting it drop back down onto his plate.

'Smoked eel, sir,' she replied in perfect English. Dan stared at her, not amused, but she wasn't about to stop and talk. Flicking her head around, causing her long hair to brush over Dan's annoyed face, she carried on serving. Dan had no one left to vent his frustration on, apart from one. Barry knew that it was coming.

'Barry, man! You can't be serious expecting us to eat this crap?' shouted Dan, as loud as he could so everyone else in the restaurant could hear.

'Do you do anything else but moan?' Barry said waving his fork in Dan's direction. 'It's just fish, for crying out loud! If you don't like it then just eat your veg.'

Mike leant across and whispered into Dan's ear. 'It's a delicacy here and everyone eats it, so don't be rude.'

'Well, I'm not everyone. You eat it if you want.' With no one else to moan at, he pushed his plate away and refused to even try it. A few others weren't too keen to eat it either, but none of them felt like moaning at Barry. Dan, as always, had done the moaning for them. Mike, on the other hand, did eat the eel and he was surprised at how tasty it was. It reminded him of smoked trout, maybe even smoked salmon. He tried to convince Dan but, as it didn't have chips with it, he wasn't interested and when the meal ended, apart from some ice cream, Dan had eaten nothing.

When the last mouthful had been swallowed Barry stood up and asked everyone to make their way through into the lounge. He wanted to break the news to them about confining them to the hotel and he needed to do it in an environment that wouldn't disturb the other guests. Before he announced the news, he thought that he would be clever and try and bribe them in order to ease the pain. He produced a DVD of the 100 Best World Cup Goals. It was the best that he could come up with given the short notice. It worked surprisingly well and didn't ruffle too many feathers at all. The majority didn't want to go out anyway; they were too tired from their previous match and the long journey. The remainder that did want to go out were swayed by the DVD, or Barry's other ace up his sleeve which was the chance to watch a movie in their room. Barry felt relief for the first time in ages; he'd worried all day about how they would take to being confined to the hotel and, all being said, it had gone better than he had expected. Only a little bit of dissent had been encountered but he'd handled it well and his mood had been given a boost. It was now time for him to relax as well.

Out of the entire group, Mike was the only one to feel miffed. He'd visited Amsterdam before with his dad to watch Newcastle play Ajax in a UEFA Cup competition but he'd never got a chance to see the city. It seemed always to be the same story wherever he went to watch football - all he got to see were the stadiums. Nevertheless, he wasn't too distraught and a night in front of the TV seemed a good alternative. A good opportunity to patch things up with his uncle, he thought. Maybe he would ask his him if he wanted to watch the footy. Looking around, he realised that he hadn't seen him since they arrived. Suddenly he felt worried that his uncle had left the tour. In a panic he got up to go and look for him.

'Where are you going?' Dan asked. 'We're putting the footy on soon.'

'To find my uncle Jim to see if he wants to watch it with us. Are you coming?'

Dan followed Mike out but, after five minutes of looking, Jim wasn't anywhere to be found.

'I'm going back to watch the footy, you coming?'

Dan said, looking fed up.

'Yeah, hold on a minute. I'm just going to look out front then I'll be with you.'

Jim Slater sat with his two colleagues a hundred yards down the street. Henri and Didier had given them all the slip and Jim was in the middle of a phone call with his Dutch counterpart, trying to organise some more bodies on the ground to cover the boys. He knew Dubois or his men wouldn't be far away, but he needed more police officers in the area otherwise the boys would be at genuine risk. At such short notice Jim was promised two men now and a further two at midnight. He thanked his colleague and hung up. Looking back towards the hotel, feeling a little frustrated by the lack of support from his Dutch colleagues, he saw Henri and Didier appear from a side street and walk in the direction of the hotel. Suddenly there was no more time for talking.

Chapter 12

When he stepped outside the hotel front door, Mike froze with fear. Without thinking, he pushed Dan back inside. His heart jumped in his chest and he thought that at any second it would break through his rib cage. Dan was confused; he didn't know what was happening, but whatever it was it was too late. Eyes had already met across the street and irreparable damage had been done. Henri and Didier quickened their pace towards the hotel. Mike followed Dan back inside, pushing him further into the hotel lobby.

'What are you doing man?' Dan shouted as he fell into a large rubber plant in the lobby. It toppled over, spilling its contents of earth all over the polished tile floor.

'It's Dubois's men - there're coming this way!' Mike yelled in Dan's ear. Dan's face went white with fear.

'They've come to kill me,' he whimpered.

'No!' Mike said as he grabbed his friend. 'They've come to kill us both.'

They ran in blind panic. The first door that they came to was open and they went through. It led to the stairwell.

'Quick, up here,' Mike shouted as he dragged Dan behind him. Dan's body was ridged with fear, frozen solid by the thought of death. Mike struggled to pull him up the stairs.

'Fuck's sake, Dan, snap out of it!' Mike slapped him across the face, and he came back instantly.

'Ok! Ok! Fucking hell, what are we going to do?'

'Up here, quick.' Mike directed them to the first floor and, as they passed through the exit door, Henri and Didier entered the stairwell. They paused to listen for their prey. A door above them clicked shut and they knew where the boys had gone.

The first floor corridor was deserted. The boys tried each room door in turn but each was locked. Panic was fast turning into terror and Mike swore out loud with each locked door. They could hear the advancing footsteps and knew that at any second the two armed men would burst through the door. Suddenly a door gave and they fell inside, hitting the floor hard. Mike kicked the door shut and turned the lock. They'd tumbled into a store cupboard. The light activated automatically and they were now surrounded by hotel bed linen folded neatly on shelves. Scampering to the back of the cupboard they sat there in silence, listening for the approaching footsteps. The store cupboard had saved them for a while but, without any other means of escape, it would only be a matter of time before they were discovered.

Mike looked around, willing there to be another exit, but there wasn't. In the corridor, door handle after door handle turned as Dubois's men methodically tried each one, coming closer and closer. Dan squeezed himself into the corner. For him, any second the door would be kicked in and his young life would be extinguished. He began to shake as the fear took him. Tucking his knees under his chin he gripped his legs tight shut, closed his eyes and plunged himself into darkness. With his mind awash with fear he began seeing flashes of his past. They were so clear and vivid that his mother and father appeared in happier times when he used to feel safe and secure. They sat together on a grassy river bank having a picnic in the warm summer sun. Dan swung on a rope swing across the water, dipping his toes with each pass. He watched how loving and tender his parents were to each other as they prepared the food. Everyone laughed and giggled without a care in the world. It was one of the best times Dan had ever had.

Mike feared the worst too, but he hadn't experienced the unbridled fear that Dubois had instilled into Dan. He looked up and saw a fire alarm button to the right of the door. Lunging forwards, he hit it with his fist. The plastic cover snapped and fell to the floor. He pushed the button, expecting to hear a bell or a siren. There was nothing, just the sound of Henri and Didier getting closer. Again and again he pressed; fury took hold of him and he hit the button as hard as he could. His hand throbbed with pain but there was no time to feel it.

'Work you bastard, work!' he yelled.

The door handle to the cupboard began to turn. His eyes widened in fright and, without thinking, he hit the button again. It worked. Immediately, a loud bell rang out in the corridor. Mike fell backward onto the floor in anticipation of the door opening, but nothing happened. Muffled sounds of feet in the corridor moving quickly could be heard. Doors banged shut and people speaking in a language alien shouted as they ran to escape, taking Henri and Didier with them. The noise of the alarm and rushing quests brought Dan back to the land of the living.

'I think they've gone,' Mike said whispering into his hands. 'The fire alarm must have scared them away.' Dan looked at Mike anxiously; he didn't believe that Dubois's men had gone so easily, but he couldn't explain why they hadn't got to them by now. The commotion died down in the corridor and Mike went forward to open the door.

'No! No, Mike, don't do it!' Dan whimpered.

'I'm not going to sit here and wait for them to come back. There's no one there now. Let's get the hell out of here,' Mike said, taking command. Dan couldn't bear to watch as Mike turned the key. Slowly it clicked and he pulled the door open an inch to survey the corridor. He kept tight hold in anticipation of someone yanking it from him but, as he had guessed, no one was there. Slowly the boys peered around the door; the corridor was empty.

Fire engine sirens grew louder as they approached the hotel. The corridor became lit with the intermittent glow of red and blue lights as the boys made their way to the window at the far end. A net curtain hung across the glass hiding their faces from the crowd outside. Mike saw Henri and Didier standing at the back of a fire engine. Barry and the rest of the team were huddled in a tiny group in the middle of the courtyard. Mike thought that he saw his uncle, but he flicked the curtain back across his face when a torchlight passed in their direction.

'We can't go that way, they're out there,' Mike said as he peered round the edge of the curtain again. 'There must be a back way out. Quick, this way.'

The last door at the far end of the corridor led to a separate staircase which was used by the staff to service the rooms. The boys ran down the corridor, stopping when they'd reached the end to orientate themselves. Turning right would take them to the front of the hotel and danger, while left would take them into the kitchen. The kitchen won. They ran through, not noticing steaming pans bubbling away on large gas hobs. Smells of all kinds hit them as they ran, but none enticed them to stop and taste. At the rear of the kitchen was a small back alley that gave access to the waste bins and incoming deliveries. Out through the alley they ran, narrowly missing a woman who was walking her poodle. Not knowing where they were going, they ran down a small side street over a bridge and into a larger street that thronged with people. Mike stopped at a lamppost to get his breath. Dan leant over a bicycle rack that was full of bikes and sucked in the air to feed his burning lungs.

'What are we going to do?' Dan said, sitting down onto the pavement looking dejected.

'I don't know, but we can't go back yet. Dubois's men will still be looking for us. Let me think!'

***

Barry's breathing was laboured. He'd ran to every room once the alarm sounded to make sure that all of his boys had got out, but two had eluded him. He found it difficult to breathe, not through physical exertion but because of the mental torture of losing two boys - the same two boys that seemed to be making a habit of getting lost. He counted heads again, pointing at each one with his finger to make sure that he hadn't missed anyone. Dennis had opened the bus and Barry directed each boy, one by one, to its safe keeping where, once on board, Dennis would keep them there. Barry needed to find the boys fast and that meant talking to the Fire Service and the police. It was going to be hard to communicate and he began to worry.

'Barry, have you seen Mike yet?' Jim said as he appeared from between two fire tenders. Barry didn't hear him, even though they were only a couple of metres apart. He was so flustered that if someone had set fire to his trousers he wouldn't have noticed. Jim shouted again and this time Barry heard, but still he did not take any notice. Waving his hand, he shook his head and automatically mouthed the word 'no' in the direction of where it came.

Jim was angry and he needed someone to shout at. He had taken his eye off the ball and the boys were in danger again. It would now be a race against time to find them before Dubois's goons did, but this was Amsterdam. Three quarters of a million people and thousands of tourists to consider, not to mention the fact that it was now night time, which was when the city came alive. There were miles of canals and tram systems and, to cap it all, he spoke no Dutch.

Superintendent Slater felt helpless; he needed to pull on every instinct that he had, but his head and heart were giving conflicting views. His head told him to wait as the boys would eventually turn up back at the hotel, but his gut told him different. Wait and you'll find them dead floating face down in a canal, each with a bullet hole through their heads. He needed more help and he needed to find Henri and Didier. If he found them he may well find the boys.

By the time the Amsterdam fire service had found out that it was a false alarm, six fire tenders and four police cars had crammed into the courtyard at the front of the hotel. Bystanders had gathered in the morbid hope of seeing some poor soul's fatal misfortune, but they soon dispersed when none materialised. Barry had managed to talk with one of the fire crews and had been told that the hotel was empty. He felt a little relief but it didn't give him any satisfaction. It would be a long night and he needed to summon Dennis and John for their assistance.

Two dark figures stood in the shadow of a doorway unnoticed. A fifth police car arrived on the scene, siren's wailing and lights flashing, which intermittently lit up their faces as it sped by. Both faces remained expressionless before the dark cloak of night smothered them once more.

***

Tiredness was beginning to take hold of the runaways. The adrenalin rush of their near death experience had all been spent and, with the light fading, both boys started to feel exhausted. Mike looked at his watch. It was 9.45pm and their situation hadn't improved.

'Where are we?' Dan asked as he looked around the street.

'How the hell should I know?' Mike spat back at him.

Night had arrived without them realising it. The street lights were on and pink and red neon lights emanated from shop windows, transforming the pavement with their rosy glow.

'Ring your uncle, he'll know what to do,' Dan said, having a bit of inspiration. Mike put his hand into an empty pocket.

'Shit! I've left my mobile in the hotel room. It needed charging.'

'Well, that's just great, isn't it?' Dan said, kicking an empty Red Bull can into the canal.

'Well, at least I've got a fucking phone,' Mike shouted.

'Pssst. Hey guys,' said a voice nearby. Both boys swung around to see who was interrupting their argument. They were a good twenty yards away but a lone figure could be seen standing in a doorway.

'Are you talking to us?' Mike said as he pointed to himself.

'Well, I don't see anyone else here, do I?' replied the stranger. He waved his hand, beckoning the boys to come closer. He wore a long black leather coat, a blue bandana on his head and carried a large leather bag over his shoulder. Dan started to walk over, but Mike grabbed his arm and held him back.

'What are you doing? He's a pervert,' Mike said keeping hold of Dan's arm. 'Think about it, Dan! It's midsummer and that bloke is wearing a full-length leather coat. You go over there and you know what will happen - he'll flash his cock at you, but if that's what takes your fancy then go, I'm not stopping you.' Mike let go. Dan looked at him, having second thoughts.

'Well, if he does get it out he can kiss his nuts goodbye because that's where I'll kick him,' Dan said defiantly as he started walking towards the stranger. 'Anyway, if he's not a perv he may be able to help us because he speaks English.' Mike thought for a little then realised Dan was right, so he followed on behind. He thought it would be a laugh to see Dan in action, though he decided he'd better stand well back just in case Dan let fly with a Kung Fu kick.

'Greetings, young men,' said the leather-clad stranger in an accent that sounded a bit American. Mike could see the stranger's face fully now. He was in his early thirties. He had a day's growth of stubble on his chin, but Dan had to contain himself from laughing because he had trimmed it so exact that it reminded him of the type of stubble George Michael would have. Dan turned away to hide his laughter. Any second now, he thought, the stranger would open his coat, produce a guitar and give his best rendition of 'Faith', but he didn't. There was a small tattoo of Popeye the Sailor Man on his throat, just below his Adam's apple which, when he swallowed, made Popeye's pipe go up and down. It was hard not to look at it without smiling. Two pirate earrings hung from each ear lobe and his fingers were covered by rings of all shapes and sizes. If he thought that he was trendy then fair enough but, according to Dan, he thought that the stranger looked like a twat and he managed to whisper it into Mike's ear without the stranger hearing him.

'My friend here thinks that you're a flasher,' Dan said with a huge grin on his face. Mike thumped him on the arm.

'Oh no, my friend. There's a lot more interesting things under my coat than flesh,' he replied slowly, opening it to reveal his goods within.

'Call me Popeye, gentlemen,' he said, lifting his head to show off his tattoo, while at the same time taking the bag from his shoulder. Mike and Dan stood, silently staring into his coat. Dan spoke first, pointing at the substances in tiny polythene bags that hung from rows of string within.

'What's all that then?'

'This is the best quality hash in Amsterdam, my friend.'

'Hash!' Mike shouted. 'You're trying to sell us drugs? Not interested. Thanks, bye. Come on Dan, let's go.' Mike took hold of Dan's arm and tried to pull him away but, like a Cobra hypnotised by the charmer's music, Dan seemed spellbound by the contents of the stranger's coat.

'Your friend doesn't share your appetite to leave, does he? Come closer, let me show you something.' Mike gave Dan a hard stare, but Dan seemed oblivious to all but the little polythene bags. 'I have everything you need to take you places that you have never been before. Take this little example I have here.' He produced a small sachet containing a grainy brown substance. It changed to yellow when he held it up to the street light.

'Come on Dan, let's go.' Mike urged his friend. 'We'll get locked up if the police catch us.'

'Don't worry my friend, what I do is totally legal and here is my licence to prove it.' The man held out an official-looking document and both boys leant forward to read it.

'You probably got that off the internet. You're not fooling me,' Mike said shaking his head.

'You forget where you are. This is Amsterdam and you are in the heart of the Rossebuurt, the pink neighbourhood where soft drugs and prostitution are legal. If you don't want drugs I can get you laid for a very reasonable price. Maybe it's your first time. I know ladies that would be gentle with you.'

Dan took it as a slight on his manhood for this stranger to think that he was a virgin. There was no doubt about it that he was, but that was his secret and not for anyone else to make assumptions.

'Hey, I've done it loads of times, right? I lost my cherry a long time ago,' Dan said, staring into the stranger's face. Mike smiled but stayed quiet; he wasn't getting involved.

'No worries, anything you say stud. But if you don't believe me, ask my colleague around the corner.'

'What do you mean? You make it sound like a business,' Dan said looking confused.

'You see the old church over there?' Popeye pointed over their heads and both boys turned to look at the huge medieval church, the magnificent Gothic structure of which rose up dwarfing the surrounding buildings. Stained glass windows, several metres tall, flickered as they reflected the street lights below.

'That is the Oude Kerk and in this district there are many like me who sell drugs legally with a licence. I wouldn't last five minutes if the police arrived and found no licence. This is my job and this is what I sell.'

Mike looked at Dan and both of them laughed.

'Shit!' Dan said in amazement. 'Imagine if this was the same in Newcastle, everyone in the big market would be stoned out of their heads and this bloke would have been robbed by now.' Mike laughed in agreement.

'You interested in what I have then?' said Popeye, holding out the same substance as before.

'What is it?' Dan inquired curiously.

'Amsterdam Delight, my favourite and very reasonably priced. It's a strong one but has a nice minty flavour, similar to the taste of one of those menthol cigarettes. Be very aware though, it will make your heart jump out of your body.' Mike knew how that felt without taking drugs. 'Or there's this one.' Out of his shoulder bag he produced a brown and black blob of a substance and he held it out before them. 'Caramello. This is the kind of spliff you really don't want to pass onto your mate! You'll wanna keep taking it down right to the very end. It's for a daydream, but if you have too much then into a deep trance-type sleep you'll go.'

Dan was enthralled by each substance that was thrust into his face. Mike was getting annoyed; drugs had gotten them into trouble the previous day and now he was being subjected to them again. Everything about them he detested. He'd been brought up to reject drugs. They weren't for him and never would be.

'Look! I've had enough. Sorry mate, but like I said before I'm not interested.' Mike turned and walked away. He knew Dan would eventually follow him so he didn't bother to look back. After about a hundred yards Mike stopped and leant on a lamppost. Dan came sprinting towards him, just like a child that had been let out of school early. Mike was still annoyed and needed to vent some anger at Dan.

'What's it with you and drugs? They seem to be dominating everything at the moment, and don't tell me you're taking them because you can stay away from me if you are.' Dan squirmed and stuttered a little when he tried to answer. Mike knew that he'd hit a nerve, so he stood staring at him, egging him on for a reply. 'That bloke was a lying bastard. Legal my arse and you fell for it, standing there with your tongue hanging out Come on! Come on! Tell the truth!'

'I'm just interested in them, ok? Is that a good

enough answer for you? And by the way, you're not my mother so it's none of your business. If you want to know the answer, then no I don't take drugs.' Mike stared into his eyes. He wasn't sure whether or not he was telling him the truth, but at the moment they needed to stay together so he dropped the subject. There would be another appropriate time to resurrect the topic.

'I don't want anything to do with drugs,' continued Mike, walking off down the street. Dan came up behind him and tapped him on the shoulder.

'Where're you going?' he said tentatively in Mike's ear.

'I don't know, but not back to the hotel, not yet anyway. I need to talk to my uncle. He'll know what to do. Let's wait until all the commotion at the hotel has died down and we'll creep back.' Dan agreed since he'd no choice. He hadn't got a clue what to do. Mike was giving the orders and he would just have to follow them.

Mike looked at his watch again. It was 10.30pm yet it seemed like a Saturday afternoon in Newcastle. There were people everywhere; some strolling nonchalantly by the side of the canal, others queuing to get into clubs and others staring into dimly-lit pink windows. There was even a group of about twenty having a guided tour; it was definitely not what Mike had expected to see and he realised it was going to be a long night.

Chapter 13

Dan suddenly stopped and grabbed Mike's arm, swinging him around with a jerk. They'd been walking slowly, trying to kill time, but neither of them had taken the time to look into the shop windows, until now.

The shop looked more like a Whitley Bay bed and breakfast with its large front door and ornate canopies over the front windows. The only difference was the unearthly pink glow from the huge fluorescent tube light that hung high upon the wall in each room.

'Take a look at her!' Dan said, eyes bulging. Mike looked up, mouth wide open and nodding in agreement. They both moved closer to the window, away from the passing onlookers, and for over a minute the two teenagers gawped at the lady in the window.

Sitting on a wooden stool directly in front of the boys, with only the thickness of the glass separating them, was a prostitute. She had long blonde hair which rested on her shoulders and hid the straps of the little black leather bra which supported the finest pair of boobs that Dan had ever seen. Her belly button entertained a small pearl stud which gracefully moved in and out with each breath that she took. The black leather G-string that she wore was barely visible as it hid between her naked thighs, and white knee-high boots swung in the air each time she crossed and uncrossed her legs.

Seeing a prostitute this close was a new experience for both of them. They knew that Newcastle had its fair share of ladies of the night illegally plying their trade. Mike had even seen some hanging around the city centre one night when his dad had pointed them out, but they weren't as beautiful as this one. Dan was speechless and Mike was blown away.

'What makes a girl as beautiful as that become a pro?' Dan said without taking his eyes off her.

'I don't know. Maybe she enjoys it. You know, a bit like a footballer getting paid for doing something that they enjoy,' Mike said philosophically.

'Yeah, I suppose so, but it seems a shame to me because she looks like she could get any bloke that she wanted.' Dan was transfixed.

'Well, we'll never know will we?' replied Mike.

'I think that if you put black hair on her she'll look a little like Mrs Taylor. What do you think?' Dan said, staring deep in thought at the prostitute. Mike slapped him on the back of his head.

'You and your fetish for your Geography teacher! You definitely have a problem, you know that? Now, there's one for you,' Mike said, walking a few yards down the street to look into another window. The blonde that mesmerised Dan blew him a kiss, which immediately embarrassed him so he chased after his friend.

Mike pointed out another window lady to Dan.

'This one's more your type,' he said trying hard to hide his amusement.

'You gotta be joking!' Dan said looking disgusted. 'She's fat. Definitely not my type, but have you ever seen a pair that big before? She could feed every baby in Africa and end a famine in an instant.'

The lady in the second window carried a little bit more weight than that of the last and, no matter how hard she had tried to make herself look sexy, Dan wasn't having any of it. Mike didn't think that she looked too bad; he preferred women with a bit of meat on them and not the usual stick insects, but he kept that thought to himself. Dan would never know.

'Sure, they're enormous, but what's wrong with that? Some blokes like women with a bit more flesh,' said Mike, making the movement with his hands as though he was cupping some boobs.

'Flesh! Is that what you call it? She must be related to the Michelin man. She's even got a tyre around her waist.'

'Oh, that's rich coming from you. You're not exactly a looker yourself,' Mike said, squeezing Dan's cheeks.

'Well, look at her,' insisted Dan. 'She's so fat, that you'd have to roll her in flour to find the wet spot.'

'You are so disgusting sometimes, you know that?' Mike replied unimpressed with Dan's observations. He continued walking down the street to look into the next window leaving Dan to take a last look.

Now that's more like it, Mike thought as he beckoned Dan to come and have a look. In the third window along sat a small Asian lady. Her tanned skin shone under the artificial light as though she had been covered head to toe in oil. Long black hair, like threads of silk, flowed down her back all the way to the stool that she sat on. It was Mike's turn to gawp, but he couldn't make up his mind whether to look at her body or her face. He was finding is hard to decide so he thought that he better start at the top and work down.

Dark eyebrows emphasised her brown but sparkling eyes. Her petite nose sat beautifully above tiny pert lips that glistened as though they were wet. A little white dress clung to every curve of her slender body and when she moved the tiniest hint of white underwear was revealed. Mike was happy to stand and admire her all night but he had to jostle with the small crowd that had gathered in front of her window. Dan pushed his way through the crowd and stood next to his friend, curious to see what kind of merchandise had taken his fancy. Dan leant to whisper into Mike's ear.

'I wouldn't touch her if you paid me. That's if it's a *she*.' Mike looked at him puzzled.

'What do you mean, a *she*?' he asked.

'Well, my old man told me that his mate Frank visits Amsterdam all the time.'

'Yeah, to get stoned out of his skull no doubt.' Mike was already dubious about what Dan was about to say, because any gossip from his dad had to be taken with a pinch of salt.

'He does like a smoke but that's not what I am trying to tell you. He's a ladies' man as well.'

'Is this going to be a long one, because if it is I'll have to find a chair.' Mike steadied himself for a long story.

'Shut up! On one visit he picked up a woman, just like her, who was from the Far East. They go back to her room and start to have a kiss and a cuddle, but when he put his hand down her knickers he nearly had a heart attack.'

'Why, was it her time of the month or something?' Mike replied, innocently.

'God, the painters weren't in, don't be thick! She was a bloody man.'

'No! You are bullshiting me'

'Yeah, she was and his hand went down straight onto his knob.'

'You're making this up, aren't you?'

'No I'm not, honest. It was definitely a man who'd had a boob job but was awaiting the full sex change. I think that they call them shemales or lady men or something.'

Mike swallowed hard and looked back towards his beauty behind the glass. He suddenly felt a bit sick. He didn't want to believe what Dan had said; there was always some kind of crap coming out of his mouth, but this time he'd really confused him. The cheek bones did seem a bit high, but it was her hands that threw him into turmoil. He wasn't sure whether they looked like a man's hands or not. Dan put his hand on Mike's shoulder.

'Don't worry, we all make mistakes,' Dan said smugly into his ear.

'Piss off! I think it's a woman, ok!' Mike said sharply. Dan started to laugh and found it hard to get his words out.

'Well, you'll end up washing your hands forever when you put your hand down there and cup a pair of hairy balls and a warm sausage, but don't say that I didn't warn you.' Mike wasn't amused.

'Don't be a twat. As far as I'm concerned she's a woman and that's final.' Mike pushed his way back through the crowd. Dan followed, but he felt it his duty to have the last word before they moved on.

'We will never know, will we?'

The next twenty minutes were spent going from window to window giving marks out of ten for the best looking prostitute, until Dan saw a face that he didn't want to see.

'Quick! In here,' Dan said suddenly, pulling on Mike's arm.

'What's up?'

'There's that Henri bloke.' Mike turned to look but he didn't recognise anyone. Nevertheless, it was too late. Dan had dragged him through the nearest door and it wasn't until he got inside that he began to wish he was outside again. Dan was adamant that it was Henri so, for the time being, they had to stay put.

The shop was empty of customers which meant that Mike and Dan drew the shop assistant's attention straight away. Mike began to feel self-conscious as the assistant looked him up and down. Dan was already perusing the goods.

There were rows of shelves down each side of the shop containing hundreds of magazines, films and sex toys. Towards the back were various role-play clothes. Nurses, French maids, naughty schoolgirls and dominatrix outfits could be seen, all neatly arranged. The shop assistant stood behind a counter in the centre of the shop and, no matter where Mike went, he could feel the assistant's eyes following him. *Why did Dan have to pull me into a porn shop, of all places?* Mike thought, almost bursting with embarrassment.

He tried not to make eye contact with the assistant and when that failed he went after Dan. It was the first time that either of them had been in such a shop and Mike thought it embarrassing and kind of intimidating. Dan, on the other hand, thought nothing of it as he was used to the odd dirty film that his dad would leave lying about and which would somehow find its way into his bedroom before it went back to the shop.

Dan picked up a magazine from the shelf in front of him. The front cover had 'Hot' and 'Horney' in big red letters at the top and a woman sitting with her legs apart over the barrel of a tank. Dan flicked through the pages quickly, laughing and giggling at each turn of the page. The contents didn't seem to bother him one little bit. Every now and then he would offer a selected picture to Mike for his opinion, but Mike wasn't impressed. He had never felt so uncomfortable.

'Why do you like looking at this crap?' Mike said, pushing a proffered picture away from his face.

'My old man has loads of this stuff stashed in his wardrobe. I'm just used to it I suppose. It just makes me laugh, especially when you see the size of some of these willies. Look at this one.' Dan showed Mike a picture of a man's penis being readied for action.

'That's not real. No one's got a dick that big!' Mike

said examining the page.

'It's definitely a fake he wouldn't be able to walk if that thing was dangling between his legs.' Dan said as he put the magazine back onto the shelf and then walked further into the shop. Mike followed amazed at Dan's sordid knowledge until they both came to a halt at the counter.

'You look like a couple of nice boys,' the shop assistant said, leaning forward, twitching his nose and squeezing his lips tight. Dan whispered into Mike's ear.

'He's a poof, but I'm not worried because I think he fancies you not me.' Mike thumped Dan on the arm and pushed him away towards the vibrators. Mike couldn't help but glance at the shop assistant; he looked so funny with his shaven head, plucked eyebrows, diamond stud in his nose, thick black leather-studded dog collar around his neck and a love heart tattoo on his shoulder.

'Can I interest you in Silvia? She'll drive you wild,' the assistant said while placing his hand on the top of a fake head of a woman that sat pride of place on his counter. Mike looked down, watching the woman's head being stroked as if it were a cat that would start to purr any second. Blonde synthetic curly hair draped over the head, falling onto the counter. Two large round eyes with false eyelashes blinked every few seconds. The lips were bright red giving off a shiny reflection from the shop lights, but the mouth was wide open forming a perfect circular shape. Mike stared at the abnormal head and thought that it wouldn't be out of place in a waxwork museum. Then, like being hit in the face by a hot wind, a rush of embarrassment filled his body. The man at the counter had flicked a switch at the back of the false head. It started to vibrate and make female moaning and groaning noises.

'You can try her out if you like,' said the assistant

looking directly into Mike's eyes. He winked and licked his lips. Mike didn't know what to do or say and for several seconds his brain had pressed the 'pause' button and wouldn't allow him to react. His body temperature had climbed to volcanic proportions and his cheeks glowed like two shiny red apples.

He was dumbstruck with embarrassment and there had been only one other time in his life that he had felt the same. That was when he had unwittingly entered the wrong washroom on a camping site when he holidayed with his parents three years ago. The signs on the doors had been swapped by an unknown practical joker and when he entered he was confronted by an elderly lady wearing nothing but a frown. Like now, he froze, not knowing what to say or do. His eyes befell a pair of saggy, drooping flat old tits and a hairy triangle that stretched from between her legs to just underneath her belly button, an image that would remain in his memory for ever. His horrified gaze only broke when a bar of Imperial Leather soap hit him on the forehead. He had turned and ran as fast as he could back to his tent. But now, in a porn shop in Amsterdam with two gangsters after him, he had nowhere to run. Looking around for his escape he saw three doors to his right. Not thinking where they might lead to, he opened the first and stepped inside, pulling the door shut and locking it behind him.

Mike slumped into the plastic chair which was positioned directly in front of a TV screen. It was more like a cupboard than a room but it didn't matter; his head dropped into his hands, his embarrassment turning into despair. The most fantastic football experience of his life was quickly turning into a nightmare. He opened his eyes when the TV in front of him suddenly sparked into life. Dan knocked on the door. Mike questioned who it was and when Dan answered he

176

unlocked the door and let him in.

'What ya watching?' Dan asked, pushing Mike to one side so that he could share half of his seat.

'I haven't got a clue. I couldn't give a shit. I just want to get out of here,' Mike said unhappily.

'You're bloody right! We're getting out of here now. Look!' Mike looked up at the TV and his eyes widened to the size of dinner plates. Two muscle-bound men were wrapped in each other's arms, kissing, cuddling and touching each other. Mike felt sick and swallowed hard to keep the contents of his stomach down. Dan flung the door open and was immediately confronted by the shop assistant.

'Room for three in there if I close early,' he said, rubbing his cheek with his finger and running his tongue along his top teeth.

'Don't even think about it, pal,' said Dan, pushing him out of the way.

The shop door opened and the boys turned their heads to look. Henri stood there, grinning from ear to ear. Mike instinctively started to back away. Dan followed, keeping his eyes on Henri who was now no longer alone. Didier had appeared next to him, shaking his finger as if he were a teacher scolding a naughty school child. Like two rats in a trap there was no way out. Dan trembled as he pushed against Mike to gain an extra inch of distance from Dubois's men. Mike watched as the shop assistant approached the two new customers. Mike knew that was their chance.

Sprinting forward, dragging Dan behind him, he ran at the assistant who by now was standing directly between them and Dubois's men. With two hands he pushed the assistant as hard as he could, sending him forward into Henri and Didier. Three tumbling bodies fell onto a rack of pornographic magazines, sending them flying all over the shop floor. Mike and Dan ran

177

out of the shop door and into the crowded street outside. Henri and Didier scrambled to get up, throwing magazines everywhere and ignoring the protests from the shop assistant who was flapping around like a seagull in an oil slick. By the time Henri and Didier had exited the store, Mike and Dan were long gone and Henri was starting to contemplate how he was going to explain all this to Dubois.

It was well past midnight and hunger and fatigue were luring Dan to stop for something to eat. Across the other side of the canal, Dan spotted a sign which read 'Coffee Shop' and which flashed in pink neon lights.

'We've lost them for now. Come on, I'm hungry,' he said, making his way across a small bridge. Mike wanted to go back to the hotel to find his uncle, but Dan was on a mission for food so Mike followed him across.

'No drugs, right? I'm not stupid. I know these places sell more than just coffee,' Mike muttered as they crossed the bridge.

'Don't get on your high horse again. I won't be smoking anything.' Dan replied as he jogged towards the shop.

The coffee shop was busy for such an unearthly hour, but the boys found a seat at the rear. The sweet smell of smoke hung in the air in such a thickness that it stung Mike's eyes when he entered. A Rastafarian man with dreadlocks halfway down his back gave them a menu.

'You eighteen?' he asked them as he walked past to serve other customers. They didn't answer. Mike only wanted a Coke, but Dan had his eyes on something called 'Space Cake'. Five minutes later Mike had his Coke and Dan had his cake.

'What are we going to do about Dubois's men?'

Mike said as he sipped from his can. Dan had his mouth full of cake and couldn't answer so he just shrugged his shoulders.

'Well, you're a great help. We've got a drugs baron and his two zombies trying to kill us and all you can do it stuff your face with cake.' Mike got up and started to walk away.

'Well, I don't know, do I? It's not the sort of question that's easy to answer,' Dan shouted back at him, spitting out bits of cake as he ran out of the coffee shop after Mike.

'Do you have any idea how much trouble we're in? They're after us and they aren't going to stop until we're dead. You got us into this so you better start thinking of a way to get us out.' Dan didn't answer; he just stood with a glazed expression on his face as though he was in a trance. Mike turned and walked away.

The street either side of the canal was still heaving with people so, to make sure no one was lurking in an alleyway ready to jump out on them, every fifteen or twenty yards Mike would stop and survey the scene. Dan was no help at all and then suddenly he began to giggle uncontrollably.

'What's up with you?' said Mike not amused with his friend's blatant disregard for their situation. Then he realised.

'It's the cake, isn't it?' Dan just giggled the more. A pathetic, gormless grin appeared on his face which, to Mike, was a red rag to a bull.

'You knew that cake had drugs in it, didn't you?' By now Mike was furious. He clenched his fist, but hitting Dan wasn't going to help. Dan had let him down big time and now, as far as Mike was concerned, their friendship was over.

'You and me are finished. Right! You're on your

own, you stupid fucking arsehole.' Mike walked off, full of rage but also hurt. Dan had pissed him off many times in the past but he had always stood by him. But when it came to taking drugs - that was it, end of friendship.

'It's just a bit of fun, man! Get a life, for fuck's sake,' Dan shouted, but Mike was too far away to hear. Dan fell backwards onto a small flight of steps leading to a shop window full of girls. He banged on the window, sticking his tongue out and licking the glass. A roller shutter descended and obscured his view. He gave up and drifted off into his own little world.

Mike hadn't gone far. He'd sat down on a bench at the edge of the canal, watching the reflections of passers by and the buildings that surrounded him. He was still fuming inside but, as each second passed, he began to calm down. The inky black water shimmered and rippled each time the light breeze stroked the surface. For a moment Mike became mesmerised by his own reflection, watching his face become distorted and then slowly, as the water settled, his image would return.

The spell suddenly broke when he saw their faces reflected in a window of a canal barge. Henri and Didier stood no more than five yards away from him, but his back was to them and they hadn't seen him yet. Butterflies began to fly in his stomach. He'd dare not turn to look so he kept his eyes on the barge window. Henri had a mobile phone to his ear. He must have been talking to Dubois because every few seconds his face would distort and he would take the phone from his ear, grimace then return it for what Mike thought was further abuse. He had visions of Dan sprawled out in a doorway and he hoped that the police may have found him. At least a night in the cells meant safety, but Henri and Didier were heading in his direction and

Mike needed to do something fast.

Running across the nearest bridge, he sprinted up the opposite side of the street to the next bridge which would hopefully get him to Dan before anyone else did. Out of breath and with beads of sweat forming on his forehead, he arrived at the place where he had left Dan. He wasn't there. Mike looked around and could see Henri and Didier walking in his direction.

'Come on, where are you, you little git!' he said as he looked up and down the pavement.

'Mate, you've come back to me!' a voice called out from a little further up the pavement. Mike looked and couldn't help but smile when he saw him. Dan lay under the rudest fountain that Mike had ever seen. It looked like an over-sized candle stick with an enormous penis acting as the candle. Dan's gormless smile appeared like the Cheshire cat in 'Alice in Wonderland' and Mike knew that he was still in cloud cuckoo land. He crawled alongside him and put his hand over his mouth. The fountain provided good cover for them both, but the pavement underneath was damp and Mike could feel the moisture soaking into his trousers. Two pairs of feet belonging to Henri and Didier walked slowly past. Mike kept his hand over Dan's mouth, just to be safe and let out a sigh of relief. *How is this night going to end?* he thought to himself as he dragged Dan from under the fountain. Dan tried to give him a kiss but Mike pushed him away and, like two drunken old men, they wobbled off in the direction of the hotel.

Chapter 14

Mike and Dan had made it into a smaller side street, one without a canal. Tall three and four-storey buildings leant at odd angles, giving the street a claustrophobic feeling and, unlike the tree-lined canals, not a bit of flora or fauna could be seen anywhere.

It was difficult for Mike to support Dan as he had turned into a dead weight and it didn't take long for him to feel exhausted. The street was narrow and bustled with people, making it difficult to walk in a straight line with his intoxicated burden. Here, at least, he felt safer and less likely to be hijacked, or so he thought. However, in reality they were worse off. There was nowhere to run and nowhere to hide. If they were spotted now they would need a miracle to escape. Mike ached all over, his legs especially. It had been one hell of a day and if he closed his eyes tight enough he could see his single bed in the five-man room beckoning him.

Dan, minute by minute, became lighter as the effects of the drug wore off and he started to take his own weight. It was then that it happened. The crowd in front of them seemed to part like a pre-rehearsed scene in a musical and a man, unknown to both, stood in front of them blocking their way.

'Daniel Sharpe and Mike,' was all the man could say before the words died in his mouth and he crumpled up in a heap on the pavement. Dan had heard his name mentioned and, without thinking, Kung Fu kicked the stranger between the legs.

'Run! Quick!' Mike shouted. Both of them jumped over the man curled up in the middle of the street. It was impossible to run in a straight line and when Mike looked ahead his eyes fixed onto another face that stared straight back at him. He assumed stranger number two was with the first man. The way forward was now blocked and the man with the swollen testicles had gotten to his feet. They were trapped with nowhere to go. Mike needed courage. He told himself that if the men had guns then they surely wouldn't try to use them in a busy street. Preparing himself for hand to hand combat was the only thing that he could do, but he had never been in a fight in his life.

Dan, invigorated by the shot of adrenalin in his veins, was now almost fully recovered. He pointed to a nearby door.

'Quick! In here! They've got to have a back door,' he shouted. Mike wasn't going to argue. Through the door they ran, not seeing the doorman to their right who was crouching down tying his shoe lace. He witnessed the two blurred figures run past him but he thought nothing of it. Quite often people, embarrassed to be seen going into a live sex show, would run past him to get inside. He stood up, lit a cigarette, inhaled and resumed his task of keeping out the drunks and do-gooders. A man, half crouching half standing and rubbing his groin area, approached the doorman.

'You seen two boys run this way?' he said, first in Dutch and then repeated in English. The doorman shook his head. The man cursed, spun around and produced a two-way radio from his pocket.

***

Jim Slater sat in an unmarked police car a few streets away. He'd managed to rope ten Dutch officers in on the task to find the boys. Henri and Didier were now being tailed again but the boys had eluded him. A voice crackled on the two-way radio in his pocket. He listened to the bad news. *Why had they panicked?* he thought. 'Bloody third rate surveillance,' he muttered to himself, then placed the radio to his mouth.

'I want a full sweep of each establishment on that street,' he said tersely. 'Try and be discrete, we don't want to lose them again. *Do we* gentlemen?' There was no reply, so he put the radio back in his pocket and settled back in his seat to await more news.

***

Once through the door, still running at full pelt, everything went black. A thin neon floor light guided their way. Slowing down to walking pace, while at the same time listening for footsteps behind them, the two boys followed the light. Passing through a heavy black curtain, they entered a dimly lit room which couldn't have been more than four square metres in size. Immediately to their left was a kiosk with the entry fee of thirty Euros printed in large white letters above the hatch. The kiosk was empty. Too much alcohol had given the woman in the kiosk a headache and when the boys crept past she was down on all fours, fumbling through her handbag for headache tablets.

Music escaped from the other side of the room, enticing them to venture further inside. Going back wasn't an option so, sticking tightly together, lips sealed, they walked into what was to be an experience they would never forget.

The lighting was subdued. In fact the room practically in semi-darkness. It gave Mike the feeling of walking into a cinema just as the film was about to start. Horseshoe-shaped booths with red leather seats encircled a small stage; they reminded Mike of an American diner that he had once visited on a holiday with his parents to Florida. To the rear of the booths, little round glass tables with designer plastic chairs accommodated the unfortunate clientele when the booths were full. The bar was the only thing that stood out in the darkness. A gleaming chrome beer pump in the shape of a 'T' had central position in the bar and, gracefully lying across the top, wearing not a stitch of clothing, a figurine with large breasts smiled lustfully at each customer as they waited to be served.

The rear of the bar was cleverly mirrored, allowing the on-stage performance to be watched from any angle, but no one left their seats to be served. Three topless waitresses, wearing hot pants and high heels, flitted between tables and booths with seductive efficiency. Each time they appeared with orders the customers would be distracted from the show to stare at the bare breasts dancing only inches from their faces.

Dan's hand gripped Mike's arm so tight when he saw the entertainment that Mike needed to unwrap his fingers and wrench it free. Then, with a rush of blood to the head, he realised the reason for Dan's grip. Over and over again he opened and closed his eyes, blinking in rapid succession to make sure that he wasn't seeing things. A warm rush of self-consciousness engulfed his body but no one saw his embarrassment - they were too busy watching the show. Two bodies, completely naked and entwined in each other's arms, rolled and writhed rhythmically on the small stage to the sound of Donna Summer's 'Love to Love You Baby'.

'Are they doing what I think they're doing?' whispered Dan.

'Yes, they are, but why are you asking me? I thought that you were the expert on shagging.' Dan didn't answer and, had the lighting not been so poor, Mike would have sworn that Dan had gone red.

'Well,' Dan said finding his voice. 'It's just a bit different in the flesh, isn't it? Anyway, I'm not bothered. I could watch it all night.'

Mike knew that Dan felt embarrassed but the big-headed git wouldn't admit it. He, on the other hand, felt comfortable with the idea of sex. He knew what it was all about but he found it hard to come to terms with the lack of intimacy in a place like this. Doing it in front of the gawping public repulsed him rather than excited him.

While Dan stared at his first live sex show and fiddled about with his hands in his pockets, Mike looked around at the barely visible faces in each booth. He wondered at the type of person who would frequent a place like this. He'd often heard reports on the news or read articles in the tabloid press of important people with highly responsible jobs having their decent, upstanding lives blown apart when some paparazzi caught them in a compromising position. He smiled to himself when he remembered the story of a High Court judge who was found in women's underwear in a brothel in South East London. Of course, everything was brushed under the carpet, but it made Mike wonder just how many High Court judges, politicians or other powerful officials were in the same room as him now.

Mike's eyes, for a couple of seconds, inadvertently focused on the pair of lovers. He was muscular, toned and glistening with sweat. She had a figure which bent and curved, adapting perfectly to suit her dominant male partner. They moved to change position now, making the shape of a sixty-nine for the audience. A naughty thought, which made him chuckle, appeared in front of his eyes as if somebody was holding up a photo in front of his face. He pictured the burger van girl slowly undressing and dropping her clothes, one by one, onto the floor in front of him. Oh, he was definitely going to ask her out when he got home, he decided as the imaginary pile of clothes grew bigger on the floor.

'I wonder how much they get paid?' Dan said, tapping Mike on the shoulder. Mike's bubble of love burst, bringing him back to reality. He looked at Dan and gritted his teeth, annoyed at his friend for prematurely putting an end to his daydream.

'How should I bloody know?' he snapped back at Dan. 'Why, you thinking of asking?'

'No I'm not! But to do that in public they must be on a good wage. Can't be bad, can it, getting paid for shagging. I might have to think of a career change,' he said, vigorously fiddling in his pockets.

'Firstly, you need to be good-looking, which you're not, and secondly you need a big love muscle, which you also haven't got. But even if you get past those two hurdles you would still struggle because you wouldn't know what to do with it.' Mike enjoyed his reply and waggled his little finger in Dan's face.

'Ha, ha, very funny. Say what you like, but I think that I could do it.'

'I tell you what,' Mike said pointing at the stage. 'Why don't you go down there, tap the bloke on his bare buttocks and ask him for his hourly rate?'

'Yeah, I might just do that.'

'Oh, by the way,' Mike said spinning Dan around to look at him. 'I haven't forgotten about you and your cake, so don't think us being here together changes anything.' Dan looked at him pitifully, like a scolded puppy looking at his master. He was just about to reply and try and get back into Mike's good books when Mike pulled him down to the floor.

'Don't say a word. Just look over there, eleven o'clock, corner of the room.' Both of them had dropped behind the back of an open booth. Dan rose slightly and peered over the top.

'What am I supposed to be looking at?' he whispered, looking down at Mike.

'Tell me that's not Barry over there?' said Mike, peering over the top to look again.

'Jesus!' Dan said putting his own hand over his mouth to stifle his amazement. 'Barry, John Dodd and fatty Dennis the driver, all in that end booth. Fuck! I tell you what, I'll make sure Barry never lives this one down. Oh, there'll be some mileage there.

'Oh, I don't think so,' Mike said. 'When I tell Barry that you do drugs you'll be out of the team anyway.'

'You won't tell him, will ya?' Dan said, looking directly into Mike's eyes.

'Give me one good reason why I shouldn't.' Dan didn't answer.

'Well, there you go,' Mike said sarcastically. 'You signed your own death warrant so don't blame me.' Dan's appetite for the show disappeared and he slumped to the floor with his back to the performance. But Barry sat with his eyes closed, trying hard not to look at the two lovers.

***

The search for the boys had proved fruitless. John and Dennis had talked Barry into taking a break, but the minute that he'd agreed to set foot in the place he'd began to regret it. It was sordid, immoral and sleazy. *Thank God no one will ever know that I'm here*, he thought to himself.

'This tour couldn't get any bloody worse, could it?' Mike said, running his hands through his hair in pure frustration. Dan wasn't listening. With the change of music, he'd regained his appetite for the show and was peeping over the top of the seat to see what position the two lovemakers were in.

'Hey! Are you listening to me, you lecherous little git!' Mike shouted as he pulled him back down. 'Start

188

thinking about what we're going to do, because at the moment the last thing I want is your hard-on sticking in my back.'

'I don't know, alright! I told you before, I just don't know.' *Fucking useless*, Mike thought.

The curtain separating the kiosk from the bar moved to one side and the man who'd had his balls kicked into orbit by Dan entered the room. Quickly the boys scampered around the other side of the booth. It was now a matter of time before they were spotted, either by Barry or the stranger. Mike glanced above the seat. The man stood talking to the doorman, his eyes scanning backwards and forwards across the room. Mike believed they were safe if the stranger didn't advance any further. For Barry to see them he had to purposely look in their direction. He told Dan to sit still and not look up but be ready to run when he told him to. Dan sat transfixed, waiting for the signal. It came sooner than he thought. Mike got to his feet a split second before Dan, who soon made up for the momentary lapse.

The stranger had produced his Police Badge, which gave the doorman no choice but to turn on the lights of the club. Mike and Dan weren't the only ones to panic when the lights revealed their identity. Like rats scurrying for cover, a number of men of all ages, and a few women, tried to hide themselves from the unwanted exposure. Others just sat nonchalantly with their drinks, oblivious to the blind panic that was taking place all around them, Barry, John and Dennis amongst them.

With the entrance to the bar blocked, Mike and Dan could only run one way and that was to the stage where the action was taking place. Mike concentrated on finding an exit but Dan, in mid sprint, looked for Barry. When their eyes met it was Dan's which had the upper

189

hand. He smiled a cheeky grin and winked. Barry, wide-eyed, dropped back into his seat. His head fell into his hands and he began to weep. A lifetime of devotion to his religion, his dead mother and clean living had been thrown away in an instant. As Mike and Dan ran in one direction, Barry got to his feet. Ignoring John and Dennis, he started to walk the other way.

With the stranger in hot pursuit, Mike and Dan needed to negotiate the stage. Mike leapt nimbly over the two bodies still entwined on the floor. Dan, on the other hand, couldn't resist having one last look. He tripped and fell, sprawling face down onto the stage. Hurting and embarrassed, he got to his feet looking directly into the male porn star's face.

'Do you make good money?' he shouted as he headed off after Mike. He never got an answer.

The boys found the backstage exit which led into the dressing rooms. Knocking over clothes racks and bumping into men with bulging biceps, six pack stomachs and genitals which donkeys would be proud of, they ran to the fire exit. Women in various stages of undress stood in shock as the two English teenagers sprinted through. Dan's eyes were nearly falling out of their sockets as he ran past the best, and only, naked display of female flesh that he had ever seen.

Mike had also taken in the sights but his main attention was on the fire exit, which gave way easily with the force of his foot kicking the bar. They emerged into a small alleyway with the choice of going left or right. Left took them into the darkness behind boxes and crates. Right took them to the busy street but it was a good thirty yards away and, with the pursuer's footsteps getting closer, they wouldn't make it without being seen. Mike dragged Dan to the left, squeezing themselves between a stack of crates and a large wheelie bin. Finding it hard to control their breathing, they watched in silence as the pursuer ran towards the busy street and disappeared into the crowd. The fire door slammed shut and the boys were plunged into darkness again.

Barry walked with the weight of the world on his shoulders. He had made the mistake of entering an establishment of sin and now he was being punished for it. It didn't matter whether it was Sharpe that had seen him. By going in that club he had forsaken everything that he had been taught to uphold. With his head full of regrets he walked into the nearest bar and ordered a double whisky. *One more sin won't hurt*, he thought as the harsh tasting liquid set fire to the back of his throat, swallowing it in one.

It was a good half hour before the boys moved from their hiding place. Slowly creeping out of the alleyway, like two infantry soldiers scanning for the enemy, they entered the busy street. There was no let up in the foot traffic. Two o'clock in the morning had come and gone and still it was like a Saturday afternoon shopping spree. A kind twist of fate had led the boys back to the hotel. Relieved, tired and dragging their feet, they approached the main entrance. Veering off like a car swerving to miss a deer, they hid behind the tour bus, squinting to make out the two dark figures that stood to the right of the hotel entrance.

'It's those bastards again,' Dan said kicking the wheel of the bus. They both squinted to see into the shadows but only the outline of a human shape could be made out. The tour bus provided the perfect cover to view the hotel and not be seen. From the driver's window they could see straight through the bus entrance door to the hotel beyond.

'What are we going to do?' Dan said, yawning into Mike's face.

'Is that all you can say? Mike said turning to look at

him. 'Don't know, what are we going to do? Where we going to go? You're like a broken record saying the same thing over and over again.' Dan wasn't too impressed with Mike's tone, even though he knew that he was right.

'Look here, mister perfect,' Dan said staring into Mike's eyes. 'I'm sorry that I don't have any answers, but I've never had someone trying to kill me before.'

'Yeah, yeah, yeah. I'm sorry I haven't got a violin, but don't worry! Mike comes to the rescue again,' said Mike with a big cheesy grin on his face. Dan looked at him puzzled. It was the middle of the night with no way of getting into their hotel and Mike was smiling. Beckoning Dan to follow him, Mike walked down the side of the bus. At about half way along he lifted a door catch and slowly the hatch to the luggage compartment under the bus lifted up, revealing the dark void beneath.

'What are you doing?' Dan said, watching in amazement as Mike climbed into the luggage compartment.

'Are you getting in, or what?' Mike said holding the hatch open. Dan followed Mike into the void below the seats. As the hatch clicked shut, Mike flicked a switch and a small light illuminated the space. The heavy smell of plastic and diesel hung in the air but, for Dan, it didn't matter for he had seen the small sleeping compartment laid out in front of him.

'I know it's not five star, but it's the best that I could do at such short notice,' Mike said lounging back onto the small mattress that fitted between the superstructure of the bus bodywork. Dan smiled, shaking his head in disbelief. He crawled forward carefully, trying not to bang his head on the low ceiling. Mike surrendered half of the mattress and the pair lay down, staring at the checkerboard underside of the bus floor.

'How did you know about this?'

'Oh, Dennis showed me when I had to hide my stinky top. He told me that he never uses it because of his size. It was either sleep here or on the street. So I chose here.'

'Thanks Mike. I do appreciate it, you know,' Dan said with a tone that Mike rarely heard. 'I'm sorry for today. I just had this urge to try some. I didn't see the harm in it. My old man smokes it all the time in the house and I have tried it occasionally but please, please believe me I'm not a druggy. Stupid yes, but a druggy no.' Mike didn't answer as him he waited for Dan to get it out of his system. 'I'm sorry Mike. I know I'm a fool, but please don't get me kicked out of the team. And I promise that I won't mention a thing about Barry, honest.'

'Look, go to sleep,' replied Mike, 'we'll talk about it tomorrow. Hopefully those two won't stand in front of the hotel all night, so we'll get back in before the rest get up, ok!' Dan agreed. He'd said his bit and now it was time for sleep and it didn't take long before both had drifted off.

***

Barry walked two steps forward and one to the side. The whisky had dulled his pain but had taken away his coordination, eyesight and Euros. Stumbling into the side of the bus, he put his hand out to steady himself. For a second he thought that he heard snoring coming from inside, but he shook his head, deciding it must be the whisky playing tricks on him. He clung to every parked car, getting the support that he needed as he headed for the hotel entrance.

The two shadows watched as the drunken Englishman fell twice while negotiating the steps and then watched in amazement as he began to cry uncontrollably, and then wet himself as he tried to get his key into the door. When he had finally disappeared inside, all that was left was a small smelly puddle and a trail of wet footprints.

Superintendent Slater called his men off. He'd received the report of the two boys running wild through the live sex show. The thought of it made him smile to himself. The streets were becoming quiet and he assumed that the boys were holed up somewhere safe. Henry and Didier had given them the slip once more and disappeared into the red light area. He decided to leave two men outside the hotel to report should the boys return, so for now there was nothing more that he could do. Hoping that the boys were safe and not in the hands of Dubois or his men, he decided to recline his car seat and settle down for a few hours sleep before the dawn chorus began.

Chapter 15

Mike woke with his face imprinted with the checkerboard pattern, his back aching and his right arm asleep. Dan had somehow muscled him off the bed and he'd spent the last hour lying on the cold hard floor of the bus. His watch told him it was 7am but he felt as though he had just closed his eyes. Little shafts of daylight like laser beams shone through the hatch seal where it had come away from the bodywork of the bus and illuminated Dan's sleeping face. Mike listened to the sound of footsteps on the pavement outside and cars passing on the other side of the bus. Feeling evil, he ran his knuckles up and down Dan's rib cage, applying pressure each time he touched a bone. It was a painful experience when you were awake, let alone being woken up by it. Mike smiled sadistically to himself, feeling good about inflicting Dan with pain.

'I'm awake, you twat!' Dan said opening his eyes and grimacing with pain. He grabbed Mike's hand and turned towards him, looking not very amused with Mike's wake-up method.

'Come on, cannabis breath, let's get into the hotel before the rest get up,' Mike said crawling towards the door.

'I'm knackered,' said Dan. 'Just another half an hour for God's sake.'

'You stay if you want, but I'm going.'

Mike pushed the hatch open and daylight flooded in, causing him to squint. A nearby street cleaner got the shock of his life as the two boys climbed out from under the bus. Mike looked at him, shrugged his shoulders and then closed the hatch behind them. The street cleaner shook his head in disbelief, then turned away to continue his brushing.

The hotel entrance was deserted and the boys had no trouble getting to their room. Little Terry Grainger woke up as they entered.

'Where've you two been?' he said, rubbing the sleep out of his eyes. 'It looks like you two have slept rough and you stink. Barry will have your nuts when he sees you. He's been out looking for you and he got the police involved too.'

'Firstly,' replied Dan, sitting on the bed next to Terry, 'it's none of your fucking business and secondly, no, Barry won't do anything to us. Thirdly, say anything and I will smash your face in. Ok?'

'Don't worry about it, Terry, it's not your problem,' Mike added as he undressed to take a shower. 'We're back now and it'll be fine with Barry. Just forget you saw us, ok?' Terry nodded and lay back down, but as Dan turned away he stuck his fingers up at him behind his back.

Barry woke up with his mouth tasting like a camel's jock strap, his head throbbing. He lay on top of his bed, still fully clothed. The top half of his body felt warm but below his waist it felt decidedly chilly. Moving his hand down towards his belt he felt the cold dampness of wet trousers. At first it didn't register, but when he smelt his fingers he sat up in shear disbelief. The sudden movement made him feel dizzy and the throbbing got worse. He looked at the wet patch extending from his groin to his shoes. The shame of the night before returned in an instant and he lay back, staring at the ceiling, his eyes slowly filling with tears as his brain went into replay mode. In all of his life he had never wet himself and to do it now, at his age, was pure humiliation. He hated himself for it.

Superintendent Jim Slater had only slept for an hour, but in his line of work he'd come accustomed to having very little sleep; it went with the job. His neck hurt as he moved his head from side to side. He slowly rubbed it with his hand to loosen it up. At the same time he sniffed his armpits and realised that his deodorant had stopped working hours ago. Nevertheless, his mood was a happy one. He'd received reports that the boys had returned to the hotel unscathed, Henri and Didier had been traced to a motel on the outskirts of the city and Dubois would be somewhere fuming. He knew sooner rather than later that Dubois would have to show his face and when he did he would feel the hand of the law. *Today would be a good day*, Jim thought and he went back to loosening his neck muscles.

***

The bus pulled into the sports ground in the small suburb of Sloten, on the outskirts of Amsterdam. Mike and Dan had slept the whole journey. Barry wore his sunglasses to hide the black coal sacks that had materialised under his eyes, and he'd already decided to leave the talking to his assistant, John. Jim had followed the bus unseen and managed to pick up a cup of coffee and a doughnut on the way for his breakfast. He had instructed his handful of men to scatter around the area and to inform him of anything out of the ordinary. For now, though, the day seemed to be progressing normally but, as before, Henri and Didier weren't going to be too far away.

Barry hadn't spoken to anybody throughout the journey, and when the bus stopped he got off almost immediately to announce their arrival. The rest of the team stayed onboard, their interested faces pressed against the glass. A hum of excitement buzzed through the bus. It was time to play their favourite game again.

Mike woke up with the sound of the air brakes being applied. He pushed Dan, who hit his head against the window.

'What!' Dan answered, wiping the dribble from his chin.

'We're here.'

'Already? Jesus, I've only just closed my eyes,' he said, turning to look out of the window. Mike joined him, but with a definite lack of interest. His brain and body weren't working together. His tired body cried out to stay where he was and sleep but his brain told him to get himself motivated. For the first time in his life the thought of playing football didn't agree with him, but he knew that as soon as he ran out onto the pitch it would be different.

Dan wasn't feeling too enthusiastic either and he squeezed the bags under his eyes, trying to make them disappear. Mike looked at him without sympathy, as he knew that Dan was an expert at finding hidden reserves of energy. He never knew where it came from and he was always amazed how Dan could run like a mad man for ninety minutes. He thought about the night before and the episode with the space cake. Suddenly he had the awful thought that Dan was taking some sort of drug to boost his energy. He shook his head in disbelief. 'Even Dan couldn't be that stupid,' he said to himself. Or could he?

Sloten for a City suburb was pretty. Trees lined every street; even the nine football pitches at the sports ground had lines of trees and bushes dividing them from one another. Typical of Amsterdam where houses, trees or roads couldn't be found, water flowed in the form of canals and streams. The suburb gave the appearance of wealth and with only six kilometres separating it from the centre of the city there was no problem for commuters. Yet, as with all nice places, there was always something that prevented it from being perfect. The team soon discovered this as they observed their surroundings from the bus. The sight of it caused jaws to drop. The excited chatter stopped and even Dennis the driver was struck dumb.

The Boeing 747 seemed to hang in the air as it passed overhead. It made everybody and everything shudder as a wave of vibration passed through their bodies. It was so low that it seemed all one had to do was reach out and touch it; then, as though something had blotted out the sun, a huge shadow cloaked them in darkness as it chased the plane on its flight path to Schipol International Airport. So that's what stopped Sloten from being perfect. It sat just two kilometres from the airport and every few minutes hundreds of tonnes of metal would pass overhead before touching down on the runway.

Mike found it hard to comprehend living under the flight path of one of Europe's biggest and busiest airports. The noise, let alone the sight of each plane, was enough to drive a person mad. Still, thought Mike, if you live with something for long enough you forget that it's there. He opened his eyes wide and for a split second he swore that he could see the passengers looking down at him. 'No, can't be,' he said to himself rubbing his eyes. Barry appeared with some paperwork in his hands, mobile to his ear and a look of thunder on his face. He threw a glance at Mike and Dan but he didn't let it linger. Dan grinned back at him, but Mike remained expressionless. Barry was starting to feel his old self again; he'd drunk some water and scrounged a couple of headache tablets from Dennis. They seemed to be doing the trick, but the news that he'd just received had been enough to clear his head once and for all. He put his phone away, climbed back onboard and asked Dennis to shut the door. The team knew

Barry well and the look on his face told them to sit down and shut up. Within seconds you could hear a pin drop.

'What I'm about to say is not my fault,' Barry said pointing his finger in the direction of everyone, 'so don't shoot the messenger.' Suddenly breaking the silence, Martin Cuthbert shouted across the bus.

'Look at him!' he said pointing out of the window. Everyone turned to look. 'He's got hair down to his arse.'

'That's because it's not a he, it's a she,' Barry exclaimed. Heads swung back to Barry, meeting his gaze, but no one had put two and two together yet.

'There's been a cock-up boys and I don't really know the best way to say this.' Barry stopped and scratched his head, unable to continue.

'Come on Barry, spit it out!' Dan shouted.

'Yes, well,' Barry stuttered, but he knew he had to tell them. Taking a deep breath, he spilled the beans.

'This tournament is an all girls' football tournament,' he said sheepishly. For at least five seconds silence reigned; then, like a busy day on the floor of the London Stock Exchange, all hell broke loose. Barry waited and watched their reactions, feeling totally useless. Questions were being thrown at him from all directions. Some in disbelief, some in amazement and some in stupidity, but the majority were in anger and all led to the same point. How had this happened and what are we going to do? Barry held his arms up and waited for calm to be restored. Eventually, though, the torrent of abuse subsided. The air of hostility died away and, luckily for Barry, females in football strips outside the bus had undermined their concentration.

'The cock-up is back home,' he shouted into the microphone. 'So there is nothing that we can do about it now, ok?'

'It's that useless Chairman, isn't it?' Dan screamed trying to incite more hostility.

'You sit down and shut up. Comments like that aren't welcome,' Barry said, now very red faced. Dan was just about to attack again when Mike pulled him back down to his seat. He gave Mike an evil stare, but Mike just stared at him until he backed down. Nothing more was said and Barry continued nervously.

'Listen to me, you lot. You have a choice because they're allowing us to play, if we want to.' The bus went quiet once more. 'Yes, you heard me right. They are allowing us to play if we want to, so decide now. Play or stay on the bus. It's up to you.'

'Surely it's against the law for male and females to play together? What happens if we sort of touch something that we're not supposed to?' Tony Fletcher shouted nervously over the noise.

'Get a grip of yourself, Tony,' said Barry. 'You don't touch the opposition now, do you? So why should it be any different against females.' Tony shrank back down in his seat, embarrassed by Barry's reply. 'The law is not important here,' Barry continued. 'This is a five aside competition and not eleven versus eleven. It's a private event and I presume it's up to them. They know that we've travelled a long way so they've given us the option of playing. You've got two minutes to decide and then I'll have to go and tell them.'

Mike stood up.

'Barry, what do you think?' The murmurs died down, and all ears were tuned to Barry.

'Look, the way I see it is you came on this tour to gain experience of playing different types of football, so all this here is a different type of football.'

'That's bollocks, Barry, and you know it,' Dan said over the silence of his team mates. 'Having to play girls shouldn't be allowed. Football should just be for men only.' Eyes flew back and forth from Barry to Dan waiting for the verbal tennis to start, but it never did.

'Well, that counts you out,' Mike said pushing him in the back.

'What do you mean, it counts me out?'

'Well, it'll be a few years yet before you become a man.' Laughs and sneers could be heard throughout the bus. Dan didn't like being laughed at, especially when the remarks had come from Mike who was supposed to be his friend.

'Very funny. I thought you were on my side,' he said angrily, but glowing red with embarrassment.

'I'm not on anybody's side. Just like Barry said, this tour is for us to experience different styles of football and this will just be a different style. So what's the problem? You're not scared of being shown up by girls, are you?'

'No, I just don't like the idea, ok!'

'Well, that's not much of an excuse, is it?'

'That's the only answer you're getting, so bollocks.' Dan sat back in a huff and Mike gave up on him. Barry was relieved and pleased all at the same time with Mike's comments. He admired Mike's positive thinking and was always happy to have him around and could see he had more to say.

'Anything else that you would like to say, Mike, before I go and tell them thanks but no thanks?'

Mike looked around the bus. Every face looked at him in anticipation. He never liked to be the centre of attention, it made him nervous, but this time the nerves weren't so bad. Winking at Dan, he addressed his team mates as though he was one of the coaching staff.

'Look, I say let's play. It won't be that bad. We can use it as a training session and just think about it - we might actually win the competition and that means a trophy to take home. Now, wouldn't that be good? As far as I'm concerned I'm up for playing, and I didn't come on this tour to be stuck on this bloody bus all the time, ok?' Mike sat down, pleased with his contribution. Barry smiled gently at him as a father would smile at a son.

'Right, let's vote on it,' shouted Barry, bringing everybody's attention back to him 'Who wants to play?' Mike put his hand up first and it seemed as though he had it raised for ages before others joined him.

'You heard Mike,' shouted Barry from the front. 'Come on you lot, decide.' Slowly, and a little unsure at first, hands began to rise. Dan sat arms folded until his arm was the only one not raised.

'Well, I think it's out of order playing against girls,' he said folding his arms even tighter. Someone further up the bus began to make chicken noises. Dan shot up out of his seat to identify the culprit.

'Hey, do that again whoever you are and it will be the last thing you ever do!' he yelled.

'Come on, Dan, you in or out?' Mike said in his ear.

'Yes, I'm in but I'm not happy about it, ok?'

With a unanimous vote to play, the tension and uncertainty disappeared and the excitement returned. Barry left to get details of their opponents and the teenage boys were left to ponder the pros and cons of playing against girls. It wasn't long before Barry returned clutching the fixture list. The noise died down and anticipation took over.

'Good! Right, listen up. There are sixteen teams in total in this competition and each stage is a knock-out stage. We're putting in two five aside teams and those not selected will be rolling subs between the two.' Dan butted in before Barry could go any further.

'Come on, Barry, give us the teams. I bet you can't

wait to see this male and female live action. You'll be getting quite used to it by now.' Barry didn't even look at him, let alone reply. He wasn't going to rise to the bait and he blinked hard to concentrate on what he had to say. The rest of the team hadn't understood the connotations; it was only for those present last night that knew what Dan was getting at. Mike kicked him in the shin.

'What did you do that for?' Dan said as he bent down to rub his leg.

'Listen to me, Dan! You don't mention anything about Barry and the club, right! And I might conveniently forget about the space cake, ok!'

'I'm just having a laugh, for God's sake.'

Mike gripped Dan's arm, right in the fleshy bit. Hurting, Dan agreed to keep his mouth shut. Barry definitely wasn't on Dan's Christmas card list but even he, with his limited brain capacity, knew that he needed the club more than the club needed him. Barry stood staring at them both, arms folded, waiting for them to finish. Mike answered for them.

'Sorry Barry, go on.'

Barry outlined the teams and, as normal, there were the customary moans and groans. Today, though, Barry wasn't in the mood for dissent and he wasn't going to take any prisoners.

'Hey! If you don't like my decision then don't play. Ok! Anybody fancy spending the day on the bus?' Heads shook and no one dared to speak, not even Dan.

'The opposition teams are unknown so you are going to have your work cut out. There may be a lot of quality on show and you only have to look at these facilities to know that they take their football seriously.' Barry had a point. The grass was like a bowling green, little privet hedges around each pitch were immaculately trimmed and the white lines on the pitches were perfect. It had all the appearance of a country park but with one exception - it didn't have the peace and quiet. The next plane due to land at Schipol shattered the illusion.

'Oh, and by the way,' Barry shouted over the roar of the jet engines. 'You'll have to get changed on the bus, as the changing rooms are for the girls. Don't worry though - you'll get a shower at the end.' Barry's last comment was like a red rag to a field of bulls. The sexist smutty comments were about to arrive.

'Any chance of sharing the showers?'

'What happens if I bang one in the net?'

'Can we swap shirts at the end?'

'Hey Terry!' shouted Dan. 'No groping the opposition. They won't appreciate it because they'll all be lesbians anyway.' Terry, as usual, was Dan's victim so he answered him with his finger.

'Ok, that's enough,' Barry said, slowly walking up the centre of the bus. 'Look, you lot. It's a friendly competition and it'll do you the world of good, because you'll have to use your brains a bit more. Less of the rash challenges and more skill please, ok! But before we get going, I want to leave you with this thought.' It was another one of Barry's motivational speeches and he knew it was bound to work.

'There is no way at all that you will ever be able to show your faces back home if you lose to girls, so you better win or be ready to keep your mouths shut when you get home.' Barry had hit a nerve, but he hoped it would spur them on and not scare them to death. There was silence and disbelief and even Dan's mouth hung open in shock. Barry had played another one of his trump cards out of his deck, and north east boys losing to girls was enough motivation to keep them running full speed all day.

'One last thing I have to warn you, and there is

nothing I can do about it. One of the female teams is semi-professional. These girls are different - they're attached to Ajax here in Amsterdam so you can guarantee they won't be push overs.' Astonished faces turned to each other, all knowing how big a club Ajax was. Barry could feel the unease returning so he carried on, not allowing them to dwell on it. 'Now, you aren't drawn against them in your first game and that goes for both of our teams. So let's hope they get knocked out before the possibility arises because, from what I hear, they're good.'

'There are no good women footballers, only bad ones,' shouted Dan. 'They won't be a problem, Barry.'

'I'll remind you of that after you have played them, shall I?'

Mike relaxed again as he listened to the comments being thrown around the bus. He wanted to play football - that's what he came on the tour for and it didn't matter whether he played girls or not. For him it wasn't important because he knew that in a five aside match the goalkeeper stayed inside his area; therefore, getting physical with the opposition was out of the question. He'd done his bit, and all he knew was that the impending football match had won over his fatigue.

Once off the bus, everyone could see that the full-sized pitches had been divided into two, but even so there was a lot of area to cover for four men. Mike had been put into the A-team and Dan the B-team. The B-team was to play first so Mike settled down on the side lines to watch. The opponents were a team from the University of Amsterdam. *Students! They'll be crap,'* thought Dan to himself. All night drinking binges and smoking dope - they'll be unfit and useless. However, he had no idea how wrong he was when they finally ran on to the pitch.

Five gorgeous blondes, with legs all the way to the

top, sports bras bursting with cleavage and all of them looking fit and agile, limbered up in front of his eyes. It was then that Dan had the overwhelming feeling of embarrassment. *How shall I tackle? What happens if I hurt one of them?* Thoughts danced in his head, but they weren't about football - they were about being nice which, for Dan, was a completely new experience. He would rather be sitting somewhere chatting these girls up than playing football with them. His motivation started to dwindle and, when the whistle went to start the match, he let the ball run through his legs through lack of concentration. The next thing he knew was a sharp pain in his right shin as one of his opponents took him out with a sliding tackle. The pain brought him back to reality and there and then he knew that he was going to be in for a tough game.

'How's it going, Mike?' said his uncle appearing from nowhere and sitting down next to his nephew on the grass. Mike didn't turn to acknowledge him but continued to watch the game.

'You look a bit tired. Are you ok?'

'Yeah, I'm fine. The last couple of days have taken their toll, but I'll survive. I thought that you'd gone anyway.'

No, not yet. I wanted to say I'm sorry before I left.'

'Don't be, ok? You were right to tell me. Now, let's forget it - there're other things that I really need to talk to you about.' Jim raised his eyebrows in surprise. He'd been struggling to find words to ease his nephew's pain and anger but had failed miserably. Mike had given him a get-out-of-jail-free card and he took it gladly.

'I'd like you to stay because I think that I need you more than ever,' continued Mike, looking up at his uncle. 'There are things that I need to tell you that are really important, and if I don't tell you now I may never get another chance.'

'I'm all ears, Mike. I'll do whatever I can, you know that?' Jim replied, moving in closer to his nephew.

'It's to do with what happened the other day on the train and, more importantly, last night. You've the right to know everything because I think that I'm in some deep, deep shit.' Jim smiled reassuringly while Mike took a long, deep breath and prepared himself to tell his uncle everything that had happened to him, right from the beginning. He only left one thing out and that was Dan and his space cake.

Jim listened and not once did he break Mike's flow. Only on one occasion did he find it difficult to hide his amusement when Mike talked about the sex show, so he pretended to have a coughing fit and turned away. Jim, though, knew everything already but he cringed when Mike told him of how close Henri and Didier had come to getting them. Mike unloaded everything onto him and there was nothing that he could do but give a consoling hug. The half time whistle blew and Mike realised that he hadn't seen any of the game. He'd been so engrossed telling his uncle about the previous night that he'd missed everything.

'What can we do? I'm so scared that they'll get to us,' Mike said with desperation in his voice.

'Don't worry, Mike, leave it with me. I'll give Inspector Sanderson a call, he'll know what to do. But for now, you concentrate on the football and keep your eyes on the ball and not these gorgeous girls!' Mike smiled, but it wasn't a happy smile; just a smile for effect. He did feel a little relief but he knew Dubois's men were still out there looking for them and, try as he might to concentrate on other things, this thought was never far away.

Jim walked away slowly, pondering his next move. He sensed his nephew's fear and with it returned his feeling of guilt for using a family member as bait. He cursed himself repeatedly, but the wheels were now in motion and there were more important things to do than feel guilty. With or without Mike, this journey was only going to end one way, and that was either prison or death for Dubois. He needed to change tack but first he had to speak to Sanderson. As the second half got underway, Jim formulated his new arrangements with the Inspector while Mike lay back on the velvet turf to watch the shambles that was quickly unravelled before him.

Chapter 16

This isn't how it's supposed to be, Mike thought as he sat on the grass watching his team mates being given the run-around by five Dutch girls. The first half had been a disaster and he was glad that he'd missed most of it; but the second half was starting in much the same way and, with his own morale at an all time low, he felt deflated. He wondered whether his motivational speech earlier on the bus had been the right thing to do, as he was now having second thoughts about the whole issue of playing against girls. He knew the lads were talented and normally would brush the opposition aside, but against these girls they were a different team. As a writer would get writer's block, the five players that stood before him had got footballer's block. They couldn't pass, couldn't tackle, couldn't even kick the ball; a total lack of ideas whatsoever haunted the players, and if a miracle didn't happen soon humiliation would be their closest friend.

Barry had tried one of his special team talks at half time. Knock them down and then build them up in the hope that they may be motivated, but it didn't seem to be working and, in any case, no one was listening to him. The shock of a looming defeat had dulled their senses and Barry could have promised them free tickets to the next FA Cup Final and no one would have known. Five zombies had left the field, and five zombies had returned. Within a minute of the restart, a lovely ball through the centre, a quick one two and a perfectly placed volley put team B of the Indispensables one goal down. Dan stood hands on hips, looking totally dejected. He turned towards Mike, who instantly tried to rally the troops, but his eyes gave him away and the only message received was 'You're up shit creek without a paddle'.

Barry, who was normally calm and collected, was beginning to break his own rules. Not only had he started to break his personal rules but now his managerial ones were being shattered too. He'd started to lose his hair in his early twenties and, by the way that he was rubbing his head in frustration, the rest was soon to follow. He looked down at his watch - there was still time. He needed to make a substitution and without hanging about decided that little Terry Grainger was to replace Mark Baxter as soon as the ball went dead. Dan showed his disdain for Barry's decision by mouthing some obscenity in his direction. Barry saw it but he was past caring when it came from Dan; he had others to think of and, anyway, he was the boss and there was no way he would be influenced by that little gob shite.

Terry, looking overjoyed, skipped onto the park as if he was chasing butterflies through a sunlit meadow. He rarely got a chance to show his meagre talents, but maybe this time he could change things. Normally, though, Terry was about as influential as a Conservative Party politician - lots of huffing and puffing and promises to succeed but all the time ending in disappointment. Why Barry sent on Terry when there were more talented players sitting by his side was a question that only he could answer.

While everyone's attention was on Terry, Barry called Dan over to the side line for instructions. Dan approached cautiously, thinking that he was going to get a mouthful, but he was surprised when all that Barry said was 'Route one, no arguments, route one. Now go and win this game.' For Barry, route one football didn't exist in his rule book. He believed that the long ball was killing the game of football. It stopped it from being a game of skill and movement and turned it into a game of tennis instead. To resort to the long ball game hurt him, but he'd run out of ideas and with just a short time remaining on the clock it was their only hope of salvation. Barry didn't understand how it had come to this, as the lads normally played with heart and determination. It never mattered if the opposition were bigger or better, once on the pitch they became a single unit and played to their strengths; this time, however, playing against girls had for some reason turned them into gibbering idiots.

Barry's arm had developed a life of its own, nervously lifting up and down every twenty seconds so that he could look at his watch. Time ebbed away and it was now or never for someone to find the equalising goal. Mike bit his nails as the tension grew and even two undercover cops that pretended to be training on a nearby pitch watched in anticipation of girls defeating boys. The rest of the team congregated around Barry. Some whispered to each other secretively, sharing their worries quietly between friends. Some stood in silence, mechanically chewing gum in awe at the spectacle that unfolded in front of their eyes, while some shouted and jeered sending derisory remarks about the opposite sex each time a girl touched the ball. Yet not one of them, even Mike, would argue against the skill of these girls. What was supposed to be a walk in the park was slowly turning into humiliation and not one of the Indispensables looked capable of changing this fact. A lasting impression was slowly being burnt into the memories of these young boys. They were making the fatal mistake, which happens at all levels of the game - you never underestimate the opposition.

Richard Green was in goal who, apart from getting the ball out of the back of his net, had stopped everything else that had been kicked at him. The ball now in his hands had suddenly become a ticking time bomb and he needed to get rid of it fast. He looked left and right, hoping to launch it into space. His team mates danced around aimlessly, not giving him any chance of a clear throw. 'Bollocks to it,' he said to himself and he launched the ball, under arm, as hard as he could, right up the centre of the pitch in the hope that one of his team mates would run onto it

Terry, who had his back to the ball, didn't see it coming. A defender tried to get to the ball first but Terry was in the way, unaware of his impending importance. Knocking Terry off balance, he fell giving the ball a little nudge with his knee. The ball spun away, heading in the direction of the goal. Every player on both teams, apart from Terry who lay sprawled on the grass clutching his left shin, froze and watched the goalkeeper who, unfortunately, had been sent off balance by the unkind deflection and was now hopelessly out of position. Diving to her left, arm outstretched, she felt the ball brush off her finger tips as it steadily but surely flew into the back of the net.

Terry disappeared under a mountain of bodies, even Dan joined in with the pile on. The relief could be seen on all their faces. It was just the medicine that they needed to revitalise their flagging fortunes. Instantly the girls looked defeated. Elation of their impending victory had been turned upside down and, even though it was now one all, a betting man would have his money on the Indispensables to be victorious.

Barry picked up a bottle of mineral water and drank hard, soothing his sore throat and giving his voice box a rest. Under his breath he thanked God for saving him from possible embarrassment and for giving his unworthy players a second chance. As the ref made his way to the centre spot to resume the match, Dan stood on the side line talking to Mike.

'I knew we'd get one back,' he said with an air of cockiness in his voice.

'It's not over yet and stop bullshitting. A minute ago you were suicidal and ready to take defeat from a team of girls.'

'Well, it's all different now. There'll be no stopping us. They've got no balls for it now. Get it!' Dan shouted as he ran back to his position. Mike let out a wry smile and sat back down to witness the last few minutes.

Barry regained his voice and shouted warnings of how a team that has just scored is vulnerable to a quick counter attack. He need not have worried because the girls were already beaten. A cruel twist of fate had taken their energy and injected it into the boys. Their smoothly shaven legs were now heavy and, with only thirty seconds left on the clock, they had to endure the final indignation of an own goal caused by a mistimed back pass. When the final whistle blew the wind of defeat wiped them off their feet and they sat on the grass watching the boys, their enemy, taking the celebration that should have been theirs. *What two-faced gits we all are*, thought Mike as he congratulated his team mates.

A few minutes later when Barry could finally get his revitalised players under control, both teams lined up opposite each other. The victorious grinned with delight, while the beaten tried to force a dignified smile whilst giving unconvincing handshakes but not one, on either team, dared to make eye contact with their opponents. Barry shook hands with the opposing manager; both smiled and congratulated each other on their teams' performance. Barry was filled with relief, but the girls' manager was filled with anger and disbelief but neither let on to the other. Within five minutes of the final whistle being blown everything had been forgotten. It was as though the game had never taken place. The girls had been beaten and it didn't matter how. For some a win was a win and that's what counts in football, they would say, but for others a bad taste remained in their mouths. Lady luck had gone their way, but they hadn't deserved it and they knew it.

***

Jim Slater ended his call to Inspector Sanderson and put his phone into his pocket. He stared at the celebrations going on in front of him but his mind was on other things. Since the boys had ran amock in the city centre he needed to keep tighter reigns on them for the rest of the tour. Sanderson had deployed a man from the gadget department to meet the Superintendent to issue him with two tracking devices. If the surveillance guys couldn't keep tabs on them then maybe a tracking device could. The only problem now would be how to get the tracking devices onto them without them knowing. He had six hours to think about it before they arrived, but he knew it wasn't going to be easy.

He strolled over to where Mike was warming up. Both acknowledged each other with a smile, then he pulled out his mobile, sat on the grass and rang Sanderson again, but this time it was for inspiration.

Dan had decided to stay away from Barry. He wanted so much to wind him up, but the last time that their eyes met Barry had sent him daggers and he'd replied with a look that had said 'You dirty pervert'. He leaned against a lighting gantry which, when lit, illuminated the main centre pitch. The cold metal made him jump as it touched the wet, sweaty patch on his football top. He lurched forward in surprise, his foot hitting one of the enormous bolts that secured the gantry to the concrete base and fell forward on to his front, landing a few metres away from one of the girl teams, who sat huddled together talking the way girls do. Five girls stared at the untidy figure which lay still, looking towards the sky, trying hard not to make eye contact. Giggling non-stop, four heads turned away, but one didn't; she kept her eyes on Dan, waiting for him to stir.

Dan would later say to Mike that the four ugly, butch lesbians turned away and only the beautiful stunner kept her eyes on him. Mike had seen the other girls and he wouldn't have called any of them ugly, butch or lesbians, but he let Dan tell his story.

Dan rolled over, making eye contact with the little Dutch blonde who still looked in his direction. Butterflies took off in his stomach and fluttered around aimlessly; unknowingly he threw her a smile. He sat up silently, not taking his eyes of her. Knowing that Dan was staring back, she dropped her head and turned slightly, obscuring her eyes from his view. The second match had started but he hadn't noticed. His eyes were fixed in one direction and one direction only.

She looked across at him again, this time looking directly into his eyes. He knew he was fixing his gaze on her but he couldn't help it. Something told him that he had to look at her and he could not but help run his eyes up and down her slender frame. The football shirt that she wore clung tightly to her body, each curve and line emphasised by the red stripe that ran all the way round her upper body. Her red shorts hung perfectly over her unblemished silky-skin thighs, which shone delicately in the natural sunlight.

To Dan it seemed like he had been staring at her for an eternity, but in reality it had only been for a few seconds. His eyes became mesmerised by her deep purple-coloured lips and he focused directly on them as she talked to her friends. Then, her stunning blonde hair took his attention as it lifted from her shoulders and fell back again as the light breeze caressed it. Her eyelashes, as long as spiders legs, teased him every time she blinked and her deep blue eyes looked as inviting as rock pools bathed by the ocean waves, calling to him to dive in. But it was her lips that held him in a trance. Like a magnet drawing everything towards it, Dan's eyes were hypnotised. He had once seen a Goth in Newcastle wearing the same colour lipstick, but God she had been ugly. Confusion reigned in his head as he tried to comprehend why he liked her choice of lipstick colour so much, but the answer never came.

Aware that he was still looking at her, she suddenly ran her tongue along her lips in the sexiest way imaginable. That was it. His concentration had gone out of the window totally. He felt tingles running through his body and his feet had pins and needles. Whatever this girl was doing to him, he had only experienced it once before and that was behind the language lab at school when an ex-girlfriend, Wendy Hall, had allowed him to fondle her boobs. This time it was different, and he didn't know whether to be frightened or excited.

She stood up and for the first time his eyes left her gaze and dropped to her legs. As she walked towards him he was in awe as she glided like a model, putting one foot in front of the other as though walking an imaginary line, and with football boots on as well. Dan was gob smacked. His assortment of pins and needles and butterflies had been replaced by a stomach full of knots, his mouth had become suddenly dry and his head filled with confusion as panic set in. She was so close now and he hadn't got a clue what to say. Normally he was confident with the opposite sex, even overconfident as Mike would say, but if truth be told Dan's contact with girls were few and far between. His life predominantly revolved around male company and it was his vivid imagination that led to countless lies and exaggerations which gave him a reputation of being a ladies' man. Now it was the real thing and he didn't know what to do. He swallowed hard. He was on his own.

'Hi, I'm Sabina,' she said in perfect English, sitting down just a few inches away from him.

'I like your lipstick,' he replied, cursing himself under his breath for making such a poor start to the conversation.

'Thanks. Purple is my favourite colour. You don't think it's too much, do you?'

'No, I like it, makes you look gorgeous.' Where that remark came from he didn't know. He just said it. Sabrina blushed, giggled to herself and Dan dug his fingers into the grass to hide his tension.

'What's your name?' Sabina asked, looking directly into his eyes. He shifted his position on the grass to hide his self-consciousness.

'Dan,' he replied in a whisper.

'Oh, I love the name Daniel, it's one of my favourites.' This time it was Dan's turn to blush. She sensed that she had hit a raw nerve.

'Dan's better though,' she said quickly, restoring the equilibrium. He agreed that Daniel was too soft, but he didn't mind her calling him that. She could call him 'little fluffy bunny' if she wanted to and he wouldn't care.

'My brother studied in England at Leeds University. Are you from Yorkshire?'

'Yorkshire, no way! I'm a Geordie.'

'What's a Geordie?' she asked looking puzzled. Dan had to think quickly and thought that he had better give the easy answer.

'Oh, it's what you are called when you come from

Newcastle.'

'Newcastle! You come from Newcastle? Did you know Bobby Robson? He used to be manager of PSV Eindhoven, where I live.' *Wow*, Dan thought, *fancy her knowing that? Gorgeous and knowledgeable about football. What a woman.*

'No, I didn't know him personally,' replied Dan, 'but he was a great manager for Newcastle and, of course, wherever else he managed as well.' It was a good answer and both smiled at each other. Dan liked this girl a lot and slowly his male chauvinistic views about women and football were being eroded away.

The rest of the team were still riding high on a wave of euphoria from the previous win and were too engrossed with the football to observe Dan and his new female friend. As this was going on, Mike stood in his goal area bored to tears, quickly losing count of how many goals they were winning by. This opposition team weren't a patch on the previous one and the game was so one-sided that it was becoming tedious. Mike looked across at Dan and Sabina sitting talking.

'Well, well, mister smoothy. You're a dark horse aren't you?' Mike said out loud as he leant on the crossbar behind him. 'You're supposed to be watching us play football not watching the wildlife.' Then he dropped his voice and continued muttering to himself. 'But I can't blame you. What you're looking at is a dam sight more interesting than what I'm doing, you lucky sod.'

Dan was proving to be better entertainment than the nine players in front of him. Mike continued looking over, trying in vain to grab Dan's attention, but the two new friends laughed and giggled in their own little world, Dan the Northeast bullshitter and a Dutch beauty. *What a combination*, Mike thought as he momentarily forgot what he was supposed to be doing.

Watching his friend and not the game had made him take his eye off the ball and when it did arrive he didn't see it until it was too late.

He reacted with the speed of an extremely slow slug and the only contact that he had with the ball was to pick it out of his goal. He kicked the goal post in frustration, feeling stupid beyond belief. To make the most basic error in football and in front of all his team mates, not concentrating on the game was despicable. *It was Dan's fault*, he thought to himself, as he threw the ball back to the referee. *If he wasn't talking to that girl I would have been watching the game.* But that was the easy excuse and he had no room for it. 'It was my stupid fault,' he muttered and he started to concentrate on the rest of the match.

'Are you alright, Mike?' Barry said from behind the goal, making Mike jump. 'Forget it, don't worry about it,' Barry continued. 'I would have done the same. Dam right boring for you, this game, isn't it? I'm sorry that I've had to put you through it.'

'Thanks Barry. It's not your fault. I thought that it would be a good idea to play in this competition myself, but I don't think it was the right decision now.'

'Me and you both, son. I thought the same. Do the lads the world of good, but it may end up breaking their spirit. There are some quality female footballers on show here today and even I have been impressed but, as always, wherever we go we find problems.'

'What do you mean?' Mike said, half looking at Barry and half scanning the pitch.

'Next round the team won't play us. Their manager isn't happy about his girls playing us, and with this match being a joke they're asking us to withdraw from the competition. I just don't want to lumber you lads with the possible disappointment of losing to a girls' team. It may scar you all for life. So I think that we'll pull out. But anyway, you concentrate, I'll talk to you all after the match.' Barry walked away and Mike realised that he'd had enough as well. He urged the ref to blow early, but the ref was a woman and she was having none of it.

Dan and Sabina sat, unaware of the turn of events going on around them. Sabina loved to talk and Dan, for a change, was prepared to listen. He was impressed by her knowledge of all things football, especially the English leagues. Her father happened to be the team doctor at PSV and she had been brought up to adore the game. Dan listened to her life and thought how exciting it must be to rub shoulders with so many famous European football stars. However, when it came to his own life story he stuttered and struggled. How could he tell her that his mother had walked out on him and his dad years ago and that his dad was a waste of time? He had to quickly fake a past and it didn't bother him at all to do it.

Sabina put her hand on his leg, making his groin tingle with pleasure and he struggled to suppress a smile that would wreck his deception. She looked sincerely sorry when she heard that his parents had been killed in a car accident and that he had been put into a children's home. The Indispensables were the only family that he really had and Barry was like a father to him. He tried so hard to look sad and he hoped that he was convincing. It must have worked; she told him how sorry she was and said he must come and visit her home one day and she would take him round the PSV ground. Dan accepted the offer and gently put his hand on top of hers. She didn't flinch or attempt to pull it away. Dan was besotted and he was enjoying every minute of it.

How long Mike had been standing there Dan didn't know. Mike had heard what he wanted to hear but, being a true friend, he wasn't going to ruin Dan's moment. There would be time later on when he could chastise him about his lies; for now though, he would break the news gently to Dan on what was happening and would leave him to say his goodbyes alone.

'I hope he's not annoying you, because if he is I'll take him away,' Mike said as he stood over them both. Sabina smiled and looked up at Mike. He could understand why Dan was smitten; she had one of those smiles that could make you go all weak at the knees.

'No, Daniel has been a gentleman,' she said turning her head and looking back at Dan while she said it. Dan swallowed. She had started to melt his heart. He had only known her for twenty minutes but already it felt like he had know her for years. Mike could see infatuation written all over his friend's face and now he had to break the bad news to him and cruelly whisk him away, just when things were getting interesting.

'I know it's a bad time, Daniel, but I need to talk to you,' Mike said leaning over to whisper in Dan s ear.

'Oh, you are fucking joking. I don't believe it.' Dan managed to keep his cool in front of Sabina. Normally he would have gone off on one, but he stayed calm.

'Look, I know how you feel,' Mike said sympathetically, 'she is gorgeous, but the bus will be leaving in half an hour and you better make sure that you are on it.' Mike didn't linger for Dan's reply; he walked off towards the showers, leaving Dan to break up the shortest relationship that he had ever had.

The team had taken the news of the early departure better than Barry had expected. The girls had frightened them and it was best to leave now and forget all about it. The general consensus was that they should put it all behind them and never mention it again because, after all, no one would have to know. Barry, too, was eager to leave; however, before he could he needed to prevent some of his players, or perverts as he called them, from spying on young ladies taking showers. Three limped back to the bus, rubbing non permanent injuries and Barry was pleased to see, for a change, that Dan was not among them.

All were aboard the bus except one. Barry made the move to the door, but Mike stopped him.

'I'll get him Barry, give me five minutes.' Dennis pushed the button and the door of the bus opened with a gentle swishing sound. Mike jumped off and disappeared from view. He knew where to find his friend.

'Come on Dan, we've got to go.'

'Just give me a second, will ya?' Sabina was frantically writing on a piece of paper, using Dan's back as support.

'I've written my address, email and phone number on the back of this flyer,' she said, spinning him round and pushing the paper into his hands. Leaning forward she kissed him on his cheek and whispered into his ear.

'I've got your number safe and sound. Please keep in touch, I would like to see you again.'

'You will, I promise,' Dan said pulling her to him and kissing her on the lips. Mike coughed and pulled at Dan's shirt. The two friends ran back towards the bus and only once did Dan turn around to look at her face, but that was all he needed in order to memorise her image.

As the bus pulled away, Dan looked at the mobile phone that Mike had produced and strategically put it in front of his eyes. He turned to Mike, grinning from ear to ear when he saw the picture of Sabina on Mike's camera phone.

'You are my best friend. I won't forget this,' Dan said putting his hand on Mike's knee and giving him a squeeze. In front of Dan's eyes was the image of him sitting on the grass with Sabina; both were smiling at each other, and Sabina looked gorgeous. As Dan lost himself in the picture, Mike decided to give him the phone to hold.

'Come on mate,' Mike said. 'Chill out, we've got a long way to go. You'll see her again, I'm sure.'

Chapter 17

The street lived and breathed before his eyes. It was the end of the working day and ordinary people with ordinary lives rushed home to their ordinary families. From his sprawling palatial office on the twentieth floor, the well-dressed man who, forty-eight hours earlier, had stood in the shadows of Dubois' office, now stood in front of the ten-foot square pane of glass observing the ordinary people below. As a bird of prey hovers over a corn field watching the scurrying mice below, waiting for the opportune moment to strike, so he too hovered above waiting for his moment.

'Soon you will all belong to me,' he said to himself, leaning forward onto the glass to get the best view of the street directly beneath his feet.

The intercom buzzed on his phone, breaking his concentration. He tapped the glass with his finger and smiled reassuringly at his reflection, which smiled reassuringly back at him. He turned and walked over to his desk and pressed the receiver.

'Yes, what is it?' he said sharply into the machine. His secretary replied in her normal manner, as she was used to her employer's tone of voice.

'I have Mr Dreyfuss for you on your private line. Would you like me to put him through?'

'Thank you, Maryse, put him through. By the way, that's all for today. You can go.'

'Thank you sir, see you tomorrow. Good night.' The line went quiet and he sat back in his executive leather chair which squeaked and moaned through over use. He could hear Dubois's laboured breathing on the other end of the line. *How I hate cigars*, he thought.

'Dubois, I have a problem and I need your help.'

Dubois, alias Dreyfuss, didn't answer but he knew that he had the Belgians attention, so he carried on.

'I have a man who has let me down, Dubois. I trusted him because I knew that if I wanted something done he was the man for the job.'

Dubois ran a nervous finger around his tightening collar. He began to get the feeling that he knew just where the conversation was going.

'But this man, Dubois, has cost me fifty million Euros.' The well dressed man paused for a reaction from Dubois but it never came. 'Believe it or not, Dubois, that I can live with. What is really hurting, though, is the fact that he has given away my identity and you know how important my anonymity is, don't you Dubois?' Once again Dubois said nothing.

'What do you think I should do, Dubois? Tell me please.' Dubois cleared his throat. He hated being talked down to but on this occasion he had no choice.

'I think that if he's been a loyal servant,' said Dubois hesitantly, 'then he needs another chance to redeem himself.'

'Yes, Dubois, exactly. I agree. He has been a loyal servant so make amends he should, but if he fails I will fill his lungs with concrete. Do you think that I'm a reasonable man, Dubois?'

'Yes you are,' Dubois replied, hating each of the three little words as they passed his lips.

'Thank you for calling, Dubois. Your help has been invaluable.' The line went dead once more. The suited man resumed his position at the window and picked up his train of thought from earlier.

Dubois sucked the smoke from his cigar in deep and blew out hard over his nine millimeter Beretta that he held in his right hand.

'Anyone thinking of making *me* eat concrete will meet my friend here,' he said to himself, pointing the gun at the water fountain and pulling the trigger. 'Click' - there was no round in the chamber, as his magazine lay on the table. There would be a bullet for his new found business partner if he ever decided to cross him but, for now, he relaxed. If everything went according to plan they would be making billions of Euros; fifty million will seem insignificant in the scheme of things. Dubois knew that they needed each other. For now, therefore, he would remain subservient to his partner.

Dubois's worries did not completely disappear, however. The unpredictability of the two English boys plagued him. Above all else, he had to get hold of the photo that they had taken before they ran. There would be no way he could dispose of them until this was in his possession. In the wrong hands the photo would mean prison or self exile for him, and there was no way he was going to let that happen. Placing the gun gently onto the table, he picked up his mobile phone and searched for Henri's number.

Henri listened and answered with his customary 'Yes Boss'. Within two hours he would have to explain to Dubois why the English boys had not been snatched and the photo found. He repeated the conversation to Didier who swallowed hard, made the shape of a gun with his own hand and pointed it at his head. Henri nodded - he didn't have to say anything, he knew his partner was right.

Didier pushed the door of the steam room open carefully. If Dubois was going to kill them, he had chosen an excellent place in which to do it. An assassin could sit directly in front of them and they would not see him. Their bodies would be thrown into the nearby canal and their blood washed down the drain. *How simple*, Didier thought, as he walked inside. He was nervous but not afraid. He knew that he would die one day, but death didn't scare him. By working with Dubois he lived with death and dealt death out on regular occasions, so he knew that eventually it would be his turn.

'If it is, make it quick,' he said to himself, stepping into the steam. Henri, on the other hand knew that Dubois needed them as there was no one else to do his dirty work.

'We've done nothing wrong, we won't be killed today,' he adamantly said to himself.

Dubois lay sprawled out on a wooden bench. As he saw his men approaching, he sat up and tightened his towel around his waist, causing his sweaty pot belly to spill over the top. He beckoned his men to him. Nervously Didier sat down next to him. He felt naked wearing just a towel. If only he had his gun. It never normally left his side. He even slept with it under the pillow. He placed his hands on his lap; beads of sweat were already forming on his body and he could feel them running down the side of his face. He waited for Dubois to speak.

Henri, feeling more relaxed, sat on the other side of Dubois. He had known Dubois since he was a delinquent teenager. Dubois had taken him in and taught him that even criminals had to live by the rules of respect. Fight hard, live hard and die hard was Dubois's motto.

'I'm not a happy man,' said Dubois leaning backwards, putting his arms on the bench seat behind him. 'There are two things that I want, Henri, and you're not giving them to me.' Henri bit his lip, afraid to answer. He paused, hoping that Dubois would continue. Dubois did and his lip became free again.

'I want the photograph and I want those boys. I have a reputation to think of. Do you understand?' Both Henri and Didier nodded in unison but still they didn't say a word. Dubois suddenly swung around. 'Meet José!'

Startled, they looked behind them. Beads of sweat shot from their heads, hitting Dubois on his chest; he didn't feel it, however, as it mingled with his own. Up until that moment Henri and Didier believed that Dubois was alone when they entered. Unknown to them a fourth person sat at the rear, totally obscured by the steam. José moved closer and came into view. He couldn't have been more than five feet tall. A chubby man in his fifties, of Spanish descent, heavily tanned and covered with body hair. A three-inch scar ran across his right cheek, from below his eye to just above his top lip. He smiled, showing tobacco-stained teeth.

'This is José, a Spanish Basque friend of mine, an expert with a knife and explosives and the best with a long range rifle that I've ever seen.' With that compliment José smiled even more, showing his full array of dirty brown teeth. Henri nodded in acknowledgement. He had known Dubois for as long as he cared to remember but he had never heard of José before. He knew about the Basques and the region between France and Spain. He knew about war being waged by the Basque Separatists Eta for their region to be recognised as an independent Socialist Basque state, and he even knew about Eta wanting to speak their own language, called Euskara, but he hadn't got a clue why Dubois would want to introduce them to an assassin from a known paramilitary terrorist organisation.

'You two get the photograph,' Dubois pointed at Henri and Didier in turn. 'And José will do the rest.'

'You mean to kill the English boys?' Didier said, immediately regretting saying anything as Dubois glared at him.

'I want those boys alive. I've got plans for them. You two get that photograph and José will put them to sleep for me. That's all.' As Henri stood to leave, Didier was already at the door when Dubois shouted a parting gesture.

'Do not fail me again, gentlemen, otherwise I may have to tell José to put you two asleep permanently.'

They heard his parting shot, but they had heard such a comment many times before. The steam room door swung shut. Didier went to get his beloved gun and Henri stood in the shower, pondering their next move.

***

Jim Slater examined the two devices that he had been sent by Inspector Sanderson and banged his head on the steering wheel in frustration.

'Sunderland! What the hell am I supposed to do with two Sunderland badges?' he shouted to himself, dialing Sanderson again almost immediately.

Normally Sanderson would answer quickly, but this time he let it ring at least eight times. He stared at the phone, unable to answer.

'I know what you're going to say guv,' he said before Jim could get any words out. 'I didn't know that they'd done it until it was too late.' Jim could sense the honesty in his colleague's voice. He knew that the Inspector wouldn't have let it happen if he could have helped it.

'The boys at the lab were under strict instructions to produce something related to Newcastle United, but they couldn't get their hands on anything at such short notice. You know what it's like here - people in London don't know what's going on North of Watford Gap, so if Newcastle was out of the question Sunderland became the next option. They hadn't got a clue. Newcastle was in the North East and so was Sunderland, so what was the problem?'

Jim Slater refrained from shouting. He knew that it wasn't going to help.

'Look Tony,' said Jim in a calm tone of voice, but Sanderson knew him too well. His boss was failing to hide his anger.

'They come from Newcastle, there're both Geordies, they've been brought up following the black and white. If you were to cut their arms off, like a stick of rock, they would probably have Newcastle United written in the middle. How the bloody hell am I supposed to get two of the most hardened fans of Newcastle United in the world to wear Sunderland badges?' Silence was the only answer that the Inspector knew, so Jim continued.

'Tony, I'm not blaming you, but just see it from my point of view. If you come from Newcastle you are a Geordie. If you come from Sunderland you are a Makem - two different areas, two different loyalties. Geordies despise Makems and Makems despise Geordies. We are knackered. These boys will not wear these tracking devises.'

'Look guv, I'll see what I can do, but I can't promise anything.'

'Just get back to the lab and tell them that two boys' lives depend on them, ok?' The Inspector never replied. As the line went dead, Jim Slater sank into his car seat throwing the two devises disguised as Sunderland badges onto the passenger seat.

'Fucking lab rats!' Jim said to himself. 'Need to get out into the real world. Useless bastards.' Jim put his mobile away and picked up the two badges and jiggled them in his hand. The frown on his face slowly turned into a smile as he thought of an idea as to how to get the boys to wear the badges.

'Caring uncle I am, caring uncle I will be,' he said to himself. 'Now I need to find those boys.'

It wasn't too long before he caught sight of the team bus on the auto route heading east. He knew that he wouldn't be missed on board - there'd still be too much tension from the day's events for anyone to notice his absence. Best thing to do would be to follow until the first rest stop then join them there. He'd get someone to pick the car up, but first he needed to call his contacts in Germany to arrange resources and briefings. He'd get Sanderson to thank the Dutch because he wasn't feeling very charitable and, in any case, he may need them again.

***

The atmosphere on the team bus was subdued. There wasn't much chatter and even Barry sat on his own in silence. The tour had been built up with such high expectations but it wasn't living up to them. Barry felt old and tired; he'd taken on the challenge of the tour with gusto but for the first time he was having second thoughts. Boys getting lost, lack of moral fiber from himself in Amsterdam and females in football. He wondered what could seriously happen next. Anger still haunted him for his own moral corruptness in Amsterdam, but at least Daniel had kept his mouth shut, thanks to Mike. He closed his eyes and drifted quickly into a deep sleep, blissfully unaware of the turmoil that young Dan was suffering a few seats behind him.

Dan had his eyes closed but he wasn't sleeping. He just found it easier to relive his time with Sabina with shut eyes. His head was dancing, with different feelings. He thought that he might be in love but he wasn't exactly sure what love was. He had never been surrounded by it. It was something that he saw on the television, not in his own life. His parents, when they were together, only argued and only on very rare occasions did they show any affection to each other. There were never any visible signs of love in their relationship at all which Dan could learn from as he grew up. When his parents' marriage had broken down his dad had fallen deeper in love with the bottle, so Dan was left to learn the important things in life for himself.

Lust and infatuation he dismissed straight away There hadn't been one second of their short time together that he wanted to kiss or touch her, or even look at her body. Being in her company and talking had been enough. For the first time in his life he had found someone that had actually taken his breath away with just their presence. She had given him the best rush that any drug could have done and instantly he had become addicted to it. In his own world, on that bus and in that moment, Dan was going through his own version of cold Turkey. His supply had been withdrawn from him and now his body and mind shouted for it to come back.

He vowed to himself that he would see her again and he vowed that the only drug that he would have in the future would be her and nothing else. Love it must be, he thought and he wanted it to be. It gave him the nicest feeling every time he thought about her. The secret would be his alone. Dan Sharpe had fallen in love with a Dutch girl who he had known for only an hour, but knew more about football than most of his mates and who looked fantastic in a football strip. Smiling to himself, he opened his eyes, pick-pocketed Mike's mobile phone and looked at the picture of Sabina's face.

'I will see you again, I promise,' he whispered to her picture.

Germany, the next stop on the tour, was quickly approaching. Dennis the driver knew his destination.

233

His maps had been studied and the bus refueled. A steady drive became his priority - he'd done so much rushing to destinations that it felt nice to slow down a little. Leaving the last tournament early meant there was plenty of time to get to their next rendezvous. He chuckled to himself. He was having a good time and being paid for it. *Fantastic*, he thought.

Barry opened his eyes with sudden surprise. Looking left and then right, he familiarised himself with his surroundings. He breathed a huge sigh of relief when he realised that he was still on the bus. He had been dreaming and it wasn't one to remember. He had woken up at the part where his dead mother's face had appeared on the body of the woman performing the acts of sex in that Amsterdam club. His mother had looked deep into her son's eyes and scowled a hideous grimace, her eyes burning into his. Waking up had taken the dream away, but the face of his mother had been stamped to the inside of his eyelids and he would be looking at it for a long time to come. Pulling out the itinerary of the tour and the details of the next stop, he flicked through the pages in an effort to take his mind off the dream. It seemed to do the trick but, in reality, it took him away from one worry straight to another.

Gelsenkirken, a large industrial town in the Nord Rhine Westphalia province of Germany, happened to be their next stop. It was twinned with Newcastle Upon Tyne and it had been arranged for the Indispensables to play against a team from the Bundeswher, the German army that was based there. They were to be accommodated in an army camp of a training regiment where they would play against young new recruits. Barry read on. It all seemed so easy this time. Sleep in the camp, play football in the camp - simple, no problems, but then he read further and it gave him the usual sinking feeling in the pit of his stomach. After the

234

match the Indispensables had been invited to a local Bierfest, apparently to give a taste of the local culture and customs. *Local culture and customs*, he thought to himself, *more like fifteen drunken English teenagers to look after. Don't Europeans realise that the majority of British kids had lost respect for anything years ago? What's to say that my boys are any different when given the chance? God help me. Here I go again.*

Throwing the paperwork onto the seat next to him, he closed his eyes once more.

'Dream about something nice, Barry,' he said to himself.

Mike was becoming concerned about Dan's silence. They hadn't spoken for over an hour. Normally it was all that Mike could do to shut him up, but he knew that the last few days must be taking their toll. He himself felt drained, so Dan must be too. Dan had been asleep but most of the time he only pretended. Mike hadn't said anything, but from the corner of his eyes he had noticed his mobile phone illuminating Dan's hand. Dan had tried to activate it without Mike knowing but, unknown to him, he'd failed. Mike let it go as he was enjoying the peace and quiet too much to give Dan an excuse to open his mouth again.

Mike started reflecting on the tour so far. A tour that had, as yet, failed to come up to his expectations. It made phoning home a nightmare and he hated himself for exaggerating how good it was going.

'God, if they only knew,' he said to himself. 'Dad would have kittens.'

Gangsters, drugs, live sex shows and, to cap it all, playing against girls and nearly getting beaten. It was going to be a long time before any of the last few days could be repeated to his parents, if ever. Thinking about home, he decided that he needed to break Dan's silence to take his mind off it. Luckily he didn't have to try too hard as he noticed that the bus was pulling into a rest area.

'Good timing,' he said, nudging his friend in the shoulder.

Barry, awake again, shouted his usual ten minutes and, like rats leaving a sinking ship, the bus emptied quickly. Mike and Dan waited, then followed the hoard towards the waiting burger bar, amusement arcade and sweet shop.

'How's it going, pal?' Mike said, putting his hand on Dan's shoulder. 'You've been a bit quiet, it's not like you.'

'Have you ever been in love, Mike?' Dan said out of the blue, making Mike raise his eyebrows and stop in his tracks.

'Why do you want to know?'

'Well, it's that girl back in Amsterdam.'

'What, the one in the sex show? Don't tell me you've fallen for a porn star?' Mike knew what Dan was on about but he thought that he would string him along for a while.

'No, you knob head, I'm not talking about *her*.'

'Oh, I know. You mean the prostitute in the window!' Mike said giggling.

'Forget it. I'm trying to be serious and all you can do is take the piss.' Dan started to walk away with a serious frown on his face. Mike caught up with him.

'Dan, I'm sorry. I know who you're talking about. I just couldn't help myself.' Dan turned and looked into Mike's eyes and Mike knew that it was going to be a serious conversation.

'Go on Mike, tell me. Have you ever been in love?' They both settled down on a bench on the edge of the car park. Dan looked at Mike with the expectation of a child waiting for a story to be read. Mike felt uneasy, not because of the question but the way that he would

236

answer it.

'I have been in love and I didn't realise it until it was over.'

'How did you feel?'

'Look, if you want me to tell you then shut up and let me tell you, ok?' Dan apologised and pulled an imaginary zip across his mouth. Mike needed to find a starting point. He looked up into the sky and paused, and then it came to him.

'I'm not telling you her name because you probably know her, but that doesn't matter. It's not about the person, it's about the feelings you get and I got them really bad. I couldn't sleep, I couldn't concentrate, and I didn't want to do my usual things. If we were together my actions were because of her and my words were because of her. If we were apart my mind and thoughts were only about her. Everything else, even football, got pushed aside. I was consumed totally, but it wasn't about kissing or feeling or touching, it was just about being near to her. I lost control of my own body and mind and she, without knowing, had gained total control over me. If she'd told me to cut a finger off I would have done it.'

Dan listened, recognising some of the symptoms in himself. Mike wasn't looking at him anymore - his gaze was elsewhere, and he was seeing and reliving everything that he was relating.

'But I didn't know that it was love until she wasn't mine anymore. It was the wanting of all the things that I've just said that hurt the most, because I couldn't have them anymore. You find yourself doing stupid things to regain them and you hurt yourself more. It's then I realised that it must have been love but I was too immature to know, but you live and learn. It taught me a few lessons, the most important being to concentrate on my football and not on girls.' Mike sat back and took a deep breath. 'Has that answered your question? Do me a favour, don't ask me things like that again, ok?'

Dan had gone red. He'd embarrassed Mike by asking him a personal question and Mike had answered better than Dan had expected.

'Thanks Mike. You know why I asked, didn't you?'

'Yes I do. If it's that girl Sabina then I can understand how you are feeling. It doesn't take long to know if you feel for someone and in your case it was an hour, but there's nothing you can do about it now. Keep your memories private and pull them out when you want but only to cheer you up, not to depress you. When the tour's over, if you still feel the same way then do something about it. But until then, let's enjoy the rest of the tour and concentrate on what we are here for and that's the football.' Mike had amazed himself with such a sensible reply, and even felt better for reliving his past for his friend.

'Thanks mate, I couldn't ask for a better friend than you. I do appreciate all you say.'

'Let's forget it now and enjoy the rest of the tour.' Mike got up and walked back towards the bus. Dan sat for a moment, watching Mike walk away. He smiled to himself, slapped his right cheek with his right hand then ran after his best friend.

Chapter 18

As Mike walked back to his seat feeling proud of the advice that he'd given Dan, a hand reached out and grabbed his arm. He looked across and was just about to tell the culprit to fuck off, but stopped himself in time when he saw that it was his uncle Jim.

'I thought you'd missed the bus.'

'No! No! I've been asleep. It's bloody tiring watching you lot prance around in a football kit, and anyway I need to talk to you.' Changing the subject quickly, Jim leaned forward to whisper so as not to let anyone else hear. 'Since we had our last chat I've spoken to that nice Inspector back in England. You know the one?' Mike nodded and moved even closer to his uncle until his right ear was centimetres from his uncle's mouth. 'He's sent something for you.'

'What do you mean, he's sent something for me?' Mike whispered sternly back into his uncle's ear, while at the same time steadying himself as the bus pulled away from the services. Jim fumbled in his coat pocket for the badges. Mike looked on, intrigued as to what the Inspector had sent him. Jim held out his hand; the badges were tightly tucked into his grip.

'Now, before you comment, please let me explain,' Jim said as he unfurled his hand. 'These are for you.'

'Sorry, I don't understand,' Mike said, backing away from the badges as though any second now they would jump at his throat and start sucking his blood. 'What would I want with a Sunderland badge, apart from chucking it in the nearest bin? 'What would the Inspector think I'd want with a Sunderland badge? You've got me confused here.'

Sliding back towards the window, Jim made room

for Mike to sit down. It gave him the time he needed to gather his thoughts. He found it hard to be the caring uncle. It was much easier being the boss, telling his subordinates what to do. He'd expected this kind of answer from Mike, as he knew that anything to do with Sunderland was a non starter. However, he needed for them to accept the badges so he pressed on with his plan.

'These badges are special.'

'Special my arse,' Mike said pushing them away.

'Are you going to let me finish, or what?' Mike apologised and relaxed, but a sarcastic grin remained on his face.

'Both these badges are tracking devices. Each has a small transmitter inside which, with the right receiver and within a three kilometre radius, will pinpoint the wearer's position to a metre.' Mikes grin had disappeared, only to be replaced with a solemn look of dissatisfaction.

'Why do Dan and I need tracking devices? I thought Dubois would be behind bars by now.'

'The Inspector said that it was better to be safe than sorry because Dubois is still at large and...' Mike threw his uncle a stair that made him stop in his tracks.

'That's it then. We'll have to go home.' Mike got up to leave, but Jim quickly reached forward and pulled Mike forcefully back into the seat. Mike grabbed his uncle's hand to prise it free, but he felt immense strength in his uncle's grip so once more he sat down.

'You can't go home Mike, what about the tour?' Jim said in a calm and gentle voice, releasing his grip. He knew that if the boys went home he would lose his chance of catching his quarry. Dubois would never enter the UK; instead, his money would pay for a hit, leaving himself untraceable. Jim Slater needed his nephew in Europe.

'Bollocks to the tour,' Mike said raising his eyebrows and staring at his uncle. 'The tour's not exactly been a phenomenal success so far, so I don't think that I would be missing much. I'll just have to go home and tell my folks the truth. I'm sure they'll understand.' Jim had heard enough. It was time to call his nephew's bluff.

'Yeah, I suppose you're right,' Jim said sincerely. 'The police are just overreacting as usual. You go home back to your folks and hope that Dubois doesn't find you there. Yeah, I think that's for the best.' Jim waited for a reply from Mike, hoping that the comment about his parents had hit a nerve. It had.

'Well, it must be bloody serious if the police want Dan and me to wear tracking devices,' Mike replied on the defensive, raising his voice. Then suddenly, when he realised that others could be listening, he toned it down. 'But tell me this, who is going to be tracking the tracking devices?' Mike asked sarcastically. 'A team of undercover cops chasing us around Europe. This is crap!'

Jim was beginning to lose patience with his nephew. If he didn't think quickly then the whole operation would fall apart.

'Look, let's not blow this out of proportion. You asked me if I could help and that's what I'm doing. From what I've been told, you and Dan got yourselves into some heavy shit in Belgium and it's not going to just blow away.' Mike listened, but Jim was unsure if he had made any headway in persuading his nephew to stay on the tour.

'Look, take these badges and stick them in your pockets,' he continued. 'Paint the bloody things black and white if you want to, but stay on the tour.' Jim stopped suddenly. Mike had turned pale and when he did speak he struggled to get his words out. Jim could hear alarm bells ringing in his head and he could sense the emotion in Mike's voice. He shut up. It was his turn to listen.

'I knew we'd got ourselves into trouble, but I never realised just how much until you showed me those badges. Everything that we've gone through seems so surreal. It's as though we're watching a TV show. Even in Amsterdam with Dubois's men following us, none of it seemed real to me, the red light district especially. The tour and playing football were the only two things that mattered, but now I understand. The tour isn't important anymore.' Jim knew that Mike was confused; he needed to lay it on thick to pluck at Mike's heart strings.

'Mike, I know that you find it difficult to understand, but you don't realise how vulnerable you are. Dubois and his men are evil. They have spent years spreading the filth of drugs around Europe, destroying lives and families. Dubois is a parasite feeding on the innocence, naivety and stupidity of young and old drug takers alike. Somebody has to stop him and Inspector Sanderson and his team are very close, but they can't do it alone. They need your help.' Mike listened. His stomach had gone tight and he felt an unnatural warm rush of blood tearing through his veins.

'But I didn't ask for all this to happen. I was just doing a favour for a friend.'

'I wouldn't expect anything else from my brother's boy. You haven't been brought up to turn your back on your friends. You just have to accept that in life things happen, sometimes good and sometimes bad. It's a shitty world out there, you have to take the rough with the smooth. Wouldn't it be boring if everything was nice, eh?' Mike didn't answer and Jim still wasn't sure whether he was winning Mike over or not.

'Now, listen close and listen good.' It was the

Superintendent talking now, rather than uncle Jim. 'Dubois is a wild animal and he's wounded. You and Dan have hurt him really bad. He's lost a lot of drugs, not to mention money, but the problem is that when a wild animal is hurt it becomes even more dangerous. You don't want to go home and take all of this crap back to your parents, possibly putting them in danger, do you?'

'No, but...'

'There are no buts. Stay on the tour, keep these badges with you at all times and understand that if anything happens a helping hand won't be too far away.'

Mike sank further back into the firm comfort of his seat. He was so confused as to what to do for the best, but he could also feel anger rising up inside him. He suddenly realised that he and Dan were being used as bait to catch Dubois and he didn't want to be part of it. Jim, on the other hand, felt as though he had won his nephew over and, for the first time in their conversation, Jim began to feel comfortable again until he heard the fatal word 'bait' spring out of Mike's mouth.

'What did you say?' Jim snapped back.

'Bait, that's what I said, fucking bait. Dan and I are the bait to catch this scum bag, aren't we? Go on, tell me it's not true. I bet you knew about it all along, didn't you?' Mike's eyes bored deep into his uncle's, but it had no effect on him. Hardened criminals had tried to unsettle the Superintendent in the past and failed, so there was no way that his seventeen year-old nephew would succeed. Jim was becoming frustrated with his nephew's attitude. It was time to counter attack.

'You need to grow up fast and realise that you are out of your depth and out of choices,' said Jim angrily.

'You were caught in a truck with fifty million Euros worth of drugs and you wonder why the police let you walk free? Get real, boy. If they didn't have a use for you then you'd be sharing a prison cell by now where some six foot seven muscle man would be using your arse as a pincushion. How would you explain all of that to your parents? You got yourself into this mess so you need to get yourself out, and if that means taking a risk or two and putting yourself in the firing line, well, that's what you've got to do.'

Mike didn't answer. He wriggled in his seat, suddenly feeling uncomfortable. Jim watched and waited for a reply but it never came. Mike picked up the two badges, got up and walked to where Dan sat. Dan smiled at him as he sat down, but Mike failed to return the gesture.

'Put your hand out,' Mike said to Dan sternly. Dan thought that Mike was playing a game and refused. It was when Mike grabbed his hand that Dan realised he was being serious. With his hand open, Mike laid one of the Sunderland badges onto Dan's palm.

'Get that shit off me!' Dan shouted, throwing the badge onto the seat. Mike, expressionless, picked it up and held it in front of Dan's eyes. In a quiet whisper Mike relayed the conversation that he had just had with his uncle.

'Well, I can't say that I am surprised,' replied Dan which was not the reply that Mike would have expected.

'What do you mean, you're not surprised?' said Mike, throwing the badge in Dan's lap.

'After Amsterdam when Dubois's goons caught up with us, it got me thinking.'

'Oh yeah, and when were you going to tell me?'

'I was, honest, but with all this Sabina stuff I forgot to talk to you about it.'

'Fucking hell, Dan, you really do my fucking head in sometimes. The shit you've got me into. And now we're fucking bait for the police. I'm this far away from going home, you know that?' Mike held his fingers up to Dan's face, showing him the smallest of gaps between his thumb and forefinger.

'Sorry Mike. If I could turn the clock back I would. I am sorry.' Dan looked about as sincere as he could, but Mike wasn't looking. Ignoring his friend, Mike left his seat again and made his way down to Barry, who was sitting in the seat directly behind Dennis the driver.

'Barry, can I talk to you?' Barry looked up from a magazine that he had just bought at the previous stop. He'd been anticipating this moment and he hoped he was ready for the grilling that he was going to get over the club in Amsterdam.

'Look Mike, if it's about the other night in that club I can explain.'

'No, it's got nothing to do with that. What you do in your own time is none of my business. Oh, and don't worry, Dan's lips are sealed.' Barry breathed a sigh of relief and gestured for Mike to sit down next to him.

'I'm thinking of going home, Barry. I've had enough of this whole tour. It's just not what I expected and my own stupidity has led me to this decision.'

'If it's because of this drug dealer that you and Dan had a run in with, then I'm surprised that you have held out so long.' Mike looked at Barry in shock. How did he know about Dubois?

'You didn't think that I knew, did you? Your uncle Jim told me he thought that it was something that I needed to know, and of course in that club I saw it first hand with that man chasing you.' Mike put his hands over his face and rubbed vigorously until his cheeks shone like rosy red apples. He was finding it hard to comprehend all that was being said to him as he had never expected Barry to know anything.

'Mike, if you want to go home I won't stop you. This tour has been a nightmare from the beginning and I would be lying if I said that I hadn't thought of going home too, but I'm still here and no doubt I'll see it through to the end.'

'I've really fucked it up for myself Barry, you know that?' Mike said, holding his head in his hands. Barry put his hand on Mike's head. Mike felt comfort in his touch and he lifted his head to look Barry in the eyes.

'Look, son,' continued Barry, 'you can't run away or hide from problems. They're always there until you deal with them. Some people spend their whole lives running and burying their heads in the sand, hoping their problems will go away, but they never do. Their lives become ruined and they end up bitter and twisted. You and Dan have to deal with this particular problem head on. I don't know the nitty gritty of it all and I don't want to know, but from what I have heard it's going to be difficult and dangerous for you. I don't like the idea either because I've the rest of the team to look after, but we have to make a stand sometimes and do what we feel is the right thing to do.'

Mike put his hand on Barry's shoulder and smiled Barry smiled back, nodding his head slowly but steadily. Mike had taken comfort from Barry's words and he realised that going home wasn't an option, but the tour had still lost its appeal. How was he supposed to motivate himself to play competitive football when he knew that one of the biggest drug dealers in Europe was after him? Barry's kind words had helped but had gone nowhere to solving the problem. Barry could see the despair written on his young goalkeeper's face, so the time had arrived for him to share a little secret with him.

'Mike, can I share a secret with you?' Mike looked

up and Barry gestured for him to come closer so that he could talk quietly into his ear.

'You are a wonderful goalkeeper with natural ability, excellent fitness, perfect positioning and the most fantastic mind for reading the game, but if you go home now you may never again get the chance to show your talents off.' Mike felt embarrassed with such compliments, but he let Barry continue.

'You know that the final game for us is in Paris?' Mike nodded in agreement. 'Well, what I need to tell you is that this game will not be any ordinary game, but will be watched by the chief scouts for Barcelona, Paris St German, Manchester United and our very own beloved Newcastle United.'

'You're kidding me! Why would such scouts want to watch the Indispensables play?'

'Because I asked them, that's why. All four are in Paris on a conference, and believe it or not two of them are old friends of mine.'

Mike couldn't believe what he was hearing. Barry, their own manager, moved in the same circles as these scouts from such huge clubs! He knew from this moment he would never utter a bad word in Barry's direction again.

'I organised the final game in Paris. The others were arranged by the Chairman - that's why they have left a lot to be desired. All of these other matches are all just gap fillers to get you all used to the European style of football. You understand, Mike, this is your chance to show how good you are. Your chance to play at the very highest level and reach the dizzy heights that your father let slip through his fingers.' Mike looked at Barry in surprise.

'I know your father well and I was there the night he injured himself. I saw a man's heart break in an instant and a lifetime of dreams disintegrate. You have that

247

chance of your own now and you can't let it get away from you. I have primed the scouts to look at you and Daniel. That's the reason I paid for Daniel to be on the tour. You two are talented and it is for you two that we are here now. This other stuff that has happened is unfortunate, but just concentrate on what you are here for and the police will concentrate on what they have to do. Ok?'

Mike was dumbfounded. His mouth was dry and his eyed glazed with emotion. A great pressure rested on his shoulders, but they were broad enough to take it. He had never heard Barry talk like this before and never in his wildest dreams could he have realised that all this was for him and Dan. What a day this was turning out to be.

'Now,' Barry said, breaking Mike's concentration. 'This was for your ears only. I know that I can rely on you to keep it a secret, can't I Mike?'

'Yes, of course I will. Mum's the word.'

'Now, go and get some rest. We will be in Gelsenkirken soon.'

'Thanks Barry. I won't forget what you're doing for me.'

'Go on, get some rest,' said Barry, dismissing Mike with a wave.

Mike walked back to his seat, but couldn't help but look across at his uncle who had caught his gaze.

'Everything alright, Mike? I saw you talking to Barry.'

'Don't worry,' Mike said, leaning over the seat in front of his uncle. 'I'm staying on the tour, so you can let your police buddies know. But make sure they are close by because I value my life too much, ok?' The things said earlier had all been taken on board by all parties, and when Mike sat down next to Dan he felt a whole lot better.

Dan turned towards Mike, grinning from ear to ear. Mike couldn't help but notice the Sunderland badge pinned to the zipper of his tracksuit top. The red stripes had been crudely penned out with black ink and, from a distance, it could probably be mistaken for the Newcastle badge.

'This is just for you. Now I'm going to take it off and stick it in my pocket, never to be seen again.'

'Thanks mate,' replied Mike. 'You know I don't like what we've got to do, but Dubois and his goons need to be taken out or we'll have them chasing us forever.'

'I know, it scares the shit out of me and I'm sorry that I got you involved. I'll make it up to you one day, I promise.'

'Look, what's done is done. We'll get through it, mark my words. Now, get that badge off or I'll be calling you a Makem.' Dan took is badge off, pretended to spit on it then put it in his pocket. Mike smiled and chuckled quietly. Then, without prompting, he did the very same thing. Together again and with high spirits returning, albeit aware of the dangerous times ahead, they laughed together as the bus approached the next leg of their tour.

***

As the stolen Audi motorcar headed towards the German border, Henri shivered in the cool night air. The stench of cigarette smoke which lingered on José's breath had been too much to bear and both Didier and Henri wound their front windows down to take some fresh air. Since leaving Dubois, José had tagged along. He wasn't much of a talker, which pleased his two colleagues; instead, he chain-smoked. His clothes reeked of it. His fingers were stained a disgusting dirty brown. He smoked constantly, even while eating.

Henri knew Didier had bad habits, but never to the extent of this Basque. The journey so far had been spent getting windswept from the gale that blew in through the open windows as the car travelled at nearly one hundred and fifty kilometres an hour. Slowly, though, the air in the car was becoming cleaner as José slept on the back seat. Didier and Henri counted their blessings and hoped that he would sleep the whole journey, but it wouldn't have surprised them if he unconsciously lit another one and puffed away at it as he slept.

'We won't be able to get to them in that military camp,' Didier said, winding up his window until only a slight gap remained.

'Yeah, I know,' replied Henri, 'but don't worry. We'll find our time and when we do we better succeed, otherwise Dubois will have our nuts served to us on a plate.' Didier cherished his anatomy and no way would he be dining on his own genitals.

The snoring grew louder in the back, so Henri flicked the radio on to drown out the noise but it didn't really work. The piercing shriek of vibrating tonsils masked everything on the radio. The journey was slowly becoming unbearable. From day one, every day had got progressively worse until now even two hardened criminals like Henri and Didier were slowly losing their will to live. The quicker they found this photo and handed the boys over to Dubois, the quicker they could get rid of José and the better they would feel.

José grunted and Henri turned and punched him in his chubby thigh. He didn't even stir. Henri shook his head and turned the radio up a little more. A song called 'Highway to Hell' played and Didier thought how apt it was. A service station was coming up and

Didier wanted to take a leak, but Henri stopped him from taking the exit. He didn't want José woken. There was enough fuel in the tank to get them to where they wanted to go, so on they went, slowly catching up with their targets.

The unmarked police car kept its distance but it needn't have bothered. Henri and Didier paid no attention to anything thanks to José in the back. Instead, they just watched the road signs, counting down the distance when they could get rid of this stinking hit man.

Chapter 19

A lone German soldier with an automatic weapon slung over his shoulder greeted the bus with a bored smile. Standing to the rear of an enormous steel gate, he waved a nonchalant arm to his gate house and the gate began to roll open. Interested faces pressed against the glass and watched as the heavy barrier moved, at a snail's pace, toward its final resting place. Listening to the metal on metal screeching on an ungreased runner, faces winced and twisted in agony as their ear drums were slowly tortured. From the splendour and character of Amsterdam with its merchant houses and picturesque canals, the Indispensables were met with the uninteresting and downright depressing sight of Camp Steiner of Ninety-nine Battalion Mechanised Infantry.

Natural daylight had long since been cloaked in darkness, and was now to be replaced with fluorescent street lighting. The small glimmer of excitement that each boy had felt at being in a foreign land began to ebb away at a remarkably fast pace. For Barry, if this was to be another catastrophe then it would probably be better to turn the bus around now before going any further, but he wasn't going to get the chance.

When the gate had finished its awful welcoming song and come to rest fully open, the lone soldier approached Dennis's window. Dennis, holding out a piece of paper that Barry had seconds before given to him, waved it in front of the soldier's face. Taking it, he turned and walked back towards his gate house disappearing from view. Dan stood up on his seat, eager to get going, but even more impatient to empty his bladder. The lack of urgency shown by the soldier on the gate and the lengthy period that he had been absent began to test everybody's patience.

'Fuck me!' Dan shouted, gaining everyone's attention. 'No wonder they lost two World Wars and a World Cup.' Laughter from Dan's comment made Barry shoot up from his seat and glare in the direction of Dan. Mike was well aware of the poor timing of Dan's comment, so he pulled him down into his seat out of view of Barry's angry eyes.

'I don't want any further comments about the war or the World Cup,' shouted Barry. 'That goes for everyone. Do you hear me, Daniel?' All eyes searched for Dan's acknowledgement but he never showed his face. Mike had pinned Dan's head under his arm and wasn't willing to let him go. Dan was going to behave himself this time. Mike was full of optimism for the rest of the tour and wasn't going to let his friend spoil it before they'd even got inside. Mike relaxed his grip and Dan surfaced, red faced and grinning.

'What you smiling at?' Mike said, pushing Dan back into his seat.

'I'm glad you did that. I thought that Barry was going to come up here and drop the nut on me or something.'

'I wouldn't have stopped him if he did. Sometimes you need to think before you open that mouth of yours. Anyway, shut up! Somebody is coming.' Everyone looked on as another German soldier appeared, this time carrying no weapon but walking with an air of superiority and urgency. He made his way over towards the bus and Barry descended the steps to meet him.

Major Wilhelm Koch, a career soldier of nearly thirty years and a lifelong football fanatic, shook Barry's hand vigorously.

'Welcome, welcome please come in,' the Major said in perfect English but with the heavy German accent on each word. Barry, for a moment, marvelled at the square chiselled shape of the German officer's chin and there was no doubt that this man was German born. The Major, beckoning the bus to enter, stood to one side as Dennis guided it into a military lorry parking bay opposite the gatehouse. Barry asked him to wait for a moment as he needed to educate his own troops on the Major's name, as loose tongues could cause a lot of damage.

Leaving the Major to supervise the closing of the gate, Barry climbed back aboard. The windows and bodywork of the bus gave a certain amount of sound insulation but it was nowhere sufficient to stop the laughter escaping. Barry listened, straight-faced, as each comment increased in laughter and volume. Dan, as normal, couldn't help himself and it was his voice that rose above everyone else's.

'He's called Major Cock, Willie Cock! You're taking the piss, Barry,' heckled Dan. Barry wasn't amused.

'His parents must have hated him as a child to give him the name of Willie Cock and now he's grown up to be a right major cock. I bet he's got a brother called Ivor Cock, get it? I've a cock.' Mike smiled to himself but he refrained from siding with the rabble. The last roar of laughter had got Dan the second angry stare, in ten minutes, from Barry and this time Mike decided against taking away Dan's liberty. He'd dug himself a hole all by himself and Mike didn't want to fall into it. Eventually Barry was able to address everyone but he didn't say much. He didn't have to - the team understood perfectly.

'If everyone is finished and got this childish nonsense out of their systems then remember this. Any piss taking or rudeness to our kind host will lead to the end of playing football on this tour. That's all that I'm

254

going to say. Now, get your stuff together and get off.'
A low murmur emanated throughout the bus, but Barry
felt confident that his warning had hit home. There
would be only one on board that was likely to cause
embarrassment so at the earliest possible opportunity he
would have to make his presence felt, but for now they
needed to settle into their new surroundings.

The team congregated in front of the whitewashed
façade of the military gate house. Barry introduced the
Major, who stood to attention and nodded his head in
true German style. A few sniggers managed to get
through to the front but Barry's stern face made sure
that they died before reaching the Major. Mike held his
finger up to his lips at the same time, grabbing Dan's
attention. Dan just smiled at him and then grimaced,
twisting his body this way and that. He held his hands
to his groin and mimicked that he needed a piss. Mike
grinned back at him mischievously wanting to poke
him in the bladder region, but even he couldn't be so
cruel.

After a quick introduction by the Major, which luck
would have it was snigger free, and a welcome to his
camp the visitors were led deeper into the world of the
Germany military. The road on which they walked
became overshadowed with four-storey barrack blocks
that stood on either side of the street imposing and
intimidating as they walked past. Lights from tall
square windows flooded out onto the pavement and
now and then faces would appear to look at the new
arrivals, but within seconds disappear. Different music
could be heard sporadically but it died as sudden as it
arrived with the passing of each block. If the
Indispensables had any cheerfulness left inside them,
by the time they had reached the end of the street and
come to a halt in front of, unlucky for some, block
thirteen, it had all but disappeared. Mike's confidence

remained, but Dan's pessimism was so great that it had even taken away some pressure from his bladder.

After climbing ninety-six steps to the top of Stalag 13, the Major produced a large key and opened a heavy metal door to the attic of the block. One fluorescent light after another illuminated a section of the large attic at a time until the whole roof area was lit. No windows could be seen whatsoever, just a door that led in and a door at the other end of the enormous roof space. Military beds with military mattresses and military pillows greeted the team. Barry enjoyed the look on his boys' faces. They were going to have to rough it for a change and it was apparent that it disturbed some of the mommy's boys among them.

Barry quickly organised them before dissent could be heard. Each was allocated a bed, two white sheets as crisp as a sheet of brown wrapping paper, two blankets as abrasive as the coarsest of sand paper and a pillow that had more feathers on the outside than inside. A small shower room with four showers and the same amount of toilets lay behind the other door. Before the Major left with Barry and the other adults for more luxurious accommodation, he announced that in thirty minutes someone would show them to the canteen for their evening meal.

Dan wasn't in the mood for back chat as he sprinted to the toilet, but he still managed to stick his fingers up as he went. None of the management saw anything as they were too busy enjoying the misery the accommod-ation was causing the team. Mike put his kit under his bed, threw the sheets and blankets loosely over the top and lay down to watch and listen to his disgruntled team mates. The majority weren't bothered at all with the accommodation - it would be quite a good laugh, all bunking down together, and the initial shock disappeared quickly. In any case, it was better than being stuck on the bus and, if truth be known, fatigue had set in a long time ago. With empty stomachs calling to be filled, some were rather glad to be there. Others called it a bag of shite and poor little Terry Grainger even had the makings of tears in his eyes.

Dan came out of the toilet looking somewhat relieved at being at least a pint of liquid lighter. He looked to where Mike lay sprawled on his bed.

'You ought to see the bog role, it's like John Wayne paper,' Dan shouted across the room. Mike looked confused.

'What the hell are you going on about?'

'It's that tracing paper stuff. My old man calls it John Wayne paper. Hard as nails and takes no shit.'

'Well, you better not have a shit then, or find something else to wipe your arse with,' replied Mike. Dan ignored him. Little Terry Grainger had taken the bed next to Mike, and Dan didn't find it amusing to be sleeping at the other end of the room away from his best mate. He picked up Terry's kit and threw it onto the floor.

'You have one of those beds up that end, I'm sleeping here.' Terry eyes were still full of tears and he was too upset to argue. With tears running down his face, he gave Dan a look of hatred, picked up his bag and shuffled up to the other end of the attic.

'You're always nasty to Terry, but never big Floyd. Is it something to do with Terry's size?' Mike enquired sarcastically.

'Terry's just a nob and he needs to know his place, and that's over there not here. His size doesn't come into it.' Mike nodded. He knew he had hit a nerve because there was no way Dan would treat some of the other team members the same way; if he did he'd probably get a smack. Chucking his bag onto his bed, Dan lay down using it as a pillow.

'What do you think of this place then?' Dan said, rolling onto his side to face Mike.

'It's alright. It's somewhere to sleep and, anyway, it keeps Dubois and his men off our backs for a while, so I'm happy.' Dan agreed, he hadn't thought of it that way. He was always too preoccupied with taking the piss and playing practical jokes that most of the time he forgot what was important.

Both friends lay back and were staring at the ceiling when the meal guide entered. It was the same soldier that had let the bus into the camp. His bored facial expression remained.

'Please follow.' He shouted twice before turning and heading off towards the stairs. The canteen wasn't very far away. It was situated in another block just like the one they were sleeping in, but this one smelt better. Queuing at the hot plate, a large tray of fries arrived which got a warm welcome from everybody The next tray contained items that Dan could only describe to Mike as steaming little cow pats. After an exchange of horrendous German and Geordie English it emerged that these were called 'Frikadellers'. Mike came to the conclusion that it was a kind of Burger or flat meatball. He wasn't going to go into the ingredients with Dan as trying to translate was too hard, but it appeared to consist of some sort of minced meat. If Dan didn't want it then there were plenty of fries on the tray. Mike took two; they smelt good so no doubt they would taste good, at least he hoped so.

Dan as predicted filled his plate with fries but, after stealing a piece of Mike's Frikadeller, he wormed his way back to the hot plate and helped himself to three of his own. Apple Strudel took his fancy next and after demolishing two, still hungry he decided to take a piece back to the attic or dorm as everyone was calling it, but the pastry split in his pocket and the flimsy napkin didn't hold the hot content. Dan had to drop his trousers in full view of everyone to extract the scalding apple that, by now, had left a large red mark on his thigh. Swearing with every step, Dan hobbled back to the dorm. However, his embarrassment hadn't been caused by the burn - it was the exposing of his love heart boxer shorts to the rest of the team that caused him more annoyance. Mike's sympathy was short-lived and, anyway, Dan had regressed into a mood so he left him to stew and take the humiliation all on his own.

***

Jim Slater needed a good night's sleep. Knowing where the boys were helped him to organise his contacts in Germany and for the first time in the last couple of days was able to get some decent food into his stomach. He and his two officers had booked into a small guest house on the advice given by the Major; it was situated conveniently across the road from the camp. With a small Imbiss next door, the German equivalent to a fast food cafe, there wasn't far to go for some decent food but, more importantly, with their receiver picking up a strong signal for the boys, he could relax as well.

It wasn't long though before Jim noticed a Black Audi with Dutch number plates cruise slowly past the entrance to the camp and stopped further down the road, turning off its headlights. Three dark figures could be seen but it was too far away to get any description. Just then, the bell attached to the entrance door of the Imbiss jingled and a tall man wearing a black leather jacket entered. On seeing Jim, he grinned and walked over to the table.

Hans Reidel was in his late forties but looked younger. He had spent his whole career in the German police force, the Bundespolizei, but was now working for the German equivalent to the American FBI, the Bundeskriminalamt, dealing with organised crime which gave him jurisdiction over the local forces. Never married but always with an eye for the ladies, he had come to know Jim when a joint drug smuggling operation between Interpol and the Polizei didn't go to plan. Hans had become weaponless and separated from his colleagues. Jim had come to his rescue before two drug heavies could spoil his good looks with a baseball bat. Even though it had been four years since they had last seen each other, Hans had remained thankful for Jim's intervention and a long distance friendship had formed between them.

Jim stood and held out his hand. Taking it, Hans pulled Jim towards him and patted him on the back as brother would greet brother.

'You look old Jim! Life still being unkind to you?' Hans said, patting him once more on the back and speaking English with a heavy German twang.

'Oh, it's nice to see you too Hans,' Jim replied offering him a chair. 'You still look as good as ever, though. Still womanising like it's going out of fashion?'

'Keeps me fit - you ought to try it.'

Both men laughed and then it was down to business. Firstly, Jim pointed out the Audi and explained who two of the occupants might be, the third being unknown, but both men agreed Dubois would not be the third. Hans knew their names well from intelligence reports. Making a quick phone call on his mobile he would have a team to watch them within five minutes.

Thirty minutes later, Hans had been given the full brief about Jim's operation. He was shocked to hear that one of Jim's relatives was involved, but Jim told him it would all come out in the wash, so he dropped the subject. Hans would give all the support that he could - he was a Captain now so authority wouldn't be a problem. The Bierfest tomorrow would cause slight worries, due to the amount of people attending, but Hans would saturate the area with men and Jim assured him that if Dubois was caught on German soil he would make sure that Hans got his share of the credit. With the Audi now being watched, the five officers settled down to eat.

***

Barry also relaxed, now that he knew his team was out of harm's way. Enjoying the splendour of the officer's accommodation and a served four course meal, he chuckled to himself then raised his glass to the forthcoming match tomorrow. The Major agreed that it would be a match to remember and even better for the fact that he would be the referee. Barry swallowed his mouthful of Riesling slowly. *He hasn't met Daniel yet*, he thought. No, let the Major learn firsthand, he decided. Tucking in to the wild boar on his plate before him, he felt content for the first time since leaving Amsterdam.

Back in the dorm, boredom had set in. A small TV set had been wheeled in for their entertainment but, with it only being able to pick up German channels, it was left virtually ignored. The majority of the team were chatting in small groups. Dan sat on the end of Mike's bed complaining, as always, about the accommodation. Mike told him to get a life and kicked him off the end of the bed. Landing on his burn he let out a cry, got up, gave Mike the finger, which was his answer to a lot of things, and hobbled off towards the TV to see if he could do any better in finding a channel to watch. Mike lay down and reflected once more on

Barry's comments from earlier that day. He was excited about the prospect of scouts watching the final game in Paris. Suddenly Dan shouted, making Mike lose his train of thought and nearly jump out of his skin.

'What is it?' Mike shouted back, annoyed.

'Come here, quick! I think I've found some shagging on the tele.'

'Haven't you seen enough? You're just a pervert, you know that? It hasn't taken you long to forget about Sabina.'

'I haven't forgotten, ok?' Dan shouted back.

Dan's comment had aroused interest from some of the others and very quickly half a dozen had congregated in front of the TV.

'What shagging? I can't see anything,' said Richard Green, leaning on Scott Dale's back to get a good view. The screen was fuzzy; two figures could be seen in the centre moving backwards and forwards, but whether or not they were having sex was questionable.

'I tell you, I saw them at it. He was going hell for leather,' said Dan twiddling with the tuner button once more. The picture disappeared completely for a couple of seconds, to be replaced by what only could be described as traditional German music. A band consisting of three men, one playing a trumpet another playing an accordion and the third a euphonium, was performing in front of a studio audience. The lady in the group played the trombone and each time she blew a note it looked as though her chest would explode out of her bra.

The Oompah music, the tight leather shorts made of goat suede, the bright red braces, the little green hats with feathers and even the over-stressed bra didn't raise many eyebrows. It was the two men dressed in similar attire that appeared in front of the band that caused the greatest amusement. As the band played, the two men

262

began to slap themselves, firstly on the feet and then on the thighs. It was when they began to slap one another across the face, in time to the music, that the laughter started. Dancing around in circles, jumping and skipping all seemed relatively normal, but the slapping was totally out of the ordinary.

'Mike, come and have a look at this!' Dan shouted across the room. Mike sauntered across slowly to see what all the commotion was about. The dance looked quite brutal; each man was really giving the other the hardest of slaps. When the music ended the audience went wild and the two red-faced dancers took the applause.

'Did you see that?' Dan said to Mike looking astonished.

'Don't be too surprised, it's a traditional dance from Bavaria, Southern Germany,' replied Mike knowledgeably. 'There're into it in a big way over here. You might even see some at the Bierfest tomorrow.'

'How do you know such crap?' said Dan as they both walked back over to their beds.

'I read books and go on the web. It's called learning and you ought to try it sometime,' replied Mike sarcastically. 'It might stop you being so critical of people and things you don't know anything about.'

'Ok, mister know it all, but I go on the computer as well, I'm not that stupid.'

'Yeah, I know you do, but only to play games. When was the last time you read the news to see what was going on in the world?'

'That stuff's boring. I look at the footy results though.'

'Well, there you go. The world could be coming to an end but you'll know if Preston North End has had an away win.' Dan paused to think what to say next, but Mike was quicker and changed the subject altogether.

'Come on, tell me what you think about this game tomorrow. It's going to be the most difficult yet, you know.'

'Don't be silly,' Dan said laughing. 'It'll be a walk in the park. They're just new recruits - we'll piss all over them.'

'Don't be too sure. They're all aged seventeen which gives them an edge and they'll be fit, which means physical.'

'Yeah? So what? We're English and we're not going to take any shit from these box heads.

'Box heads! Where do you get that saying from?'

'Oh, that's what my old man calls Germans. Box heads.'

'Well, start making up your own mind when you've actually met a few. I'd hate to think what they would call you if they knew you.'

'I couldn't care less what they might call me. Tomorrow we'll see - it'll be a breeze.' Mike laughed out loud while shaking his head from side to side.

'I'm going to take a shower before bed. I've had enough of this stimulating conversation.' He picked up his wash bag and walked off towards the bathroom. 'You crack me up sometimes, you know that Dan?'

Chapter 20

At 7am the lights in the dorm came on. Mike rubbed his eyes to clear the sleep; they felt sore and the bags underneath hung heavy. He needed at least another couple of hours to make him feel normal, but he knew that was never going to happen. Sleeping in that dorm had been virtually impossible. If it wasn't the snoring, the farting or the schoolgirl giggling that kept him awake, it was the full-blown argument between little Terry and Miles St John that seemed to be never ending.

Dan, for once, had been the calming influence and had got out of bed to separate the duo. Miles had accused Terry of playing with himself under the covers because of the constant rustling noise that came from Terry's direction. Terry denied it and argued that the blankets didn't agree with his skin and made him itch. It was when Miles called him a wanker that Terry plucked up the courage, jumped out of bed and tried to show Miles his blotchy skin. That didn't change Miles's point of view and the two smallest players on the team squared up to each other. Dan intervened threatening them both with bodily harm, and the dorm went silent once more.

Three hours later, Mike was happy to run out onto the football pitch to find his own space once more. It wasn't the best pitch that he had played on; the goal mouths were a bit patchy but, with a running track encircling the pitch, it gave a greater feeling of freedom. Since waking up, the morning for Mike had been one constant headache. Queuing for a shower and then breakfast, listening to the perpetual moans and groans about the water being too cold, the food being crap etc. *What a bunch of whingers*, he thought. At home some of these boys probably lived and ate worse than this. It only took one to set them all off and the morning had been one constant whine after another.

He welcomed his moment of solitude in his goal mouth and took a moment to study his surroundings, but that didn't take him long. The same ugly barrack blocks where the team had spent the night were on one side. Opposite was a small assault course which ended next to a gymnasium. Next, a long garage-type building with military vehicles parked up out front which led onto a large drill square, and all surrounded by a German housing estate. Mike thought how bizarre this little bit of Gelsenkirken looked, as a football came hurtling in his direction.

Barry felt rejuvenated after his five star treatment the night before. The team had sat gobsmacked in the changing room, listening to a poetic Barry extolling the virtues of a shoulder barge and a sliding tackle in the way that a ballerina would pirouette and dance. Bewilderment and disbelief held them and you could hear a pin drop as he droned on. Mike helped him snap out of his reverie by asking politely if he could tell them what the team would be. Reading out names one after another from a slip of paper he had prepared the previous night, he informed them that he had picked the strongest team that he could, but he'd left Dan on the bench to the amazement of some of the others. Eyes darted around the room as everyone looked for other facial expressions, but no one dared to let their emotions show. It was a well-known fact that Dan was the best centre forward and goal scorer that the team had, but he sat quietly, nonplussed in the corner of the dressing room.

This was totally out of character for Dan, as it had been known for him to dish out a fair share of verbal abuse to whoever picked the team if it didn't agree with him, even to the extent of stomping off and throwing pieces of kit in all directions. However, this time he just sat smiling, making no attempt to reply. Mike knew the reason why Dan was on the bench; it was he himself who had persuaded Barry and both had concerns for his welfare. Dan was a tenacious player with an enormous amount of guts and nine times out of ten he wouldn't shy away from a tackle. He always gave everything if he was in the right frame of mind, but this game was going to be tough.

The German squad were all raw recruits, but to make matters worse they were all conscripts, boys of seventeen who had no choice but to serve in their country's military. Barry knew that the Indispensables were in for an extremely physical game as his evening with the Major had enlightened him to some of the German squad and, if the word 'animal' was anything to go by, the German team would be full of them. The Major had informed him that it had been known for recruits to purposely injure themselves to get discharged early and therefore there may be a slim chance that a member or two of his team might be in the same frame of mind. Barry thought that the Major was talking rubbish just to worry him but, he couldn't take the risk of ignoring the information. If someone in the opposition team was looking for their early exit home and were going to use the Indispensables as their ticket, Barry didn't want Dan being part of it. Their game in Paris was too important and Dan had to be fit to play any injury caused by rash challenges, or Dan's stupid attitude could destroy a chance of a life time. Barry had put too much into this tour to create this fantastic opportunity for his best boys, and he had no choice but to sideline his centre forward.

The Indispensables had a mild sweat on when the

German team jogged arrogantly onto the pitch. Barry urged his team to continue warming up, but jaws had already hit the turf, Mike and Dan's included. The Indispensables consisted of a mix of two fifteen-year-olds, a majority of sixteens and two seventeen-year-olds. As they watched the German team arrive, even Barry had to look twice. Not one was less than six foot with one even having the makings of a beard. Barry wasn't happy with what he saw. The Major had extolled the virtues of his team the night before, but Barry never expected this. He made his way over to the Major who was warming up with his assistants.

'I must question the ages of some of your players, Major,' Barry said politely at first.

'You have a problem with my team, Herrn Ellis?' replied the Major arrogantly. 'They are all recruits of seventeen, I assure you.' He smiled irritatingly in Barry's direction which instantly annoyed Barry.

'That one there,' Barry said pointing at the one with the beard.

'Oh Wolfgang, yes. It is unusual to see a boy of that age with such a large amount of facial hair. His mother is German but his father is Turkish and I believe it is quite common for boys of Turkish descent to have hair on their faces at the age of ten.' Barry had no answer.

'That one there then, he's got to be older than seventeen. I've seen younger looking players in your national squad,' Barry said, pointing at another six-footer with thighs the size of tree trunks.

'That's Helmut, he's been bodybuilding since the age of eleven. He is quite a big boy isn't he?' Barry smelt a rat. His temperature started to rise but he couldn't argue against anything that the Major had said, but he knew that the wool was being pulled over his eyes.

He turned to walk away, not knowing what to do.

Should I refuse to play? he thought. He couldn't do that, but the welfare of his boys was his primary concern. He wasn't bothered about losing face; it was a totally unequal match and it would be his boys that would suffer.

'Call it off. Yes, that's what I'll do,' he said to himself, turning back to the Major. However, the Major's next comment changed his mind completely.

'Herrn Ellis, I have to admit that there is one piece of information that I forgot to tell you. My players are the pick of the whole fifteen thousand recruits that are available in this intake. I hope that this news doesn't worry you.' Barry, hurt with anger, clenched his fists tightly. *You arrogant bastard!* he thought to himself. *We aren't going to walk away. We'll show you how to play football!* He smiled a polite smile at the Major.

'Good luck, Major,' Barry said confidently, holding out his hand. He shook with a grip so hard that the Major tried to pull away early. 'May the best team win,' Barry said, as he turned and jogged back to his boys.

'Oh Major,' Barry shouted back from his dugout. 'If you can give me another five minutes to talk to my team I would appreciate it.' The Major waved his aching hand in acknowledgment. Barry, full of anger and determination, needed to give the quickest and best team talk of his life. David and Goliath this match would certainly be.

Calling his team around him, he could see the look of worry on their faces. His boys were scared and it showed. 'Time to inspire,' he said to himself and he apologised to God for the language that he would be using.

'Now, if any of you don't want to play for your own personal reasons then it's alright with me. Nobody will think any the worse of you.' He had to say that first, but he knew it would take a very strong character to stand up in front of their friends and team mates and pull out. No one replied. *All credit to them*, thought Barry and he felt overwhelmed with pride. It was just the spur he needed to start motivating. Sitting and crouching on the grass, fifteen faces looked to him for inspiration. He took a deep breath, smiled his biggest smile for ages and began.

'We only have a short time before kick off so listen to me. I don't want any interruptions, ok Dan?' Nodding in unison, Barry's boys listened. 'A long time ago a large army had gathered for war against Israel. The two armies faced each other, camped for battle on opposite sides of a steep valley.' Hearing something religious, Dan looked at Mike and frowned, but Mike mouthed for him to listen. Taking a deep breath he did as he was told.

'There was this philistine giant measuring over nine feet tall, much bigger than any of those over there,' Barry said pointing at the German squad. 'This giant of a man wore full armour and came out each day for forty days to taunt and mock the Israelites, challenging them to fight. Now, this giant was called Goliath and he scared the shit out of everyone, especially the King of Israel. A young boy called David appeared one day and was sent to the front to get news of his brothers. He was probably your age and your build, Terry,' he said looking at the little winger. Terry nodded in agreement. 'Now, this Goliath wasn't known to David and he wondered why this man should be shouting his mouth off so much. He was just a large clumsy idiot, but nevertheless Goliath was doing a fantastic job of scaring everyone to death. David saw the fear around him he persuaded the King to let him fight the giant. People laughed at him. How could a boy so small fight a man so large? He would get killed without a doubt.

So, without battle armour because he was too small to fit into any, he confronted Goliath with only a sling shot and a bag of stones. That's a catapult nowadays. The giant swore at him and tried to humiliate him in every way, trying to get him to run away, but David couldn't care less what Goliath said. To him, he only saw another man, just like himself. So what if he had a spear, shield and armour? David was younger, quicker, accurate and more intelligent than him.

'Goliath by this time had had enough of this boy and came at David, lunging with the spear. David was quick and nimble, dancing around Goliath, making him look stupid and making him tired. David was slowly wearing him out and when the opportunity arose he struck. He reached into his bag, pulled out a stone and, using his sling shot, he hurled it at the giant. Boom! The stone knocked Goliath out cold. David cut off Goliath's head and his side won the battle, but I'm not going to go there.' Barry hoped that some of them at least could draw a comparison with the opposition at the other end of the pitch.

'Look boys, the point that I'm trying to make is this - it doesn't matter if they are bigger and stronger than you, it's what you have in here that counts.' Barry pointed to his head. 'Yes, you are in for a physical game and for some of you it will be painful, but David defeated Goliath by using his talents and his brain. He must have been frightened, any man would be stupid not to be when faced with a giant, but he went out there with confidence and a positive attitude. You are Indispensables,' Barry paused and pointed a finger at each one of his boys. They looked back at him transfixed, lost in the moment and the momentum of Barry's wise words.

'Each one of you is here on your own merit. You are all excellent footballers playing for a club, and now for a country, with a reputation to uphold. This club was founded by men who had just fought in a war. They had seen their friends die in front of their very eyes, had lost everything that they held dear, yet they had the courage to survive and the self belief to succeed. You are like them; you have the skills to beat anyone, no matter who they are. We are on their turf and playing under their spotlight. What better time to take our football to them and prove that the country that first invented the game is still the best at playing it. We come from the Northeast of England, we come from Newcastle, we pride ourselves on being part of a fantastic football heritage. Let's show these bastards what we are made of. Now go and make us all proud to be an Indispensable.'

Jumping to their feet, shouting and patting each other on their backs, the boys showed the type of resolve that the underdog needed. Each player ran onto the pitch full of enthusiasm, courage and the knowledge that no one could stand in their way. Barry turned to John Dodd who had just touched him on the shoulder.

'Fine speech Barry, you've given them hope.'

'For all our sakes let's hope these Germans aren't as good as they look. If they don't score too early and we can hold our own for the first quarter of an hour then we just might stand a chance.' Barry sat down in the dugout, his heart still beating fast fuelled by the adrenalin of his speech. He put his hands together and prayed for courage. They were going to need it.

Within the first two minutes a crunching challenge on Martin Cuthbert, the left back, had him writhing in agony and clutching his ankle. Barry ran onto the pitch with John and the medical bag, fearing the worst. Even the Major saw the cynical side of the foul and booked the player who had committed it. Barry made eye contact with the Major who found it difficult to look back. He knew the odds were stacked against the Indispensables but until now he had been swallowed up in his own team's greatness to realise what the English boys were up against. Clamping down on any further stupid tackles, the match turned into a flowing game with both sides having their share of the ball.

Mike was in his element; it was just what he needed to boost his confidence. Many goalkeepers wanted a game that tested their ability, put them under pressure and made them pull out the saves. That was what being a goalkeeper was all about. Mike had to concentrate; he was the last line of defence and he made sure that he controlled his defensive line with authority. He had watched so many top class goalkeepers on the television that were just shot stoppers. They had no idea, in his opinion, how to control their defence. If the defence had confidence in the ability of the goalkeeper to organise from the back then it took pressure off them and, in turn, improved their performance. Mike did what he did best and the Indispensables were holding their own against a superior force.

When the half time whistle blew they came of the pitch annoyed at having to stop for the break. Barry encouraged and inspired each player as best he could. Legs were bruised and bleeding but passion still fuelled their engines. They wanted to win so bad now that, even before the ref blew for the second half, most of the team were back on the pitch waiting for the restart.

The German team, on the other hand, were feeling demoralised.

'Why are we struggling to beat this team of children?' said the assistant manager to the row of bowed heads. 'You are a disgrace to this regiment and your country,' he told them pushing them back out onto the pitch. Not the best motivation for anyone to be told that they are a disgrace. So the best eleven German conscripts went back onto the pitch feeling even worse than when they came in before the break.

Barry told Dan to warm up. He, too, saw a possible victory looming and the time seemed right to bring on their secret weapon. Dan buzzed with enthusiasm to get on. He'd been silent the entire first half and, like a greyhound out of a trap, he sprinted onto the pitch with a sense of urgency that Barry had not seen before.

The first time he touched the ball he tasted grass and the second time he tasted grass again. He was too quick for them. He was the David to their Goliath. Even though the tackles flew in at him every time he got the ball, it was only through their clumsiness that he suffered. Barry questioned his decision. *Dan should still be on the bench*, he thought. *I'm risking his future for my glory now.*

Dan shone and excelled each time he had the ball. His fresh legs had spurred his team mates on and, when the Indispensables finally put the ball in the back of the net, it was Dan who put it there. A midfield ball over the top of the Germans' square defensive line beat the offside trap. Dan took it down majestically with his right knee and, without letting the ball drop, volleyed it hard and low into the bottom right corner. He sprinted at top speed back to Mike, who caught him running at full pelt and they both ended up on the floor, celebrating in typical football fashion, until the rest of the team arrived and did the usual pile on.

The game had turned their way under incredible odds. Whether it was Barry's speech or the determination of his players, both could take some credit. The Germans came back at them; they now had three pairs of fresh legs on the pitch and they badly needed the equaliser. Ten minutes remained and the Germans won a corner from a deflected shot that, if it had not been deflected, would have gone into orbit.

Mike organised a man on each post and stood on his toes, poised to make the ball his if he could. In it came, whipped in viciously towards the penalty spot but out of reach of Mike, who was blocked by the amount of German players that flooded the area.

Tony Fletcher, the tall centre half, rose with an equally tall German attacker but he didn't manage to make contact with the ball, which enabled the attacker to glance it towards the goal. As the ball spun towards the net, Mike knew it was his. Diving with both arms, he caught it cleanly and held it firm. He didn't see the German lunging towards him until it was too late. The force of the incoming body pushed Mike into his goal. He knew that he had to keep the ball from crossing the line and he stretched, placing it down on the ground still in his six yard box, even though his body lay over the goal line. He stood to throw the ball to one of his team mates in order to quickly get the ball back into play. When he heard the whistle blow and the ref point to the centre spot his shoulders dropped.

'No way', he shouted out loud, 'you can't do that. I kept it out.' Every Indispensible on the pitch confronted the ref, not maliciously, just in honest complaint. Ushering them away, he told them that his assistant had deemed the ball to be over the line as he himself was not in a position to see, so he must take his assistant's word and award the goal.

Dan, known for acting before thinking, was full of pent-up emotion and anger. He didn't like what he had heard and definitely didn't like being dismissed by 'that fucking box head' which he later denied saying but, in reality, the whole of the camp would have heard him say it. He pushed the ref on the chest, sending him off balance and falling to the ground. Mike had seen it coming but couldn't get to Dan quick enough. He managed to grab hold of him and walk him away, but the Major being a military man needed to keep face in front of his men. He sprinted to where Mike held Dan and thrust the red card in his face, shouting something in German. Mike held him fast as he wriggled to get free.

'How could the linesman have seen from where he was? There were too many bodies in the way,' Dan said to Mike, still struggling, then shouted towards the ref. 'You blind cheating bastard.' He yelled but the ref ignored him, brushed himself off and walked away.

Barry, normally calm and reserved, exploded into life on the touch-line. His fuse had been lit earlier and had been burning in secret all through the game.

'That was never over the line and you know it,' he yelled, pointing at the ref who just apologetically pointed to his linesman as if to say 'sorry, not my fault'. It was inevitable that Dan's team mates would voice their opinion at the linesman, but it would fall on deaf ears as he spoke no English. So, with a group of angry British teenagers shouting abuse at him, he turned and calmly walked away totally oblivious to it all.

'Cheating scumbags,' Barry said to himself as he walked over to escort Dan back to the bench. He wanted so much to lay into the Major but he held himself back. He couldn't air his opinion - it wouldn't be right for tender ears. But more importantly he was the manager and he needed to set an example to his players. The decision had been made, like it or not, and if his team could see their manager acting like a gentleman then hopefully it would rub off on them. He began experiencing the swan syndrome. On the exterior he looked calm and collected, but underneath, inside his head, he paddled like fury with anger.

'Right you lot, forget it,' Barry shouted. 'Concentrate! It's not over yet. Come on, dig deep.' It was too late though. The goal had knocked the stuffing out of them and no matter what encouragement Barry gave he could not raise them out of their depression. Hope had not been lost altogether, though, because the German side had lost interest also. They were blatantly aware that their Major and referee had cheated for them. Recruits they were, but stupid they were not. An opposition which, on paper and in the flesh, they should have annihilated had wiped the floor with them. Being given the goal was an insult to the better team and they all knew it. The fighting spirit of Britain against Germany had disintegrated through unfairness and the match ended in a lifeless one all draw.

At the final whistle Barry's boys looked to him for an answer, but he had none. He only had pride for a team that had shown so much courage and bravery against overwhelming odds. He could not but have admiration for them. A draw would have to be acceptable to them, like it or not, but Barry would make sure that this match would be remembered by Indispensables of the future. Putting his arms around each of his boys he consoled their loss, wiped tears from their faces and instilled pride in the fact that what they had achieved should not be tarnished by the result. They had slain Goliath. They were heroes.

'You were all Davids today,' he shouted. 'Well done!'

Chapter 21

Mike sat alone in the dressing room. The rest of the team had left a few minutes earlier, many of them subdued and quiet, still coming to terms with their disappointment. He carefully picked the mud from his football boots and threw it into a nearby bin. The smell of sweat mingling with shampoo and soap hung in the air as it slowly drifted towards an open window, wafting on the last remaining clouds of steam from the shower room.

'That was a hell of a game you played,' Jim said, standing in the dressing room doorway. 'Don't be too disheartened Mike, you should be pleased with your performance.' He walked forward and sat down on an old wooden bench next to his nephew.

'Oh, I'm not pissed off,' replied Mike, 'I enjoyed every minute of it. It was never a goal, but so what. We all performed well and these sorts of games you don't get to play every week. No, I'm sitting here savouring the moment. I couldn't leave with the rest, they were all depressed. So I decided to stay here a while.'

'Gave me flash backs of the World Cup goal of sixty-six, you know,' said Jim chuckling to himself. 'These games against the Germans always seem to court controversy. It must be just one of those unexplainable things. Still, it was a great spectacle to watch, no matter what the outcome.' Mike gave his uncle a friendly smile and nodded in agreement. Putting his boots in his bag, he pulled the zipper across and let out a sigh at the same time.

'What's up?' asked Jim, putting a caring hand onto Mike's shoulder.

'This thing with Dubois worries me. No matter how

much I try to put it to the back of my mind, I can't stop thinking about it. I can't relax anymore. I'm scared Jim, really scared.' Jim pulled his nephew in closer.

'Don't be scared Mike, everything's going to be fine,' Jim said as reassuringly as he could. 'Dubois and his men won't get within a mile of you today. The Inspector told me on the phone last night and I believe him.' Mike tried to smile but Jim could see the strain behind his eyes. Jim hated himself again for what he was doing. He felt so close to his nephew now, with their relationship growing stronger each day. He wanted so much to tell Mike the truth about himself, his German friends, the operation - everything, but he couldn't. He had no idea what that sort of knowledge would do to his nephew. The pressure on him would be immense and Jim needed Mike's innocence to catch Dubois. However, he knew that, on the day of reckoning, he would have some explaining to do and it wouldn't be easy. For now, though, he needed to put his personal misgivings aside and concentrate on catching Dubois.

'Anyway,' continued Jim trying to sound light-hearted, 'you need to think of only one thing and that's Paris.' Mike looked at him puzzled.

'You know about Paris?' Jim knew every movement that this tour made. It was his business to know.

'Yep, the scout's everything. Paris should be uppermost in your mind, not Dubois. Now, come on, let's go and enjoy this Bierfest,' he said jovially, scrunching Mike's hair and pushing him away. 'I believe that there will be quite a few young ladies there too. That'll take your mind of things.' Mike laughed and pushed him back and together they left the dressing room, oblivious to the storm that lay ahead.

***

279

When they reached the dorm, to their surprise they were met with excited faces. Dan saw his friend and raced over to him as though he hadn't seen him for years.

'What's going on with you?' said Mike. 'The last time I saw you I thought you were going to commit suicide or something.'

'Oh, I'm alright, thanks to Barry. He told us that we'd played against the best of the best out of all of Germany and still they couldn't beat us. We rubbed their noses in it today, right in it. The Indispensable are world beaters.' Raising his hands into the air, Dan yelled at the top of his voice 'Indispensables!' As if rehearsed, the whole team, even Barry, held their hands up in the air and echoed 'Indispensables!' The noise reverberated around the Dorm and Mike wouldn't have been surprised if the whole of Gelsenkirken had heard them. The team was jubilant once more thanks to the master of motivation and, by the looks of things, Dan's new friend Barry.

Beckoning them all to the door, Dennis shouted that the bus was outside. He just managed to get out of the way before being knocked down the stairs as the team exited the dorm in record time, leaving only Mike, Jim and Barry to turn off the lights and close the door. Mike followed, bemused by the change in atmosphere, but Barry put him at ease when he told him that he had promised to buy everyone a beer for their excellent performance, but only one. After that it would be soft drinks and nothing else. Mike informed him that at German beer festivals they only served beer in a two litre glass called a stein. He laughed when Barry grimaced, realising that he may have made an error of judgement. Jim came to the rescue, but it didn't help.

'I'm sure they'll make exceptions to the rule, Barry.

Even the Germans wouldn't want fifteen drunken Geordie boys on the rampage in their town.' Jim looked at Mike and both laughed. Barry, on the other hand, didn't share their amusement. His face remained straight when he climbed aboard the bus. *Poor Barry!* Mike thought.

When the bus reached the main gate to the camp, the door opened and the Major climbed aboard. A few boos were heard but Barry, like a headmaster in assembly, stood and shouted silence. The Major asked Dennis for the microphone and everyone went silent as he began trying to make amends for his poor decision making. In perfect English, but with his heavy German accent, the Major made his announcement.

'I would like to thank you all for a performance that I and my team did not expect. You are a great credit to your club and country and I am honoured to have you here in my camp. As you say in England, the beers are on me.' The bus erupted in cheers and shouts and the Major stood, clapping his hands in support of his fearless opposition. Barry's eyes rolled at the thought of more beer flowing, but he did manage to smile when he shook hands with the Major and managed to hold a pleasant conversation with him as he sat beside him.

The festivities had begun early as the bus made its way through the streets. It seemed that all of its residents were making their way to the Schloss Berge and the Sommerfest. A three-storey, eighteenth-century German manor house that was now a hotel opened its doors and grounds once a year to hold a pop festival and fair. The Indispensables had luckily timed their tour to coincide with the festival. The depression from the earlier game had lifted and, with the sight of girls in short skirts and the thought of beer coming their way, a wave of euphoria washed backwards and forwards inside the bus.

With a military vehicle in front as escort and the German Major giving the unofficial tour guide with the microphone permanently glued to his mouth, all eyes except for Jim's looked forward. Jim slyly peered behind and, as he thought, cars which only he knew looked out of place followed from a distance. 'Back to work,' he said to himself and began texting instructions to his colleagues.

The Major seemed to relish the task of tour guide, even though no one was really taking much notice of him, especially after he'd spent five minutes talking about Gelsenkirken being twinned with Newcastle. No one was in the slightest bit interested in the coal production of the two cities. It was only when the bus passed the Veltins Arena where the German football team FC Schalke played that the boys' ears tuned into his voice. Everyone on board looked on in admiration at the magnificence of the ground. It dwarfed everything around it. With a sixty-one and a half thousand capacity, a retractable roof and a slide-out pitch which enabled the turf to flourish under natural conditions, it was classed as a UEFA Five star rated football stadium.

The Major was starting to score brownie points with the Indispensables but then blew it in one statement. He pointed out that St James' Park, the home of Newcastle United, isn't a five star rated ground and that Old Trafford, Manchester United's ground, is the only one in England. He didn't realise his error and when the bus passed by some houses belonging to the old mining community of Gelsenkirken everyone had turned away again, paying no more attention to him.

The streets had started to become busy with people on their way to the festival and the opposite sex had taken the Indispensables' interest. Barry kept eye contact with the Major but he was only pretending to be interested in what he was saying. His mind was in overdrive and his stress levels began to grow as he worried about the forthcoming event. John Dodd had fallen asleep, Dennis was concentrating on his driving and Jim carried on sending his texts. The Major was definitely talking to himself.

A marshal wearing an orange bib waved the bus forward as it edged towards the party. Swallowed up by a wave of moving bodies and other vehicles, it eventually came to rest behind a catering lorry. A perfect summer's day greeted them as they descended from the bus. Dan shoved Mike, who turned to see him pointing at Dennis's back. Mike cringed when he saw the state of the driver's shirt. For a big man on a warm day and on a hot bus, to be wearing a light blue shirt was definitely the wrong choice of clothing.

Dan held his nose as he walked past. Dennis glared at him, made a fist, punched the palm of his hand and pointed at Dan. Dan didn't hang around to see if Dennis would carry out his threat; he jumped off the bus and quickly followed Mike. The Indispensables with the Major leading the way weaved in and out of the crowd that thronged around the entrance to the festival, leaving Barry to nervously fuss around his boys.

The team was led into the biggest tent that Dan had ever seen. He'd been to a wedding once where the bride's parents had erected a marquee in their garden for the reception, but this one was a hundred times bigger. The team were greeted by the smell of smoke, sausage and sauerkraut which gave their nostrils the first real taste of Germany. The tent was packed with people of all ages who sat at long tables on wooden benches. Some ate, some drank and many sang to the drinking songs that the typical German Oompah band played.

Like an infant school teacher being trailed by six-year-olds, Barry and the Indispensables meandered between tables that were packed with noisy party revellers waving glasses of beer. There were waiters carrying trays of steaming sausages covered in sauerkraut and waitresses carrying the biggest glasses of beer that any boy from the North East of England had ever seen. Dan couldn't help but stare at the cleavage of one of the middle-aged waitresses as she squeezed past him displaying her wares. Her breasts were pushed up so high that it was probably possible to balance two full steins of beer on top. She knew where Dan's attention was and winked at him brazenly. Dan tried to act macho but his cheeks had gone red in embarrassment and the waitress chuckled to herself.

Arriving at the only empty table left in the tent, the Indispensables crowded around it, sitting on the wobbly ten-foot benches that ran down either side. Everyone seemed to be lost in the atmosphere of the occasion and mouths were shut as each one examined their surroundings. With the Major shouting orders to a small rotund potbellied German dressed in a white shirt, dark green embroidered waistcoat and a black apron which hung a couple of centimetres from the floor, it wasn't long before the same steaming sausages and sauerkraut began to arrive at their table. Dan looked at the food before him, turned to Mike then looked at it again. He flipped the sausage over and over, examining its brown shiny skin, with each turn wincing as though he was in pain.

'I thought maybe a steak or some roast boar,' Dan said unimpressed again. 'Maybe even some chips, but Jesus, sausage and stinky wet cabbage? You must be joking.' He held up the eight-inch long sausage and sniffed it from a safe distance. Mike sympathised with him as the sight of the brown, slightly curved sausage floating in the cabbage looked about as appetising as a shiny wet dog turd in a pile of old mouldy grass. Stabbing it with his fork and biting into the end, with his eyes closed, the salty juices within mingled with his taste buds and he was pleasantly surprised by its flavour. Talking with his mouth full he urged Dan to taste his. Dan, however, thought it more humorous to make rude gestures with it, but he quickly put it back in his bowl when his eye caught an elderly lady on a nearby table who had been watching him. Picking the sausage up with his fork and knocking the cabbage from it, he took a bite. Mike laughed at him as, once more on this tour, the food actually tasted better than it looked.

When the beer arrived, Barry let out a sigh of relief as it came in four large pitchers and each boy was given a half litre glass. He could hear mumbles of discontentment over the noise in the tent but they soon disappeared when the beer hit their lips, as each boy downed their share of the amber nectar in record time. Mike sipped at his, soaking up the atmosphere and purposely ignoring Dan, who had swallowed his without it touching the sides. Asking for more, Barry scowled at him across the table. Dan took it as a 'no' but craftily stole some of little Terry's when he wasn't looking. Mike shook his head in disbelief at Dan's nerve but quickly went back to watching nearly two thousand Germans and his team mates tuck into their sausage, cabbage and beer.

***

Henri peered through a tent flap on the catering side of the tent. He could see the Indispensables but they were too far away and it was too crowded for him or Didier to approach. He looked around for other inspiration, but he lurched back suddenly when he saw a man talking

285

into his collar, and when he strained his eyes he could just make out a wire behind the man's ear. *We've got company*, he thought. He knew that it would be only a matter of time before the police would show up, but were they watching the English boys or were they just police at the festival? Either way they needed to tread carefully. Withdrawing from view, Henri, Didier and José made their plan.

The white shirt and waistcoat fitted José perfectly and as Didier dragged the unconscious body of the pot-bellied German waiter away, dropping him behind a huge green wheelie bin, Henri tied the apron around the bulbous stomach of José. The German leather money pouch provided perfect cover for the syringe and hypodermic which carried the knock-out dose of chloral hydrate and which would enter Daniel's blood stream and in seconds put him to sleep. With Dan being taken to the medical tent, Mike would be sure to follow and, according to Henri, it would be easier to abduct both of them from there. All three agreed that it sounded like a good plan; it was their only plan, and they didn't have an alternative. Holding the tent flap open, José left to do his work.

The tent relentlessly bustled with diners all through the afternoon, and it was when the time came for the team to leave that José chose to strike. Dan and Mike rose from the table together. Barry had given his orders to be back at the bus for nine o'clock, which gave them four hours to see the sights of the festival. Jubilant to be away from the table Dan, following Mike, made his way towards the nearest exit. Reidel nodded to one of his officers to follow. Nodding his head back to his boss, the officer started to make his way towards the boys from the other side of the tent.

Nonchalantly, but making a point of squeezing his body next to Dan, José pushed the inch long needle into

Dan's neck. The chloral hydrate entered the carotid artery, sending it immediately to the brain. Being famous for its date rape properties, within seconds Dan had lost his balance and dropped to his knees. His body felt as light as a feather; his vision blurred and noises became muffled. The blackness took him. He lunged for Mike's ankle, falling forward onto his face. Mike turned on feeling his trouser being pulled and saw his friend, face down on the dirty beer-soaked floor. Initially he laughed and reached down to help his friend up.

'Come on, piss head,' shouted Mike above the noise of the diners. 'I know you can't take your drink but you've only had one glass. What a lightweight!' Grabbing him by the hand he pulled, but Dan was a dead weight, totally unconscious. A flush of fear ran through Mike's mind when he realised Dan wasn't faking. Mike's eyes became alive as the adrenalin rush hit him. Looking this way and that for a friendly face, and hoping against finding an unfriendly one, he struggled to raise Dan to his feet. *Why won't somebody help me?* he thought, making eye contact with the nearby onlookers who looked but made no effort to help. So many drunks had fallen already that afternoon that another didn't raise any eyebrows. Slapping Dan on his face to try and revive him, he slung his limp arm around his shoulders and slid him towards the exit.

Jim caught sight of them as they passed into the daylight through the open tent. He could see Mike supporting his friend but they were too far away for him to get to them. He looked at Hans for help but he was too busy watching his subordinate failing to make progress across the tent. The German officer was struggling to catch up with the boys because it seemed that two thousand people had decided to leave the tent at the same time, and it was impossible to make any ground in the throng of bodies. Hans immediately radioed for assistance, barking orders to colleagues as he watched them disappear from view.

Outside, Mike squinted as his eyes adjusted to the bright light. People moved from left to right and back again in a constant flow as they made their way to and from the huge fairground that dominated half of the festival site. Mike didn't know what to do. Should they stay where they were, hoping the tracking devices would lead their protectors to them, or to lose themselves in the crowd? What if Dubois got to them first? Where was Uncle Jim? Dan could be dead. *Fuck, what shall I do?*

Looking above the heads of the passersby, he noticed by chance a small red cross inconspicuously positioned between a stall selling Bratwurst sausages and a large children's merry-go-round. 'First Aid, a Doctor, anybody,' he said to himself. He pushed his way through the crowd, dragging the lifeless body of his friend behind. He could hear his mobile ringing in his pocket but he had no way of answering it. He knew that it would be Jim so he had to try to answer it.

Supporting Dan the best he could, he reached with his right hand into his left pocket. His fingers touched the plastic casing and he could feel the vibration against his finger tips. Stretching to his limit he managed to manoeuvre it between his index and middle finger. It wasn't the best grip but, if he remained steady, he would be able to twist it around and take a better hold of it once it was out of his pocket. He never got the chance. With the constant interruption of bodies knocking into him, the phone slipped from his grasp. Watching it disappear under foot he had no choice but to go on without it.

Swearing under his breath for the loss and dragging Dan with renewed vigour, he moved ever closer to the

Red Cross tent. After finally breaking free of the crowd he stood, chest heaving, sweat running down his face and body, in front of a small white First Aid tent no bigger than a typical ten-man Scout tent. A young girl wearing a Red Cross arm band greeted them in German when Mike's face appeared in the opening of the tent. The smile soon disappeared when Dan came into view and she realised that he appeared to be suffering from more than a minor cut.

Mike dropped him as gently as he could into a wheelchair, propping his head with a blanket against the corner tent pole. Asking for help, the girl now in full panic herself mimed the best she could for them to stay there. Feeling Dan's brow, checking his pulse and sensing the breath from Dan's mouth on the back of her hand, she said in English 'get help' and ran out of the tent. Mike shouted for her to come back but she was long gone.

He decided to check Dan himself. He knew First Aid from the numerous courses that he had taken with his dad. Taking his pulse, checking his breathing and looking for any injuries he quickly but systematically came to the assumption that Dan was alive, but why unconscious? It wasn't the alcohol, so it must be Dubois. Putting his head out of the tent, he looked for help which he hoped would arrive soon.

It was Didier who he saw first. The same sickly feeling that he had had in Amsterdam welled up in his stomach. Didier looked Mike straight in the eyes and began to hurry, sending bodies flying to the ground as he ran towards the tent. Mike slung the flap open at the other end of the tent and wheeled Dan outside. This time there was more room to move, as the tent backed onto other stalls from the other side. Pushing Dan over power cables, ruts made by lorry tyres and discarded litter, he entered the moving crowd. Forcing his way through, he pushed Dan out of sight, coming to a stop behind an attraction similar to the Waltzers in England. Dance music pumped out from a nearby speaker but Mike didn't care. Propping up Dan's head once more, he peered cautiously back in the direction of the tent to search for their pursuers.

Didier, revolver drawn, stormed into the tent. With Henri close behind and José bringing up the rear, panting heavily, they ran on through coming to a stop at the mass of bodies in front of them. Mike watched from his position of relative safety as the three of them cursed in anger at their loss. With a look of frustration on his face, Didier went off to his right. Mike thought it best to go in the opposite direction as his choices were extremely limited.

After all the commotion Mike thought that he better check on his casualty. Still lifeless but alive, Dan sat like an unhappy Guy Fawkes waiting for the bonfire to be lit. Mike straightened him up and tried to get his bearings, looking around in each direction. It was always the same - happy people laughing and enjoying themselves wherever he looked. He was frightened and angry but now he had a new emotion - jealousy. He wanted to be like everyone else, but it wasn't to be.

'This is all your fault, you little bastard,' Mike shouted into Dan's ear, but he wasn't hearing anything at all.

Mike dropped his aching shoulders and looked up to the heavens.

'If you are there, God, help me please,' he whispered under his breath. Nothing happened. He waited a few more seconds, again nothing. 'Thanks for nowt. It looks like I'm fucked then, doesn't it? Lost and fucked.' He hit his head firmly three times on the metal framing of the Waltzers; it hurt but he was past caring. He began to wander aimlessly between the attractions but all of the time in the back of his mind he hoped for a friendly face to appear. He rubbed his pocket; the sharp metal tracking device in the form of a Sunderland badge could easily be identified under the light material of his trousers. 'They'll find us,' he whispered to himself. 'The police will come. I know they will.'

***

Jim banged the receiver with his hand. It sent a shooting pain up his arm but he didn't care.

'What's going on Hans? How the hell could we have lost them?' Jim shouted, this time banging his fist down onto the table. 'For God's sake, we've got more officers out there than civilians. We're going to get these boys killed, I know it.' He rubbed the stubble on his chin hard with both hands and looked at Hans, anxiety written all over his face.

'Jim there's too much electrical interference with all the attractions for us to get a close fix on them, but we know that they are still in the park.'

'Well, tell me something I don't know,' Jim said sarcastically. Hans didn't rise to his remark.

'We'll find them, trust me,' he said looking through the one-way glass in the Polizei control centre at the multitude of people that passed by. 'I have good men out there. Believe me, we will find them.' His words sounded hollow and he knew it. With thousands of party goers, attractions and with time running out he started to doubt his own words. They needed some luck and they needed it fast.

Chapter 22

For a short time Mike became caught up in the atmosphere of the festivities. The smells, the noise, the music and the rides - there were too many to take in. It took hold of his senses and, for an instant, which felt longer, the enemy was not in his thoughts. Dan let out a groan bringing Mike back to reality. He bent down to rouse his friend, gently tapping Dan on his right cheek. Almost immediately a German man selling candyfloss only a couple of feet away cried out in pain as the tranquilising dart embedded in his chest. Mike didn't have to guess who that was aimed at - he knew it was for him.

He pushed Dan into the crowd, wanting for them to disappear again. The enemy were gaining on them. Mike needed Dan to wake up otherwise it would only be a matter of time before they were caught. Mike had no time to feel exhausted; the football match earlier in the day had taken its toll, but now he was running on his reserve tank and he wasn't sure how long he could go on for.

Henri whispered 'Imbecile!' under his breath, just loud enough for José to hear it. José turned towards him.

'This gun is for sleep,' he said, holding up a small green tranquilising gun which looked more like a child's water pistol than a tool for putting animals to sleep. Then slowly, reaching into his inside pocket, he withdrew another gun. 'This gun is for death. Be careful what you say, Belgian.' Holding a black nine millimetre Beretta, just the same as Dubois's, José gestured to shoot Henri. Henri shook his head and smiled. He wasn't afraid of this man - he wasn't afraid of anybody.

'Come on, we're wasting time. They won't be far, let's go,' Didier shouted as Henri and José stared at each other with hatred. With Didier pushing them on, the three gunmen ran after the boys. The argument would have to be finished another time.

Kicking a wooden bench in frustration, Jim stood up and began to pace around the control room. The noise of the wood hitting the hard floor startled the German officers who were viewing the monitors of the CCTV system that overlooked the fair. Hans said nothing. Jim, seeing a packet of cigarettes, asked the German owner if he could have one. Taking it gently, he rolled it between his fingers.

'I didn't know you smoked Jim,' said Hans pulling out his own cigarettes. 'You only had to ask.'

'I don't smoke, well not for a long time anyway. And who said that I'm going to smoke it? When the shit hits the fan then I'll light it.' Looking at the cigarette, it rekindled memories of his youth when smoking was as natural to him as walking. Putting it between his lips, he bit down with his teeth on the filter. For now, he had made the first step on a road that he didn't want to take, but the smell and taste agreed with him. Feeling more relaxed almost immediately, he picked up the bench and sat back down to wait for the imminent sighting report.

Hans answered his two-way radio with lightning speed. Jim looked up, urging his friend to tell him what was going on, but Hans was oblivious to his English colleague as he spoke in his native language.

'Move quickly, we've got a lead. Come on!' Hans shouted to Jim. Instinctively jumping to his feet, the cigarette dropping from his mouth, he ran after his German colleague.

'What's going on?' Jim shouted as they raced

towards a nearby car.

'I'll tell you on the way.' With lights flashing and sirens wailing, the police car slowly made its way through the crowd. Jim, sitting in the back seat, willed the surging crowds to get out of the way but, with nowhere to go, the progress became painfully slow.

'Someone's been shot,' Reidel shouted from the front seat.

'What do mean, someone's been shot?' Jim shouted back in panic.

'Don't worry, it's not one of your boys but they have been spotted close by. Somebody shot this guy with a tranquiliser dart, it nearly gave the poor sod a heart attack. It must be the work of Dubois.' Jim gripped the back of the driver's seat as the thrill and fear of the chase took hold of him.

'Come on you fuckwits, move out of the way,' Jim yelled out of his window. No one cared because no one understood.

Mike pushed but the wheelchair wouldn't go through the metal barrier; the gap was just too narrow and the barrier wouldn't budge. He tried to reverse but the wheel caught again as it came back. Shouting and swearing, pushing, pulling and kicking the barrier with his foot, he wrestled to free it. Sweat ran down his brow, stinging his eyes. He looked around. They were going to get them.

'Shit, shit. Come on! Come on!' he screamed. He anticipated the pain of the bullet hitting him in his back so, with one last pull, he gripped the chair and heaved with every bit of strength that he had. It wasn't coming out. Dan groaned and Mike gave up. Tears ran down his cheeks as the fear gripped him. Taking Dan by the arms, he dragged him over the top of the wheelchair and both ended up crumpled in a heap on the floor.

'Mike, is that you?' Dan whimpered.

'Come on mate, get up. We need to go.' Dan made no effort so Mike shouted into his ear. 'Come on you lazy shit! Let's go.'

The loud encouragement made Dan react, giving Mike the little help that he needed to get Dan to his feet. Putting him over his shoulders just as a fireman would carry his rescue victim, Mike ran towards the back of some black trucks that stood, without guard, nearby. The air whistled as the dart passed only inches from his head. Hitting one of the trucks, it embedded itself into a canvas tarpaulin. Mike didn't have time to stop and examine it.

He stumbled unceremoniously through a large black double door, dropping Dan onto the floor. The words *Geistzug Verboten* in bold white letters were clearly plastered over the two doors. He had no time for reading signs, and it didn't mean anything to him anyway. If he'd paid more attention in his German lessons at school he may have understood it, but 'Ghost train forbidden' would never have been high in his vocab list. Self-preservation was his only priority. Dan would have to forgive him later for the rough treatment. A broom once supported by the door lay at his feet. Picking it up, he thrust it behind the horizontal bar-closing mechanism, jamming the door shut. From the beautiful summer's afternoon they were consumed by the semi-darkness and silence within.

As the two stumbled on, not knowing of what lay ahead, Mike could hear the door rattling behind.

'Hold, you bastard, hold,' he said to himself finding a second wind of untapped energy which made him tremble. He knew the old wooden broom wouldn't last long and sooner rather than later Dubois's men would break through.

When it happened, his heart jumped like a crazed monkey in a cage banging to get out. Even Dan, who was slowly coming out of his big sleep, flinched in surprise. Lights flashed on and off in psychedelic waves disorientating him. Groans and moans, shrieks and screeches deafened him. Sweating profusely, he lurched backwards in fright as the skeleton thrust itself forwards, opening its mouth, groaning and spewing out smoke. Then, as quickly as it had appeared, it disappeared back into its coffin-shaped box.

Turning away, his legs feeling weak, the thin veil of a spider's web caressed Dan's face. He blinked again and again, waving his free arm to get it off. Mike didn't see the thin iron rails at his feet and he tripped, throwing Dan forward, himself landing by his friend's side. In trying to save Dan's fall, Mike had fallen heavily, hitting his head on a metal pole. Everything went dark.

His dad appeared lying in a coffin and everyone was crying. He could see his mother being comforted by Uncle Jim as she cried uncontrollably on his shoulder. Jim had his hand on his mother's backside; he wanted to go over and tell him to remove it but instead he froze, seeing himself as ten-years-old walking slowly towards where his father lay. The young Mike stepped up to the coffin and leant over the top to say his last goodbyes. Brian Slater had been laid out in a full Newcastle United strip, his hands were across his chest but his eyes were wide open, staring at the ceiling. Brian's face was white, his lips dry and flaking, his hands cold and clammy to the touch. Mike lent down to give his father a farewell kiss; tears were streaming down his face, falling onto his father. Suddenly, Brian sat up, grabbing his son by the neck and began to strangle him. People clambered on top of the coffin trying to pull Brian off his son, but his grip was too strong and everyone watched, Mike as well, as the life was slowly squeezed out of the ten-year-old with Brian all the time shouting.

'You let me down, you failed, you killed me.'

'No, no it's not true,' Mike shouted back. 'No, no I've always done my best. You know I have, dad. Please.'

'Mike, Mike it's me, Dan. Come on, you're alright,' Dan said, slapping him on the face. Mike opened his eyes to see his friend looking down at him. He suddenly remembered where he was and knew there was no time to reflect on his vision now. Touching the bump on his head, he winced with pain and then felt relieved to be looking at his conscious friend again.

'Let's go, quick,' Mike shouted, getting to his feet and running towards a small railway car with the face of a gargoyle on it. Dan, still feeling nauseous and not having a clue what was happening, followed his friend.

Suddenly the broom shattered, sending shards of wood in all directions. Daylight flooded back in highlighting the three figures that stood at the door, silhouetted like three cowboys waiting for the draw. The small ghost train car was enough to hide the boys. They'd managed to jump in as it moved slowly between a wax dummy of a man waving a severed arm and an old hag mixing her potions in a black cauldron.

Dan's head throbbed in rhythmic time with the car as it passed over the rails below. The chloral hydrate was still doing its best to slow him down and he would need more time before he was fully recovered. Still only semi-awake, he tried to get up and peer over the top of the car, but Mike pushed his head back down.

'Fuck's sake!' Dan whispered angrily into Mike ear. 'Will you please tell me what's going on?'

'Shut up and keep still. It's Dubois's men.' The instruction didn't immediately register and Dan carried on talking.

'I remember eating the biggest sausage in the world

297

and that awful cabbage, but after that it's all blank.'

'I'll tell you later and you can thank me then. Now shut the fuck up or you'll get us both killed.'

'It's like that Indiana Jones film, you know the one, where they have to escape in a miners' railway cart. I can't remember what it's called though, but you know the one?' Mike managed to turn and look at him with a face like thunder. Dan shut up.

Dubois's men were not far away. Mike could hear them shouting as they stumbled around in the darkness looking for them. When the car finally hit the rubber stops on the exit door a wave of relief rushed over Mike. They were still in danger, but being back in daylight raised his hopes again of getting away. Even before the car had come to rest Mike and Dan had jumped out. The ghost train cashier looked then looked again, confused and bemused, as he didn't remember their faces on entry, but it was too late as the boys had gone. Relaxing back in his cubicle, he lit a cigarette and leaned back on his seat, waiting for the next thrill seekers. Almost immediately he dropped the cigarette in his lap in shock when the three killers came charging out of the ride. He looked out through the paying hatch shouting obscenities in German, but he soon stopped when he saw a gun. Dropping to the floor, he waited until they'd gone. It was the cigarette burning through his trousers that made him get up again.

Running straight through the large crowd, Mike and Dan had inadvertently run to the front of a queue waiting for another ride. There was no way that they could turn and backtrack as their pursuers were gaining on them. Pushing on through, they took the last two seats on the Magic Carpet ride. They were right at the back and maybe, if they were able to, Mike hoped, they could climb over the side and escape. The metal restraint bar came down blowing their chance and they both watched, full of fear, as Henri, Didier and José stopped at the front of the queue with no interest in getting to them.

Mike was confused. Why would they stop? They had guns, they could stop the ride. Then he realised. 'We're going nowhere. They'll just wait until we come down,' he said to himself. He hung his head. He had no more energy in him to fight. Even the fear of what lay ahead could not overcome his fatigue. They were as good as caught.

Dan had more pressing things to worry about as the ride speeded up. The Magic Carpet ride was basically a large platform in the shape of the mythical Arabian flying carpet. Supported by a single arm, it rocked backwards and forwards slowly at first and then sped up until it went around one full circle but always staying level. Dan had been on such rides before at the Hoppings on the Town Moor in Newcastle, but never before having been drugged with chloral hydrate.

As the carpet swung to and fro his nausea grew. He swallowed again and again, trying to keep the contents of his stomach where it should be. Forcing his hand over his mouth to help stop the force of the exodus, he closed his eyes praying that it wouldn't happen, but as the ride began to do its first full loop the inevitable happened. The foulest, evilest demon ever to puke would have been proud of Dan's projectile vomit. Helped on its way by the rocking motion of the ride, half-digested sausage, sauerkraut and stomach acid rained down on the people waiting in the queue below.

Unfortunately for the onlookers below, the vile substance hit them full in their faces as they looked up towards the carpet. Screaming women and children ran for cover. Fathers covered their loved ones the best they could. Vomit splattered onto the control booth of the ride, saving the operator from being covered. While the people on the ground could escape, the people on the ride could not. Spraying nearly all those around him, Mike included, the ride turned into chaos. Others started to be sick with the stench and the knowledge that someone had puked on them. People tugged at the restraint to get off but, until the ride stopped, it was in vain.

As the ride began to slow, so Dan became empty, and only drool could be seen dangling from his mouth. His face was as white as one of the ghosts on the ghost train and he sat sobbing quietly to himself. Mike could see Henri & Co wiping the vomit from their clothes, faces full of fury rather than disgust. The ride slowed to nearly a stop. Mike waited and held Dan back as the panicking riders fled off the ride. There was no trying to escape - Dan was in a bad state and going nowhere. Mike gave up all hope and sat back, closed his eyes and anticipated their fate.

The screams had become fainter but the stink remained when Mike heard the siren. Opening his eyes he could see a German police car forcing its way through the crowd. He watched as Dubois's men conceded defeat and mingled with the bystanders that had gathered to watch the spectacle, soon disappearing altogether. Mike thought it impossible but, looking down at the police car, he saw his uncle getting out from the back seat. Feeling safe once more he looked up towards the heavens.

'Maybe you were listening, but you took your time,' he whispered to himself finding some energy to chuckle. Dan sat motionless, oblivious to everything.

***

Jim put the phone down after speaking to Barry. Mike and Dan were safe in his care but they wouldn't be joining the rest of the team that night. Barry thought twice about asking questions; he knew Jim's secret. Mike and Dan were with Jim and that was all he needed to know.

The hospital room felt safe and secure, if not a little sterile as Mike sat on the end of the bed. Both boys had been brought in for observation as they'd had a rough day. Scrubbed clean, clothes taken away for washing and wearing awful blue striped pyjamas, the sort a geriatric would wear, the boys were placed under police guard in a two-bedded room in a privately run hospital somewhere in the centre of the city.

'Jim, I've had enough,' Mike said taking a sip from his hot chocolate bought from a vending machine in the corridor. 'I feel like I'm someone's toy. The police don't seem to be able to protect us no matter where we are and they're not even trying to catch Dubois's men. They get away each time, at the tunnel, Amsterdam and now here. I sometimes think that Inspector Sanderson wants us to get caught. I'm fed up with it all and I would like to get home in one piece.' Swallowing the last drop of hot chocolate and throwing the paper cup into the bin, Mike waited for his uncle to reply. Dan had fallen asleep once more, unable to back his friend up. This time, however, it was under the control of hospital drugs to help him recover.

'I don't know what to say, Mike,' Jim said sitting down next to him on the bed. 'This state of affairs that he's got you into,' Jim said looking over at Dan, 'was never going to be easy to get out of. But the way I see it, you have no choice but to remain on the tour and see it out to the end. Like it or not, the police are the only friends that you've got.' Mike shook his head in disagreement and was just about to answer when the door opened and in walked Hans, ending their conversation and letting Uncle Jim off the hook from having to justify the situation again.

'I am Captain Reidel. I am in charge of your protection while you are here.'

Mike smiled sarcastically at him. 'Well, you don't seem to be doing a very good job so far, Captain Reidel,' Mike said raising his eyebrows, urging the captain for a reply. Hans could see the family resemblance between Mike and his uncle and, if Jim was anything to go by, he thought that he better not rise to any bait.

'There will be a police guard outside your door all night, so get a good night's sleep and we'll talk about our plans tomorrow.' Turning, Hans left the room to talk to the guard.

'Not a man of many words,' said Jim trying to play the uncle role again.

'I'm too tired to care,' Mike said lying back onto the bed. Jim said his farewell and thought it a good time to leave. He didn't want any more heavy conversations, mainly because he didn't have any answers. A few minutes later, Mike had drifted off to sleep and Jim was talking to Hans at the other end of the corridor.

'I only had to walk through the door and I could see you in him,' said Hans, 'and when he opened his mouth - well, he was just like you.' Jim didn't know whether to take that as a compliment or not. Hans sensed he had hit a nerve. *Maybe a skeleton lurking in a cupboard*, he thought, and dropped the subject.

'Here's the information on the third man with Henri and Didier,' Hans said, handing a sheet of A4 paper with a photo and description on it.

'Well, that accounts for the tranquiliser darts, doesn't it?' Jim said studying the photo. 'But why would Dubois want to get a Basque hit man to do his dirty work? It doesn't make sense.'

'Yes, it confuses me too, but this one is dangerous.

302

Henri and Didier have their methods, but José comes out on top of the nasty bastard list. Come on, I need a drink,' Hans said steering Jim to the elevator. Jim reluctantly stood his ground and looked back towards the ward.

'Don't worry,' continued Hans, 'no one can get to them here. They're in safe hands. Come on Jim, I'm thirsty.' Leaving the two boys sleeping and the single police guard outside the room Jim left reassured that the boys were out of harm's way.

***

The ambulance was unlocked and unguarded, making it easy for the three killers to climb inside and be perfectly hidden from prying police eyes. *What a perfect getaway car*, Didier thought as he wired the ignition, kick starting the engine into life. The gowns and wheelchair would make perfect cover for Henri and José to enter the hospital, deal with the guards and take the boys. Didier would make sure their escape route stayed clear.

It was midnight when Mike woke. The same nightmare kept reoccurring, the one with his father lying in state. With sweat dripping from his nose, he got out of bed to get a drink. He carefully opened the door a few centimetres to look down the corridor. The police guard stood opposite, laughing and flirting with a nurse. Mike went to the bathroom attached to their room. He washed his face, dried it on a towel which had the texture of a sack cloth and filled a small plastic cup with water. The sign above the basin said in German and English not to drink the water, but he thought that one little cup wouldn't hurt. He filled it to the brim, drank some, then topped it up.

Sitting on the bed, propped up by three pillows, he

303

sipped at the cold liquid and recalled the terrible events of the day and thought about Paris. His head wanted so much to go to Paris but his heart wanted to go home. They needed to argue it out some more so he decided to settle down and try and get back to sleep.

Hearing a muffled thud, he woke up in surprise. Getting out of bed, still half asleep, he opened the door and peered through a half inch gap to view the corridor. The guard wasn't there. He didn't know how but he knew something was up. Turning to Dan, he shook him hard to get him to wake from his second drug-induced sleep.

'What did you do that for?' Dan said rubbing his eyes. 'I was on a beach with this beauty queen. I was just about to take her bra off and you went and spoilt it.'

'There's something wrong, I know it. Come on, get ready to go.'

'Go where? We're wearing bloody Hitler's pyjamas.'

'Shut up. Look.' Mike held the door ajar, just enough for two sets of eyes to see. The corridor was empty apart for an orderly in a mask pushing a man in a wheelchair. Mike knew those eyes - he'd seen them so many times before. He was certain that it was Henri. Slowly closing the door, pushing a nearby chair under the handle to prevent it from being opened, he went across to open a window. Dan followed and peered out into the night. Their room was situated on the third floor. It was too high to jump to the ground and it had no other means of escape. The branches of a large horse chestnut trees hung in reaching distance. It was their only way down - they had no choice but to take it.

Climbing out on to the window ledge, Mike could feel the sudden cool air rushing through the light cotton pyjamas. He shivered, holding onto the window frame for support.

'You must be joking,' said Dan watching his friend balancing on the ledge outside.

'You can stay and talk to Dubois's men if you want, but I'm going.'

Without looking down and arms outstretched, Mike jumped for the closest branch. As soon as he felt the rough bark on his palms he grabbed hold as tight as he could. With his weight acting on the branch it bent and swayed, bouncing him up and down into the foliage of other branches. Hand over hand he made his way towards the trunk where he could get a good foot hold. Turning to Dan, he beckoned him to follow. Dan hesitated; it wasn't the natural thing to do in the middle of the night unless you were a cat, and he definitely wasn't a cat.

The door handle turned behind him. It gave him the encouragement that he needed. Jumping into the night, he reached for the branch. It wasn't there. He felt himself falling but had no time to panic - the branch below caught him in the stomach. He draped over it like a pillowcase on a washing line. The heavy landing had taken his breath away, but he was safe with all but a few scratches. Two minutes later, both boys felt the damp grass between their toes, but it was impossible to run away. They had no clothes, shoes or money and they wouldn't get far before they were caught. Back towards the nearest ground floor entrance of the hospital seemed their only choice.

Meanwhile, the chair gave way and the door swung open, hitting the wall with an ear-splitting bang. Henri sprinted to the open window. Looking ahead and to the left he saw nothing. José checked the bathroom but it was empty. It was then Henri spotted them, a hundred yards away, their blue pyjamas a dead giveaway. Shouting to José, Henri sprinted out of the room to the staircase. José tried to keep up but his years of smoking and his age slowed him down. In less than a minute Henri would be down stairs and the boys caught. They needed a miracle.

Chapter 23

The hospital corridor was deserted. Voices could be heard at the far end, female voices. *It must be the nurses' station,* Mike thought. Racing through the first set of double doors, the sensor above their heads activated the lights. A small anti-room was illuminated with three large stainless steel basins. The light to the next room had also been activated showing the boys a modern operating theatre fully kitted out with instruments and equipment ready for use. Next to the steel basins green trousers, white gowns, masks and headwear all hung on a row of hooks. White plastic clogs in little sterile packs sat immaculately on a shelf not far away.

'Put these on quick,' Mike said to Dan throwing the outfits at him. It didn't take them long to get changed and the pyjamas were discarded in a waste bin almost instantly. Mike shuddered as the cold garment touched his skin. He never liked wearing trousers without underpants but in this case he would make exceptions. A commotion could be heard at the end of the corridor. Mike carefully pulled back the swing door to look. José had a gun pointed at the nurses while Henri methodically opened every door in the corridor.

'Get on this,' Mike said, to Dan pulling an operating theatre trolley towards him. Dan looked at him bemused but Mike had no time to explain. Pushing Dan onto the trolley he covered him up totally, from head to toe, with a white sheet. Quickly donning his mask, Mike wheeled the trolley out into the corridor nearly hitting Henri in the process.

'Entschuldigen,' Mike said in the finest German that he could muster, hoping that he'd remembered the right word for excuse me. Dan lay still, holding his breath; he closed his eyes and concentrated hard to keep his body from shaking with nerves. Henri, not interested in hospital staff, pushed past and continued his search further down the corridor. Mike continued walking towards the exit, the one through which they had just entered. Any second he expected Henri to appear again, but he never did; both he and José had disappeared along the other end of the corridor. Once outside, Mike pushed Dan to the end of the pavement, whipped off the sheet and, without making a sound, they disappeared into the night.

***

The mobile phone rang and vibrated against the small dolphin-shaped lamp which sat on the bedside table, waking Jim immediately. Hans broke the news. Jim searched for his clothes. A car would be waiting downstairs; no time for pointing the finger now. Dressed and downstairs in record time, Jim swore during the whole duration of the journey to the hospital. 'This was getting out of hand,' he said to himself. People had died this time.

Hans stood behind the Polizei crime scene tape, hands in pockets in deep contemplation.

'Hans, what's going on?' said Jim. 'Tell me you haven't lost them. Does Dubois have them?' Hans didn't answer. His mind seemed to be elsewhere.

'Hans, for God's sake, talk to me. What kind of show are you running out here?' Striking the wrong nerve, Hans swung around and glared at his English friend. Jim knew that in his frustration he'd said the wrong thing, and he regretted it almost immediately.

'I've lost three good men tonight. Two with throats cut and one suffocated with a plastic bag. Three wives

308

and five children left without husbands and fathers. Do not say a word to me, Superintendent.'

'Look Hans, I'm sorry, forgive me. I know it's not your fault.'

'But it is my fault, Jim. I underestimated these men. Blame goes to the top and that's where I sit.'

Hans was suffering deeply. Jim realised it would be best to wait a while before talking to his friend again. There were other officers around who could explain the circumstances, and anyway Hans would have his hands full for the next few hours notifying relatives of their losses. Jim knew from experience how awful that would be.

***

Mike stopped running, doubling over to catch his breath. Dan lent against a lamppost to stop himself from falling over.

'Where are we going?' asked Dan, taking one of the rubber shoes off and rubbing his foot.

'I don't know, but I think we need to get back to the camp. We'll be safe there,' Mike said, walking towards a town map which fortuitously stood a few yards away. 'We are here and the camp is there,' he continued, running his finger across the map.

'That's bloody miles away. How the hell are we going to get there? We've got no money.'

'Dan, stop asking questions. You do some thinking for a change. I've had it up to here,' said Mike, holding his hand to his forehead. 'I'm sick of all this running, sick and tired.' Mike crouched down on his haunches. Dan decided to study the map - maybe he would get some inspiration from it. He didn't really know what it all meant - it might as well have been written in Chinese as far as he was concerned.

Mike got to his feet again. Pushing Dan to one side, he concentrated on the map.

'Right, we are here, there's the camp and that black line goes from here to there. Bingo. We'll take the Stadtbahn.'

'We'll take the what?'

'It's the local light railway, or tram system. It'll take us right to the camp.'

'But we've got no money for tickets,' Dan said looking defeated already.

'Don't tell me you've never been on the Newcastle Metro before without paying?'

'Yeah, all the time, but when you get caught on the Metro they don't do anything to you. What happens if we get caught here?'

'Well then, they'll call the police and we'll be safe in their hands, ok? You got any better ideas?' Dan shook his head.

'Right, the train stop should be over there. Come on, keep up.' Running again, they headed off to catch a train.

***

Jim lit the cigarette that he had been given. He went a little light-headed as he breathed the smoke into his lungs. It had been a long time since he had smoked, but the shit had definitely hit the fan tonight and he needed it to take his mind off the thought that Mike and Dan were either lost in Gelsenkirken or in the hands of Dubois.

Earlier that evening, Hans had placed two of his officers in an unmarked car to watch the front of the hospital. José and Henri had got to them. José, using a method often used by him, sliced the throat of the officer in the driver's seat. Henri had thrown a bag over

310

the other officer's head, pulling it tight around his neck. José's kill had taken seconds for the life to drain out of his victim. Henri, on the other hand, had struggled with his victim for over a minute, slowly starving the officer of air. José had despatched the officer guarding the room in the same inimitable fashion and dumped the body in a storeroom. All three deaths had been unpleasant to say the least and totally unnecessary.

Why kill? Why not just incapacitate? Jim thought. This whole business with Dubois was becoming ugly. If police officers could be killed with such disregard, then Mike and Dan's deaths would be easy. Jim began to wonder how he would explain his nephew's demise to his brother and sister-in-law. He cringed at the thought.

***

The small train station, if you could call it that, was deserted. It consisted of a ticket machine next to a perspex bus shelter affair. The only saving grace for the boys was that there was a clock and there happened to be one more train tonight before it stopped until the morning. At 1.30am the train arrived. Stopping for only a few seconds, the doors opened. The boys got in and it moved off again.

The single carriage would normally have accommodated around thirty people, but at this time of night there were only three other people onboard. It was modern, clean and lit up like a Christmas tree with electronic advertising everywhere. Mike compared it to some of the English trains that he had travelled on. He sniffed the air. It was clean, not like some of the English carriages he travelled in, which smelt like people had urinated in them. This one was a different class.

An old couple in their seventies sat side by side, holding hands for security and reassurance. Mike and Dan sat opposite. The old man looked at the two fake hospital workers and nodded politely. Mike dipped his head in response but said nothing. Dan wasn't paying any attention to them; he was studying a chart giving the number of stops before they had to get off.

The third passenger was a young punk rocker with a bright green Mohican hair style that stood a good eight inches off the top of his head. Mike thought he looked like a parrot as he also had a big nose, but he'd not seen many six foot parrots drinking beer on a train before. The punk nodded his head in recognition when he made eye contact with Mike. Mike replied back with a gentle raising of his eyebrows, hoping not to annoy him as he looked quite intimidating. Too late! The punk rose from his seat, walked down the train and sat next to Mike. He had a swastika on each of his military-style boots, his tartan trousers were so worn that they must have been originals from the seventies and his ripped leather jacket had 'Fuck off' written all over the front and back.

'He's probably on drugs,' Dan said into Mike's ear.

'Well, you should know,' Mike answered stiffly. Dan didn't appreciate the reply and threw himself back in his seat in a huff.

The punk, without saying a word, ripped the cardboard apart on his box of beers, took two cans out and offered them to Mike and Dan. Thinking it bad to decline the offer, Mike took two cans from him, passing one to Dan and said 'thank you' in English.

'English, I like the English. You strong, you beat us,' said the punk, picking his nose and wiping what came out on the seat. Mike hoped to God he was on about the World Cup; he couldn't be on about the war, surely.

'You want come to a party?' said the punk, taking a long drink from his own can.

'No thanks, we need to get back to Camp Steiner very quickly,' said Mike trying to sound manly but uninterested in the offer.

'Lots of girls, like English boys, you come,' he said making the shape of breasts with his hands. Dan looked across at Mike.

'Don't get any ideas,' whispered Mike into Dan's ear. 'We're going back to the camp, ok?' Dan was intrigued with the offer but he knew Mike was right.

'Just a thought,' Dan whispered back.

'Well, just keep it that way.'

Two more beers came their way and Dan was struggling to keep the offer under wraps.

'You doctors?' said the punk offering the third. Mike had forgotten about his appearance.

'No, not doctors. Students, yes medical students,' Mike said, plucking the answer out of the air. Dan looked at him. Mike shrugged his shoulders. Dan pointed at the diagram with the train stops; lucky theirs was next. Rising to their feet, they stood waiting for the train to come to a halt. Mike thanked the six foot parrot for the beer, who nodded back without saying anything and then spat phlegm over the floor. Mike was glad to be getting off.

Henri watched as the train stopped and the two lone figures descended and walked towards the main gates of Camp Steiner.

'We've got you now,' he said out loud, turning the ignition of the car. Didier and José, who were both dozing, woke with the noise of the engine turning over. For a change it was Dan who saw them first. The cigarette end flying out of the window like a tracer bullet from a machine gun caught his attention. He knew it was them. They'd found them! With no time to be frightened, he shouted to Mike, who was slowly lumbering towards the gate suffering from a complete lack of energy after the day's events.

'Run!' shouted Dan turning back towards the train.

The doors were still open and with luck they might get back on. Mike had found hidden energy and ran only a few yards behind Dan. Seeing the English boys run, Henri floored the throttle. Tyres screeching, burning rubber spewed out from behind the car as it sped towards the boys. Mike's chest burnt as his muscles and lungs worked overtime to sustain his escape. Dan reached the train first but the door had already closed. It was moving away, slowly picking up speed and momentum. Stretching for the button for the door, he lunged forward and pushed but nothing happened. He banged on the window for someone inside to open it, but it was no good - the old couple sat there in fright and the punk, with beer in hand, just smiled and waved.

'You fucking wanker!' Dan shouted, hitting the window with his fist. Eventually he had to let go or be dragged as the train sped away on its journey. Both boys were now in the wide open street, vulnerable to José and his tranquilisers. No other cars or people moved; there was no one to help. Twisting and turning between parked cars, they sprinted for their lives. Henri had narrowed the distance between them to only four or five car lengths. José had his window down, aiming his little green gun at Mike, but with Henri's erratic driving he was finding it impossible to take aim.

'Keep the car steady,' José shouted from the back seat. 'You drive like a woman.'

Henri heard him, but driving steady was not his priority as the boys had the luxury of being able to twist and turn, jump cars, gates and fences to evade them. He counted on fatigue and error to capture the boys, not that stupid vet's gun. Didier was helpless. To contribute he hung out of the front passenger window, ready to fling himself onto one of the boys and take them out.

Mike was slowing down. Every muscle in his body shouted for help and his lungs were ready to split. Seeing a small, dark alleyway between a bank and a pharmacist, Dan shouted to Mike but he was suffering and the enemy were in grabbing distance. Instinctively, without realising what he was doing, Dan stopped running, picked up a metal litterbin that had been placed outside the bank for all those discarded receipt slips and ran towards the oncoming car. Henri was concentrating on Mike and didn't see Dan. Didier tried to attract Henri's attention but he failed to do it in time.

Throwing the bin with all his might into the path of the oncoming car, Dan immediately jumped onto the bonnet of a parked car to escape being hit. The bin hit the bonnet and spun off with tremendous velocity, embedding itself in the windscreen. The shock of the impact caused Henri to swerve. The car spun sideways hitting the curb, throwing the passenger side into the air. Didier, who was perched on the door, flew out of the car flailing his arms and legs in midair, coming to an abrupt stop in a shop window. Glass smashed and covered him from head to toe but he was conscious, if not a little shaken.

The car by its own momentum had been raised into the air and spun upside down before landing on its roof. José hung onto the passenger seat for support but ended up on the ceiling of the car, which had now become the floor. Henri, belted in, hung like a poor excuse for a puppet, upside down, struggling to free himself. The upturned car slid headlong into a stone wall, taking out a lamppost on the way. Bricks and rubble exploded onto the street, car alarms activated with the carnage and lights from apartment buildings were suddenly switched on by residents woken by the noise. As the boys made their escape the car came to rest. The rear wheels spun out of control, the engine screamed for mercy and a plume of steam and smoke rose from the radiator. Dan and Mike quickly disappeared into the dark alleyway. It would be a few more minutes before the three pursuers were in a fit state to chase, but Dan knew they would. They needed to push on further into the back streets and, when the emergency vehicle sirens sounded far enough away, they finally stopped. Totally exhausted, soaking wet with sweat and still shaking, they sat down together on the steps of a lower level basement hidden from the pavement above, breathing heavily. Neither spoke.

Suddenly Dan burst into laughter. Mike looked at him confused.

'Did you see what happened back there? Did you see what I did? Fucking hell, that was unreal.' Only Dan could get a kick out of what had just happened. Mike was too tired to even talk, so he just ignored him. Dan sat quietly chuckling to himself.

***

Jim arrived at the upturned car with a colleague of Hans, who identified it as the stolen car driven by Henri. Sighing with relief, Jim was happy to know that the boys were out there somewhere and not in the hands of Dubois. Their precise location was unknown, but he was sure they would reveal themselves soon to the right people. For Henri, Didier and José the net would be tightening as Hans would throw every resource he had in finding them. If they were wise they would get out of Germany now, but Dubois would be a greater threat to them than any justice system and Jim knew that they would be lurking in the darkness somewhere.

***

The body heat from their exertion had disappeared and the chill of the night air bit into their lightly covered bodies. The hospital clothes had served their purpose well but offered no form of insulation. Black-eyed and weary, Mike and Dan walked aimlessly through the streets. The time was unknown, the streets were unknown and the city they walked in was unknown. They were lost. The city slept while they walked but their predicament wasn't hopeless. Dan had an idea.

'Why didn't I think of this earlier?' Dan said out loud, picking up the pace.

'Think of what?' replied Mike, walking quicker to keep up. Dan didn't answer; he was on a mission and jogged off in the direction of a shopping precinct. Mike tagged along behind, making no effort to understand what Dan had in mind. He hoped it would be good because at the present moment in time he was completely out of ideas. Dan suddenly stopped in front of a row of shops, lent against a lamppost and contemplated his idea. His eyes darted backwards and forwards to an area on the street that was having repairs and the brightly lit coloured façade in front.

'What are you going to do?' asked Mike standing next to him.

'Give me a minute, I'm thinking,' snapped Dan.

Mike turned away and began admiring a Rolex watch that sat in a jeweller's window behind him. It was gorgeous, with a diamond encrusted bezel, platinum face and platinum strap. It looked very expensive. His eyes nearly burst out of their sockets when he saw the price. Ten thousand euros! He chuckled to himself. What a waste of money, he thought, for something that spends most of its life

317

covered by a sleeve.

Turning to watch Dan, he yelled at him to stop but it was too late. Dan's brilliant idea had been set in motion. Mike watched in horror as Dan hurtled a red paving brick at a shop window. The glass broke immediately, sending shards of glass into the shop and onto the pavement. The brick continued inside, coming to rest in the hands of a female mannequin in a bikini. The crash of glass on stone sent a shockwave of noise into the street. Mike had his hands over his face, not to protect himself from flying glass but in shock at what he had just witnessed. The alarm sounded as the red light on the alarm box flashed angrily, on and off in time to the high-pitched whine.

'What the fuck did you do that for? Are you stupid?' shouted Mike, spinning Dan around and glaring into his face. Dan stood there laughing, totally nonplussed at what he had done. Mike grabbed him by the shoulders and shook him.

'What are you playing at? Don't you think we're in enough trouble?' Dan pushed Mike away.

'You don't understand, do you? Think about it.'

'Understand what? There's nothing to understand. You've just smashed a shop window for nowt.'

'Look, Sherlock. We need help and to be somewhere safe and that means the police. We could have spent all night looking for a cop shop and if we'd found one what would we say? I don't know what we'd say, do you?' Mike listened over the howling of the alarm, stuck for words. He thought that he may be starting to understand the reasoning behind what Dan had done, but he needed some more convincing

'I remember reading this story about a tramp in Newcastle on a freezing winter's night without anywhere to go,' continued Dan. 'Every place he tried to find shelter he would be moved on by the police.

They just wouldn't listen to him or help him at all. It was late in the evening, the coppers' shift was ending and the tramp was unimportant to them. So guess what he did?'

'Don't tell me he smashed a window?'

'Correct, you win first prize. You see, the police had to act now as he'd broken the law. He was arrested, locked up in a nice warm cell, given a hot meal and a bed to sleep in. It'll be the same for us, but we'll just ask for Captain Reidel. It's great, nothing will happen to us. Reidel will come and get us and Dubois men won't be able to touch us.' Dan finished his tail and grinned at Mike. 'Trust me, it's in the bag.'

At that, Dan scraped a patch of pavement clean and sat on the floor. Mike understood now, but he still couldn't believe what he had seen. Sitting together on the hard pavement they listened to the approaching police siren.

The handcuffs hurt, but the heavy two-foot long torch into the stomach didn't create a great deal of respect for the German police. Bundled into the back of a half green, half white VW Passat, Mike looked at Dan and mouthed 'wanker' in his direction. Dan told him to fuck off, but was then met with the torch again as one of the officers hit him in the ribs with the blunt end. Dan fell onto the seat, howling in pain, not able to rub his throbbing chest. Mike cringed in sympathy.

'You fucking kraut bastard,' Dan shouted. Mike nudged him to shut up. The officer raised the torch to hit Dan again, but when Dan cowered away he lowered it down and turned around. The German police obviously weren't as politically correct as their British counterparts. The rule of law still existed in Germany, England had lost theirs years ago. Dan, moaning and whimpering, didn't say another word as the car sped off towards the police station.

One out of three was the best that the boys got in custody. No bed and no hot food, but safe they were. Sitting in a six foot by six foot cell on a stone bench that was moulded into the wall and handcuff-free, Dan rubbed his chest. Mike, leaning forward, elbows on knees, propping his head up with his hands, looked thoroughly fed up. A single bulb on the ceiling in a protective metal cage gave off a depressing light which did nothing for their optimism. Conversation had died in the car, but at least on arrival Mike had been able to ask for Captain Reidel. Whether the message would be delivered he could only hope. For now they had to wait for their rescuers to come.

Chapter 24

Like two drunken tramps on a park bench, Mike and Dan sat propping each other up. Falling asleep individually, they had slowly drifted off together and were now supporting each other shoulder to shoulder. With heads drooped and saliva dribbling onto the floor from Dan's mouth, they were finally getting the sleep that they had yearned for.

The heavy bolt of the cell door striking the lock mechanism sent a deafening boom around the cell. It was loud enough to wake the dead. Mike sat up straight, eyes wide and for an instant not sure of his surroundings. Dan, losing his support, fell forwards onto the hard floor. Getting up, shaken but not hurt, he sat back onto the bench, rubbed his eyes and wiped his dribble away. Together they looked to the door, hopeful that a familiar face would walk through, but they were immediately disheartened when the same police officer that greeted them when they arrived in custody walked in. Their disappointment, though, lasted only for a second when Captain Reidel walked in close behind.

'Guten Morgen my young English friends,' he said, trying not to laugh, amused at what they were wearing.

'Herr Slater, you may come in now,' Reidel said, quickly remembering not to call him Superintendent. To the boys' relief Jim appeared at the doorway. However, he failed to restrain his amusement and burst into laughter when he saw their medical clothes.

'Oh, you think it's funny do you?' Mike said feeling aggrieved at being the cause of his amusement. 'So much for the police protection, or lack of, I should say,' he continued, directing his frustration at the Captain and his colleague. Reidel didn't answer, instead he ushered Jim into the cell, who sat down next to his nephew.

Whispering into Mike's ear, he asked if he was alright. Mike nodded and whispered a relieved 'yes' back to his uncle. Dan, not wishing to be left out, decided that it was his turn to air some of his complaints.

'Yeah, thanks a lot for the German hospitality. More like police brutality,' he shouted, holding up his shirt to show a large cluster of bruises on his ribcage. Reidel, seeing the marks, came over to take a closer look. His face showed concern but, behind his eyes, anger was growing. Dan pushed his chest out at the Captain who responded by gently pulling Dan's shirt back down. Turning to face his subordinate, he glared into the eyes of the police officer at the door. Dropping his head, not able to keep eye contact, the officer swallowed hard and prepared himself for the consequences. Dan, still in full swing, shouted out as the Captain walked away.

'No toilet, no food, nothing to drink and not even a mattress or a pillow. I don't like the Brit police but you lot are a disgrace.' Mike put his hand on Dan's leg, stopping him in his tracks before he said something that he might regret, if he'd not already done so.

'Shut up, Dan, that's enough,' Mike said, feeling weary and exhausted. Not wanting to alienate his saviours further, Mike tried to ease the tension that his friend had created.

'Thank you, Captain, for your help and we are sorry for the damage caused. That is what my friend really wanted to say, wasn't it?' Mike said, gripping Dan's thigh and squeezing. Dan looked at him and Mike just shook his head like an annoyed father at a mischievous son.

Reidel heard, but his course was set and no intervention, kind or malicious, would stop him from dealing with his subordinate. Any humour or laughter that remained had disappeared. His night had started badly and was ending even worse and the officer at the door was going to take full brunt of his wrath. No one knew what was said, but it wasn't friendly chat. The officer stood with his back pinned to the cell door, humiliated and threatened by his superior, who unleashed a torrent of abuse into his face. The officer tried to reply, stuttering to get his words out, but the Captain silenced him each time. He had no time for excuses.

Having finally finished, the Captain dismissed his disgraced colleague. As the officer scurried away into the custody suite to lick his wounds Reidel, feeling relieved and de-stressed, grinned at his English friends. Mike and Dan looked at each other, feeling a little embarrassed to have witnessed such a dressing down. They hadn't exactly been angels themselves that night and it wasn't that particular officer's fault anyway; it was the two who brought them in. Jim had seen it all before and no doubt dished out the same kind of justice to incompetent colleagues back home, but nevertheless he sat there slightly impressed by the show that he had just witnessed. Hans Reidel was definitely not a man to get into an argument with.

'Forgive me. My colleagues have forgotten their duty and they will pay for their errors. Do you need attention for your injury?' he said looking sympathetically at Dan.

'No, I'll live,' Dan replied bluntly. Mike squeezed his leg again. 'Thank you Captain, I'm fine.' The Captain nodded in agreement.

'Do not worry yourselves about the window, I have a friend in the British police who will be footing the bill,' he said, grinning at Jim. Jim looked at him in surprise and shook his head, but he couldn't reply. He realised very quickly that he had been stitched up and when he knew the boys couldn't see him he looked at Hans and wagged his finger in jest. *Anyway who cares?* he thought, the force had deep pockets.

'Look, can we just get out of here?' said Dan, standing up and stretching his legs. Reidel ushered them out of the cell and, after a short walk down two corridors and up a flight of stairs, they entered an office with a comfortable reclining seat and settee which the boys pounced upon almost immediately. On the way, Mike had been able to tell Jim about their movements. Jim listened, taking in the facts, but he already had a fair idea of what had gone on. However, for Mike's sake he let him tell his story.

Jim, on the other hand, needed to tell Mike and Dan about the three dead police officers. Dubois had upped the stakes and the boys needed to know that tonight widows and orphans had been made. The timing would never be good and when they were sitting comfortably he told them. Both boys took the news of the deaths badly and they instantly realised that their predicament had not got any better. Luck had been on their side so far and if Dubois was to be caught the luck would have to remain with them.

Mike was lost for words. He looked over at Dan, who looked away in shame. Dan knew that, because of him, his father and drugs, three men had been killed. He lay down and covered his face. Tears flowed but he hid them well. He cursed his father and hated himself. Lying there, shielded from view, he swore that if he got out of this alive he would make his father pay.

It had taken an event of evil proportions to show Dan the error of his ways. Mike would say later that, on that night, Dan changed for the better. He couldn't put his finger on it but Dan woke up a different person. Part of the boy in him had died and a man had taken its place.

Mike, finding it hard to sleep, looked across at the Captain. He regretted what had been said earlier and felt uncomfortable with himself for doubting the abilities of the police. Dubois and his men were killers and it had taken three deaths for him to realise that Dubois had to be stopped. There was definitely no going back now. If he had to put his life on the line to catch or kill Dubois then so be it. He apologised to Jim for having got him involved, and thanked him for hiding the events from his parents.

Jim swallowed hard; he was glad that this charade was coming to an end. He hugged his nephew and tried to allay Mike's fears, giving him reassurance that in the end Dubois would be caught, but he despised himself more and more for the lies and deception. Reidel watched and understood the heartache on both sides. Sometimes life could be cruel, but for an undercover police officer life could be hell.

After hot coffee and vending machine sandwiches, Hans and Jim left the boys to sleep. Their worries were still out there, but the noose was slowly tightening around Dubois's neck and, sooner rather than later, he and his men would be theirs.

***

The lamppost wasn't working at the far end of the service station car park. The black Mercedes, with its even blacker windows, was barely visible to the early morning motorists stopping for their breakfast.

'Be assured,' said Dubois, talking hands-free into the microphone clipped to his collar, 'they will not leave Paris. You have my word.'

'I hope you are right, Dubois, for your sake,' said the voice on the other end. The line went dead. Dubois sat back into the plush leather seat, feeling tense and frustrated at being treated like a third rate common criminal. *Why were these boys so hard to catch?* he thought to himself. He felt the bulge made by his revolver under his jacket. It was never far away from him and it wouldn't let him down if he needed it. It was the only thing left that he could trust and be sure that it would do what was asked of it. The feel of it made him relax. Pulling it from its holster, he checked the magazine, chambered a round and applied the safety catch. *Best to be prepared*, he thought, *you never know what might happen.*

The headlights startled him and he shielded his eyes from their glare as the vehicle approached. Driving full circle around the black Mercedes, the strange car came to a halt and turned off its lights. Henri stepped out, walked to the Mercedes and got into the rear. Closing the door he looked across at Dubois. He did not fear Dubois. Dubois was the father that he never had. Take his punishment he would, and if it was to be his life then so be it. Sitting in silence, he waited for Dubois to make the first move.

'Henri, you have been with me nearly all of your life,' Dubois said cool and collectedly. Henri did not reply but looked down at the floor. It was his time to listen. 'I have nurtured you and taught you everything I know. You have carried out many tasks for me and have never questioned them or failed to deliver a result. Why is this, I ask? It is because I have guided you, Henri. I have guided you as a father guides a son, and I shall guide you again and together we will succeed where alone you will fail.' Leaning over, Dubois kissed Henri on his forehead like a priest would kiss a child in his congregation. Henri lifted his head but still remained silent. They had business to do.

Giving instructions to Didier and José, Henri and

Dubois left together in the Mercedes. Paris would be their next stop and there was much work to do.

***

It was 8.30am when Jim and Reidel reappeared. Mike and Dan were woken from their slumber and presented with breakfast. Fresh bread, ham, cheese and two enormous cups of hot chocolate were placed before them. Dan was quiet. Mike knew that he was troubled but he left him alone, wrestling with his own demons. Clothes arrived next - their own clothes, washed and ironed immaculately. *Even better than what mum would do*, Mike thought, but he'd never tell her that.

At 9.15am they left the police station. A red unmarked BMW sat at the main entrance of the police station with doors open and engine running. Mike looked around, taking in the scene. He had in his head a vision of what he thought the police station might look like in the day time, but it was nothing like what he had imagined. In the dark, lights and shapes had moulded into one, making the building appear old and shabby - or so he had thought, having spent most of the time doubled over with his hands cuffed behind his back. Now, though, in the light of day the building glistened with glass. Pleasantly surprised and feeling rather positive about his imminent future, he got into the back of the car. Dan was still silent. His face was straight and lacking emotion and it stayed that way as the car pulled away. Captain Reidel drove and Uncle Jim sat next to him, looking nervous, twice starting to say something but stopping each time.

Nothing was said as the car made its way through Gelsenkirken. Traffic was heavy and every traffic light that could have turned red did so. Everything he saw was alien to Mike as he watched as commercial

327

buildings gave way to suburbs, and suburbs gave way to open fields. The sun slowly climbed in the morning sky and for once Mike felt relaxed and at peace. He was safe for the time being and happy to soak up his security.

The car had been driving for an hour when it pulled into a secluded lay-by. Coming to a stop next to a picnic table, Reidel and Jim got out and opened the rear doors for the boys. Dan climbed out and immediately strolled away from the car and sat under a small sycamore tree. Mike walked over and sat next to him, waiting for Dan to say something, but he never did.

'You know, it's not your fault,' Mike said putting his hand onto Dan's shoulder. Dan flinched. Mike could feel the tension in his body.

'You didn't kill those police officers. I did,' Dan said with pent-up emotion in his words.

'Don't talk bollocks. You didn't put the weapons in their hands,' Mike replied annoyed with what Dan was saying. 'People like that kill because they want too, because life to them is cheap. They don't need reasons. If things we do had predictable endings then the majority of them wouldn't be done in the first place. You and I are part of this stupid game. We didn't start it and we have no control over it, but we can help to end it. We've come too far these past few days to be sitting here blaming ourselves. Oh, I could sit here and blame you for getting me into this shit, but I don't. What's done is done. Now come on, let's concentrate on what we came here for, you agree?' There was no reply.

Getting up, Mike walked away. He knew Dan had heard him but Dan had made no effort to respond. Whether Mike's words would make him feel any better he didn't know. He left him to think it out for himself.

Jim and Hans stood by the car, smoking. Both men

looked serious and when they saw Mike approach their cigarettes were stubbed out.

'I didn't know you smoked,' Mike said wagging a finger at his uncle.

'It's a long story. You don't want to know,' replied Jim, putting the cigarette packet into his pocket. Walking around the car to face Mike, he leaned against the side, anxious at what he was about to do.

'It's about time that I told you what's going to happen next,' Jim said, sounding anxious. Mike looked at him puzzled. Why should his Uncle Jim be telling him what's happening? *What's it to do with him?* he thought.

'Come over here, I need to talk to you.' Jim began walking away from the car towards a picnic table several metres away. Mike followed and sat facing opposite, intrigued by what his uncle was about to say. Jim had been pondering the subject of telling Mike the truth all night. The bottle of Schnapps shared with Hans had helped a little but, in the end, he had decided that it would have to be now or never if he was going to do it. The stakes of the game had been raised and it was time for his nephew to decide whether he wanted to play his part any more.

'Mike, I owe you the truth,' Jim said, staring Mike full in the face. Mike, suddenly feeling nervous, waited for his uncle to continue.

'I'm not an accountant and never have been one. It was all a lie to hide my real job.' Mike squirmed on his seat, uncomfortable with what he was hearing. 'You see Mike,' Jim began and then immediately stood up and hit the table with his hand in frustration. 'God this is difficult!' He shouted out, staring up at the sky and cursing under his breath. Mike's eyes widened in shock and he felt decidedly uneasy with this display of anger. 'I'm a police officer, alright! I always have been since I left school and no doubt I always will be.'

'What are you trying to say?' Mike said, showing his first sign of rage that was steadily building inside him.

'What I'm trying to say is that I'm a police Superintendent, part of the Serious Organised Crime Agency and attached to Interpol. This is my job, Mike. I catch scumbags like Dubois and close their drug operations down.'

'I don't believe what I'm hearing,' Mike said, slowly shaking his head. 'Why have you kept this a secret from me? Why couldn't you have just told me in the first place? Did you not trust me, or was it because you thought I was a child, not mature enough to be told?'

'You don't understand, Mike. I couldn't tell you. It wasn't that simple.'

'Bullshit! The truth is always simple.'

'You couldn't handle the truth,' Jim shouted back at him. 'You were heading for prison. Your life was ruined before it had even started and you blame me for not telling you the truth? You better think again.' Jim was right, but he was still confused as to why he hadn't been told the truth.

'I hear what you say, but you still should have told me. I'm family,' Mike said standing up face to face with his uncle.

'My point exactly,' replied Jim staring back. 'Family we are and from the moment that I stood behind that one-way glass and saw you sitting there in that interview room, like a common criminal, family was all that I had in my mind. I didn't believe what I was seeing - my brother's boy caught red-handed with millions of pounds' worth of ecstasy. It wasn't possible for me just to let you go with an apology and a slap on the wrist. And it definitely wasn't possible for me to see you thrown into jail. What was I supposed to do, Mike? Tell me, because if you have any better ideas I'd like to hear them.' Mike sat back down. The first knockout blow had been dealt and he was silenced. Jim sensed Mike's confusion and relaxed his tone once more.

'Do you know what would have happened if my superiors had found out that you were my nephew?' Mike shook his head. 'Off the case straight away and you and Dan would be facing a long prison sentence and a ruined life. Come to think of it, me being there saved you from prison. You understand that, don't you?'

'Yes, I do, but it was all an accident. Surely any court in the land would have seen that we were innocent?'

'No Mike,' Jim replied bluntly. 'Any court in the land would have convicted you. Nearly fifty million euros of class one drugs which you, yourself, had witnessed being loaded at Dubois's headquarters. Your fingerprints all over it and his father involved too, using his son and you as couriers. No, Mike, you were finished, believe me.' Mike's anger quickly subsided as he realised that everything Jim said was true.

'I'm not an angel, I know,' continued Jim. 'I'm a single man tied to his career, but I'm good at what I do, so please believe me when I say I had your welfare at heart. You wouldn't have come back on the tour if I had revealed my true identity in England. You would have been finished. The only way we could succeed was if I came on the tour with you as your dutiful uncle and hope that you unknowingly would flush Dubois out from his hiding place.'

'Bait, is that what we are? Bait?'

'Yes, bait if you want to call it that. But think about it. It's the only way you can clear your name and stop

Dubois from coming after you. Dubois is ruthless. You've seen him in action. His men have killed, and all in the course of trying to get to you and Dan. He won't stop. He's a man driven by revenge and hatred. And remember this - if he can't get to you he will get to the people that you love the most.' Mike's eyes shot up as he realised the enormity of what Jim had said.

'Yes, you're starting to understand now, aren't you?' Jim said smiling confidently. 'Your mother and father, destroyed by you throwing your life away or destroyed by Dubois. It's a horrible thought, isn't it? You have no choice and I had no choice but to use you.'

'What about mum and dad? Do they know?' asked Mike, his voice stuttering in panic.

'For now they know nothing and I hope that we can keep it that way. I've got a team watching them round the clock. They'll be ok, trust me.' Mike could feel tears welling with the immense burden that he now carried.

'Look Mike, I know that you are angry with me and you've got every right to be, but there was no other way. Why am I telling you all this? Isn't that what you want to know?' Mike looked up. Jim didn't need a reply to his question; he could see it in Mike's eyes. 'I'm giving you the choice, Mike. You've earned it. I thought that we would protect you better than what we have, but we didn't and I'm sorry. You've come close to being killed and it is now your right to decide your fate, not mine anymore.'

Mike didn't have to decide. He knew there and then what he must do, he always had, but he sat silently listening.

'You can go home, carry on as normal and I will do everything in my power to protect you and your family from Dubois, but I cannot change the law. You would still have to face the consequences of your actions. Or, you can stay with the tour, play your football, show those scouts who you are and leave the rest to me. Paris is where your future lies, not at home. But remember, Paris is where the danger lies also. Dubois and his men will still be there and your life will be on the line.' Jim waited as Mike soaked it all up. 'Two difficult choices and not one of them better than the other, but one is the right way and one is the wrong way. You're not stupid Mike, you're like me you want justice and to do what is right. Those families of the murdered policemen would not want you to walk away now. I know that you will do the right thing and I am sorry for hiding the truth from you.'

Jim walked away towards the car, leaving Mike alone. Mike stared at the wheat field in the distance. The wind caressed it gently, giving it the appearance of a golden ocean rocking and rolling. How simple to be a wheat plant, he thought. Dan sat down beside him and gave him a friendly nudge.

'I'm so sorry for all this shit that I have caused,' he whispered. 'People are dead and it's my fault.' Mike wanted to say 'yes it is' but he couldn't. In silence they sat together and watched the wheat sway in the breeze.

'Captain Reidel told me everything,' Dan said quietly into Mike's ear. 'It's not your fight anymore. I've caused you too much agro and I want you to get out and go home.' Mike turned and grinned at his friend and then pushed him over onto the grass.

'If you think that I dragged you across Amsterdam and through that fairground for nothing then you've got another thing coming. I've lost count how many times I've had to save your arse. Just face it, you need me.' Dan smiled back, the tension had been broken. Both boys laughed out loud and rolled on the grass. Mike rubbed Dan's hair into the ground and Dan squealed in pain. Everything was back to normal and the friendship as strong as ever. Jim and Hans watched and smiled from a distance. They knew the outcome. It would be in Paris where they would catch Dubois.

Chapter 25

Barry had become tired of the constant questions regarding the whereabouts of Mike and Dan. Picking up the bus microphone from the dashboard he announced to everybody, once and for all, that they would be making their own way to Paris. For some members of the team even that didn't quash their curiosity and they heckled Barry to tell more. Not being in a very talkative mood he told them to mind their own business, sit down, relax and enjoy the trip as it was going to be a long one.

He found it hard believing his own words and sat down feeling uneasy. He'd kept his mouth shut, forced himself to bite his tongue on a few occasions and even managed to keep his opinions to himself about Mike and Dan's predicament. He blamed himself. They were his boys. Given to him by trusting parents to look after and protect from danger. They were on the tour because of him and, if the truth be known, the tour was because of them. They were his adopted sons and he'd let them get into trouble and he couldn't do a thing about it. He desperately worried for them both as the bus slowly made its way towards Paris.

***

The atmosphere in the car had improved. Mike listened to Jim and Hans talking while Dan sat, much happier, looking out at the German countryside. Mike didn't hate Jim for what he'd done; he knew that Jim had his best interests at heart. Since being told the bombshell, keeping his parents safe and in the dark about everything was now the most important thing to do. He hated to think what his parents would be going through if they knew the truth. When all this had blown over and if he was still alive, he thought smiling to himself, he would need his mum and dad more than ever. Now, though, it was on to Paris with three top football scouts waiting to watch him play. Hopefully he would arrive in one piece and be in a fit state to impress them.

Hans had been given permission by his superiors to travel to Paris. The deaths of three of their men had been the decisive factor in letting him go. The authorities in Paris had been notified and they would be waiting for their arrival. The French guillotine would be primed and ready to separate Dubois's head from his neck. Hans smiled to himself when he thought of the Belgian's fate but, in reality, he knew that if Dubois was taken alive he would sit in a prison cell and be pampered by the over-politically correct justice systems that controlled Europe today. Dubois needed to die - it would be the only way to get real justice. Nevertheless, picturing Dubois having his head cut off the old-fashioned way did cheer him up for a while.

The burden of keeping the truth from Mike had gone and with it a heavy weight had been lifted from Jim's shoulders. For the first time in days he felt happier in the knowledge that he could concentrate on the task in hand without worrying about playing out his charade. He still remained unsure, though, about the coming events but happier nonetheless. Reaching into his pocket, he took out his packet of cigarettes. Looking at them, he chuckled to himself. Then, in a flash, he threw them out of the car window.

'I won't need those things again,' he said laughing.

'Hey, I would have had those,' said Hans in surprise.

'No you wouldn't. You need to give up too,' replied Jim. Both men laughed, unaware of what a cigarette packet hitting a windscreen at 90km/h could do. The two German police officers three cars behind didn't appreciate the packet of Marlboro Lights disintegrating in front of their eyes, and appreciated even less being told off by a senior officer of the Bundeskriminalamt for interfering with an undercover operation when they pulled the red BMW over.

Initially, Hans thought about playing innocent with the two officers, but he didn't like the tone of voice that one of the officers was using so out came his identification. Next came the how-to-embarrass method of interrogation, when the two officers had to listen to a barrage of reasons why you shouldn't stop an unmarked police car, particularly one of your own. Jim and the boys sat quietly watching Hans do his work. Dan smirked at one of the officers when it was all over, but they were in too much of a hurry to get away to take offence.

'You like giving uniform a hard time, don't you?' Jim said grinning at his friend.

'Keeps them on their toes, the bloody idiots. They needn't have stopped us. If they'd done a check on the car they wouldn't have come anywhere near us. Anyway,' Hans said, pointing his finger at Jim, 'for launching that packet you can buy the beers in Paris. What do you think boys?'

'Oh definitely,' said Mike.

'Yeah thanks Jim, it's very kind of you,' Dan shouted from the back seat, patting the Superintendent on his shoulder at the same time.

'Ok, ok, the beer's on me, but after we get Dubois. Thanks, Hans, you're a pal.' Hans looked at his friend winked at him, then turned back to his driving. With the fun and games over, Jim went back to his mobile phone making arrangements for their arrival. It was another ten minutes before he finished his calls and

Mike was eager to know what was going to happen next.

'Where are we going anyway?' asked Mike. 'I thought Paris was to the west and we've been going east for the last half hour.'

'Do you want to tell them Jim, or should I?' Hans said looking in the rear-view mirror at the boys in the back.

'Well, it's thanks to you Hans, so go for it,' replied Jim.

'Gentlemen, I will ask you just one question,' Hans said playfully. 'If you had the use of a private helicopter would you be driving a car to Paris?'

'No way!' shouted Dan in excitement. 'To Paris by helicopter? You're joking, right?' He looked at Mike in amazement. Jim turned around with a huge smile on his face.

'It's all to do with connections, boys. Hans has a lot more than me and they're bigger, richer and more powerful than mine.' Hans looked at Jim, shaking his head in jovial disagreement with Jim's comments.

'A stroke of luck, that's all. But don't get carried away, it might only have two seats and two of us might have to sit outside on the skids.' Everyone laughed.

The thought of flying to Paris by helicopter was the first bit of good news the boys had had in a while and, as the car sped towards their destination, they sat excitedly chatting like a couple of schoolboys. Mike looked across at Dan. His excitement spilled out into the car. Grinning from ear to ear, fidgeting and looking in anticipation at the route ahead, Mike was happy to see his friend in good spirits again.

The airfield was smaller than Dan had imagined and, even though he was excited, there was a slight disappointment when he realised that he wouldn't be walking across the runway of an International Airport

338

with everyone looking at him getting into his private helicopter. It was totally the opposite. It wasn't an airport at all but a field with a wind sock. It was as small as an airfield could be, with a name that no one but Hans could pronounce, consisting of two buildings, a small hangar with two wingless gliders and an ancient Cessna. There was a small hut attached to the end of the hangar which served as the club house, bar and control tower. Dan managed to hide his disappointment, but it would only be short lived.

It was late morning and not a soul was to be seen. Hans drove the car into the hangar, out of sight, and pulled up next to the Cessna. Birds that perched in the rafters, chirping, fled as the echoes of footsteps on concrete drowned out their morning singing. Dan raised the alarm first when he heard the drumming of the rotor blades in the distance. He ran around looking for it but, with the reverberation of the sound, it was difficult to tell where it was coming from. Jim and Hans paid no attention to it. For them, helicopters were a part of their job, but for Mike, and especially Dan, a helicopter ride was something special, a once in a lifetime occurrence that needed to be enjoyed and savoured.

The noise grew louder and louder and then, without warning, it appeared over the wood line at the rear of the airfield. Hanging in the sky for moment, like a Kestrel hovering above its prey, the helicopter made a circuit of the airfield and then gracefully landed in front of the hangar where they all stood. The down draft from the rotor blades threw up dirt grass and dust and all four onlookers had to shield their eyes and turn away until the blades stopped rotating.

Hans led the way with Mike and Dan following, Jim bringing up the rear. Climbing in, Hans handed everyone a set of headphones and demonstrated how to fasten their seat belt. Jim sat down next to Mike. With a crackle and a whine, the intercom came alive and Hans spoke to the pilot and co-pilot. The expectations of the two-seater helicopter that Hans had described had been blow away with the pure luxury that surrounded them. This was in no way a standard police helicopter, Mike thought, rubbing his hand up and down the armrests. The carpet on the floor was an inch thick. The seats were of cream coloured leather and reclined for extra comfort. Walnut trim adorned the door panels and, to top it all, there was a drinks cabinet with Champagne inside.

'Hello, my name is Gunter Kohl and I am the Pilot,' said a voice in best pigeon English. Mike and Dan looked to the front and saw a large man with dark sunglasses waving at them. 'This is Yan Schwarz and he is my co-pilot.' An equally large German waved back at them. Both boys gave a nervous wave and sat back as the rotors began to turn again.

'Please feel free to talk into the microphones and ask any questions that you would like,' said the voice again. 'Enjoy the trip.'

Mike and Dan sat in silence as the speed of the rotor blades increased and the engines roared into life. With a small amount of vibration and without warning the helicopter lifted gently off the ground, turned one hundred and eighty degrees, dipped its nose and moved off gaining height as it flew. The sensation of gaining altitude in such a short time made the butterflies return to Dan's stomach. Mike listened to the pilot and co-pilot talking to air traffic control and found it weird that they spoke in English and not German, but he later found out that English was the universal language for pilots and he understood why.

The countryside seemed to pass slowly underneath them and now and again it would disappear completely when they entered a low cloud. Dan sat glued to the window, marvelling at everything that he saw. Hans spoke to the crew and Jim closed his eyes to grab some well-earned sleep. Mike wanted to know what this flight was all about and was just about to ask, when the pilot started to tell everyone the full details of the aircraft.

'You are in a Sikorsky S76 C++ five seater executive helicopter,' he said sounding impressed by his own words. Dan butted in before he could go any further.

'But this isn't a police helicopter, is it? It's too posh,' he said as he took a nosy look inside the drinks cabinet. Hans thought that he better tell them why they were flying in such luxury.

'This baby belongs to the European Union, so don't go thinking that the German police travel around in this style, ok?' Jim, not yet asleep, tapped Mike on his shoulder.

'You know when your dad complains about all the money that the Government wastes?' Mike nodded his head in agreement, as he knew very well how much his dad hated all politicians. 'Well, this is where some of that money goes,' Jim continued. 'It flies all of those Euro Members of Parliament back and forth across Europe. What would you expect? For them to catch a cheap flight on Ryan Air from Stansted? No, of course they don't. Wasting tax payers' money is their speciality. Not bad for a freebee, is it? Go on, ask the pilot what one of these babies cost to run.'

Mike could sense bitterness in his uncle's voice when he spoke about politicians, but for him they were just faces on the television that got accused of lying all the time. Mike asked his question and was bombarded with an assortment of technical answers - max speed 287km/h, two turbine engines and a cruising altitude of 2149metres, but his jaw fell when some of the financial costs were outlined. He looked across at Jim with astonishment. Even Dan was amazed at hearing some of the figures. The helicopter that they were flying in was ten years old but would still cost to buy today about £6 million. The average cost per hour was between £2500 and £3000, this flight costing about £6000. Jim looked at the boys and laughed when he saw their faces. He wished he had a camera with him. *What a picture it would make!* he thought.

The two-hour flight seemed to pass in no time at all. Dan asked if he could have some Champagne, but when the pilot told him it would cost him a hundred and fifty pounds a bottle he quickly changed his mind. Water was offered instead, but at five pounds a bottle he decided that he wasn't thirsty anymore. Paris soon arrived and the view was tremendous. The River Seine snaked through the centre with the magnificent Notre Dame Cathedral sitting majestically on its own small island. The sky was clear and both boys looked for the Eiffel Tower. The pilot pointed it out and kindly turned right so that the boys could get a clearer view. Towering over Paris like a child's giant Mechano set, you could just about see the people on the top level. Dan waved to see if anyone would wave back but the helicopter turned again, putting the tower behind them and headed for the main police headquarters with its private helicopter landing pad.

It was the smell and sounds of Paris that hit them first as they descended from the helicopter. The early morning start in Germany had been in the countryside surrounded by fresh summer air and silence. Now they were in Paris one of the most beautiful cities in Europe. The smell of diesel fumes, coffee, bread and cheeses greeted them, together with the noises of car horns, screeching tyres and a man shouting angrily in the distance. How different it all seemed.

The boys were led by a French Gendarme into a grey, anonymous-looking building and asked to wait in a small office. Jim and Hans disappeared with the officer and the boys were left alone. Five minutes passed when Jim returned followed by a short man in a grey suit with an extremely large nose. Francois Lachaise introduced himself to the boys. Head of the Europol Division in Paris Lachaise was at the top of the tree, only one down from the Police Commissioner himself. As Commissaire Divisionnaire, he would be in charge of operations whilst they were in Paris but, as always, Jim knew the man well and knew the boys would like him.

Intelligence reports had learnt from an undercover source that Dubois was coming to Paris to carry out some business. Mike and Dan looked at each other and then at Jim, who mouthed 'relax' back to them while Lachaise still spoke. Outlining the resources available to him, he assured the boys that in his city they were safe. Dubois and his men would either be in custody or dead, he didn't care which. Shaking their hands, he left the room more quickly than when he'd arrived, leaving the boys feeling slightly vulnerable. The word 'dead' hadn't made the boys feel any better. Jim saw the look on their faces and he knew what they were thinking.

'Hey!' Jim shouted to get their attention. 'I think you two better have these back.' Tossing the Sunderland badge transmitters over to them, Mike caught his and put it straight into his pocket. Dan, on the other hand, toyed with his for a few seconds, pretending to drop it onto the floor. Jim looked at him, not amused at his antics Dan caught it once more, spat on it and then rammed it unceremoniously into his pocket.

'What's going on Jim?' said Mike suspiciously, feeling that he and Dan were being left in the dark.

'Nothing is going on. Everything is under control.'

'Well, I don't know about Dan but I'd like to know just what it is that's under control.'

'Mike, you trust me don't you?'

'Of course I do, but...'

'No buts, ok? This time you have the whole of the Parisian law enforcement behind you. I need you to act normal.' Dan butted in before Jim could finish.

'Normal with what's going on? How are we supposed to act normal?' Dan shouted out in annoyance.

'Do you really want to know?' Jim said, staring furiously at them. Both nodded back in unison.

'What I want you to do is, go back to your team and play your football. There is no doubt that Dubois will try and get to you, but he will fail.'

'But we were told that in Germany and look what happened,' said Mike striking the wrong cord with his uncle.

'What did you think was going to happen when you got here, eh? Dubois wants you and he will try anything to get to you. You concentrate on your football, never go anywhere alone and you can rest assured that there will be a friendly face not very far away.'

'But what if Dubois gets to us first?' said Mike looking straight into his uncle's eyes. Jim began to feel annoyed, but he couldn't hide his own thoughts and Mike was reading him like a book. Everyone in that room knew that it was a possibility Dubois could get to the boys first, but Jim was trying his best to convince them otherwise. Failing this, he came closer and whispered. All three heads were together when Jim said his parting shot.

'If Dubois succeeds you will need to be prepared to use your wits and strengths. Whatever you do, do not lose those transmitters. They will be your lifeline. But most importantly, do not give up hope, no matter how desperate things might seem. I will find you and that's a promise.' Looking up he broke away. 'It won't come to that. Now, come on,' he said breaking the tension. 'Let's get you to your hotel. I hear it's a good one.'

They left the police Headquarters in a police car disguised as a taxi. It wouldn't have been ideal for any of Dubois's informants to see them arriving at the hotel in a marked police vehicle. On a map, the hotel was only two kilometres away but in the Paris traffic it seemed more like fifty kilometres. Winding their way through the heart of Paris, sights that any tourist would want to see passed them by unnoticed. They didn't care for any of it. Jim's words reverberated around in their heads and deep down they knew that it would be only a matter of time before Dubois made contact. Mike closed his eyes and wished for it all to end. Dan's thoughts were a little bit more ruthless. He wanted to pull the trigger himself and watch Dubois's brains spray all over the pavement. That was his wish and he sat with his fingers crossed in an effort to make it come true.

When the car turned into rue St Jacques and they saw the stadium of the Parc Des Princes, their spirits lifted enough to take their minds off Dubois. The magnificent 48,000 seater stadium home of Paris Saint Germain stood before them. Since being demoted to stadium number two in 1989 when the Stade De France had become France's national stadium, it had not lost any of its splendour and Mike thought how in real life it looked even more majestic than in the pictures. He nudged Dan and asked him what he thought. Dan gave his usual reply of, when comparing anything against his beloved Newcastle, 'not as good as St James'. Mike, being more open-minded, was impressed nonetheless.

The hotel didn't fit the criteria of what Mike and

Dan were used to. It looked big, modern and expensive. Not the normal cheap establishment that the Indispensables frequented. Jim turned around from the front seat to give the boys the good news.

'You were supposed to be staying at a small Chambre d'hôte, that's a bed and breakfast for you northern boys, but thanks to Her Majesty's Constabulary, Interpol and the Bundeskriminalamt, you and your team mates have been moved here as it is easier for us to look after you. I know you're impressed,' Jim said grinning at them. 'But there's no need to thank me, it's the least that I could do.'

'Thank you, it's about time you did something right,' Mike said sticking his tongue out. Jim didn't take offence; he just called his nephew a smart arse. Laughter rang out from the car as it pulled up at the entrance to the hotel. Built of concrete and glass and only a stone's throw away from the stadium, it was the perfect accommodation for anyone using the Parc Des Princes. Mike noticed that the team bus sat parked at the rear of the car park. He was pleased that his team mates were here already and no doubt Dan would bore everyone senseless with his helicopter story. A friendly face greeted them when the sliding door revealed the interior of the reception. Barry had been notified by Jim of their arrival and he rushed over as soon as they stepped inside. Hugging Mike first and then Dan, he was sincerely pleased to see them.

'Come over here, I've got something exciting to tell you,' Barry said leading them away to a comfortable seating area in the lobby.

'Barry,' Mike said as soon as he sat down. 'We're sorry for all the bother that we've caused you. Isn't that right, Dan?' he said nudging his friend.

'Yeah, as Mike said, sorry all the crap we've caused Barry,' Dan said unconvincingly, but Barry was too overjoyed to let Dan bring him down.

'Look, it doesn't matter. You're here now and that's all I care about,' he said patting them both on the knees. Mike and Dan could see the excitement in Barry's face. 'Right, I've got two things to tell you. Firstly, tomorrow night the Indispensables will be playing football in the Parc Des Princes.'

'You're having us on, Barry, surely?' said Mike, amazed at what he'd just heard.

'No it's true, believe me. Originally we were to play one of their youth teams at their training ground, but they're replacing the turf in the stadium so they are letting us play in there instead before they rip it up. How fantastic is that?' Barry said, rubbing his hands together like an excited child. Mike and Dan hadn't seen him this happy for a long time. It was truly great news, but with everything that had gone on they found it hard to feel so excited.

'The second thing is that I had a phone call today from one of the scouts,' continued Barry, leaning towards them as if he was going to tell them something secretive. 'He would like to meet you both this evening. It appears that your reputations have preceded you. So at seven tonight the three of us will be dining at a small restaurant just along from the stadium to discuss your futures. What do you think about that?' Mike and Dan looked at each other in disbelief. Mike, feeling cautious, needed to know more.

'Why does a scout want to meet us even before he's seen us play? It sounds a bit weird if you ask me.'

'Don't worry,' Barry said. 'He's a good friend of mine and it won't be time wasted, I promise. Your uncle knows what's going on. It'll be fine.'

'You know about the police involvement?' said Mike, astonished by Barry's comment.

'Yes, I know what's going on. You don't think I'm

paying for this hotel do you? This is the reason you are not going alone to night. I'm going to be stuck like glue to you two. I'm not going let you out of my sight again.'

Dan looked at Mike, but Mike was quick in putting his hand over Dan's mouth to stop him from spoiling the occasion.

'Everything is going to be ok,' Mike said, slowly releasing his hand from Dan's mouth. 'Now let's get something to eat. I'm starving.'

Chapter 26

The story of their helicopter journey had gone down extremely well with the rest of the team, except for one. Miles St John, or snobby rich bastard as Dan called him, explained that his stock broker father regularly flew in his company helicopter to London from their home in Northumberland. It happened to be bigger, faster and more expensive than the one Mike and Dan had just flown in but, to cap it all, St John's father had his own brand new one on order. Dan had never liked St John, but stealing his thunder deserved punishment. Dan knew only one way to punish somebody and that meant physically. Lucky for St John, Jim arrived before any harm could be done.

'Mike, Dan,' Jim shouted over the chatter. ' It's time.' Dan gave St John a hard stare as he left with Mike. He would deal with him another time.

Down in the hotel lobby, Hans waited with a very nervous Barry who stood attacking his fingernails again. Monsieur Lachaise had requisitioned the hotel manager's office and, when the boys entered, he stood in deep discussion with Jim. Taking the nearest two seats, they sat down and prepared to listen to the night's proceedings. Mike looked at his uncle concerned at his facial expression. He knew that Jim wasn't happy with them leaving the safety of the hotel but they needed to get Dubois into the game. Lachaise's plan had become their only choice but nevertheless Jim tried everything to persuade Lachaise otherwise but to no avail. Sitting down next to Mike he gave his nephew a reassuring nudge. Mike smiled but made no eye contact. Abruptly coughing to clear his throat Lachaise started the briefing. The room went quiet and Mike swallowed hard.

A taxi would drive Barry and the boys the short distance to the restaurant. Police marksmen would be positioned on rooftops along the whole route, including the front and back of the restaurant. Once inside, their table would be positioned in such a way that, if a quick exit was required, nothing would block their route. The restaurant staff, of course, would all be undercover police and fully armed. Local street CCTV cameras had been seconded to cover the restaurant and all footage was being relayed back to a covert police surveillance vehicle from where Jim, Hans and Lachaise would control the operation. Mike rubbed his brow nervously and Dan let out a long sigh. They were part of something big and there was no way of backing out now.

'Do you understand everything, boys?' Jim asked, once the details of the operation had been laid out. Subdued and apprehensive, they both nodded.

'And just think,' Jim said, chuckling to himself. 'If nothing happens you get a nice meal at a swanky French restaurant for nothing. Can't be bad, eh?' Mike and Dan didn't appreciate Jim's optimism and only managed feeble smiles. Leaving the office, Jim shook Barry's hand and patted him on the back.

'Good luck, Barry. Take care of my nephew, will you?'

Barry nodded but couldn't answer. His nerves were so bad that he'd clamped his mouth shut, biting his bottom lip to stop it quivering. As he left the room he made the sign of the cross on his chest. Jim just smiled and patted him on the back once more.

'Good luck, Mike,' Jim whispered into his nephew's ear. Gripping Mike's shoulder, he hoped to give him reassurance. 'It'll be alright, believe me. Probably an over-the-top reaction to nothing. I'll see you later.'

Mike didn't react, but carried on walking to the taxi. His mind was spinning so much that he felt light-headed.

The taxi, with engine running, sat at the entrance with a plain-clothed, armed officer at the wheel. Barry climbed into the front passenger seat and the boys got into the rear, watched from a distance by Jim. As it pulled out of the hotel car park, Mike looked back at his uncle who stood behind the sliding doors trying to stay out of sight. He put his thumb up to his nephew. Mike nodded nervously back at him and smiled the best he could. Jim looked into his nephew's eyes and saw fear. Turning away, he hid himself in case Mike could see the fear in his.

Seeing his uncle turn away unnerved Mike, but it was too late for him to read anything into it and it would just be another worry to add to his already growing list. The taxi turned the corner and it was time to concentrate on other things. Looking at each other for the umpteenth time, but without saying a word, both boys knew that they had jumped into deep water. Mike held up crossed fingers in the hope that there would be no sharks swimming in it.

The Belle Époque was no different from a thousand other Parisian restaurants. Situated in a small street, it comprised the whole ground floor of a six-storey, hundred year old French apartment block. It was well away from the main tourist routes and therefore survived on its regular clientele. Set meals at lunch time for office workers and quality evening à la carte menus enabled it to thrive extremely well. The only down side for the restaurant, if it was a down side, was the amount of traffic that used the road out front. In the summer, people wanted to eat outside but with a small pavement and wall to wall cars, two tables and four chairs were all that they could manage. Nevertheless, traffic brought customers and customers brought profit.

The taxi turned the final corner into Rue Daumier and approached the restaurant slowly. Behind it a line of cars, with their occupants ignorant of the importance of the leading vehicle, travelled their regular routes on their way home from work. Jim stood behind Lachaise studying the TV monitors of the CCTV cameras. They could see the taxi approaching and Lachaise informed his men. Jim had watched a thousand operations just like this. It was always business to him and even if they went wrong or failed he could pick up the pieces, totally remote from any personal concerns. This time, though, it was different. Mike made it different. Family involvement was taboo in his line of work and he stood nervously behind his colleagues, praying that nothing would happen.

Like any other taxi ride in a big city there was so much to see, different faces, architecture, the feeling of grandeur and opulence. Mike saw it all. A young attractive French girl pushed a baby in a pushchair, stopping at every window to browse. Mike thought that she must be a nanny as she was too young and gorgeous to have a child. An old man with a black French beret precariously balanced on his head sucked hard on his Gauloise cigarette. His face carried the lines of a hard life as he stood motionless and expressionless, watching the World go by. How different it all looked compared to Newcastle. Grey Street in the city centre back home was beautiful with its tall elegant Georgian buildings, but here in Paris every street seemed architecturally glamorous.

Mike was in deep thought when it happened and he wasn't prepared for it. No one, not even Lachaise, was prepared for the coming chain of events. All the focus had been placed on the restaurant - no one would surely attempt something in broad daylight in a busy French street. Jim saw it happening first. Something didn't quite fit and his gut instincts, built up over the years, were beginning to shout at him again.

'There's something wrong,' he said putting his finger onto the screen of the monitor. They could see a man wearing dark glasses walking hurriedly, with his head down, towards the taxi. Watching with eyes wide, Jim saw the man slowly withdraw something from his jacket. His stomach turned when he realised what the object was.

'It's a grenade!' he yelled. 'He's got a bloody grenade.' For an instant everybody in the van froze as they watched the stranger pull the pin from the grenade and roll it under the taxi. Everyone in the car was blissfully unaware of what was going on as they sat, oblivious to the nightmare that was about to unfold. As the grenade came to rest it immediately began to spew out smoke which curled upwards in the light evening breeze, slowly enveloping the taxi.

A white lorry that had been parked further down the street headed in their direction. On any normal day, the lorry would have passed by without anyone taking notice, but the driver of this one had other intentions. Swerving directly into the path of the taxi, the lorry smashed into it head on. Pushing the taxi back violently, the shockwave threw everyone inside around like rag dolls. Barry lost consciousness as his head struck the passenger window. Blood began to pour from his brow as he slumped forward, doubled over in the foot well. Dan sat dazed, holding his head. Mike frantically tugged at his seat belt to get free but, in his panic, the easiest of tasks was proving impossible.

The police driver, shaken and bruised, instinctively, through his years of training, thrust the gear stick into reverse. Escape and evade was his only priority. Save the passengers at all costs. With screeching tyres and burning rubber, the taxi reversed in the cloud of smoke that filled the street behind them. Another sudden violent jolt and the car stopped. They had nowhere to go; the taxi was hemmed in with the traffic piled up behind. The ramp of the lorry dropped with a loud clatter as it hit the road surface and two armed men, wearing respirators, appeared from behind and ran towards the stricken taxi.

Jim had had enough of watching the events unfold in front of his eyes. As Lachaise shouted orders to his men, Jim and Hans leapt from the back of the van. They were at least two minutes away if they sprinted, but the blocked road and panicking civilians would make their run harder and longer. Nevertheless, with gun in hand and his old German friend to back him up, he sprinted to where his nephew was in danger. Giving the orders for the two masked men to be taken down, Lachaise stood in silence for his men to confirm the shoot. No confirmation returned, the smoke was too thick and, with panicking civilians in the area, no officer would risk taking a shot. He ran his hands through his thinning hair in frustration and shouted French obscenities at the TV monitors.

The police driver fumbled for his side arm, but he slumped forward almost immediately as the 5mm round entered the side of his temple and exited through his neck. His death was instant. Blood and tissue sprayed onto everyone around him. Dan screamed as droplets of blood and pieces of skull hit him in his face. Mike, in shock, stared mesmerised at the piece of scalp that had fallen onto his lap. His brain shut down in shock and with it went any survival instincts that he may have had. He was seeing everything but not believing what he was seeing. Comprehending nothing, he was too far gone to even care about what would happen next.

Dan, still very much aware, kicked and punched

anything and everything as he was violently hauled from the car. The needle that punctured his skin and allowed the knockout drug to enter his body didn't cause him any pain at all. Still struggling as he was dragged along the road, his captor decided that it would be easier if he put him to sleep the old-fashioned way. The punch did the job and Dan lost consciousness immediately. Mike felt a sharp twinge as the needle stuck into his flesh and it momentarily woke him from his trance, but it was too late.

The engine roared as the black Range Rover drove at speed out of the back of the lorry and screeched to a halt in the road. The two boys were unceremoniously dumped in the back seat by the masked men, who jumped in behind. The doors slammed shut and the Range Rover sped off towards the end of the road. Lachaise held his head in his hands. Not one shot had been fired by his own men; the whole operation had gone sour and there was nothing that he could do about it.

Jim and Hans arrived on scene. They were covered in perspiration and panting heavily but they had no time to rest. The smoke was slowly clearing as they approached the crumpled taxi. Hans went left and Jim right, simultaneously aiming their weapons at the interior of the car just in case a bad guy remained. The boys were gone. Barry lay where he had fallen and what was left of the driver hung propped up by the steering wheel. Jim cursed and kicked the side of the car. They were too late. The tyres of the Range Rover screeched as the driver threw it sideways, turning right at the end of the road. Jim, for his age, reacted like an athlete in his twenties. Shouting at Hans to look after Barry, he sprinted after the Range Rover.

The courier hit the pavement before he realised that his motorbike had been liberated by a mad English policeman. The road in front of Jim was blocked, but the pavement wasn't. Releasing the clutch with maximum revs, the rear wheel spun as he threw the bike around and headed off in pursuit of the getaway car. Screams and yells went up as the innocent flung themselves out of the way of the motorbike. Jim tried his best to give a warning, but there was no way he could slow down as he would lose his quarry.

At the end of Rue Daumier the road widened as it joined onto the quayside. The traffic was much heavier here as everyone made their way towards the next bridge over the Seine. Jim could just make out the black rear of the Land Rover swerving in and out of the traffic. *This was it*, he thought, *you're mine*. He accelerated, weaving through the cars in front. Every second he would make ground only to lose it again as he negotiated traffic lights and cars turning into his path, unaware of his existence.

Behind the wheel, José thought about easing up. He looked into his rear-view mirror as a final check to see if they were being followed. The motorbike zigzagging in and out of the evening traffic with a helmetless rider changed his mind. Telling Didier that they had company, he put his foot to the floor and the V8 super charged 390hp engine did what it was designed for, but the short blast of speed ended abruptly when a lorry blocked their route. Jim's confidence grew when he saw the Range Rover held up by a lorry.

José saw him coming. Gunning the engine, the Range Rover mounted the pavement, demolishing a newsstand and a small ice cream stall that was busy minding its own business. Papers and magazines fluttered into the air and ice cream sprayed onto the windscreen. José switched the wipers on max speed and the vanilla smeared as it mixed with the screen wash. For Jim it was impossible for the bike to follow as debris was scattered everywhere. Without thinking he headed for the lorry, blocking the road. There would be at least two and a half to three feet of clearance under the flat bed trailer. He had no choice - he would have to risk it.

Easing off the throttle, he laid the bike on its side. Sliding along the road, his momentum carried him under the trailer. The engine fairing of the motor bike protected his leg from being ripped apart by the tarmac below and the handlebars limited the damage to his upper body. Stopping in the centre of the junction, he was at the mercy of oncoming vehicles. He had nowhere to run and he shielded his head from the imminent impact of an approaching car. The driver, upon seeing the motorbike and rider before him, hit his brakes hard. All four of his tyres locked up leaving a trail of black rubber lines on the road behind. Stopping only feet away from Jim, the driver sighed and rested his head on his steering wheel in relief. However, the following vehicles failed to brake as quickly and car after car rammed into the back of each another.

Safe and sound, Jim lifted the bike from the road. Luckily the engine was still ticking over. Jumping back on, he sped off after the Range Rover leaving several angry French people shouting insults at him. Plastic and metal hit against his leg as the damaged fairing of the bike flapped helplessly in the wind. His shoulder and arm were bleeding from the fall but his adrenalin masked his pain. The Range Rover was still in view but the chase began to die. The fuel line of the bike had been ruptured and slowly the bike lost power. It coughed and spluttered and then died. He tried in vain to restart it but it was no good. Watching the Black vehicle disappear, he threw the bike to the floor and fell to his knees. The traffic stopped as Jim's lonely figure and the motorcycle sat in the road. Horns were sounded and people yelled for the stranger to move, but Jim was oblivious to it all. His nephew had gone and he had been unable to prevent it.

'The tracking devices!' he said to himself, springing to his feet. Leaving the bike where it lay, he ran back in the direction where he had come from. It wasn't too late, there was still hope. 'Please Hans,' he said to himself, hoping that Hans would have had the same thoughts and be heading in his direction with the receiver.

He was right. The sirens grew louder as they forced their way through the traffic. Hans saw the dishevelled figure of his friend staggering towards him. Jim jumped in while the car was still moving and they headed off, following the directional arrow shown on the receiving unit.

'You ok Jim?' Hans said as he manoeuvred through the traffic. 'You look like shit.'

'Yeah, thanks for the compliment,' Jim replied, at the same time holding the receiver up and looking at the way a head.

'Where's Lachaise?'

'He's going airborne. We should see him soon,' replied Hans calmly as he negotiated the Parisian traffic. Jim scanned the skies for the chopper but it wasn't there. Swearing under his breath, he went back to watching the receiver. The signal had intensified and he realised that the boys weren't far away.

The factory door opened as soon as the Range Rover came into sight. Once inside, the door closed. An old dirty mattress lay on the floor. Didier dragged it over to the car and one by one the boys were laid on top. Without thought of any kind of dignity, the unconscious bodies were stripped of their clothes, wrapped in blankets and placed into the back of a white Renault Van. Leaving the getaway car where it stood,

Didier and José climbed into the van and drove out the rear exit of the empty factory. The traffic was moving steadily and the white van disappeared, joining the thousands of other white vans driving around Paris.

The signal grew stronger and Lachaise came into view, hovering a few hundred feet above the road in front of them. Jim's optimism grew and, together with his anger, he was prepared for anything. Turning off the busy main road, Hans slowed to a crawl. Before them stood an abandoned factory destined to be demolished and the site redeveloped with modern riverside apartments. Only a weak temporary fence and gate had been erected to stop trespassers and part of it lay to one side of the entrance, giving clear access to all who wanted it.

It wouldn't be long now, Jim thought as he reached for his side arm and checked the magazine. The boys were there, they must be as the signal was at maximum. Hans, using a high gear and low revs, silently entered the site and pulled the police car up to the first warehouse. The helicopter kept its distance so as not to alert any occupants, and Lachaise watched on the high tech camera that hung like a giant wart on the under belly of the chopper. Getting out of the car and leaving the doors open, Jim and Hans, in support of each other, made their way to a personnel door. Part of the frame had rotted away over the years and it gave just enough of a gap for Jim to look through. Squinting to focus, he saw the back of the Range Rover. His view wasn't wide enough for him to make out any persons. Giving the ok to Hans, he gave the after three symbol. Hans stopped him.

'We need back-up. We don't know how many there are,' he whispered.

'We don't have time to wait. Let's go,' Jim hissed, positioning himself to break down the door. Hans shrugged his shoulders. He would follow this man anywhere.

Positioning himself, Hans released the safety catch of his weapon. The door fell to the floor with no effort at all. The hinges were rusted through and a gust of wind would have eventually done the job for them. Covering Jim, Hans stood to the side of the doorway. Jim rushed to the nearest cover of some oil drums, allowing Hans to follow. When they were both together, Jim made a dash for the 4 x 4. It was empty. Slamming the driver's door shut, the noise reverberated around the empty building until it died away, only to be replaced by the footsteps of Hans who walked over to join his friend. They were the only ones there. Apart from the empty car, the dirty mattress and pile of clothes, the warehouse was deserted. Their worst fears had just been confirmed. The boys were gone and they had no way of tracing them.

Jim felt defeated; he was so sure that the boys would be there. The signal was so strong. Maybe they hadn't searched thoroughly enough and the boys were still there somewhere, hidden, just waiting to be found. Jim's final glimmer of optimism died when Hans called him over to the pile of clothes. They belonged to the boys. Picking up each garment, Hans quickly checked the pockets. He knew what he was looking for and it wasn't long before he found them. One after the other Hans produced the two transmitting devices. He threw them to Jim. Gripping them tightly in his hand he fell to his knees, crying out in pain. If any hope remained, finding the transmitters had erased it completely. The boys were on their own in the hands of a killer and Jim was powerless to act. As the helicopter flew overhead he rubbed away the tears that were forming in his eyes. Without saying another word, he got up and walked away. *God help them*, he thought.

Over and over again the CCTV footage was replayed for any clue that might give them a lead. Jim sat staring blankly at the wall. The Superintendent in him had returned and he was running scenario after scenario through his head for clues. Out loud he began to ask himself questions.

'Why does Dubois want these boys alive? He could have killed them a dozen times over. It's not for money, they don't have any. It's just not making any sense.'

'Maybe they have something that belongs to Dubois,' pitched in Hans from the other side of the room.

'Yes but what? What could two English teenage boys have that would upset Dubois enough to kill four times?' Both men sat in silence until Jim broke it.

'It's got to go back to the beginning when they first met Dubois. I've missed something that will give us our clue.' Pulling his mobile from his pocket, he dialled Inspector Sanderson who took the news of the boy's abduction badly. He had tried so hard, from a distance, to protect them. He offered to take the blame but Jim would have none of it and quickly changed his tack.

He asked Sanderson for a copy of the transcript of the interview that the boys gave when in custody back in England. He told him the fax number and bid him stay by his phone. A frustrating fifteen minutes passed before the fax machine sprung into life. Page after page appeared and Jim read each one, passing the page to Hans when he had finished. Nothing stood out. No names, places, events - nothing to put an ounce of flesh onto their bare bones.

Laying them out on the table, Jim started again whilst Hans left for coffee. When he returned, Jim had the transcript spread all over the table. On a white board, provided by Lachaise, Jim had written bullet points relating to the boys' movements in Belgium. Hans stood behind his friend and watched as Jim systematically went through each of his points, leaving the ones that he wanted and putting a line through the ones that he didn't. He began to talk out loud once more; it helped him focus on the task in hand.

'We know that it can't be because of the loss of the shipment of drugs because there's no reason for Dubois to keep them alive. He could have had them killed many times before but he didn't. Now that he's stooped low enough to killing cops that tells me it's a whole lot more important than a shipment of Ecstasy.'

'So, if it's not about the drugs and the money, what is it about?' said Hans, passing Jim his coffee.

'I'm coming to that. It's got to be something that happened when the boys were at Dubois's place.'

'Maybe it's the package that the boys were supposed to bring back to the UK, for Dan's father?'

'No, it can't be,' replied Jim putting a circle around Dubois's name. 'The package contained the same drugs that were in the shipment. Dan's dad and his associates in Newcastle are small time criminals. Dan was just there as a mule to pick up that box and I honestly believe the boys when they said that they ended up inside the lorry by mistake.'

'Maybe they saw something that they shouldn't have,' Hans said throwing his idea into the pot.

'It's possible, but Dubois would have killed them, sending the secret to the grave. No, this thing is tangible, but what I don't know.' Jim sat down and ran his hand through his hair. He knew the answer was right there in front of him but he wasn't seeing it.

'Each time I read the part about Dubois's place,' said Jim trying to focus again, 'I keep coming back to this unknown figure that stayed in the background in Dubois's office. The boys said that they only got a fleeting look at him when the shutters were opened. But it was long enough for them to notice his features and clothes. Back then we assumed that he was just another one of Dubois's goons and took it no further.'

'Maybe he is one of Dubois's men, maybe he isn't. I don't understand what you're getting at,' Hans said losing track of Jim's line of thought.

'I think that the stranger means more to Dubois than we realise. I don't know what, but my gut instinct tells me he is. Anyway, let's look at it from a different angle. Why did they panic and run?'

'Maybe they were scared. I know that if I was sixteen and someone was running towards me with a gun, I'd run as well,' Hans said grinning as he remembered himself at sixteen years old.

'Yes, you're right, my friend,' Jim said nodding his head in agreement. 'And that's where we made another assumption and never bothered to look into it further.'

'So what made them run then?'

'Here, look at this,' Jim said putting his finger under a passage in the transcript. 'It's what Dan said that interests me.' Jim began to read the passage out loud.

'We were leaving and nearly out of there when this English weirdo who was there for the tabs (cigarettes) asked me to take a picture of him and his mates. Dubois shouted from his window and set those two bastards on us - the ones that had roughed us up when we arrived. Fuck this for a lark I thought and I ran.'

Jim leapt to his feet, making Hans jump in shock. 'That's it! I think I've got it,' he shouted. Hans was lost. Jim wasn't making sense but he listened anyway, intrigued at where Jim was going.

'The photo! It's a bloody photo, Somebody on that camera is the reason why Dubois wants the boys.'

'But what camera?' said Hans. 'There's no mention of a camera. He must have given it back to the tourist.'

363

'Ah, but he didn't, there was no time. Seeing Dubois's men he ran, taking the camera with him.' Jim suddenly hit his head with his fist. 'I don't fucking believe it,' he said pacing up and down. 'Dan had a camera in his possession when he was brought in for questioning. We had it in our hands and we gave it right back to him, but it all makes sense now. Dubois wants the boys because he needs what's on the camera, or should I say *who* is on the camera.' Jim ran to the door to get his jacket. Putting it on, he pushed his side arm into his belt.

'Hans, when the boys left the hotel earlier on did any of them have a camera on them?'

'No, I don't think so.'

'Good. So the camera is still out there somewhere. You can guarantee that Dubois's men have already gone through the boys' possessions with a fine tooth comb and come up negative, otherwise why would he still want them?' Heading off along the corridor like a man on a mission, Jim raced to find Lachaise. Hans followed behind.

'The boys are still alive, Hans,' Jim said with optimism in his voice. 'Dubois needs them to get the camera and if I know that Dan it won't be too far away. Mark my words, Hans. The boys will deliver Dubois to us and we will be waiting for him.'

Chapter 27

Mike opened his eyes slowly, his senses coming alive once more. He'd entered his captivity full of despair, but the thoughts of the previous nine days had taken him away from his desolation and given him hope. Hope in staying alive, hope in being found and hope in escaping. There were people out there that cared for him and who he cared for. *I haven't even started to live and I'm not going to die here*, he said to himself.

'Where do you think we are?' Dan said in a whisper.

'I don't know,' replied Mike getting to his feet.

'Do you think they're going to kill us?'

'If they'd wanted to kill us we'd be dead already, don't you think?' Dan didn't answer, he knew Mike was right. Mike put his ear to the door to see if he could hear anything on the other side. Nothing at all; everywhere was ghostly silent. He tried the door handle. It was firm. He pulled and pushed in an effort to open it, but it was tightly shut and locked from the other side. He came back and sat next to Dan.

'You know what Mike?' Dan said, sounding a little less depressed than he was earlier. 'After everything that we have gone through, Dubois's place, the lorry, getting locked up, running through that sex show...' Mike smiled when Dan mentioned the sex show, 'and the fairground in Germany. Well, I've not once said thank you to you for being there and helping me.'

'Don't be silly, you're my best friend and best friends go through good and bad together. You don't need to thank me.'

'Oh I do,' Dan said looking at his friend. 'You've kept me right and looked after me like a brother. Whatever happens I won't forget it.' Mike felt emotional, not through fear but because Dan's words had touched him deeply. They were brothers. Not through blood or family, but through their shared experiences. Their friendship had grown stronger and they were bound together for life.

'Do you believe in God, Mike?' Dan suddenly blurted out in the silence.

'I don't know. Why'd you ask?'

'Well, do you believe in the afterlife or heaven?' Mike struggled to answer straight away; he thought it a weird question coming from Dan but, under the circumstances, the question wasn't that strange.

'I'm not sure that I believe in anything,' he replied. 'To say that there is this old boy living in the sky whose got a long white beard and is watching over us all the time. No, that's all crap.'

'I know that bit's crap, but what about the soul and getting your sins forgiven and heaven and all that? You know, when you die.'

'I think that there probably was a God once,' Mike said philosophically, 'but he gave up and left when the world became too nasty and complicated. I don't think there's anybody or anything that is worried about your sins - there's too much shit happening everywhere for anyone to be worried about a squirt like you. No, God left a long time ago. So you're going to have to forgive yourself.' Dan laughed at Mike's comment; it cheered him a little.

'But what about death?' Dan said forcing the issue.

'I think that death is the end,' Mike carried on. 'It would be great if your soul went to another place and you were born all over again, to start another life from scratch. And yeah, no doubt when I face death I'll suddenly believe in it all, but right now I don't expect to die for a long time and you shouldn't either.' Dan smiled. Mike's words definitely made him feel better.

He wanted so much to believe them, but he was finding it hard to think of a future at the moment. Mike, who was now so full of self belief decided to stay on his soap box a little longer.

'Dan, faith in yourself is your God,' Mike said prodding his finger into Dan's chest. 'It's what you do that counts and it's up to you to decide if it's right or wrong. You make your own destiny. People point you in the right direction, good or bad, but you decide where to go. I know what you're thinking,' Mike said, making Dan look up at him. 'Because you've done bad things, particularly for that old man of yours, you think that you will pay for it when you die.'

'Well, I might,' Dan replied nervously. 'But they've not all been my fault you know. I've had no choice.'

'Stop, I don't want to hear this shit. We are not going to die. When we get out of here and we will get out of here,' Mike said forcefully. 'You have to promise me that you will concentrate on one thing, your football ok? Forget that old man of yours and put yourself as number one. Do you promise?' Mike said holding out his hand. Dan stuttered and Mike thrust his hand into his. They shook hands and Mike patted him on the back for reassurance.

'Right, quiet. Someone's coming,' Mike said putting his finger up to his lips. The footsteps grew louder as they approached. Dan gripped hold of Mike and whispered 'thank you' into Mike's ear. Mike's optimism was beginning to dwindle but he meant what he said.

The door opened and fluorescent light hit the boys full in the face. Shielding their eyes, they looked up to see two silhouettes filling the doorway. One by one they were lifted to their feet, blindfolded, and walked out of their confinement.

The two boys didn't have to be told that Dubois was

in the room - they knew from the smell of his cigar. Dubois stood at the far end with his back to them. The boys were marched up to all but a few metres away from him. Henri and Didier placed two chairs behind them and pushed them down onto them. Their hands were placed onto the armrests and strapped, thus preventing them from moving. First Dan then Mike had their blindfolds removed.

Squinting until his eyes became accustomed to the light, Mike looked around. The room was large with an ornate fireplace at one end. It looked as though it hadn't seen a fire in years and the rest of the room showed the same signs of neglect. For anyone familiar with Paris, there had to be another ten thousand rooms like this one. It oozed Parisian charm but, for Mike, Parisian charm was not on his mind. The room had only one window with two heavy stained, dusty, damp, velvet curtains that stopped the outside from looking in. *At least it's daytime,* Mike thought, seeing the sun peeking out from behind. The dampness in the air mingled with the smell of acrid cigar smoke, and Mike could taste the awful mixture as he breathed.

'You two are quite remarkable,' said Dubois turning around to face the boys. They lifted their heads to see the face that they hoped they would never see again.

'What do you want with us?' said Mike defiantly.

'Oh, it's your turn to speak this time. Young Daniel seems to have lost his tongue.'

'Fuck you Dubois!' Dan shouted. Dubois smiled.

'That's more like it,' Dubois said, coming closer.

'Now Daniel and Michael – oh, I hope I can call you by your first names,' Dubois said sarcastically. 'We have been through so much together these past few days that it feels like I have known you for a lifetime.'

The boys didn't respond. Dubois produced another long Cuban cigar from his pocket. Next he produced a small cigar cutter in the style of a French guillotine. Cutting the end from the cigar, both boys watched as the discarded piece fell to the floor. Henri produced a lit match and Dubois sucked on the cigar until the end of it burnt red hot.

'You know boys,' said Dubois blowing smoke in their direction, 'I have worked hard to get where I am today. I have bribed, cheated, tortured and killed to get here and you two have put it all at risk.' Dubois came closer and leant down in front of them. Mike could smell his foul smoker's breath as he came near him. Closing his eyes, he tried to switch his senses off but failed.

'You have cost me money, lots of money,' Dubois said, walking between them until he stood at their rear. 'You have cost me merchandise, but most of all you have cost me my reputation. But I can be a reasonable man. You do something for me and I'll do something for you. I cannot be fairer than that, can I?'

'What do you want from us?' Dan said, trying hard not to show fear when all of the time he trembled within.

'I want your camera and I want it now.'

'But we don't have a camera. I don't know what you are talking about,' replied Dan looking across at Mike. Mike shook his head and then spoke.

'It's true. Just as Dan said we don't have a camera. Please believe me, it's true,' he pleaded, looking Dubois full in the eyes. His voice trembled as he spoke.

'Oh, I would love to believe you, but I don't,' Dubois said, gripping Dan's chin and squeezing hard. Dan resisted. 'You will tell me where your camera is now!' Dubois shouted, pulling Dan's head back by his hair. Dan cried out and closed his eyes with the pain of his hair being nearly pulled from his scalp. Letting Dan go, Dubois walked away for Henri to relight his cigar.

369

'I hate sport and I hate sportsmen,' continued Dubois with his back to them. 'Money is what life is all about and with money comes power. Sport is for the weak. It's for those that need some alternative existence for their dreary lives, but I can be persuaded to play sport if necessary. Henri and Didier like sport, don't you gentlemen?' They didn't answer. Dubois turned around with a huge smile on his face.

'What do you think? Shall we play some sport together? Henri, are you ready to play some sport?' Henri didn't reply, he just made his way to the other end of the room out of sight of the boys. Dan had his head bowed, but Mike looked at Dubois trying to show some defiance.

'I understand that you are a centre forward, Daniel, and you are a goalkeeper Michael. How fascinating. How lucky you are to be talented.' Dan looked across at Mike for some reassurance, but Mike didn't look back.

'You're a fucking lunatic!' Mike shouted, pulling on his restraint at the same time. Dubois put his hand in his pocket. Dan thought that he was reaching for his gun, but when his hand reappeared it cupped a coin.

'This game I made up myself. I hope that you will like it. It's called hurt a friend, but I'm not sure which friend to hurt.' Dubois flicked the coin into the air and caught it again. 'Heads we break Dan's toes. Tails we break Mike's fingers. A centre forward with smashed toes stops being a centre forward and a goalkeeper with smashed fingers will never catch a ball again.' Dubois chuckled to himself. 'Isn't this exciting? I think I've invented a new sport.' Mike struggled again. Dan looked up, his eyes full of tears.

'Where is the fucking camera?' Dubois shouted.

'We haven't got a camera,' shouted Mike. 'You're making a mistake. Please, it's true.' Dubois, ignoring

Mike's reply, flicked the coin into the air again. Both boys watched as it spun, then dropped to disappear into Dubois's hand.

'Oh dear,' said Dubois showing the coin to his captives. 'Daniel loses. How tragic for such a promising rising star to have his career ended before it's even begun. Oh, how devastated you must feel Daniel, you lost.' Dan squirmed and struggled to get out of the chair but his restraints were too tight.

'No, please don't. Please, I beg you,' Dan cried, his voice quivering with fright. Tears began to run down his cheeks. He had started off so strong but his resolve had died with the knowledge that his football career would be over. His football was all that he had; without it he might as well be dead. The tears flowed quicker now and his head fell in despair.

'You fucking bastard, Dubois,' shouted Mike, struggling to free himself but failing. Managing to balance with the chair strapped to his back, he got to his feet and ran at Dubois. Henri kicked him to the ground and, with no hands free to save himself, he landed face first hitting the cold, hard, dirty floor. For a split second he was dazed; the room spun and wobbled as his eyes tried in vain to focus. Henri picked him up and slapped him around the face to revive him.

He came back to reality and with it came the pain. Blood trickled from his nose, running into his mouth. It mixed with his saliva and ran between his teeth. Mixing the saliva with his spit, he spat the red transparent liquid at Dubois with as much force and hatred that he could muster. As it landed on Dubois's shoe, Henri reacted without prompting and punched Mike in his stomach. Mike lurched forward and cried out in pain. His stomach was rammed into his chest cavity, causing his diaphragm to push every last ounce of breath from his lungs. He wretched but nothing came out as his stomach was empty. He coughed as his own blood ran down his throat and tried hard not to choke.

Didier, who had been standing at the other end of the room observing everything, walked forward towards Henri carrying a canvas sack. Holding it open, Henri reached inside and withdrew a hammer. Didier then placed a small wooden crate in front of Dan. Taking hold of Dan's right leg, he pulled it forward and placed Dan's foot onto the crate. With his courage ebbing away, Dan lashed out with his other foot. Why? He didn't know. His situation was hopeless; maybe he could cause Didier some pain before he felt his own, not that it made any difference to Didier as he would be used to pain working for Dubois.

Nevertheless, he swung and caught Didier full in the face with the heel of his foot. Didier took the force of the kick in his stride as though a feather duster had been run across his face. Roughly he took hold of Dan's leg once more and positioned it onto the box. Dan was finished as, in that moment, any amount of courage that he possessed had faded away. Pleading in a whisper as the tear drops fell quicker, he begged Dubois not to do it.

'Where is the camera?' Dubois said, only inches away from his face. Dan could feel the droplets of spit hit his cheeks and he turned away. 'Daniel, tell me now and your foot will keep its toes.'

'I've told you I don't have a camera,' he replied whimpering under his words. Dubois stepped back and gave the nod to Henri who walked forward with the hammer.

'No! No! Please no,' Dan yelled. Shaking with fright and eyes wide at the sight of the hammer, he screamed again but no one was there to hear him.

Raising the hammer above his head, Henri looked across at Dubois. Dubois nodded. Dan struggled to release his leg from Didier's grip but it was held firm. Like lightning, the hammer was thrust downwards. The horror in Dan's eyes, as the hard cold metal fell towards his foot, was too much for Mike to bear. He closed his eyes, not wanting to see the outcome. There was a loud bone-breaking crack as the hammer made contact. Dan screamed but the pain never came. He looked down at his foot and saw that it was untouched. The hammer had fallen only millimetres away and was embedded into the wooden crate. Dan looked across at Dubois, hopeful that he wouldn't do it for real, but he was mistaken.

'Next time he won't miss,' said Dubois. 'Do you understand me? Next time the skin on your toes will split like an over ripe tomato. Your bones will shatter and splinter just like that wood beneath your foot. You will never walk properly again. Now, for the last time, where is the camera?' Dan's head dropped and he muttered incoherently, anticipating the pain. Henri raised the hammer again. Mike couldn't let it happen. Dan was his friend, his brother.

'I'll take you to it,' Mike shouted. Henri's hand stayed where it was. 'I've hidden it,' Mike said hoping to God he could bluff.

'Tell me where it is,' said Dubois, gripping Mike's face by his chin and pulling him forward.

'Tell him to drop the hammer. I will take you to it.'

'And why should I do that?' said Dubois flicking his ash onto Mike's lap.

'Because if you don't it will end up in the hands of the police anyway.' Dubois let go of his face and stepped back in surprise.

'You're talking in riddles,' Dubois said, scowling at him. Mike knew that he could only bluff for so long. He needed to keep up the pretence or Dubois would know that he was lying.

'If Dan and I don't return, the police will seize all of our property. The police believe we work for you. We are criminals found with your drugs in your shipment. All our stuff will be seized and they will find the camera.' For the first time Dubois sounded uneasy.

'My men have searched everything you have. You are lying. They found nothing.'

'That's because your men failed to search everywhere. If they had we wouldn't be here now.' Mike watched as Dubois looked at Henri then Didier. Neither of them looked Dubois in the eyes. Dubois scowled and Mike knew that his bluff might work.

'Let me put it this way,' continued Mike, his confidence growing. When the police find the camera they will examine it, hoping to find information of our whereabouts. And what will they find? Well, your guess is as good as mine. You need us, Mr Dubois, and you need us in one piece. Dead or injured, the police get the camera and you lose. The two of us alive, unharmed and able to take you to it means you go your way and we can go ours.'

Dan looked across at Mike. He was confused but something told him that it was going to be fine. Dubois was silent. He reverted back to sucking on his Cuban cigar as he thought about Mike's offer. For a split second Mike saw evil in Dubois's eyes and his new found confidence wavered a little. He pleaded, in his head, to the God that he didn't believe in to give him courage in the hope that Dubois would go for his plan. He didn't know what he would do next if this failed, but if it gave them a chance of escaping then it would have been worth it.

'I like your style,' Dubois said smiling at Mike. 'Thank your friend here, Daniel, for saving your future. But I warn you, if at any time you try anything funny I will shoot you both dead.'

Dubois walked out of the room and his men followed. As the door closed Mike began to cry. The mental pressure of his lie had been tremendous and he had to let it out. Dan cried with him and together they released some of their fear. A minute passed by and the tears eventually stopped.

'I don't know where that camera is that I stole,' Dan said, sniffing, trying to wipe his nose on his arm. 'What are we going to do?'

'Calm down,' replied Mike. 'I know where it is.' Dan looked at his friend, not knowing whether to believe him or not. 'You remember that night we spent in the coach in Amsterdam? You had it in the pocket of your tracksuit top. Each time you turned in your sleep the bloody thing poked me, so I removed it and hid it. It was stolen property and I didn't want you running around with a hooky camera in your pocket, did I?'

'But where did you hide it?'

Mike dropped his voice to a whisper. 'It's still in the bus. I hid it in Dennis's pillow. Until I saw that hammer over your head I didn't realise that was the camera they were looking for. Christ, if I'd known from the start I would have told them.' Mike gave Dan the most reassuring smile that he could muster. 'Now cheer up. We are going to get out of here.'

Dubois and his men returned and the blindfolds were quickly replaced. Untying their hands, the boys were pulled to their feet. Dan stumbled forward as his legs failed to take his weight. The strain that he had endured had taken its toll on him and his legs had gone numb with the stress. Being instantly pulled up onto his feet again, he managed to steady himself.

They knew that they were outside when the warm air hit them and the sharp gravel under foot dug into their bare feet as they walked. Being pushed into the rear of a car, they fell together on the back seat. The

375

fabric was soft and it felt wonderful after their ordeal. It wasn't until a few minutes into the journey that the blindfolds came off. It was broad daylight and the sun was high in the sky. The midday traffic was heavy and the car made poor time as it crossed Paris. Mike gripped Dan's leg and gave him a reassuring smile. Dan, in turn, gave his friend a small nudge. There was still hope and they knew it.

***

Jim was growing impatient with the French search teams. The search operation was taking place behind closed doors so as not to alert Dubois of their presence and it was painfully slow. No camera had been found in any of the boys' belongings. Their team mates had been questioned, their cameras confiscated and then they were all confined to their rooms. Now it was time to prepare for the arrival of Dubois. Jim's hunch had been taken seriously by Lachaise, but Jim still questioned himself all the time. Hans reassured him that it was a good hunch and he felt exactly the same. The support of his friend helped, but not a lot.

Lachaise had saturated the hotel with his men. This time there would be no foul-up. He had just returned from the home of the parents of his murdered officer and his mood was awful. Standing with a cigarette in his mouth, he listened to the reports of his men.

'Search everywhere again,' he yelled. 'We need to find that camera!' Saluting their superior, they scurried off like frightened rabbits to resume their search.

Jim broke his recent promise and lit a cigarette to calm his nerves. He was a worried man. Dubois was no fool - he wouldn't leave himself wide open to capture. He'd be expecting the police to be waiting for him. All Jim's instincts had told him Dubois would show but, as the time passed, he began to doubt himself. He hoped that the lack of success by Dubois's men in capturing the boys would have been enough of an incentive for Dubois to do the job himself; even more than this, he hoped that the boys hadn't mentioned his and Lachaise's presence. If Dubois knew that nearly the whole of the French police force would be there he would definitely not show. Everything now had become a gamble put together by guess work, intuition and gut instinct. The time was ebbing away - Dubois *had* to show. Jim crossed his fingers in hope.

It was 3pm when the second search concluded with another negative result. Lachaise's mood hadn't improved and he barked orders at his subordinates to keep them on their toes. Everywhere and everyone were ready. The hotel and each rooftop that overlooked it had police marksmen ready and waiting. There were dog handlers, plain clothed detectives acting as guests and even a detachment of the GIGN (Group D'Intervention Gendarmerie Nationale), an elite counter-terrorism and hostage rescue unit. They were the military but, when a man with the power of Lachaise asks, he gets. The police helicopter was on standby half a kilometre away and could be with them within three minutes of being summoned. Police were also positioned on any road that could possibly be used for a getaway route. This time there would be no escape. Dubois would be theirs.

Chapter 28

At 3.15pm, a private ambulance drove into the hotel car park. Each officer in turn reported its position and was instructed to observe only. This was the dilemma that caused the most irritation to Lachaise. The hotel car park had to remain open. It had to look as though it was carrying on as normal, otherwise Dubois would know it was a setup and drive right by.

Pulling up next to the team bus, the ambulance switched its engine off. No one got out. The driver and passenger, who both wore dark sunglasses, straight away climbed into the rear of the ambulance making it impossible to identify their faces. Lachaise knew that it could just be a couple of medics on their break, or it could be something more sinister. All eyes fell upon it. Five minutes passed and the ambulance was forgotten.

'It's just two harmless medics skiving off work,' Lachaise said over the air and eyes were positioned elsewhere. Jim wasn't going for it. Why would the ambulance park right next to the team bus when there was a whole car park to choose from? He didn't like it.

Thirty minutes went by and still nothing. Everything coming into the hotel and going out was scrutinised by fifty pairs of eyes. Jim still had concerns about the ambulance but they had started to diminish when the vehicle check had come back clean. It seemed that it was local to the area and, according to hotel staff, it regularly parked in the car park. Even so, Jim wasn't taking any chances and every few seconds he would glance back to the solitary vehicle.

Barry watched the police operation from the comfort of the hotel manager's chair. His head hurt, throbbing in time with his heart beat. A bandage covered his wound and most of the top of his head, which had caused extreme amusement to the rest of the team. 'Barry's got a turban on!' was the favourite cry and all he could do was laugh it off. The doctors had advised him to stay in hospital under observation due to the concussion that he had suffered, but he was having none of it. Telling them that his responsibilities were to his fifteen boys and not himself, he had signed his discharge papers and left. Two nurses looked him up and down as he walked out in disbelief that such a man could have fathered fifteen boys. Momentarily, however, he forgot his pain when one of the Special Forces officers entered the room with Lachaise.

He realised how serious everything had become. How endangered his boys were. Looking at the knives, guns and grenades attached to the officer's uniform, he began to blame himself again for the whole thing. He needed to pray. Closing his eyes, he asked for Mike and Dan to be returned safe and sound and he apologised to God for letting himself wander from his path. Taking another pain killer, more than the recommended dose, he began to pray some more.

At 3.45pm a black Mercedes drove into the car park. Didier was at the wheel. Radioing his men, Lachaise confirmed the sighting. They were to act on his command only. All eyes fell onto Didier, the assumption being that Dubois must be in the vehicle as well. At the same time, the side door of the ambulance slowly slid open. Unseen and unheard, Henri stepped out, lifted the luggage compartment door to the bus and climbed inside. The black Mercedes had proven to be the perfect decoy and, when it sped away at high speed, Lachaise gave his order to pursue. The GIGN were tasked to take out the car but to be aware that the boys may be inside. The focus of the operation had changed and nobody except one was looking at the ambulance.

'It was all wrong,' Jim said to himself. It was too easy, too predictable. He didn't like it. Initially it didn't register in his mind, but he looked again. The view he had from the manager's window across to the bus wasn't the best, but he saw that the luggage hatch was now definitely open.

'Hans, they're in the ambulance!' Jim shouted, fumbling at the window latch to get it open. Hans ran to the door. His weapon was in his hand, ready to use. The window gave and Jim jumped out. Lachaise, hearing Jim's shouts, directed what manpower he had left towards the ambulance.

Jim was running at full sprint towards it when it began to move. José behind the wheel swung the ambulance around violently. The engine answered José's demand for power and accelerated towards Jim. Caught in the open, he was easy prey for José. Within two seconds of death, Hans threw himself at Jim and pushed his friend out of the way. Jim rolled on the tarmac but Hans wasn't so lucky. Catching Hans on his right side, the force of the impact threw him onto a stationary car. Whether he felt much pain was unknown, as his body lay broken on the windscreen of the parked car. Jim looked across and saw his friend motionless. He wanted to go to him but he couldn't. The ambulance was leaving and Jim couldn't let it leave without him.

Negotiating the last bend of the car park, the ambulance had to slow a little. Jim ran across the beautifully manicured flower beds to narrow the distance. Jumping the last few metres, he reached out and took hold of the rear door handle just as the ambulance began to accelerate away. Luckily for Jim, the ambulance had a disabled lift which stowed away underneath. Enough of the metal deck to the lift butted out, giving him a foot hold. With Jim gripping on for dear life, the ambulance, now with full sirens blazing, began to manoeuvre at speed through the Parisian traffic. It became the perfect getaway vehicle as everyone in front moved out of the way to let them pass. The rear windows were blocked out and, as Jim could not see in, no one inside could see out. However, more importantly, José couldn't see the English Superintendent clinging onto the back door.

Dan was strapped to a stretcher. Dubois stood over him, gun in one hand and camera in the other. He had the look of contentment on his face, as at last he had what he wanted. Soon the ambulance would be lost in the traffic and it would be time to dispose of the boys. Mike lay on the floor, while Henri stood over him with his foot on his chest. His breathing was laboured with the downward pressure of Henri's boot and, with the motion of the vehicle, he began to feel dizzy and nauseous.

José hit the brakes when he saw the roadblock. Everyone and everything flew forward. Henri released his foot and Mike breathed again. Dubois, needing a hand to steady himself, let go of the camera. He watched as it fell onto the ambulance floor and slide under one of the medicine compartments. He would get it later, he reasoned to himself. Sticking his head through to José, he too saw the roadblock.

Jim took his chance to get to the side door. Sliding it back, his eyes met Henri's. Henri raised his gun but Jim, without hesitation, aimed his own and fired at Henri. At the same time, José floored the accelerator and the ambulance sped away. Jim ran but the ambulance was too quick for him. Falling forward onto the road when his hand missed the door handle, he cried out in anger. He aimed his gun at the back but he knew he couldn't shoot in case he hit the boys. For the second time in twenty-four hours he was left stranded in the Parisian traffic and this time there would be no Hans to come to his rescue. Getting to his feet, he started to run once more but this time he wouldn't give up.

Henri started to fall as his nervous system reacted to the gunshot wound and his body began to quickly shut down. The bullet had entered his chest, shattered a rib and punctured a lung, but luckily missed his heart. Blood began to colour his clothes as it oozed between skin and cloth. He fell next to Mike on the floor, wheezing and spitting blood. The hole in his chest gurgled and fizzed as it became his new windpipe. He was dying, slowly drowning in his own blood as his chest filled with the red liquid. Mike knew he had to do something. Whether this man had tried to kill him it didn't matter, he couldn't just sit there and watch him die.

'Untie me,' Mike shouted at Dubois.

'Why should I? You'll run,' replied Dubois pointing his gun at Mike.

'I can help him. Untie me quick, he's going to die.' Dubois hesitated. Mike stared into his eyes, not in anger but in compassion, compassion for the man who Dubois had treated like a son but was now lying bleeding to death on the ambulance floor. It did the trick. Even Dubois, with his heart of stone, couldn't just watch his man die.

Kneeling down, Dubois pulled the rope from around Mike's wrists. Quickly opening one of the medical pouches, Mike rifled through looking for a large dressing. In frustration he tipped the bag up, emptying its contents over the floor. The dressing was there. Taking it out of the wrapper, he placed the wrapper over the wound and pushed against it. He wanted Henri to breathe normally and therefore he had to seal the hole in his chest. The plastic wrapper would do the job, but he needed Dubois to hold it on the wound while he secured a bandage around Henri's torso.

'Hold that there and press hard,' Mike said to Dubois, who again hesitated.

'Please, he'll die. Hurry!' Mike said looking up into the killer's eyes. Wrapping the bandage around Henri's chest, Mike placed the dressing over the plastic wrapper which Dubois was pushing against the wound. Onto that he placed a notepad that he found lying on the floor. Pulling tight, forcing the note pad, dressing and plastic over the wound, the hissing and gurgling stopped. Henri coughed again as his windpipe began to work once more.

Rolling him over so that his wound was underneath him, Mike instantly heard Henri's breathing improve a little. Hopefully his good lung would be enough to keep him alive, but only if the bullet hadn't caused anymore irreparable damage. There wasn't any sign of an exit wound so the bullet was definitely still in there somewhere.

'He needs a doctor,' Mike shouted at Dubois. 'Let us out, you have what you want. We'll take him to a hospital.'

'Shut up! He'll be fine,' replied Dubois pointing his gun a Mike.

Mike's fury was just about to explode when José began to shout from the front that the roads were blocked in every direction. Dubois wasn't in the mood for excuses. He yelled at him to get through. José didn't like it. Any minute now the entire police force of Paris would converge on them. He was a wanted man throughout Europe and a life sentence would mean life. Looking ahead, a small gap appeared on the pavement where it widened for a seating area for a restaurant. That was their way out. Gunning the engine once more, José rammed into the stationary car in front to make room for his getaway. People dived for cover as the ambulance drove along the pavement with siren wailing. Tables and chairs disintegrated instantly as the ambulance mowed them down. Desperate to escape, José would drive over anything or anybody to get away.

Dan, still strapped to the stretcher, was slowly working his restraints loose. Dubois was concentrating too much on Mike and on steadying himself as the ambulance bounced, swerved and destroyed anything in its path. Mike wasn't going to try anything; he was too busy with Henri, protecting him from all the flying objects inside the ambulance. Looking across at Dan, he saw in the corner of his eye Henri's gun sliding about under the stretcher. He looked into Dan's eyes, then at the gun, then back to Dan. Dan understood. His hands were nearly free but he was in no position to be able to get off the stretcher, pick up the gun and take Dubois out. Moreover, he had never fired a revolver in his life. He'd seen them at close quarters before but to pick one up, aim it and shoot at another person was a frightening proposition. He hated Dubois, but could he kill another human being? He swallowed hard and tried to persuade himself that he could.

Dubois stood between the head of Dan's stretcher and the back of José's seat. If Dan was quick enough he could push off with his legs from the medical cabinet and trap Dubois between the stretcher and José. If luck was on his side, it would give him enough time to grab the gun. Taking a deep breath, he kicked off the cabinet. Dubois yelled in pain as the metal end of the stretcher rammed into his legs. Dan dropped to the floor and slid his arm underneath the stretcher for the gun. Desperately thrashing with his hand, he felt the cold metal. Within a second he was on his feet and pointing it at Dubois. Dubois froze when he saw the gun in Dan's hand.

'It's over Dubois, drop it,' Dan said gesturing with his gun. Dubois began to smile but kept hold of his weapon.

'Go on, Daniel, shoot me,' Dubois said laughing.

'Drop the gun. I'll do it, I will. I'll kill you.' Dan shook as the adrenalin mixed with fear and hatred surged around his bloodstream.

'You haven't got the guts. You're just a stupid little boy.'

Mike watched from his position on the floor. He didn't know whether Dan had it in him either.

'Put the fucking gun down, Dubois. I'll count to three and then you die. One, two,' Dubois had no intention at all of dropping his gun.

'Three!' Pulling the trigger nothing happened. Fear instantly gripped him and he pulled it again, but still nothing. Dubois, laughing, snatched the revolver out of his hand.

'You are a stupid little boy, aren't you? The safety catch is on.' Being called stupid for the second time lit Dan's touch paper. His hatred had suddenly turned to rage but he was no match for Dubois and he knew it. The odds had changed back into Dubois's favour and Dan could only stand by and do nothing. Dubois, on the other hand, was beside himself with laughter and he waved the two weapons in the air, taunting Dan. At the same time, José froze as a police car came out of nowhere. His reaction wasn't quick enough to apply the brakes and, with nowhere to turn, the outcome was inevitable.

When the ambulance hit the side of the police car the whole vehicle shuddered and everyone inside flew forward. The violence of the impact was enough to throw Dan onto Dubois. Dubois dropped one gun to use a hand to save his fall, but managed to keep the other one close. Dan went for the gun in Dubois's hand. A sixteen-year-old Geordie boy struggled against a killer in his fifties who was muscular and had a history of violence using his hands. It was an unequal match to say the least. Dan thought that he had the advantage as he was on top, but he'd thought wrong. Dubois's strength was just too much for him and, even though Dubois was trapped between the trolley and the front seats, he brushed Dan off like he wasn't there.

Mike, watching from the floor, knew that he had to get involved. Leaving Henri, he came to his friend's aid and together they wrestled Dubois for the gun. Mike began to punch Dubois anywhere he could, whilst Dan tried to prize the gun from Dubois's flailing hand. Dubois panicked and pulled the trigger, hoping to hit one of the boys. Dan flinched in shock, his ears rang and the smell and residue of cordite stung his eyes. Mike froze for an instant, but he was relieved to find he had no pain - Dubois had missed.

The bullet, though, had another purpose. Hitting the valve of the small oxygen cylinder, the cylinder ruptured. The gas, escaping at such a velocity, turned the cylinder into a mini Exocet missile and it flew across the ambulance. Missing the three heads in the back by inches, José never saw it coming. Hitting the back of his neck, it smashed his vertebrae which in turn severed his spine. There could only be one outcome and, by the time his head slumped forward onto the steering wheel, he was dead.

Jim's lungs started to burn and his pulse raced. He cursed his desk job because his fitness wasn't there when he wanted it. Years ago he could run for miles after a suspect but now, due to his sedimentary lifestyle, he was struggling to run anywhere. However, with Lachaise's roadblocks doing their job there remained a chance. Jumping onto car bonnets and leaping from car to car, he slowly gained ground. The police helicopter appeared overhead, so he wasn't far away now. His confidence started to relieve his fatigue when he heard it.

'Bang!'

It was a sound that he knew so well. He didn't have to guess where it came from either, he knew. Practically dying on his feet, he ran on, hoping to God that Mike wasn't on the end of that bullet. Their fate was in their own hands and Jim could only watch it unfold.

With the awesome and frightening sight of four armed men prepared to abseil from the chopper above, people fled in panic. Dirt and dust flew into the air and the noise of the chopper drowned out the approaching police sirens. The whole street was in chaos. Paris, the city of love, had turned into a war zone.

With no driver in control of the ambulance, it ploughed into a shop front sending shards of glass and metal in every direction. Customers and shop assistants ran for their lives to escape the metal intruder. With siren still wailing and lights flashing, it came to rest in a partition wall deep inside the premises. Dan still had hold of Dubois's hand, but he couldn't prise the gun free and it perilously waved around. He felt weak and it would be only a matter of time before Dubois succeeded in loosening the teenager's grip. Dan had one last hope and there was no flinching or apprehension. Putting Dubois's arm in his mouth, he bit down hard. Dubois screamed as Dan's teeth sank into his flesh. Dan tasted blood, but he wasn't going to let go until the gun fell from Dubois's hand. Squealing like a pig before the slaughterman's bolt, Dubois let go. Dan had given him no choice. Picking up the gun, Dan placed the barrel onto the forehead of Dubois.

'Click.' The safety catch was off and Dan was going

to kill him.

'Do it!' Dubois shouted defiantly. Dan pushed it into the skin of Dubois's forehead. With his finger slowly applying force to the trigger, Dubois shouted again. 'Do it! Do it now!'

Dan withdrew the gun from Dubois's head and thrust it into the killer's mouth.

'Shut the fuck up, you piece of shit and say goodnight,' Dan shouted back at Dubois, whose eyes widened as Dan looked into them. Dan hesitated, seeing no fear in Dubois's eyes. They were deep bottomless pools of blackness. The man had no soul and wasn't afraid to die. Mike put his hand onto Dan's shoulder.

'Don't do it Dan, he's not worth it. It's over, it's finished.' Dan didn't react, but his finger, still applying pressure to the trigger, began to tremble. His anger had total control and any rational thoughts had been pushed from his mind. Dubois, with a mouthful of steel, grinned at the boy who had the power to take his life and he believed from the look on Dan's face that he would pull the trigger.

'Do it Dan, pull the trigger. You kill me?' Dubois mumbled with his teeth, gripping the weapon.

'It's over Dan,' Mike said calmly. 'Killing him is too easy. Let the law decide.'

'The law is shit and you know it,' replied Dan angrily.

'That's not up to you to decide. You kill him and you become as bad as he is. Now, come on, drop the gun.' Tears ran down Dan's cheeks as Mike gently put his hand on his friend's shoulder. 'Come on pal, you know it's wrong.'

Dan wanted so much to pull the trigger. His heart was baying for blood but his head said no. Suddenly, the door of the ambulance slid open and two men, dressed all in black, appeared with automatic weapons and 'Police' in bold white letters across their chests. Mike put his hands up straight away, but Dan had put the gun back onto Dubois's head and was squeezing the trigger once more.

'Dan, drop it or they'll kill you,' Mike shouted.

The standoff seemed to last forever, but only a second passed before Dan uncurled his fingers away from the trigger. Slowly placing the gun onto the floor, he slid it out of the door and watched it fall onto the debris-strewn shop floor. Mike was dragged out through the shop and onto the road. Dan followed, manhandled roughly until he was face down next to his friend on the black tarmac.

'They're friendly!' Jim shouted as he ran towards the ambulance. Witnessing the boys being dragged out like a couple of common criminals pissed him off, but to the security services it didn't matter who they were. Until the area was secure everyone would be treated as hostile.

Then Dubois was dragged out and thrown to the ground next to Dan. Dan watched as the handcuffs were applied and he grinned at the Belgian. Dubois began to laugh.

'You're dead!' Dubois shouted. 'I will find you and I will kill you. I will kill your family. I will kill your friends you will cease to exist. You should have pulled the trigger when you had the chance. There's no jail that will hold me. Remember what I say, English boy, remember.'

Dan didn't respond. Dubois was prostrate on the road, in handcuffs, ranting and raving, while Dan was now being helped to his feet. Walking over to Dubois and using as much force as he could, he kicked the Belgian in the ribs. Howling in pain, Dubois writhed around in agony. Dan was just about to kick him again when Mike stopped him.

'That's enough, Dan. I think he's got the message.'

Dan crouched down to within inches of Dubois's face. For a moment he watched Dubois's distorted facial expressions, getting satisfaction at the Belgian's pain and misfortune. Eventually, Dubois opened his eyes and saw the sixteen-year-old staring at him. Dan didn't give him time to say anything else. Crouching down, he whispered into his ear.

'Rot in hell, you bastard.' Then he spat in Dubois face, got to his feet and walked off.

Dubois never got a chance to reply. With saliva running down his face, he was dragged off, struggling all the way to the police van.

Jim, slowly recovering from his epic sprint, smiled at his nephew as he approached. Mike grinned back, looking like he had been twelve rounds with a heavyweight boxer. The bruises around his eyes from his fall had started to develop, but he didn't care one little bit.

As the helicopter circled overhead and every police vehicle in Paris converged on the wrecked ambulance, Jim hugged his nephew. Mike held out his hand to his best friend and together the three of them embraced. Dubois was history.

Chapter 29

Mike didn't mind being substituted. He'd given his all and now he was physically and mentally drained. The past few days had taken its toll so, with two black eyes that a Panda would be proud of, he strolled off the pitch of the Parc Des Princes. Barry, who still wore his turban, sat in the dugout popping painkillers as if they were going out of fashion. He'd been reluctant to let Mike play, but he couldn't stop him - he'd earned his place on the pitch and, with him going through so much to get here, Barry hadn't got the heart to make him sit on the bench. Giving Mike a warm smile, Barry patted the seat next to him.

'I'm proud of you, Mike, I really am. You played your heart out and I hope that the scouts liked what they saw.' After a few minutes Barry continued. 'I'm sorry I let you down this past week and that I wasn't there for you when you needed me.' Mike looked across into his manager's eyes. Barry sounded so sincere, but he wasn't having any of it.

'Don't talk daft, Barry man. If it wasn't for you I wouldn't be with the club in the first place. My old man has pushed and pressured me to get where I am, but you've guided me. You gave me confidence, gave me hope, inspiration and belief in myself and without that I wouldn't have gotten through this week at all. It's me that should be thanking you, so none of this sorry talk, ok? Barry you're one in a million, a true professional and a true gentleman.' Mike put his arm around his manager and gave him a squeeze.

Barry was lost for words and overwhelmed with emotion. Squeezing Mike's hand in return, he nodded his head and bit his bottom lip to stop it quivering. He could have shed a tear, but he turned to watch the match once more. *Oh, if I'd had a son, I would have wanted him to be like Mike*, he thought to himself.

Dan had tried to push the memory of Dubois as far away as he could. He'd played his usual tenacious game and he'd run until he couldn't run anymore. When the final whistle blew he felt relieved that it was over. Dan had changed. The result, the opposition, others' opinions weren't important to him anymore - he'd done his best and enjoyed himself doing it. The days of arguing with referees, throwing insults and brawling with other players were behind him. As far as Dan was concerned he was the same person that he was before the tour, but to others he had matured beyond belief.

Sitting on the grass, he began to untie his boots and he marvelled at his good luck. He'd come so close to never playing again that from now on he would cherish every game he played.

Mike walked over to him and offered him his hand to pull him up. Dan took it.

'You didn't play too bad. The scouts may even pick you for a girls' team if you're lucky,' Mike said, letting Dan go when he was half way up. Dan fell back down, laughing. Lying on the soft turf, he stared at the sky.

'You know what, Mike?'

'What?'

'I'm just happy to be here, you know.'

'I know what you mean pal, I know what you mean,' replied Mike, helping Dan to his feet this time. The two friends revelled in their good fortune and, with arms around each other's shoulders, they laughed as they walked their last few steps across the Parc Des Princes.

'Don't you think that you'd better go and talk to her?' Mike said giving Dan a nudge.

'Talk to who?' replied Dan.

Mike pointed towards the tunnel. Dan stopped dead in his tracks when he saw Sabina. Those butterflies that he thought would never return took off again in his stomach. He smiled, without realising that he was smiling. The purple lipstick had gone but her eyes… oh how Dan loved those eyes! Walking on air to the girl that had stolen his heart in less than an hour, Mike was instantly forgotten about. Not that Mike cared - Dan was happy but, if truth be known, he felt a little bit envious. She was gorgeous.

Standing alone in the Stadium of Princes, Mike looked around and savoured his moment. The pitch and terraces were deserted. The team and Barry were in the dressing room and Dan was floating around somewhere on cloud nine with his Dutch beauty. Filled with the overwhelming feeling of humility, he was genuinely thankful for his life and the gifts that he had been given. Maybe next time, though, there would be a crowd of fifty thousand standing on the terraces to watch him play but, if not, it wouldn't be the end of the world.

Feeling happier than he could ever remember, he turned to walk the last few yards to join his friends. Three men stood at the tunnel entrance. They began to clap as Mike approached. Jim, Lachaise and a heavily bandaged Hans congratulated the boy who had become a hero and a man all at the same time. As the last floodlight was extinguished, the four men disappeared into the darkness.

***

His father's armchair was warm and soft. A log slowly smouldered on the fire and Mike felt safe and secure back in the familiar surroundings of his home. The envelope that had been delivered that morning lay on the table where Mike's mother had put it. He knew that it came from one of the scouts in Paris but he wasn't ready to read it yet. He'd looked at it, touched it and even smelt it, but to open it he needed the right moment.

Picking up another newspaper to take his mind off the letter, he began to chuckle out loud. He looked again to confirm that he hadn't made a mistake. There they were in full colour - Mike and Dan both wearing cheesy grins over the heading of *'Geordie Hero's defeat Drug Lord'*. Once the police had released the story to the press they had been besieged with callers and reporters, all wanting to interview the boys who had brought one of Europe's biggest drug dealers to justice.

Mike sat happily, looking at his own picture, but to be called a hero didn't seem right to him. Dubois was behind bars because they were lucky. He felt proud of the courage that he had found within himself, but they had entered Dubois's world stupidly and it was definitely down to a large helping of luck that they had come out of it unscathed. It had been a learning experience from start to finish and had taught him some valuable lessons, but now he just wanted to get on with his life and put the whole episode behind him. The court case would be months away so he wasn't going to start worrying about that, but in the security of his own home he would allow himself a little indulgence and enjoy his five minutes of fame.

Mike's mum ran into the living room in a panic. Mike looked up from his self-admiration and saw his mum switch on the television.

'What's up mum? Everything ok?'

'Yes dear, I'm fine, but I thought that you had better watch this.' Mike put down his paper, picked up the remote control and turned up the volume. French police were escorting a smartly dressed man towards a waiting police car, while hoards of photographers were swarming around like an angry pack of wild dogs after their prey. As the man was bundled into the waiting police car, Mike sat stunned in disbelief at what he was seeing. He didn't even feel the remote control falling from his hand. He knew who the man was. The same suit and the same coloured hair - it was the man standing in the background in Dubois's office. Mike was sure of it. The newsreader read out the details of the man's arrest and Mike's heart pounded in his chest.

'Phillip Christophe Legrand, French Interior Minister and possibly the next President of France, was arrested on suspicion of Conspiracy to Supply drugs, money laundering and several other charges relating to forgery, deception and kidnapping. The popular politician and winner in a recent poll for the most likely man to become the next President in the forthcoming French Presidential elections was being taken away for questioning. Rumours surround him regarding his ties to a recent Belgian drug dealer who was arrested earlier this week.'

Mike turned it off. He'd seen enough and it had all suddenly become clear. Dubois had been right - the drugs and the money weren't important. It was the high ranking politician that they had caught on camera by mistake that had been the cause of all their problems. A future President of France involved with supplying drugs, through Dubois, to any country in Europe! And Mike and Dan, two Geordie boys on a football tour, had spoilt their whole operation. Mike sat back and sighed. What would happen next, he dreaded to think.

Picking up the envelope, he ran his finger under the top fold, ripping it open. Tenderly pulling out the letter headed paper, he stopped and put it down. He couldn't read it. Brian, who had been watching from behind the kitchen door, came over and sat next to his son.

'Would you like me to read it for you, son?' he said, picking up the letter.

'Please dad, if you would.'

Reading slowly from top to bottom, Brian finished, folded the letter and placed it back into its envelope. Valerie watched from the doorway. It must be bad news, she thought, as there was no reaction. Mike looked at his father, fearing the worst. Brian, overcome with emotion, found it impossible to hide his joy and smiled back. Jumping from his seat, Mike punched the air in elation and Brian began to laugh uncontrollably. Mother, father and son hugged. Mike, at last, was a step closer to his dream.

The End

Lightning Source UK Ltd.
Milton Keynes UK
UKOW051017040713

213198UK00002B/7/P